COUNTY LIBRARY
LANCASTER ROAD
KNOTT END-ON-SEA
Tel. 810632

D0708268

TRIPLE CROSS

By the same author

The Cambridge Theorem
The Last Defector

TONY CAPE

Triple Cross

HAMISH HAMILTON · LONDON

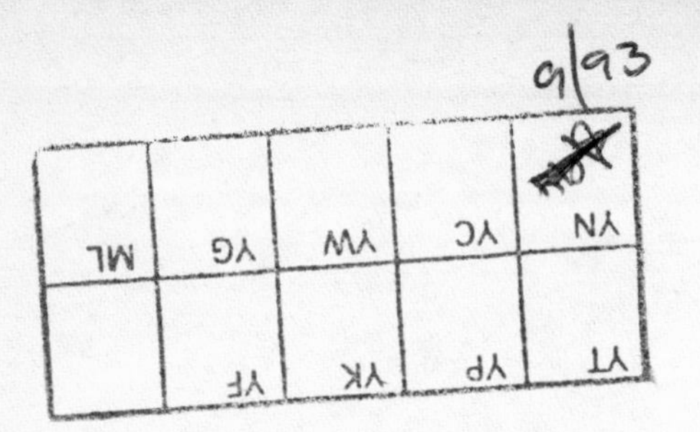

For Alice and Norris Tibbetts

HAMISH HAMILTON LTD

Published by the Penguin Group
Penguin Books Ltd, 27 Wrights Lane, London W8 5TZ, England
Penguin Books USA Inc., 375 Hudson Street, New York, New York 10014, USA
Penguin Books Australia Ltd, Ringwood, Victoria, Australia
Penguin Books Canada Ltd, 10 Alcorn Avenue, Toronto, Ontario, Canada M4V 3B2
Penguin Books (NZ) Ltd, 182–190 Wairau Road, Auckland 10, New Zealand

Penguin Books Ltd, Registered Offices: Harmondsworth, Middlesex, England

First published 1993
1 3 5 7 9 10 8 6 4 2

Typeset by Datix International Limited, Bungay, Suffolk
Filmset in 11/13 pt Monophoto Sabon
Printed in England by Clays Ltd, St Ives plc

A CIP catalogue record for this book is available from the British Library
ISBN 0-241-13295-9

I

Audrey Cole accelerated her Fiat away from the lights and swung out into the fast lane. The rush-hour traffic along London's North Circular Road had thinned, and she was eager to complete her task and get home. She was an attractive woman with full, sensuous lips and thick auburn hair which she pushed back from her face with an impatient gesture. The rain had begun falling in sheets and she flicked the tiny car's wipers on to high speed. A large handbag sat awkwardly in her lap.

The big Manor Cottage roundabout at the top of the hill often caused long delays, but tonight, despite the rain, the traffic was moving freely. She paid no attention to an elderly Morris Traveller in the oncoming lane that backfired as it coasted down the hill. Neither did she notice the tool-boxes jammed haphazardly inside its gaping rear doors. The petrol tanker, however, she saw immediately.

It seemed to approach the roundabout above her at outrageous speed, its huge silver trailer swaying alarmingly as it straightened up down the hill. She instinctively slowed, bracing her arms against the wheel, then saw the glint of the crowbar on the wet road just before the tanker's nearside wheel passed over it. She heard the report of the tyre as it burst, and looked up in horror as the tanker driver, panicking, struggled to control his careening vehicle. Then, as the huge machine lurched towards the kerb, Audrey Cole saw something that made her blood freeze in terror – the back end of the trailer was skidding into her lane as the tanker jack-knifed out of control. As she saw the driver throw his hands in front of his face, she screamed with all her force and stood on the brakes of her tiny car. The instant that the rear wheels slammed into her, she too threw an arm in front of her face, a futile reflex of self-protection. Witnesses said later that the sound of the impact was like an explosion, but the scene then fell eerily silent, except for the sound of the falling rain and the splashing of hundreds of gallons of petrol on to the glistening road.

*

The vast, floodlit compound of the Royal Ordnance Factory at Burghfield in Berkshire had a particularly sinister aspect at night. For safety reasons, many of the individual buildings were half buried under turf and were connected by a contorted network of heavy-gauge steel pipe. The glistening hummocks intersected by their tubular barriers gave the impression of an obstacle course constructed for the offspring of giants. At very least the ghostly, deserted site with its central clump of prefabricated buildings was a fitting home for its macabre, radioactive residents: its uranium, thorium, tritium and, most celebrated isotope of all, its plutonium-239, a fissile element with a half-life of twenty-four thousand years, present at ROF Burghfield in sufficient quantity to cause cancer in every living being on the planet.

Unlike its more famous sister plant at nearby Aldermaston, the Atomic Weapons Establishment at Burghfield was not, strictly speaking, a nuclear bomb factory. It was more a nuclear service station, where individual weapons from the British arsenal were taken for refit after deployment. As such, it played no lesser role in maintaining Britain's status as one of the five official nuclear powers. Nuclear weapons, unlike their conventional counterparts, decayed at a steady clip and were in need of continual maintenance.

The Burghfield compound was, of course, impregnable. A single chain-link, barbed-wire fence ran around its perimeter, monitored by a sophisticated movement sensor. An internal road ran inside the fence, which was lined with a duplicate fence system. As a fail-safe, attack dogs patrolled the compound twenty-four hours a day. Signs at regular intervals around the outer fence warned the public that photography and sketching were prohibited. ROF Burghfield had seen its share of demonstrations in its lifetime, but never, in forty years of operation, a single breach of security. Not until, that is, this particularly mild night in early June.

Oddly, the Reading Civil Service Sports Association's facility lay just beyond ROF Burghfield's western perimeter, although since the members were mostly Burghfield employees, they found little incongruity in playing their football, snooker and darts next door to such a lethal enterprise. Behind the single-storey clubhouse was an archery range, and just past its three straw targets a concrete access road ran alongside the security fence where it made a ninety-degree turn to the south. Inside this section of the perimeter stood the kennels and training ground of Burghfield's canine protectors. At three fifty-five on a balmy June night, a plain brown van passed unnoticed in front of the archery range, turned on to the slip road and coasted past the guard dog compound, then stopped noiselessly behind a high hedge. A side door slid open and two men jumped to the ground and began silently checking equipment by the pencil beam of a miniature torch.

The men were dressed in light-grey, tight-fitting overalls and wore cotton Balaclava helmets, the exposed part of their faces camouflaged with grey paint. Around their shoulders each wore a webbing harness, and they wore curious, calf-length boots secured by multiple clasps and straps, the most unusual feature of which was that, despite their Russian manufacture, their treads bore the imprint of boots belonging to US Navy SEALs, its elite commando unit.

The two men did not speak as they rehearsed their tasks. They stowed their equipment into small flat packs which they clipped to each other's shoulder harnesses. Their final act was to reach back into the van for a pair of Heckler and Koch submachine-guns, which each man clamped on to the spring clip on his chest. They practised the action twice, releasing the catch with their left hand and catching the stock as the weapon leapt across their chests in their right. They checked the magazines, then the smaller of the two crouched and his companion removed a compact pair of bolt-cutters from his pack. The squatting man cocked his wrist and after holding up his right hand for less than a minute began counting off seconds on his fingers. At the count of twenty both men stood and walked confidently into the glare of Burghfield's perimeter floodlights.

Soon both were running in a crouch towards a huge underground building to the right of the central office complex. Four minutes later a muffled explosion was heard, then the distant wail of an alarm. After an elapse of seven minutes, both figures could be seen running in a fast crouch back towards the breached perimeter. The awkwardness of their gait suggested their packs were considerably heavier on the return journey. Silently the men slid through the flaps in both fences and ran to the van, whose engine started as they approached. They leapt in the open side door as the van moved slowly away across a cricket pitch towards a gate on Grazeley Road, beyond which lay the A33 and the M4 motorway back to London. The entire operation had taken just thirteen minutes.

Police Constable Stanley Orme didn't get back to the Golders Green police station until well after nine, but he wasted no time in finding the inventory forms for the contents of Audrey Cole's handbag. He'd thought it odd the deceased woman was holding such a large bag in her lap when her passenger seat was empty, and he'd also noticed she'd only thrown one arm in front of her face on impact, when normally you'd expect her to use both. The senior officer from the traffic unit had asked him to baby-sit the body to Whittington Hospital at Archway, and he'd made a quick check of the bag's contents on arrival while the hospital staff went through the formalities of pronouncing life extinct and transferring the remains to the mortuary. He'd called in Audrey Cole's identity to his duty inspector as soon as he found her laminated House of Commons ID card, but said nothing about the document he'd found in an unmarked envelope, since it was stamped Top Secret and he wasn't sure he ought to read it. But he'd seen two names that made the hair on his neck stand on end – Trident and Faslane – both of which he knew referred to Britain's nuclear submarines.

The pile-up on the North Circular had been one of the biggest the Finchley emergency teams had handled in some time. The road had to be closed in both directions as the heavy gear came in to pry the two vehicles apart. The tanker driver had apparently climbed out of his vehicle unaided, merely bruised and shaken, but there was no point rushing the work on the driver of the Fiat – to an experienced eye, she had obviously been killed immediately. The thing about the fatally injured was they didn't bleed, and from the lack of blood in Audrey Cole's car, given the extent of her injuries, the first emergency workers at the scene knew there was no need to hurry. They also had to be careful with the cutting gear, considering the amount of petrol on the road. Luckily the rain had prevented any sparks on impact, or God knows how many might have been killed.

PC Stan Orme was only back-up at the scene and was not directed to take statements, but he heard allegations from witnesses that the tanker driver, who looked a bit of a cowboy, had taken the Manor Cottage roundabout too fast. But anyone could see the direct cause of the accident, since the crowbar was still sticking out of what was left of the tanker's nearside front tyre. It meant some jockey with an unsafe load was directly responsible for the death of an innocent woman, although the likelihood of ever finding the culprit was about zero. Stan Orme doubted the cowboy in the tanker would even face a reckless driving charge.

Orme felt a sharp pang of regret when the front of the Fiat was finally cut away and the woman's body removed, although he made sure none of his colleagues noticed. The driver had obviously been an attractive woman in the prime of her life, going about her private business, then *bang!* – her life had been snuffed out. It was then he noticed the bag in her lap, which he took from the traffic unit chief when told to ride shotgun in the ambulance. Only a doctor was permitted to pronounce life extinct, and the police were obliged to preserve continuity of evidence in order to safeguard any subsequent criminal proceedings. Stan Orme had never been wild about baby-sitting stiffs, but he didn't betray that to the unit chief either.

Back at the Finchley Road station, Orme took his paperwork and evidence bags into an interview room and tipped out the bag's contents on to the table. The plain, unsealed envelope was the first thing he picked up, having already resolved he'd better read its contents properly in order not to make a fool of himself. It appeared to be a memorandum written by Wing Commander Somebody, head of an outfit called the Special Safety Organization, addressed to the permanent under-secretary at the Ministry of Defence. It detailed the delivery schedule of Trident missile warheads from Faslane in Scotland to the Royal Ordnance Factory at Burghfield in Berkshire, beginning the previous month. There were technical references that made no sense whatever to Stan Orme. What did make perfect sense, however, was that regardless of Audrey Cole's status at the House of Commons, it was very unlikely that she was authorized to be driving along the North Circular on a Friday night with a Top Secret document in her handbag. Very unlikely indeed.

Stan Orme scanned the document a second time and, after locking up, went looking for his duty inspector, Jack Trevor. He found him in the communications room and, raising his voice over bursts of radio traffic, asked him whether they'd positively identified the dead woman from the tanker crash yet. Inspector Trevor guided Orme out into the hallway before answering.

'Yeah. I got on to the back hall inspector at the Yard, and he got on to Commons security, and it seems she was secretary to Gerry Stap, that Conservative MP. He just got back to me to say that Stap is on his way to Archway to identify the body.'

'Anything to do with defence, is he, then?' asked Stan Orme.

The inspector looked puzzled. 'I dunno, Stan. Why?'

Police Constable Stanley Orme handed over his envelope and stood back as the inspector removed the document and read it.

'It was in her handbag. Which was in her lap, not on the passenger seat like you'd expect. Noticed that when they pulled the car off of her,' he said, trying not to sound cocky.

The inspector's jaw slackened. 'Bloody hell-fire!' he said. 'What else did she have on her?'

'Don't know for definite. Haven't finished the inventory yet.'

'Then bloody well get on with it,' said Jack Trevor, pushing past him. 'Bring it to me right away. In my office,' he said, leaving Orme alone in the corridor, feeling chagrined.

2

'That bloody snip!' said Standiforth, tossing a document on to the table in front of him in disgust. 'What a stupid waste of time.'

Roger Standiforth, head of British counter-intelligence, was conducting his regular Monday morning meeting of section heads. The British Security Service had its own distinct argot, and male Jews, of whom there were very few working for MI5, were always 'snips'. At least, they always were to Standiforth.

Derek Smailes, the new head of K9, swivelled awkwardly in his chair and craned his neck against the newness of his collar. He looked down at his hands and inspected his cuff-links. Try as he might, he had never quite got used to the casual insolence with which MI5's old school treated those whose origins and activities lay outside its own narrow compass. He picked up a pencil and looked across at his former section chief, Brian Kinney, head of K5, the Russian counter-intelligence section. Kinney was one of the few individuals in K Branch with both the clout and the guts to stand up to Standiforth.

'I don't know, Roger,' Kinney said mildly. 'I don't think we should dismiss the idea of executive powers out of hand. If we had powers of arrest, like the FBI, we'd get rid of our dependence on those clowns over at Special Branch.'

'If we became *enforcers* of the law, then we'd end up *answerable* to the law, wouldn't we?' Standiforth replied with derision, as if the argument was self-evident. 'That's the last bloody thing we want. There would have to be grievance procedures, watchdog groups, all the rest of it. No, if you ask me, he's barking up the wrong tree. The wrong bloody tree entirely.' Standiforth picked up the document again, then leaned over and crushed out his cigarette in a large glass ashtray. He pushed his hair back from his forehead, reached into his suit pocket, took out a silver cigarette case and immediately lit another.

Derek Smailes studied his boss. Roger Standiforth was still in his early fifties, but a twenty-year span at the top of British counter-intelligence had begun to take its toll. The fair hair was still full but had now turned almost completely white, and deep lines ran along the wide brow and on either side of his raptor-like nose. If anything, Roger's tall, stooped frame had grown more cadaverous in recent years, and his cheeks and neck were deeply hollowed. Smailes was aware he had made one forlorn attempt to stop smoking the previous year, but was now back to his steady, forty-a-day habit. Smailes turned back to look at Kinney, but he too was studying the memorandum.

Former policeman Derek Smailes, not quite forty, had been elevated to MI5 management quite early in his career, which gratified him. However, as head of the department which investigated those who left sensitive government jobs unexpectedly, Smailes had the nagging feeling that Standiforth had both promoted and marginalized him at the same time. Smailes and Standiforth shared a long history, characterized on Smailes's part by this continuing doubt as to whether his boss saw him fundamentally as an asset or a liability.

The 'snip' to whom Roger was referring was Sir Herbert Carne, the celebrated intelligence expert, who had recently been enlisted by the Conservative government to conduct a post-Cold War review of Britain's intelligence apparatus. Few questioned Carne's unique credentials to spearhead such an inquiry, since he had served with distinction in both MI5 and SIS, the British foreign intelligence service, and had acted as an intelligence adviser to both Conservative and Labour administrations. Roger Standiforth, however, was a sceptic, distrusting both Carne's Jewishness and his service in SIS, MI5's deadliest rival. The memorandum outlining the scope of Carne's review was the first item on his agenda that morning, and the source of his uncharacteristic animation. However, none of the section heads in the room believed for a moment that the issue of executive powers was the real reason for Roger's outburst.

The truth was that Carne's memo was the opening salvo in what could become a life-or-death struggle for MI5 itself, and everyone knew it. Indeed, his very first paragraph referred to a possible 'rationalization of counter-intelligence functions', a phrase that had particularly enraged the head of K Branch.

Counter-intelligence – spy-catching – was the heart and soul of MI5, and had been since its creation to fight German espionage during World War I. SIS operated its own counter-intelligence department, concerned mainly with its own internal security and offensive operations abroad. Scotland Yard's Special Branch, originally set up to deal with the Irish problem, also operated in the field. But since MI5's charter had first been codified, it had been uniquely charged with defending the realm against both espionage and sabotage. As such, K Branch was its elite department, and Roger Standiforth, arguably, the second most powerful man in the organization, after the Director-General himself. The realization that his fiefdom was about to be subjected to independent scrutiny, and by a man like Carne over whom he had no leverage, was clearly for Roger Standiforth an intolerable prospect.

But the unnamed fear which stalked the room that morning was Roger's 'nightmare scenario' – that Carne might recommend to the Prime Minister a single, reconfigured intelligence agency, which would save money and simultaneously extinguish the endless turf wars between MI5 and SIS. SIS, the self-proclaimed senior service which traced its heritage back to Queen Elizabeth I, would doubtless hold the reins in any such new agency, and Roger Standiforth, whose ambition knew no bounds, would probably be out of a job.

Standiforth began to outline his strategy for responding to this threat, which was to entail both written and oral submissions. But at this juncture Marjorie the tea-girl came in with her trolley, and Roger called a five-minute break. It was typical that in MI5 parlance Marjorie, who was well into her sixties, should be known as the tea-girl. Smailes was bantering with her as he took his cup when Standiforth came up behind him.

'Step in and see me when we adjourn, will you, Derek?' he asked, his voice, despite the tobacco consumption, the timbre of an oboe.

'Of course, Roger,' said Smailes, turning and feeling his neck chafe again against the newness of his collar. 'What's up?'

'A sudden death. Came in this weekend. K9 business.'

'Right,' said Smailes, returning to his seat.

Roger Standiforth's office was a traditional affair, eschewing the vinyl and chrome that younger division heads preferred in favour of mahogany, leather and sporting prints. There were none of the photographs taken with public figures that less secretive men tended to display, and almost no expression of personal style beyond the slightly worn gentility of clubland that Roger's office suggested. Except for the absence of professional certificates, it could have been the office of a Harley Street specialist or a successful barrister. Roger's office had one other distinguishing feature: its high, curtained windows were lined with sheets of clear plastic adhesive, as were all the exterior windows in Curzon House, for protection against bomb attacks.

Roger took his seat and lit a cigarette, indicating that Smailes should take an armchair. He had calmed down considerably as his morning meeting progressed, but Smailes thought it wise to let his boss set the pace.

'Did you hear the news about the accident on the North Circular on Friday night? The Conservative party worker?' Roger asked, coming straight to the point.

Smailes thought for a moment. 'The woman who was Gerry Stap's secretary? The pile-up with the petrol tanker? Yes, I saw something in the Sunday paper,' said Smailes. He didn't specify the *Observer*, the paper his wife Clea insisted on taking, since it was left of centre and its mention would irritate Roger.

'Yes, well, former secretary would be more accurate,' Roger continued. 'In his constituency. Since the last election her official title has been researcher, at his Commons office. Her name was Audrey Cole.'

'I see,' said Smailes, waiting for more.

'You know Stap's position?'

'He's a junior defence spokesman, isn't he?'

'Correct. Specifically Navy, royal dockyards, the Trident programme.'

'That makes sense,' said Smailes, still waiting. Standiforth lifted the flap of a manila folder on his desk and removed a document, which he handed across his desk to Smailes.

'When the contents of her handbag were examined by the Golders Green police, she was found to be carrying this. It's a duplicate of the numbered copy circulated to the Minister of Defence. Gerry Stap would undoubtedly have seen that copy.'

Smailes blew out his cheeks. The document originated with the RAF's Special Safety Organization, which Smailes knew was the outfit responsible for the transportation of all Britain's nuclear weapons. It detailed that month's delivery schedule of Trident warheads from their Scottish base to ROF Burghfield near London, for something called 'permissive action link retrofit'. It was clearly political dynamite.

'What's your thinking?' Smailes asked.

'Copying the document and removing it from the Commons were both Section 1 offences. Either she was acting on her own initiative, or she was acting as Stap's courier. To whom she was delivering it, I don't know. The envelope wasn't addressed,' said Standiforth, adding a thin smile.

'Stap?' said Smailes, thinking aloud. 'Who would he be passing this to? He's a rising star, isn't he?'

'Very good question,' said Standiforth. 'I think the likelihood is Miss Cole was acting unilaterally. Perhaps she was a secret left-wing sympathizer, one of Nukewatch's sources, for instance. They're always publishing the SSO convoy schedule, and we've never been able to determine exactly where they get their information.'

'She was positively vetted, surely?' Smailes asked.

Roger shrugged, indicating that PV meant nothing. Almost every spy of significance MI5 had caught in twenty years had been positively vetted. But then he hesitated. Clearly, there was more to come.

'Except,' said Roger, choosing his words carefully, 'it would appear Miss Cole's relationship with her employer was somewhat ... irregular. In fact, my sources tell me they may have been conducting an affair. Seems to have been common knowledge. And the post-mortem results indicate Miss Cole was seven weeks pregnant at the time of her death.'

Smailes was impressed. 'Stap's married?'

'Of course,' said Standiforth. 'He's MP for Wembley and Harrow, but his family home is near Reigate in Surrey. Flat in Dolphin Square. Two teenagers,' he said.

'Common knowledge, you say?'

'Apparently. The give-away was his bringing her on to his Commons staff after the election. You see, junior ministers usually have secretaries only in their constituency. In the House they retain an assistant, who's called a researcher. Standard practice is they're whiz-kids straight out of university, with various specialties. Miss Cole was in her thirties and didn't even have a degree.'

'So that increases the likelihood of collusion, doesn't it?' said Smailes.

'It means it can't be ruled out.'

'You want me to handle it personally?' Smailes asked.

'It came to the Deputy DG's attention. He suggested you,' said Standiforth.

Smailes was surprised. Deputy Director-General Alex Corcoran was someone Smailes hardly knew, and he was not aware Corcoran particularly favoured him. Still, it was not illogical that K9 would be asked to assume responsibility in such a sensitive case. The alternative would be to toss it to someone in F Branch, the domestic counter-subversion department, and Smailes knew that in the bitter public rivalry between Standiforth and F Branch chief Miles Bingham, Corcoran tilted towards Standiforth.

'You have any suggestions, Roger?' asked Smailes dutifully, knowing Standiforth would have several.

'Get up to Golders Green and take an impression of her door-key, then get Les Townsend to cut you one. She lived alone, apparently. Check out her flat thoroughly. Interview Stap. Let him know we know everything about him and Miss Cole. If he prevaricates, tell him we have pictures.'

'Do we?'

'No, but he won't know that. Lean on him, he may let something slip. Tell him we're going to have to inform the Whip's office, anyway. Talk to her father. He's a retired brigadier, lives in Hampshire somewhere – the police will know. Keep me informed how it progresses,' he said, passing the entire folder across to Smailes.

Smailes got up to leave, reflecting that he wasn't surprised, either by the politician's affair with his secretary, or that Roger's sources had told him of it. After twenty years at the head of British counter-intelligence, Roger Standiforth ran personal agents in all walks of British life, in the print and broadcast media, in the three major parties, even, Smailes knew, at Buckingham Palace. What was more surprising was that a mature woman, a positively vetted Conservative party worker no less, would risk her career to betray Britain's nuclear secrets.

As Smailes walked from Coulsdon South station to his suburban home that evening, he realized to his dismay that his heart was sinking. Derek and Clea Smailes had moved out to the Surrey suburbs shortly before their daughter's birth two years earlier, choosing Coulsdon since it was just a ten-minute drive from Clea's parents' home. Somewhat to Smaile's surprise, his wife had elected to stay home with their baby for the first two years, reflecting the depth of Clea's traditional values, despite her vocal feminism. Clea, a diplomat at the Foreign Office, had reasoned that a two-year commitment was a small sum to pay in the context of a thirty-five-year career, and had dutifully arranged for extended leave. Smailes was well aware, however, that full-time motherhood had proved extremely taxing for his wife, who complained progressively of the claustrophobia and intellectual paralysis entailed in raising an infant. She was eagerly anticipating her return to the Western European desk in September when catastrophe had struck. Three months earlier Clea had become pregnant again.

It had been a genuine mix-up, but Smailes chivalrously accepted the full weight of blame she heaped upon him. In keeping with their scrupulous egalitarianism, Smailes and his wife took turns to don prophylactic devices prior to love-making. Their rules of engagement, however, were insufficiently detailed to cover circumstances in which appetite demanded more than a single course. During an encounter in March, Smailes had dutifully fulfilled his responsibilities during what turned out to be the main dish. But it soon became clear that Clea Smailes was interested in dessert, and during the ensuing engagement no protection had been used. Clea, most inconveniently, had fallen pregnant again and was now in a turmoil of conflicting feelings about her condition, and the relatively harmonious Smailes household had become riven with strife.

At the core of Clea's conflict was her unwillingness to accept her husband's insistence that she hire a full-time nanny and return to work. While desperate to re-enter the adult world, Clea could not bring herself to short-change their future son (she was convinced of his sex, thereby further damning the pregnancy) by relegating him to a child-minder, when Lucy, their first-born, had enjoyed two years of undivided parental attention. To Derek's tentative suggestion that they still retained the option of postponing any second child for many more years, their original plan, Clea had responded with horror, thereby compounding Derek's carelessness with the sin of moral turpitude.

Smailes opened the front door and called out with forced gaiety as he advanced towards the kitchen. He thought he could hear Lucy upstairs, but Clea, to his surprise, was seated at the kitchen table, leaning on her elbows, her head buried somewhat melodramatically in her hands.

'Hi, how're you?' he said, carefully avoiding sarcasm. He glanced quickly around the kitchen. It was in some disarray.

Clea looked up. She looked fraught, but was not crying as he had feared.

'I've had a bloody awful day. Lucy's been terrible.'

'Where is she?' asked Smailes.

'Up in her room, bossing around her animals.'

Smailes suppressed a smile, in deference to his wife's mood. The description of his daughter's activities sounded quite in character.

Confrontations between Lucy and Clea, he was aware, often arose because they were temperamentally so alike.

'What happened exactly?' he asked, opening the fridge and reaching for a bottle of wine.

'Oh God, Derek,' said Clea, 'she's getting impossible. Absolutely everything went wrong. We went over to Jane's this morning, and she was an absolute pig to Alex. Then she refused to take a nap and in the end I had to give up and take her out for a walk. Then we went to the supermarket and she managed to throw two tantrums, lasting about ten minutes each. Then she chucked most of her supper on the floor.'

'Mmm,' said Smailes. It sounded like hell.

'She's absolutely exhausted and is being a little bitch. I can't handle her any more.' She looked up at him plaintively. 'Put her to bed, will you, darling? I'll heat up the supper.'

'Okay,' said Smailes contritely. 'No bath?'

'She's too tired.'

Smailes took a quick swallow of wine and loosened his tie.

'See you soon,' he said, leaning towards her. Clea pecked his cheek dutifully.

'Welcome home,' she said weakly.

Smailes mounted the stairs slowly and stole noiselessly into his daughter's bedroom. As Clea had described, Lucy was hauling her stuffed animals from their roosts on the bookshelf and dumping them on to her bed, maintaining a continuous stream of prattle at them.

'Hello, gorgeous,' he said quietly.

'Hi, Daddy,' she said, not turning round, to indicate she knew he'd been there all along. As she swaggered past him, a large brown donkey beneath her arm, he detected a familiar warmth in the air.

'Daddy,' she said, her tiny wrist swinging away from her in her lady-like way. 'I did poo.' Then, with an exquisite sense of timing, she added over her shoulder, 'Big poo.'

'Ah yes, so you have,' said Smailes. 'Let Daddy change these clothes and we'll take care of you.'

'Lucy help,' she said, running after him.

'Lucy, were you a good girl to Mummy today?'

'Yes,' she said indignantly, affronted by his doubt.

Half an hour later Smailes came back down the stairs in cords and a sweater. There was an enticing aroma emanating from the kitchen, and Clea was seated at the table, having poured herself a glass of wine and set two places. She'd also straightened up the kitchen and had recovered herself somewhat. She'd run a brush through her short dark hair in an attempt to bolster her morale, but Smailes could still see Lucy's sticky paw-prints on the shoulder of her cardigan.

'Sorry, darling,' she said. 'Sometimes I just can't wait for you to get home so I can get a break from the little monster.'

'No problem,' said Smailes, negotiating a pan of vegetarian lasagne from inside the oven. It was typical of his wife, and her unyielding expectations of herself, that despite a totally chaotic day she had managed to prepare an elegant dinner for them both. 'No Fidelma today?' he asked, referring to their teenage baby-sitter.

'Not on Mondays.'

'Oh, right,' he said. 'I forgot. You haven't eaten?'

'No, I was waiting for you. How was *your* day?' she asked with undisguised hostility.

'Interesting,' said Smailes, ignoring the taunt. Although Derek and his wife both enjoyed the highest level of government security clearance, by mutual agreement Smailes only gave Clea the barest outline of his work. Even that was overstepping MI5 guidelines, they both knew. It didn't seem fair for him to elaborate further at that point, given Clea's misery – the contrast might seem too great. He served two plates and came to sit down. Suddenly he noticed what looked like a bowl of bird food in the middle of the table.

'What's that?' he asked, pointing with his fork. Smailes thought it looked like quinoa, a dubious legume Clea had brought home from the health-food store one day, describing it as 'the sacred grain of the Aztecs'. Smailes, who didn't share his wife's dietary fancies, responded that there weren't any Aztecs in Coulsdon, and to his knowledge the stuff had stayed in the cupboard ever since.

'That's Tweetie's supper,' said Clea, despairing. 'It was the only way I could get Lucy to eat any of hers.'

'Who's Tweetie?' asked Smailes carefully.

'That's him over there,' said Clea, pointing to a grotesque yellow canary seated on top of the microwave.

'Ah,' said Smailes. 'I see.'

'That was the cause of the second tantrum. Tesco's was selling a huge bin of them and Lucy refused to leave the store unless I bought her one. I told her no, but in the end I capitulated.'

Smailes shared his wife's dismay. Clea usually restricted Lucy's soft toys to items of the most careful taste, but this brute was a three-foot-high monstrosity in fluorescent yellow nylon.

'And Lucy was making a place for him upstairs . . .' said Smailes.

'I suppose so,' said Clea.

Smailes finally snorted with laughter, but Clea could only manage a weak smile. His wife's spirits had to be really low, Smailes reflected, for her not to appreciate the humour of the situation.

Clea seemed unusually preoccupied during the meal and Smailes did most of the talking, mentioning the announcement of Herbert Carne's review and Roger Standiforth's violent response. He thought it wise to say nothing about the Audrey Cole business, not knowing where that investigation might lead.

'What's up?' said Smailes finally. 'You seem unusually down.'

Slowly, Clea told him that she and Lucy had been going through old clothes in the box-room that morning, looking for items they could salvage for the new baby.

'Yes?' said Smailes, unsure what was coming.

'We found a box with your cowboy boots in it, and that lovely rawhide jacket I bought you in New York.'

Smailes put his cutlery down, immediately defensive. 'So? I know where I put them. There's no room in my wardrobe, if you didn't realize,' he said sharply.

'I don't know, Derek,' said Clea, her eyes averted. 'It just seemed symbolic. You never wear them any more. Expensive suits and handmade shirts to work. Casual trousers and moccasins at the weekend. That new shirt you were wearing today – it has french cuffs, hasn't it?'

'So?'

'You never used to wear french cuffs,' she said quietly.

Smailes, as the first member of his family ever to wear a suit to work, was indignant. 'What's the problem if I order shirts with french cuffs? Your bloody father gave me cuff-links for Christmas, didn't he, for Christ's sake? Anyway, I prefer the fit,' he said angrily, aware he hated any imputation of vanity. 'Besides, you're a fine one to complain about expensive taste in clothes,' he added foolishly.

'When was the last time I got to dress up?' she retorted.

'That's not my fault.'

'It *is* your fault.'

Despite his best efforts, Smailes had become exasperated by this argument. 'Look, it takes two to tango. You started it, the night we got pregnant.'

Clea glared at him, her eyes narrow with fury. 'Well, if you'd bloody well been able to satisfy me the first time, I wouldn't have had to, would I?'

Smailes was speechless, and Clea put a hand to her face, shocked by her words.

'God, Derek, I'm sorry. That's a horrid thing to say.' She started to cry, and Smailes's indignation melted. He didn't resent her gibe, since he knew their ability to communicate the harshest things to each other was perhaps the most important facet of their marriage. In fact, there seemed to Smailes almost a perverse generosity in his wife's willingness to pillory him for everything from his political correctness to his skill in bed. He and Yvonne, his first wife from a different lifetime, had never been able to talk about anything, which had doomed the marriage from the start. And Yvonne had never stood up to him, which was never in danger of happening with Clea Smailes.

Derek got up and went to her, resting a hand on her shoulder. 'It's okay. I know I'm a dud in bed sometimes. You have to remind me to slow down.'

Clea hugged him around the hips. 'You're a wonderful lover,' she said quietly. 'I didn't mean it. I just wanted to hurt you.'

'What's the matter?' he asked gently.

'I just feel so hopeless, Derek,' she confessed. 'I don't have anything left for myself. Lucy treats me like a doormat. I don't have a career. I don't have any mind. I don't even have my own name.'

'I didn't ask you to change your name.'

'You expected me to.'

'Not true,' Smailes lied. There was a pause. 'Why did finding my Western gear upset you so much?'

'Like I said, it just seemed symbolic. I'm afraid we're going to end up like my parents. You travelling up to town every day in your pinstripes, reading *The Times*. Me stuck in the suburbs with the kids like my mother, growing more embittered and eccentric every year.'

'I wouldn't call your mother eccentric.'

'I don't know about that, Derek. She called today. Now she's begun meditating and calls herself a Buddhist.'

'No!'

'I'm serious. She's become a follower of a some jet-set Tibetan lama. She says they're the master race.'

'Who are?'

'The Tibetans.'

'Good Lord. Well, I don't think there's any danger of that happening to you.' Smailes thought for a moment. He was aware Clea's criticism was partially true. His personal habits had grown more conservative since his transfer to MI5 headquarters, and although he hadn't realized it, he hadn't touched his cowboy gear in years.

'Listen,' he said. 'I've been thinking. Maybe Fidelma would look after Lucy and the new baby full-time. She probably makes as much working for us as she does in that waitress job.'

Clea sighed. 'You don't think I haven't thought of that? Fidelma loves Lucy, obviously. She'd probably jump at the job. But she's still just a child-minder. I believe children need a parent, not a nanny, as their primary attachment.'

Smailes knew there was no point arguing with her. He'd tried it too often before.

'There is another option, though,' said Clea quietly. 'Jane brought it up today.'

'What's that?' asked Smailes suspiciously.

'You're a parent too. You could take a couple of years off and let me go back to work. I make more money than you do, you know.'

Smailes felt a surge of panic. Clea's bloody feminist friends! he thought angrily. Jane Randall was a neighbour who had interrupted a law career to stay at home with her year-old son, Alex. Her husband was a merchant banker – he couldn't imagine Jane prevailing upon *him* to stay at home and become a househusband. 'Darling, I don't know about that,' said Smailes slowly. 'I just couldn't see . . .'

'Why not? Because you'd lose face at the office?'

'No, it's just . . . my career, my promotion prospects . . .'

'You don't think mine have suffered because of this leave?' Clea was growing animated again. Smailes had no option but to tell the truth.

'I know that, darling. I just couldn't make the same sacrifice you have. I know myself, and I just couldn't do it.'

'Well, why did you want to have children in the first place, then?' Clea snapped, lifting their plates and walking over to the sink. Smailes leaned back in his chair, unable to muster a response.

3

As the unmarked van passed through the sleeping Berkshire village of Grazeley in the early hours of Tuesday morning, an ordinary black saloon cruised past the archery range and turned left on to the concrete slip road. The car pulled up outside ROF Burghfield's dog-training compound and its occupants got out awkwardly. Unlike their predecessors, they were bulkily dressed and made no attempt to conceal their presence.

'I'm getting too bloody old for this lark,' said Ted Brock, a stocky man with a Lancashire accent, stamping out a cigarette. 'What time is it?'

'Ten past four,' said David McGillicuddy quietly. He was the younger and taller of the two, with an accent that suggested he was in charge. 'We go in in five minutes.' He patted the padding strapped to his thigh. Neither man had trusted the repeated assurances that the dog patrols would be at distant parts of the compound by four fifteen. Brock reached back into the car, then struggled into a donkey jacket with HOME OFFICE emblazoned across the yoke.

'What's that noise, then?' he asked, cocking his ear at the distant siren.

'Don't ask me,' replied McGillicuddy, intent on buttoning his own jacket. 'Maybe it's a back-up that goes off when they shut down the perimeter alarm.'

'What time was that again?'

'Four o'clock, Reynolds said, didn't he?' said the younger man irritably. 'Back on again at half past.'

'Right, four o'clock. Where are those bolt-cutters? In the boot?'

'No, Ted, you put them on the back seat.'

'Right, then, let's get this over with,' said Brock, straightening up, the long callipers gleaming in his hand. Then he noticed something that made him pause. 'Hang on a minute, Dave,' he said, pointing down the fence. 'Looks like Reynolds already cut us an entrance. Look, over there.'

'Honestly,' said McGillicuddy, following his partner's gaze, 'can't we get anything straight? We were supposed to cut our own entrance. He knew that.'

'What the hell?' said Brock, setting the cutters back on the lid of the boot. 'No point messing up two sections of fence. Let's go,' he said, looking at his watch. 'It's that big building over there on the right, isn't it?'

'That's it – the retrofit lab,' McGillicuddy confirmed, following Brock down the fence towards the opening. 'You're sure you've got that combination on you?'

'Right here,' said Brock, patting a breast pocket.

Edward Brock and David McGillicuddy were two members of MI5's F Branch, which, while not directly in charge of Burghfield security, was theoretically responsible for its defence against terrorism. Operation Wakefield, the codename for the mock attack which Brock and McGillicuddy were conducting, was designed to test Burghfield's readiness against that threat. While a little anxious about the dog patrols, the two MI5 men felt no danger from the Burghfield security force itself. Most were unarmed, and the pair had interviewed the entire crew one at a time at the start of its midnight shift, as part of what had been described as a routine security review. In their distinctive Home Office jackets, the pair would be immediately recognized by whichever guards were first at the scene, and understood to be part of an official test of their readiness. Burghfield's security chief, Frank Reynolds, who under standing rules was the only Burghfield employee indoctrinated into Wakefield, would also be quickly at the scene to straighten out any misunderstandings. It was an exercise Brock and McGillicuddy had already performed at several secret installations that year, and apart from a few subsequently rolling heads, there had been no injuries to date. Tonight promised to be similarly routine, which is why they saw nothing immediately unusual in a breached perimeter fence or a faintly wailing alarm.

As the pair approached the entrance of the huge retrofit lab, however, they experienced their first doubts. The alarm was growing steadily louder, and as they rounded the massive hummock of the underground building they smelled the distinctive odour of plastic explosive. When they saw the huge steel door itself, blown off its hinges and lolling in a buckled heap against the sloping turf, they panicked. They rushed into the fluorescent glare of the lab to find themselves confronted by an ashen-faced guard whose name they remembered was Cutler, wielding a telephone in one hand and his peaked cap in the other. His face was bathed in sweat.

'Who the hell are you?' yelled Cutler in terror, but McGillicuddy, who had the presence of mind to be already brandishing his warrant card, barked 'Home Office,' and demanded to know what was going on. Cutler recognized the two intruders and his body sagged with relief. He spoke again into the phone.

'It's all right, Mr Reynolds. It's those two Home Office blokes from earlier tonight.' He looked around the lab in anguish. Papers were strewn everywhere. In the centre of the room was a huge containment tank in which robotic arms stood silent guard over a partially dismantled warhead.

'I've no idea, have I?' Cutler said into the phone. After a pause he added wretchedly, 'Because it had to be a false alarm, didn't it? I spent nearly ten minutes trying to override and reset, and when it didn't, I radioed the dog patrol, and I came over. Dr Walker? No, I don't. How would I know?'

McGillicuddy reached for the phone. 'For God's sake, let me speak to him,' he said, but Cutler had hung up.

'He's on his way,' the guard said. 'After he calls Dr Walker.'

'Who?'

'The scientist in charge of the lab.'

'Where's Reynolds?'

'In his office. Don't ask me why. He came into the control room just before four, checked the panels and left. Gave me a real shock, I can tell you.'

'He was shutting off the perimeter alarms,' said McGillicuddy mechanically. 'That's how they got in.'

'Who? Who got in?' asked Cutler fearfully, but McGillicuddy said nothing.

Ted Brock sat down heavily. The magnitude of what had happened had just hit him. He put a hand over his eyes. 'What's missing?' he asked the guard.

Cutler cast an arm over his head. 'How the hell would I know? I'm just security. Same stupid question Reynolds asked me.'

Brock's mouth had gone dry and he looked first at the immobilized figure of his partner, then around the lab with a sense of dread that they might already have been exposed to lethal radiation. The containment tank didn't look breached, but how would he know?

The two MI5 men listened distractedly to Cutler's contorted

attempts at self-justification. He'd worked at Burghfield seven years, he said, and there were false alarms in the labs all the time, but there was always an explanation – a ledger falling off a shelf, equipment vibrating too hard, once, of all things, a mouse. You simply overrode the signal, reset the circuit, then went over to check. It was always a false alarm – it had to be, didn't it, since Burghfield was airtight, wasn't it? He repeated the forlorn claim several times – exactly the kind of psychological lapse the MI5 mock attack was designed to expose. Cutler's lament was suddenly interrupted by a dog-handler arriving at the twisted door, restraining a snarling Alsatian with difficulty.

'Home Office! Keep the hell out!' yelled Brock. The dog-handler stepped into the lab, ignoring him.

'I said get the hell out,' Brock yelled again.

'What's this, then?' asked the handler, whipping the dog with its leash and reducing its hysterical barking to a whimper. 'Mock attack?'

David McGillicuddy was coming slowly back to life, and he turned to look at the dog-handler, as if seeing him for the first time. As yet, however, he was unable to speak. Ted Brock spoke up from his seat. 'There was nothing bloody mock about this attack, mate,' he said. 'This was the real thing.'

Smailes presented himself at the St Stephen's entrance of the Houses of Parliament shortly before three. The high, wrought-iron gates represented the main entrance both for members and for the public, but the guard seemed uninterested in Smailes's pass and waved him through to the huge oak portal beyond the small car park. At the door a police officer looked at his warrant card more carefully and listened to his account of his business. Then he was ushered through to the security checkpoint itself.

Smailes found himself in a cavernous stone lobby, waiting behind a party of nervous tourists who were being scanned by a security wand. Then each visitor was guided through a gateway which stood next to the modern, prefabricated office where the security force, a special detachment of the Metropolitan Police, had its headquarters. The tourists, duly cleared, began to cluster around their guide. Beyond, Smailes could see where long stone steps led down into the vast chasm of Westminster Hall, the site where Charles I had received his death sentence from Parliament, and where countless statesmen and royalty had lain in state before their funerals. Smailes waited patiently while his clothing and briefcase were checked for explosives, then leaned into the window to explain his business. An officer inspected his pass, made a phone call, then waved him through the gateway. A second officer watched an instrument panel as Smailes passed through, then told him to make his way down a gallery to the Central Lobby and report to the guard at the barrier. Someone would meet him there.

Smailes had spent most of that morning in Audrey Cole's flat near Wembley stadium, and although he had examined her possessions with minute attention, he'd found nothing to suggest she was anything other than she seemed – a loyal Conservative party worker with few outside interests. He discovered a photograph album containing wedding pictures taken, he guessed, about ten years earlier, suggesting Miss Cole was either widowed or divorced. Her bedside table contained a diaphragm in its plastic clam-shell and a tube of contraceptive jelly, and Smailes wondered whether the unfortunate woman's pregnancy had been a total accident, like his wife's. Her condition at the time of her death made him feel an odd connection with her, which he did not welcome.

He copied a number of documents he found in a table drawer in the sitting room, including bank statements and letters originating from Australia, apparently from a brother. Cursory inspection showed nothing unusual in her financial or personal affairs. Finally he copied a list of phone numbers pinned next to the telephone in the kitchen, reasoning they might provide future leads, if necessary. There was no left-wing literature anywhere in the flat, nothing to suggest Audrey Cole had conducted a double life. He hoped the worthy Gerard Stap, MP, might provide him with further enlightenment.

Smailes passed along a high-ceilinged, vaulted gallery lined with dusty oak panelling and emerged into an enormous circular lobby with a domed ceiling. High around its perimeter stood the heraldic shields of Britain's patron saints. An elderly guide surrounded by a gaggle of tourists was pointing out marble statues of bewigged eighteenth-century prime ministers, which stood in recessed plinths around the walls. Smailes strode over to a large podium, where a policeman stood next to a telephone. Smailes announced his business again, and the policeman made a call and told him the Conservative party's press officer would be right down.

Anna Burns turned out to be a brisk, business-like woman in her early forties, with short hair, a dark suit and careful make-up.

'I can't find Gerry anywhere, I'm afraid,' she said, shaking Smailes's hand. 'He's probably in the Chamber. But if you come up to his office, I'm sure he'll turn up, if he's expecting you. Follow me.'

Smailes dutifully followed her down another gallery to the smaller Members' Lobby at the entrance to the Commons Chamber itself. The double doors, flanked by bronze statues of Lloyd George and Churchill, were closed, but he could hear the drone of a voice from within – Smailes thought it sounded like the Prime Minister. He followed Anna Burns down another passage to their right, passing statues of Attlee and Thatcher, captured in suitably hectoring poses. He jogged a step to draw even with her.

'The corridors of power,' he said jokingly. 'I've never been here before.'

'Oh no,' she said, returning his smile. 'Those are in Whitehall. You should know that. You're a civil servant.'

The passageway was lined with lockers and dusty, glass-fronted bookshelves. The tile floor was dirty and the whole environment had an aura of conspicuous neglect, as if the mother of parliaments had no need to tart herself up in deference to anyone's expectations. It was a wholly different feeling from the US Capitol, which Smailes had also visited, which was all gleaming mahogany, marble and deep-pile carpet. At the end they turned left down another corridor.

'Members' tea-room,' she said, pointing through a glass-fronted door. Smailes glanced inside. It was exactly as he would have expected – battered leather furniture, low coffee-tables, men in dark suits. It looked just like Roger Standiforth's club.

Anna was walking quickly. They passed the office of the Clerk to the House, then emerged into another lobby which Smailes guessed was at the back of the Chamber. A policeman immediately stepped forward.

'This is not line of route, Miss,' he said officiously. Anna Burns was wearing a laminated card on her lapel, and the guard was obviously objecting to Smailes.

'Oh, he's with me, that's all right. He's Home Office,' said Anna Burns.

'It's not line of route, Miss,' he reiterated. 'He needs a pass.'

Anna Burns sighed. 'You'd better show him some identification, Mr Smailes.'

'MI5,' said Smailes quietly, showing his warrant card. The officer stepped back sharply, with a nod of acknowledgement. 'Go ahead,' he said.

Anna Burns led him past the open door of a crowded office. 'Leader of the Opposition,' she said. Then they rounded a corner and the décor suddenly became modern, or at least became twentieth-century. They were in a narrow corridor, flanked by half a dozen doors on each side, a closed-circuit television screen at the far end relaying the action from the Chamber itself. Smailes saw that it had indeed been the Prime Minister he'd heard speaking.

'These are the government front-bench offices,' she said. 'You can wait in Gerry's office.'

Smailes couldn't believe his eyes. The corridor looked like something from the seedy town hall of a particularly impoverished municipality, and made his own place of work look positively palatial.

'A bit cramped, isn't it?' he said.

'Oh, I know, it's hopeless. But it's just the way it is. Here, have a seat. I'll make some more calls and see if I can find Gerry,' she said.

She ushered Smailes into a tiny office, which contained two desks, a typewriter and a computer terminal. There was a small, cluttered bookcase against which leant a silver-bladed spade, with which Gerard Stap, MP, must have turned some ceremonial sod. There were some recent photographs on the wall of constituency events, an older one of a rowing eight, and on the larger desk a family portrait, presumably of the Staps. Suddenly Smailes heard voices in the hallway.

'Well, what's he bloody well doing in my office? I didn't want to meet him here,' a male voice remonstrated.

Anna Burns responded heatedly. 'How was I to know, Gerry? You didn't leave any instructions.'

The door opened and a man Smailes recognized as Gerry Stap entered. 'You're early,' he said without ceremony. 'I don't want to talk to you in here.'

Smailes shrugged. 'Of course,' he said, 'wherever you want.' He was quite used to being treated as if he carried a professional disease, which, in a sense, he did.

'Follow me,' said Stap. 'We'll sit out on the terrace.' Stap gave Anna Burns a final glare, then led Smailes back into the maze of Commons galleries. Nothing more was spoken as Smailes followed Stap down corridors and staircases and finally through double swing doors on to an outdoor terrace. Smailes blinked against the sunlight, then oriented himself. With the spires of parliament behind him, the view across the River Thames to the South Bank was arresting. An open pleasure-boat filled with tourists passed below them. Weathered oak furniture stood in clusters, in which sat parties of parliamentary staffers. Stap pointed out a table well removed from the nearest group.

'Take a seat. You want tea, beer?'

'Tea would be fine. No sugar, thank you,' said Smailes, moving to sit down. Stap walked over to a bar beneath a red striped awning, then returned with two cups of tea. Smailes realized as Stap approached that he hadn't formulated a strategy for this interview. Given his ammunition, he didn't imagine it was going to be difficult.

It was a blustery June day, but mild enough to sit outdoors without coats. Smailes watched Stap as he pushed his red tie into the top of his trousers and buttoned his double-breasted suit jacket. Although quite bald, he was of athletic build and probably not unattractive to women, Smailes reasoned. He sat down and glared at Smailes.

'So what's all this about? This dreadful business of Audrey's death? I already gave a statement to the police on Friday night. I can't see why MI5 should be interested.'

Without altering his expression, Smailes went into his briefcase and produced the SSO document from Audrey Cole's file.

'Do you remember seeing this memorandum, sir?' he asked.

Stap looked at it in silence for what seemed a long time. 'Yes. Yes, of course,' he said eventually. 'It was circulated to me at the beginning of last week. I thought Audrey had returned it to the permanent secretary's office. At least, I told her to.'

'She did. This is an unauthorized copy which we assume she made. It was found in her handbag when her body and effects were removed from her car.'

Stap's eyes widened. 'Good Lord. Well, I have no idea where she was going with it, if that's what you mean.'

'You didn't ask her to deliver it on your behalf, did you, Mr Stap?' asked Smailes quietly.

'How dare you?' asked Stap in a low, strangled voice. 'Audrey Cole was fully vetted and had access to all the same papers as I did. If she took some unauthorized action, she did so without my knowledge or approval. I trusted her completely. But apparently I was wrong.' Somehow, Smailes always found simple denials more persuasive; Stap's indignation seemed theatrical.

'It was a little unconventional, wasn't it, sir, to bring her on to your staff after the election?' asked Smailes, changing tack.

'What do you mean?'

'Well, most research staff are much younger than Miss Cole, with greater qualifications, aren't they?'

'Audrey Cole was fully qualified . . .' said Stap.

Smailes continued in the same, reasonable tone. 'But then we have reliable information that you and Miss Cole have been conducting an affair . . .'

'That's a damn lie,' snarled Stap in the same low voice.

'We have photographs taken outside your flat in Pimlico and at hers in Wembley which indicate that it is not,' said Smailes evenly, looking out across the grey water to the arches of Westminster Bridge. He didn't particularly like Stap, but neither did he relish this role as harbinger of the destruction of his career. He looked back at Stap, who had fallen silent and was also looking at the river. When he turned back he spoke bitterly.

'My God, you really are guttercats, aren't you?'

'I'm sorry?' said Smailes. He wasn't familiar with the term.

'Guttercats. Sneaking around with your cameras and filthy minds.'

'It's routine, I'm afraid, Mr Stap. You occupy a highly sensitive position . . .' The argument was so obvious, he didn't pursue it. 'Did you know Audrey Cole was pregnant at the time of her death?' he asked, more gently than he intended.

Stap paused, as if affected by the change in Smailes's tone. 'Yes,' he said eventually. 'I offered to help, if she wanted to get rid of it. She hadn't decided.'

'You were the father?'

Stap sighed, as if deciding to come clean. 'Audrey said so. I suppose it was all going to come out, sooner or later. I knew people were starting to talk. Audrey wanted me to divorce and to keep the baby. I wasn't sure . . .' said Stap, his voice trailing off. He looked Smailes directly in the eye, allowing him a glimpse of his grief.

'I'm sorry,' said Smailes. 'I take it you deny all knowledge of her copying and removing this document.'

'Totally.'

'And you have no idea why she would do such a thing? Did she ever express anti-nuclear sentiments to you, for instance?'

'Good Lord, no,' said Stap. 'Audrey Cole was completely loyal both to me and to the party. She had worked for me for six years. She comes from a military family. Her husband was a major.'

'She was widowed, sir?'

'Yes. Ambush in Northern Ireland, eight years ago.'

'And how long had you been involved romantically?'

'About two years,' said Stap mechanically. 'What are you going to do?'

'I will write a report of our conversation, which I'll ask you to sign. A copy will have to go to the Chief Whip's office, and the Cabinet office also, I'm afraid.' Smailes knew Stap was staring at oblivion, if not public scandal. 'But first, I have some further questions.'

'Well, yes. Yes, all right,' said Stap, slumping back and passing a hand in front of his face. 'Go ahead, Mr . . . I'm sorry, I've forgotten your name.'

'Smailes, sir,' he replied. 'Derek Smailes.'

The ice cubes rattled against Sal Imodeo's stubbly top lip.

'You want another one, Sal?' asked Smailes. 'What is it? Gin and tonic?'

Imodeo shook his head. 'No. Gotta get goin', Derek. Softball practice,' he said sheepishly.

It had become one of the more bizarre sights of modern London, the teams of mixed-sex Americans playing their watered-down but frantic baseball in Hyde Park. 'You're trying to tell us the US embassy fields its own softball team?' Smailes asked, incredulous.

'Nah,' said Imodeo, trying to keep his face straight. 'I play for Goldman Sachs – you know, the bankers. We have a six-thirty practice.' Seeing Smailes's expression, he added, 'Hey, it's a good way to meet people,' and they both laughed.

Sal Imodeo, FBI London liaison, was one of those Americans that Smailes instinctively liked and trusted. Like Smailes, he was by temperament a law enforcement officer, slightly out of place in the compulsive world of intelligence. A free-wheeling Italian bachelor, he was also something of an anomaly in the button-down world of the US diplomatic corps, which further enhanced him in Smailes's eyes. Like his CIA counterpart Loudon Strickland, Imodeo was an almost daily visitor at Curzon House, and he and Smailes had struck up an easy friendship. Smailes knew that Sal had a personal proscription against office romances, and it was typical that he would have signed up for what Americans called 'co-ed team sports'.

'Do your fellow players know you're London's top G-man, Sal?' Derek teased.

'They think I'm a legal adviser – it's close enough,' Sal replied with a shrug.

Smailes and Imodeo were drinking in the staff bar in MI5's basement, and Smailes asked Imodeo whether he knew the identity of a party of Americans he'd seen touring K Branch earlier that day. He'd guessed their nationality from their dress, and also from the fact they were escorted by Peter Tennant, Roger Standiforth's personal assistant. Standiforth usually accompanied visiting dignitaries himself, except for Americans, for whom he had a legendary disdain.

Imodeo paused. 'One of them was a little guy, black hair, face like a potato?'

Smailes thought for a second. 'Sounds right.'

'That's Wexford. Must be the PEEFAB reps. I heard they were in town.'

'Who?'

'Senator Paul Wexford. Formerly the ranking Republican on the armed services committee. Had to resign in that big banking scandal last year. Now he heads up the President's Foreign Intelligence Advisory Board. It's a consolation prize the White House dishes out.'

Wexford's name rang a vague bell for Smailes. Imodeo stood to leave and offered Derek his luxuriantly hairy hand. 'Hey, I heard you've got a big birthday coming up – commiserations.'

Smailes, who turned forty in two weeks, accepted Imodeo's handshake with a grimace, not pausing to wonder how on earth Sal knew of his forthcoming birthday until he was already at the door. He drained his own glass and checked his watch, but then caught himself as he saw Brian Kinney making his way towards the bar, accompanied by a tall woman he did not recognize. Kinney spied Smailes and steered his companion over to his table.

'Hello, Derek, meet Judith Hyams. She's joining us from KY. I twisted Roger's arm for the transfer. Judith, this is Derek Smailes, head of K9.'

Smailes stood and accepted a cool slim hand. Judith Hyams was a bony woman in her late twenties who had to be at least six feet tall. She looked him squarely in the eye. 'Unexplained departures, right?' she asked, the vowels distinctly north London.

'That's K9 all right,' said Smailes.

'Can we join you?' asked Kinney. 'Were you leaving?'

Smailes's curiosity was piqued. 'No, I've time for another,' he said casually. He and Judith ordered lager and took their seats, and Smailes studied his new colleague. Once he got used to her unusual height, Smailes saw she was quite attractive. She had thick, mid-brown hair pulled back from her face in a simple clasp, dramatic eyebrows, a long nose and a wide, good-natured smile. She wore a standard business suit and blouse, and while extremely thin, her figure was not without shape. He guessed she was Jewish, which together with her sex made her a doubly unlikely K Branch recruit.

'So how long have you been with KY, Judith?' he asked genially, feeling an instant affinity with her. KY was the more orthodox movements-analysis section of K Branch, where most recruits were required to cut their teeth. It occupied its own floor and Smailes had little contact with its staff.

'Less than a year.'

'And what've you been doing?'

'Oh, you know, reconciling watcher reports, that sort of thing.'

'And with K5?'

'A real caseload now, I hope,' she said enthusiastically.

Kinney returned with their drinks and sat down. 'Judith is one of KY's high-flyers,' he explained. 'I told Roger that until we get some new people on board, I needed three internal transfers immediately. Judith was my first choice.'

Hyams sipped her drink modestly, but was clearly flattered. She set her glass down and Smailes noticed a slim wedding ring on her left hand. 'I've wanted to work in K5 from the start,' she confessed. 'I'm thrilled to bits.'

'This man can be a terrible taskmaster,' said Smailes with mock severity.

'Oh, I'm used to it,' said Judith, grinning.

Actually, Brian Kinney was the single individual at MI5 Derek Smailes admired most. A former army intelligence officer, Kinney had been 'burned' by the IRA in the mid-seventies and transferred to a desk job with MI5. Though educated at Marlborough and Sandhurst, he exhibited none of the prejudices Smailes found so objectionable in MI5's old school. He ran the crucial former Soviet section with both vigour and fairness, and had a detached, thoughtful perspective rare among senior staff. He also exhibited a physical and mental discipline Smailes found depressing. He ran every morning and looked as if he had not gained a pound since his teens, and was a firm but never inconsiderate boss. Again atypically, his wife was a doctor, and the Kinneys had a daughter at Oxford and two others at boarding school. Smailes privately hoped Kinney might go all the way to the top at MI5, and that he, Smailes, might be towed upwards in his wake.

'So what are the prospects for some new recruits?' he asked.

'Just about zero until Carne completes his review,' said Kinney gloomily. 'They've got to be approved by the Ad Hoc Committee, and they won't go begging to the Treasury until Carne prognosticates. And meanwhile, the Russians are killing us . . .'

Smailes knew the argument only too well. Under the pretext of establishing its own embassies, Russia had been beefing up its diplomatic complement throughout the West, under which cover the reconfigured KGB had been drastically enhancing its London *rezidentura*. And while supposedly cowed and defanged, the 'reformed' KGB had actually redoubled its industrial espionage effort. Technobanditry, MI5 called it, and all the evidence pointed to its dramatic increase throughout Britain. Consequently, the watchers of A Branch were at full stretch and MI5 had been screaming for more funds, particularly for counter-intelligence. The Treasury, however, remained sceptical that MI5 was not merely crying wolf, so Number Ten had dished up Bert Carne as arbiter. In the interim, MI5 had to try and cope with its existing resources. Smailes wanted to ask about developments, but was reluctant to put Kinney on the spot in front of such a new recruit. Kinney, typically, took the initiative himself.

'Did you hear about the Farnborough air show incident?' he asked, exasperated. Smailes shook his head. Judith Hyams listened wide-eyed.

'Last weekend, four "tourists" approached a British Aerospace rep for an explanation of the Harrier's D/F system. He didn't trust their curiosity and went to fetch security. By the time he came back, they'd shot several rolls of film of the cockpit interior. Totally blatant. Claimed to be Danish, but, of course, they were all Russian. We couldn't arrest them, but we confiscated the film and got Special Branch to boot them out. And surprise, surprise, no mention of any complaint to the Danish embassy . . .'

'Tourists,' said Smailes. 'That's a new one.'

'What's D/F?' asked Judith meekly.

'Radar direction-finding systems,' said Kinney. 'NATO's way ahead in that area.'

'I don't know how Whitehall can keep denying the obvious,' said Smailes. 'How many did we expel after that electronics show in Birmingham?'

'Only three,' said Kinney. 'It could easily have been double that number. You know how it is. The Foreign Office has to believe its own rhetoric about new eras of cooperation. It simply ignores the size of NATO's restricted list and what we're required to do to protect it.'

Smailes was far from being an anti-Russian diehard, but he knew what Kinney said was true. The evidence was the Russians had infiltrated dozens of new intelligence officers into Britain, which, to MI5's deep annoyance, it had always viewed as the weak link in the Western alliance.

'We stopped by your office to introduce you today,' explained Kinney. 'Godfrey said you were out.'

'Yes, Westminster,' said Smailes casually. 'So what will you have Judith working on?' Despite heading up his own section, Smailes actively missed working with Kinney in the thick of counter-intelligence operations.

'We need to follow up watcher reports much more promptly. That's priority. Which means improving search-and-identify techniques. Judith has a background in computing, which should be a big help.'

'Well, accounting actually,' said Judith, reddening. Thanks largely to television satirists, accountancy had become the laughing-stock of the British professions.

Kinney smiled. 'That should help too,' he offered.

Smailes finished up his drink. 'I've got to be off. A pleasure to meet you, Judith,' he said, standing. 'Maybe we'll be running into each other.'

She smiled across at Kinney and then up at Smailes, grateful to them both for their chivalry.

4

Graham Booth hitched up his plaid shorts and padded up the slow incline of Kensington Palace Gardens towards Bayswater. London's early summer weather was a little brisk for such dress, but in his guise as an American tourist Booth was a complete professional. He wore a blue sweatshirt with the logo of the Seminoles, the Florida State University football team, a camera around his neck and a belt-pack on his hip. He squinted through the ornate iron railings at the sprawling expanse of Kensington Palace, which had been the Prince of Wales's London residence before his much-publicized separation. Then he consulted a tourist pamphlet from his pack and continued up the tree-lined avenue.

Booth, one of A Branch's most talented watchers, was on individual assignment – 'trawling' – rather than part of a 'box' or surveillance team. His target was any of half a dozen newly registered Russian diplomats – his guidebook contained clandestine shots of four of them. Movements analysis was a painstaking process, but the most scientific way for MI5 to determine whether a given individual was legitimate or not. And it was no secret that MI5 believed most of the recent Russian arrivals to be spies, plain and simple.

The Russian embassy had supplanted the former Soviet mission in its attractive Georgian mansion set back from the avenue behind a low iron fence. A mock Gothic turret gave the building a pleasing, asymmetrical façade, and a small stand of birch at the entrance added an ethnic touch. The Russian tricolour flew above the front door, but, in keeping with former Soviet practice, the embassy was not further identified, with a conspicuous absence of physical security compared with the consulate building on nearby Bayswater Road. However, the antennae and microwave dishes on the roof confirmed the site of the KGB *rezidentura* and hinted at its darker activities.

There was some lunchtime pedestrian traffic, as personnel from the two dozen or so embassies in the private avenue strolled up towards the security gate and the Notting Hill shops beyond, or returned with plastic carrier-bags filled with purchases. As Booth drew opposite the Russian embassy, a cry gave him pretext to turn round, and he saw a teenager in a track suit race down the drive and make a mock attempt to vault over a burly figure clad in a business suit who had just reached the gate. The diplomat made a good-natured attempt to swat the boy away, who then raced up the road towards the consulate on the corner. Booth thought the individual, a silver-haired chap about fifty, might be one of his charges, and stopped to consult his booklet as the Russian ambled up the street on the opposite pavement.

'Lubyanov,' said Booth under his breath. 'Got to be.' He watched the broad-backed figure pass the security barrier a hundred yards ahead, then turn right towards Bayswater instead of left towards Notting Hill Gate, as he would have predicted. Booth quickened his pace.

In front of the Russian consulate building traffic pounded along Bayswater Road in both directions, and two bored-looking policemen stood guard opposite a bedraggled posse of demonstrators, whose placards proclaimed something about independence for the Tatars. It reminded Booth that just as the once-mighty Soviet Union had proved itself a fragile empire, the now-dominant Russian republic was hardly a monolith, either. Booth spied the man he thought was Yuri Lubyanov pause to look around, then make a sudden right turn into the public park of Kensington Gardens.

Booth stopped to photograph the ornate gates at the top of the avenue, beneath whose heraldic shield a West Indian security guard sat in a control booth, watching cricket on a miniature television. Then he made his way up Bayswater Road, passing a tourist coach park on his right. He entered Kensington Gardens by Orme Square Gate, passed two stone groundskeepers' lodges, then quickly spotted his target heading towards a children's playground in the middle distance. The next development made Booth's heart leap. A female figure emerged from the forest of swings and climbing frames and greeted Lubyanov by touching his hands, then fell in alongside him as they moved around the perimeter fence. Booth quickly checked his guidebook again. Lubyanov and his wife had been captured by a clandestine camera at Heathrow, and whereas the woman who had just greeted Lubyanov was dark blonde, the British surveillance shot showed that dour Madame Lubyanova was emphatically black-haired. Booth walked nonchalantly across to a small cupola topped by a weather vane on the south side of the playground. Over to his right he could make out the rear of the Russian embassy and, beyond, the expanse of Kensington Palace itself. Through the trees ahead he could see the grey water of the Serpentine, where Kensington Gardens became Hyde Park. Over on his left, on a park bench well out of sight of the embassy's rear windows, Booth spotted Lubyanov and his friend, seated with their backs to him. He removed a tourist map from his hip-pack and oriented it with a flourish, struggling to maintain his aplomb.

'Bloody hell-fire!' muttered Booth to himself. 'Will you look at that?'

Comrade Lubyanov and his unknown companion were locked in an impassioned embrace, hands cradling each other's heads, oblivious to everything around them.

'See you again soon, Yuri, old chap,' Booth promised him quietly. 'Box, cameras, the works. Then let's see if you play Romeo again.'

Booth put his map away with difficulty and retraced his steps, controlling an urge to skip. 'Honeytrap time,' he told himself with glee.

Smailes took the M3 motorway south-west from London towards the horse pastures of Hampshire. This was also military turf, Smailes reminded himself as he turned off towards Aldershot, an obvious location for Brigadier Alec Cole to choose for his retirement. Cole's directions had been simple – right after the town of Farnborough to Church Crookham, then left at the big pub in the centre of the village. Rose Cottage was a quarter of a mile down on the left, and Smailes found it with ease.

Smailes interrupted Cole in his flower-beds as he climbed out of his car. The old soldier straightened up with a slight grunt as his visitor entered the gate, wiping his palm on the back of his trousers as Smailes approached.

'Good morning,' he said, extending a cold, firm hand. 'Any difficulties?'

'None at all, Brigadier. I'm Derek Smailes.'

'Yes. Yes, of course. Do come in, Mr Smailes.'

Alec Cole's home was a tiny thatched cottage of exposed timber and low bedroom gables that Smailes could almost reach up and touch. A trellis of wisteria climbed around the front door, through which Smailes had to duck sharply to enter. Cole, a short, square-shouldered fellow, led his guest through a dark, low-ceilinged sitting room into a bright, modern kitchen at the rear of the house. Smailes stood up to his full height with relief and accepted Cole's offer of a seat. Cole went over to the sink and snapped on an electric kettle.

'So, what's new with the Service these days? What's Bingham up to?' he asked, taking a seat across from his guest.

'Still ruling F Branch like a medieval potentate,' said Smailes, attempting to be jocular.

'Bloody good fellow. Served on a counter-insurgency committee with him once, in the days when the country was properly led,' he said forcefully, referring, Smailes assumed, to the Thatcher era. 'So this must be in connection with Audrey's death, I assume. I understand that you didn't want to speak on the phone. No irregularities, I suppose?' he asked, suggesting that he suspected there were.

Smailes studied his host. Cole was around seventy, he guessed, a stocky fellow with thin white hair and a stubby grey moustache. The leather buttons of a fawn cardigan strained across his paunch, and his complexion was florid from outdoor activity – Smailes could tell from the flower-beds and the rimmed dirt beneath his nails that gardening was the brigadier's passion. He had a glassy, pale-blue stare in which Smailes could see the fresh wound of his grief. Clearly, Brigadier Cole understood that MI5's interest in his daughter's death could hardly be routine.

'You live here alone, Brigadier?' Smailes asked.

'Yes. My wife died last year. Cancer,' he said simply.

'Audrey was your only child?'

'No. She has a brother. Works for Lonrho in Australia.' Smailes recalled the letters he had found in Audrey's flat. He realized his beating about the bush was both pointless and unkind.

'Did you know of Audrey's relationship with her employer, Brigadier Cole?' he asked.

Cole blew out his cheeks and folded his hands across his stomach. 'Stap?' he said with resignation. 'Yes, yes, I'm afraid I did. Told Audrey she was a bloody fool. He would never jeopardize his career with a divorce. Told her so countless times. Bit of a bone between us, I'm afraid.'

Cole stared into the distance over Smailes's shoulder and Derek could sense the pain of the unhealed rift between this stern man and his daughter. He also recognized something else – the mute indignation of those whose children are taken before them. The kettle began to boil, but Cole ignored it.

'Did you know she was pregnant at the time of her death?' Smailes asked more quietly.

The old soldier actually winced at this news and looked at him sharply. 'Good God,' he said. 'Did Stap know?'

'Apparently so.'

'The police were certain her death was an accident . . .'

'Oh yes, there's no question of that. I wasn't meaning to imply . . .' Cole stood and turned away to the sink, as if suddenly in need of privacy. He busied himself making a pot of tea and extracting a milk jug from the fridge. When he sat down again he held himself ramrod stiff, as if in need of greater control. He poured tea in silence.

'She was a grown woman,' he said eventually. 'Old enough to make her own decisions. I didn't always see eye to eye with her, of course. Parents seldom do.'

'Did she ever express anti-nuclear sentiments to you, by chance?' Smailes asked carefully.

Cole was aghast. 'Good Lord, no! What on earth are you implying, man?'

'When she died, your daughter was found to be carrying a classified document relating to the Trident programme. She was not authorized to remove it from the Commons.'

Cole suddenly understood Smailes's presence at his home. He took a moment to try and suppress his rage, and failed.

'Listen, if Audrey was engaged in anything illegal, she was doing so on Gerard Stap's behalf. That bloody man! She was completely besotted with him – she'd lost her judgement entirely. I warned her it could only end badly.'

Cole struggled with his emotions in silence, then continued forcefully. 'Look, Mr Smailes, my daughter comes from a long military tradition. Both her grandfathers were colonels. I was in uniform my entire life. Her husband was an infantry major – murdered by the IRA, no less. I am treasurer of the local Conservative party, and she herself had worked for the party for six, seven years. You think it possible she could be be knowingly disloyal to the Crown? It's absolutely out of the question.'

Cole fumed for a moment in silence. 'Was the document sealed?' he asked eventually. It was Smailes's turn to pause.

'I'm not sure. It was in an envelope. I don't know whether it was sealed or not.' Smailes kicked himself – it was an obvious question to ask.

'I'll bet it was. I'll bet my daughter didn't even know what was in it. She was delivering it on Stap's behalf, obviously – she was his secretary, after all. What was she doing on the North Circular in Finchley anyway, on a Friday night? The police asked me – I hadn't a clue.'

Smailes took a drink of his tea and looked across at Cole. It was an instinctive parental response, he knew, this need to exonerate a child, no matter what the circumstances – particularly given the added guilt over an estrangement. But as he reflected further on Audrey Cole's death and what he had learned of her background, Smailes thought it very likely her father had spoken the truth.

The most striking feature of Sir David Williams's office was its computers. There were two terminals on a credenza behind the huge desk, which linked the Director-General's office to the Department of Social Security in Newcastle and the Vehicle Licensing Centre in Swansea. On a typing table to his right was a relay to his secretary's word processor, and on the desk itself a terminal of MI5's own registry, and then his personal laptop. The combined ranks of these machines gave Williams access to almost thirty million files, representing half the British population. In fact, information management was one of Williams's foremost accomplishments, and the phalanx of mute grey screens a statement of his credentials. Sir David, only the second outsider ever to head MI5, was a former chief constable who had had to face bitter resentment from colleagues who had also coveted the job.

A crisis meeting was in progress in Sir David's suite, at which three such senior aides were present: the head of counter-espionage, Roger Standiforth; the head of counter-subversion, Miles Bingham; and the Deputy Director-General, Alex Corcoran. These four comprised MI5's executive committee, the tight group which actually ran the organization. There were three others present: a Briton, Peter Starling, head of the Ministry of Defence's Nuclear Accident Response Organization; and two Americans – Loudon Strickland, London CIA chief, and Lieutenant-Commander Byron Unger, US naval attaché from the Pentagon's Defense Intelligence Agency. News of the Burghfield break-in had reached Curzon House that morning, and the mood in Williams's suite was grim.

The DG's seventh-floor office was unremarkable except for its enormous size. It housed bleak institutional furniture that Williams had never bothered to replace, and dreary lace curtains that shrouded tall windows of yellowing bomb glass. Williams, flanked by his secretary Gwyneth Rees, was reclining in a huge leather desk-chair as Unger, seated at the conference table that extended at right angles into the room, tried to explain the gravity of the theft. Unger, a beefy man with a military haircut and a beet-red face, spoke with a proprietary indignation, even though the theft had occurred at a British lab.

'The main threat, as we analyse it, is that any competent technician could determine from reverse engineering how to construct duplicates, or, worse, bypass a PAL on an existing weapon,' Unger announced.

Deputy DG Corcoran had parked his wheelchair directly opposite the American, and spoke for the Britons present. 'Can you explain what these things actually do, Lieutenant? It might help us work out who might want to steal them.' Corcoran had a twisted, slightly hunched frame, and looked remarkably like Laurence Olivier in the role of Richard III. He spoke with a weary, supercilious air and deliberately misstated Unger's rank, using the British pronunciation 'Left-tenant' as if to emphasize on whose turf the discussion was taking place.

Unger was clearly exasperated by Corcoran's tone and turned to Starling. 'You wanna take that, Peter? You've been in on this from the start.'

'Yes, well, if I may begin at the beginning,' said Peter Starling, clearing his throat. 'When the decision was taken to replace Polaris with Trident in the eighties, we were extending our policy of using an exclusively American missile system in our SSBNs.' He looked up and saw a puzzled look on Williams's face. 'In our nuclear submarines, that is,' he said, without addressing Williams directly.

'Modifications were needed for the new warheads, but these too were to be accomplished from American blueprints – it all goes back to an agreement between the Thatcher and Carter governments.' He looked around again to see if he was being followed.

'Permissive action links were developed by the Americans in the sixties after a congressional inspection tour found that the two-man rule wasn't working on NATO's front line. You know, that each nuclear weapon had to be physically unlocked by an American officer and one from the host country. In fact, security was found to be incredibly lax. One Turkish officer who later turned out to be a KGB agent was discovered flying around with a plane-load of nuclear bombs and both keys. Naturally, President Kennedy was a bit upset . . .

'Anyway, the permissive action link device was developed at the Sandia weapons lab in New Mexico as an electronic lock within the bomb's firing circuit. It could only be unlocked by insertion of a code from central authority – you know, the information the US President carries around in his football.'

Unger interrupted. 'Which is the black briefcase that the President's military aide carries . . .'

'Yes, right. Thank you, Byron,' said Starling, momentarily losing his train of thought. 'Well, anyway, successive presidents thought it wise to install PALs on all nuclear bombs, no matter where they were based, and then, when ICBMs were developed, on those too. So that, basically, American nuclear weapons are inert without launch authority from central command. However, there have been two historical exceptions. The first was the host of tactical weapons across all the services. They were considered too small and numerous, and since both sides are in the process of scrapping them, it's no longer particularly significant.'

'Then there were the Navy weapons,' said Unger, interrupting again. Clearly, he didn't quite trust Starling to get this part of the story straight. 'Neither the US nor the Royal Navy nukes have ever had PALs. That is, not until the process that began a couple of years ago.'

'Naval weapons were never locked? Why ever not?' asked Williams, genuinely surprised. Unger seemed affronted by the question.

'A host of reasons, Sir David,' he said testily. 'Primarily, the difficulty of communicating with submerged submarines in time of war. The only foolproof method had been the ELF transmitter in Wisconsin, and that's very slow indeed. Then, it was felt the Navy's PRP was sound enough . . .'

'Personnel reliability program,' Starling chimed in, taking his turn to prompt Unger.

'And I suppose in both countries it was also tradition. Both navies are the senior service, and the Navy command felt it ought to be trusted.'

'Two developments changed the thinking both in the Pentagon and in Whitehall,' said Starling, now accepting this presentation had become a double act. 'The first was during the Falklands crisis when the task force reached Ascension Island before the War Cabinet learned it was carrying unlocked nuclear depth-bombs. They ordered a hold-over of several days so a frigate could go out and offload them. Mrs Thatcher was quite peeved. Then there was the development of blue-green lasers. Byron, I think you'd better explain that.'

Unger looked around the room. Most of the expressions were non-committal, except for Sir David, who was frowning. Unger swung his massive head from right to left, then slowly resumed.

'Blue-green light is the only band of the electromagnetic spectrum in addition to ELF and VLF that can penetrate sea water. The Pentagon had developed a blue-green optical transmitter for communications satellites, of which the shuttle has deployed three, giving coverage in seventy per cent of the world's oceans. So it was felt that there was now sufficient communications redundancy that PALs could be installed on SLBMs without compromising their readiness. With the end of the Cold War and the renewed emphasis on nuclear security . . .' Unger shrugged. 'I guess Annapolis felt it had to bow to the inevitable. Which meant, since the British Navy had already upgraded to Trident, its missiles had to be retrofitted with PALs, too.'

'Why so?' asked Corcoran.

'Because in the event of the destruction of British central command, launch authority reverts to Strategic Command at Omaha. So the systems have to be completely compatible.'

'And so this was what was stolen from Burghfield?' Williams asked. 'The PALs for the Trident warheads?'

'And for the surface ship depth-charges,' Unger added, looking down at a report. 'It says here they got the hardware, engineering manuals and computer software. They sure the hell seemed to know what they were after.'

Miles Bingham, seated next to Roger Standiforth, had been silent up to this point, but was growing agitated. He was the physical opposite of Standiforth, a short, jowly man with a wide flap of a mouth and a high-pitched, nasal voice. As head of F Branch, he was responsible for the botched 'attack' which had led to the Burghfield break-in, and was eager to distance himself from its repercussions.

'Well, it wasn't terrorists, was it?' he declared petulantly. 'They didn't touch the plutonium, did they, which is what any terrorist group would go after, isn't it? It has to be someone who already possesses nuclear weapons and wants to make them safer. What about the Russians?'

'Russian strategic weapons already have PALs,' said Starling.

'Well, what about the unofficial powers – there's a ton of them, isn't there, Peter?' he asked, turning around. Clearly, as head of counter-terrorism, Bingham wanted to point the finger at a foreign government, a K Branch responsibility.

Before Starling could answer, CIA chief Loudon Strickland cleared his throat and spoke. 'Ah, there is one terrorist scenario we can't discount, I'm afraid, gentlemen. Commander Unger and I haven't discussed it yet, but it ought to be considered.'

All heads turned to Strickland, who was seated at the foot of the conference table. He was distinguished from his colleagues by his pale-grey suit, pale-grey face and thin blond hair. He wore thick, black-rimmed spectacles of the type that had gone out of fashion in the late sixties.

'I'm referring, Peter, to the Oldham Three of two years ago.'

Starling's face suddenly blanched with recognition.

'What on earth are you talking about, Loudon?' asked Williams, his Welsh accent becoming more pronounced as he grew animated. 'Let's talk in English, can we, for goodness' sake?'

Strickland paused before continuing. 'Oldham Three is NARO's designation for the most serious type of nuclear weapons accident – one that involves release of radioactive material and consequent safety hazards.'

Starling, understanding Sir David's aversion to acronyms, elaborated. 'That's my unit, Sir David – the Nuclear Accidents Response Organization. We use double-syllable towns from the north of England for all our codenames.'

'Which is why the Burghfield test was Operation Wakefield?' Williams inquired.

'Correct.'

'You want to do this, Peter?' asked Strickland.

'You explain the accident, Loudon. I'll explain the response.'

Strickland cleared his throat. 'Two years ago there was a freak accident in the skies over Norfolk. A Royal Air Force Tornado bomber was returning from routine patrol over the Skagerrak straits. It was armed with two WE177s – that's the basic free-fall nuclear bomb that NATO aircraft deploy. As the pilot began his descent into RAF Honington in Suffolk, he had to take violent evasive action to avoid a mid-air collision with a US aircraft that was taking off from RAF Mildenhall – it was an A-10 Thunderbolt, wasn't it, Peter?'

Starling nodded.

'Anyway,' Strickland continued, 'there's some dispute over which pilot was on the wrong flight path, but the navigator of the Tornado was thrown to the floor by the g force, and when he looked up, he saw the ground but no horizon. Believing his aircraft to be out of control, he ejected. But the ejection selector, which is housed in his cockpit, was switched to "Both", so the navigator and the pilot – who must have been pretty surprised – were both ejected clear. The plane went into a stall, then a steep dive, and crashed in a fireball into a Norfolk marsh. The pilot and the navigator both parachuted to the ground safely. Peter?'

There was silence in the room as Starling picked up the narrative.

'We have a multi-track response network given the severity of a given accident,' Starling said, aping Pentagon Newspeak. 'First reports indicated that this was definitely an Oldham Three, that although neither of the bombs had detonated, they were probably severely damaged and that radioactive material had escaped. So the first unit at the scene had to be the IRT – the Initial Response Team based at St Athan in south Wales. Then the nearest Special Safety Team, in this case from Mildenhall, and the Nuclear Emergency Team, also at St Athan, follow up. Given the distance involved, there was a one-hour delay before the crash site could be inspected and cordoned off. It was found that both bombs had been thrown clear of the wreckage and that in fact the titanium case of the first bomb had not been breached and there was no release of radioactive material. Luckily, we were able to convince the local press that the whole thing was a training exercise, and the story barely made the national news.'

There was a pause, after which Williams asked the obvious question. 'What about the second bomb?' he said.

'It was never found,' Starling said quietly. There was a lengthy silence.

'Let me explain, Sir David,' said Starling, with a willed lightness of tone. 'Since the dawn of the nuclear age there have been scores of accidents involving nuclear weapons in the Western arsenal. But none has ever resulted in an accidental detonation, largely because of the multiple safety devices built into the weapons themselves. But quite a few accidents have involved the physical loss of the weapon itself. Some SLBMs have been lost at sea. There were two crashes in Greenland which involved the loss of free-fall bombs. In each case, the physical integrity of the weapon has been ensured and the remoteness of the site has ruled out any danger of theft. The strong likelihood is that the second WE177 bomb was also thrown clear and sank into the marshy terrain around the crash site – wreckage was strewn over a kilometre radius. Despite extensive monitoring and a two-week search, we could never locate it, and eventually had to give up. However . . .'

Here Starling paused, as if picking his words with particular care. 'We have never been able definitively to rule out that the second bomb may have been discovered and stolen from the crash site. It weighed about a ton and could have been removed by agricultural machinery. Naturally, we interviewed all the locals who had visited the crash site before we got there, and no one spoke of anything being hauled away. But we cannot be one hundred per cent sure.'

Here Starling looked over at Strickland, who had removed a gold pen from his breast pocket and had begun playing with it. 'Go on, Peter,' he said.

Starling was beginning to look distinctly uncomfortable. 'Yes, well. When the recovered bomb was examined, it was found that all its ENDS switches had closed. I'm sorry – the Enhanced Nuclear Detonation Safety switches. These are the safety mechanisms that ensure that a weapon will detonate only if it is delivered in the precise way for which it was designed – in the WE177's case, these are gravity and barometric pressure switches that arm the bomb only when it is in free fall from a precise height. Well, it was discovered that the descent of the Tornado into the marsh so precisely mirrored the free fall of the bomb's design that all the safety switches had closed. The only thing that prevented detonation on impact and the creation of a nuclear wasteland in eastern England was the bomb's permissive action link, which functioned as designed and prevented the final arming of the bomb's firing circuit.'

Suddenly, Commander Byron Unger sat bolt upright in his chair. 'Good God, I see what you mean, Loudon,' he said.

Sir David Williams was clearly struggling against a mounting fury. 'Commander?' he asked with difficulty.

'The WE177 has an identical design to the Navy depth-bomb – they're essentially the same weapon. The group that stole the PALs from Burghfield might be able to figure out the submaster code and unlock a PAL on a parallel weapon. If they got hold of the missing Norfolk bomb – hell, they could detonate it with a car battery!'

'Wait a minute,' Bingham interrupted. 'The depth-bomb is a tactical weapon, isn't it? I thought we'd agreed to get rid of all of those.'

Unger sighed. 'There's a secret protocol allowing us to keep a handful on both sides. It was a Russian condition – the nuclear depth-bomb is the most potent anti-submarine weapon available, and they're still worried about our superiority in SSBNs. Burghfield was going to fit Category D PALs to the depth-charges, and the more sophisticated

Category F PALs to the strategic warheads. The raiders took both.' Unger looked around the room at the rows of stunned faces.

'But look, I just wanna stress that I agree with Miles Bingham here. This could not have been a terrorist operation – it was just too sophisticated. My money's still on the Russians – sure, they've got pretty tight command and control, but their actual PAL hardware sucks. You wanna know what Soviet fail-safe devices are like – go ask the residents of Chernobyl! Believe me, the Russians would kill for our PAL technology, and we know it. In fact, there's been one holy row in Washington over this. The Pentagon has been pouring money into dismantling Russian nukes, and State and the CIA have both been arguing in favour of handing over our PAL technology to enhance the safety of those limited weapons they get to keep. But so far, the Pentagon has vetoed it on security grounds and the White House has agreed. But I guess the real question is, who leaked Operation Wakefield? Find that out and maybe you'll figure out who pulled off the theft.'

David Williams decided it was time to reassert control over both his emotions and the meeting. 'How many people were indoctrinated into Wakefield, Miles?' he asked carefully.

'Officially, six,' replied Bingham. 'Here, just yourself and myself. At Grosvenor Square, these two gentlemen here today. At Burghfield, just Reynolds, the head of security. At the ministry, the permanent secretary for defence, that's all. He no doubt informed the Minister, who probably also circulated the Shadow Cabinet.'

'Really?' asked Strickland.

'I'm afraid so. Since the Labour party recovered from its unilateralist spasm,' Bingham said in a voice thick with sarcasm, 'it's been bipartisan policy to share all information concerning the nuclear deterrent. Against our wishes, I might add.'

'What about staff?' asked Corcoran.

'Well, you have a point. I would think for each individual indoctrinated there might be between five and ten subordinates who saw the information.' Bingham thought for a moment. 'I have six, for instance.'

'So a total of between forty and sixty,' said Williams.

'Sounds right.'

'Well, we've got a lot of work to do.'

'Listen, there's another possibility,' said Starling.

'Yes?' said Sir David.

'Some of the unofficial nuclear powers would also be very interested in PAL technology, I would think. Particularly in unstable parts of the world, like the Middle East, it's just too risky to keep unlocked warheads and delivery systems mated together except in the stage of highest alert. We know for a fact that during the Gulf War Israel didn't mate its weapons together until they thought Tel Aviv was about to be hit by poison gas. And you've got Iran, Libya and Syria who are all thought to be on the verge of developing their own nukes, not to mention Iraq. Don't you agree, Commander?'

'You can't rule that out,' said Unger. 'A few of them could put together some pretty impressive commando squads, too.'

'Well, we'll begin our investigation right away,' said Williams, obviously anxious to conclude the meeting. 'I meet with the Cabinet secretary in one hour. What about you, gentlemen?'

Unger consulted his watch. 'Well, Supreme Allied Commander Europe and the Secretary-General should be arriving from Brussels about now. We need to get back to Grosvenor Square.'

Strickland picked up his pen and pushed his chair away from the conference table. 'We'll begin an immediate investigation at our end,' he said. 'And any way we can help, you know where we are.' The Americans stood and, since handshakes did not appear in order, nodded to their British counterparts.

'We'll keep you informed,' said Sir David as they turned to leave.

'You need me further?' asked Starling.

'I don't think so,' said Williams coldly. He turned to the unnoticed figure of his secretary, who had been dutifully scribbling shorthand. 'Excuse us, will you, Gwyneth?' Williams asked. There was a pause as the four of them filed out of the room.

Williams waited until he heard the outer door close, then exploded. 'Why the hell was I never briefed on this Norfolk accident?' he yelled at Corcoran.

'Frankly, I didn't know you weren't, Sir David,' said Corcoran mildly. 'I assumed Sir Henry would have informed you. It was his responsibility.'

Bloody typical, Williams told himself. Ever since he had accepted this thankless position as a favour to the Prime Minister, he had had to tolerate the deliberate efforts of his subordinates to undermine him. Now he learned that his predecessor had failed to brief him on the gravest nuclear accident in Britain's history. And the Burghfield incident meant that not only had MI5 been party to the most egregious security lapse ever at a nuclear facility, but he had had to learn its full implications from the bloody Americans. He felt his anger rising again.

'How dare the Americans sit here and lecture us, as if they owned our bloody deterrent?' he exploded again.

'Well, because in a simple sense they do,' said Bingham. 'Wilson tried to develop an exclusively British system in the seventies, but the Treasury simply couldn't afford it. If the Americans didn't sell us off-the-shelf systems at a big discount, we would no longer be a nuclear power. If you ask me, it's better than being back with the wogs.'

'Look,' said Williams, regaining himself. 'Where do we start? We have forty or so individuals on our end who could have betrayed this information.'

'Well, there's an obvious candidate,' said Standiforth, finally breaking his silence. 'Gerry Stap, or his assistant. We have proof that top secret nuclear information was leaking through his office, from the document we found in Audrey Cole's car. He's the government spokesman for the Trident programme, after all, and would no doubt have been circulated on Operation Wakefield.'

'Yes,' agreed Corcoran. 'I was thinking the same thing.'

'Now, wait a minute,' said Bingham, objecting. 'I've known Gerry Stap for ten years, and the man is a patriot and a gentleman. It's out of the question he would betray our nuclear secrets to a foreign power.'

'Well, but there's the secretary, isn't there? I have some question whether she was an inside source for Nukewatch,' said Standiforth.

'That rabble are all anarchists,' said Bingham with contempt. 'They would betray anything they got, just from spite.'

'Who do you have on the Stap inquiry?' Williams asked Standiforth.

'Smailes.'

'Well, we can't watch the secretary – she's dead. What surveillance have we ordered on Stap?'

Corcoran, who as Deputy DG had responsibility for adjudicating watcher bids, appeared embarrassed and shifted position in his wheelchair. 'Working hours only, I'm afraid,' he said.

'Why so?' asked Williams. 'He must be a prime suspect in the delivery schedule leak, surely?'

'Well,' said Corcoran awkwardly, 'we're overstretched. Roger has asked for twenty-four-hour surveillance on a recent Russian arrival. He may be KGB, and he may be conducting an illicit affair . . .'

This was too many 'may be's for Williams, who had an aversion to MI5's traditional entrapment activities. 'Switch the order,' he commanded. 'Working hours only on this diplomat. Twenty-four hours on Stap. Who's performing the scene-of-crime analysis?'

Williams's subordinates winced. 'Scene-of-crime' was a police CID term, not part of MI5 vernacular.

'Reynolds's people at Burghfield, along with SSO from RAF Locking,' said Bingham.

'Have Smailes liaise with them. Miles, I want you to prepare an exhaustive list of every individual on the British end who saw this information.'

It was Standiforth's turn to object. 'This is not really a K9 matter, Sir David, and Smailes hardly has the seniority to be indoctrinated into Wakefield.'

Williams glared at him. 'Do as I say,' he said icily, reaching for an intercom button. 'You can come back, Gwyneth,' he spoke into the machine, signalling the meeting was over.

Standiforth knew there was no point in remonstrating – Williams often bestowed favour on other former policemen, as a way of asserting independence. As he and Bingham got to their feet, he countered with a favourite method of patronizing the untutored Williams.

'Audaciam virtutem esse ferunt,' he bantered in Latin.

Corcoran deftly manoeuvred his wheelchair towards the door. 'Audacia an stultitia agitur,' he responded over his shoulder.

'Haec credo,' said Standiforth smugly. Corcoran laughed.

Williams glared at the door as it closed. 'You bastards!' he spat. 'You toffee-nosed English bastards!'

5

Smailes worked it out on the drive home from the restaurant – how Sal Imodeo had learned of his birthday, and why his best friend Iain Mack had called that day, asking for his wife. He'd thought it odd that Clea had arranged this birthday dinner with the Randalls on a Saturday night, when it was difficult to bribe Fidelma to forgo her waitress shift and baby-sit Lucy. Then, suddenly, it all became clear. The ruse had been to get him out of the house, of course, so Clea and her co-conspirators – Sal, Iain, the Randalls – could complete their preparations for a surprise party. His actual birthday didn't fall until the following week, but Saturday was the obvious night for such an event. And despite Derek's insistence that turning forty didn't feel like anything to celebrate, that a quiet dinner was all that was necessary, Clea had obviously been working on her plans for weeks.

Derek glanced at his wife in the rear-view mirror and felt a surge of tenderness. Despite her dismay over the ill-timed pregnancy, Clea had obviously devoted considerable care to the deception. As he turned into their street, Smailes pointedly ignored Iain's Saab parked on the corner, and another car with diplomatic plates that probably belonged to Imodeo. The Randalls accompanied them into the house for a supposed nightcap, and Smailes found the living room empty, although he could hear Lucy squawking somewhere. Then Clea suddenly yelled, 'Surprise!' and about a dozen of their closest friends trooped out of the dining room, brandishing drinks.

Smailes turned to his wife and hugged her. 'Darling, I told you not to . . .'

'Did you guess?'

'No!'

'Well, I ignored you.'

Iain Mack came up and pumped his hand. 'Happy birthday, Coulsdon Man,' he said, peering up at the bald spot on Smailes's crown. Smailes was genuinely delighted to see him.

'Yes, well, your turn's coming, mate,' he said, aware of something odd in his friend's appearance. Then he was immediately distracted by the wailing form of Lucy, who was being hoisted with difficulty by her baby-sitter.

'Daddy tell story,' Lucy howled.

Fidelma Magrath was a dumpy teenager with a bad complexion whom Lucy treated with bottomless disdain. She was obviously embarrassed. 'Honestly, Mr Smailes, I tried to get her to sleep before everyone started arriving. But she knew something was going on, I swear it.' Despite repeated injunctions, Fidelma had never been able to call him Derek.

'Were you in on this, Fidelma?' Smailes asked, cocking an eyebrow and accepting the squirming mass of his daughter.

'Yes,' she answered sheepishly.

'That's all right, love – I'll put her to bed. Stay and have a drink.'

Lucy put her head on Smailes's shoulder as he manoeuvred his way towards the stairs.

'People,' she said.

'Yes, Lucy. Lots of people.'

In the kitchen Clea was chatting with Sarah Sutcliffe, a friend from her Oxford days, who was manipulating a large platter of hors-d'oeuvres.

'Hello, Sarah,' he said with forced enthusiasm. Sarah lived in a women's collective in Peckham and treated Smailes like a thought criminal. Clea volunteered there two afternoons a week, to Derek's chagrin. He hoped Sarah hadn't fixed the snacks herself – they would be buckwheat groat balls, or some such dreadful vegetarian fare.

'Happy birthday, Derek,' she said moodily.

'Just putting this one to bed,' he told Clea.

Clea came and kissed her daughter. 'Night, night, princess,' she said. Lucy pushed her face away with a sticky paw.

On the top landing, Smailes spied Sarah's bag on the box-room floor. 'Bloody hell-fire,' he told himself. 'She's spending the night.'

By the time Smailes retraced his steps, the party was in full swing. Willie Nelson wailed from the stereo and a bar had been set up on the dining room table, next to which Smailes found Sal Imodeo and an immaculately groomed companion.

'You nearly blew this, you know, Sal – congratulating me on my birthday last week. Couldn't work out how you knew.'

'I know,' said Imodeo guiltily. 'I realized on my way out the door. Derek, this is Laura Kowski. She's with Goldman Sachs.'

Smailes accepted an elegantly manicured hand, which he couldn't quite imagine clutching a baseball bat.

'Thanks for coming,' said Smailes. 'It's a bit of a drive.'

'Hi, Dad.'

Smailes turned to confront Tracy, his twenty-year-old daughter from his first marriage. Rail-thin, Tracy was now an art student in south London and a rare visitor at her father's home. She was squired by an androgynous-looking bloke with tight leather trousers and a prominent Adam's apple, whom she introduced as Dave. Smailes loved his eldest daughter, but realized he hadn't a clue how she lived. He accepted her peck on the cheek, noticing that her figure seemed to have filled out a little and that her latest hair colouring was starting to bleed out at the roots.

'Hi, Tracy. It's great to see you again. Nice to meet you. Dave,' he said to her sullen consort.

'Hullo,' said Dave casually, heading over to inspect Smailes's tape collection.

'How've you been?' Smailes asked his daughter.

'Oh, great, Dad,' she said, nervously watching Dave's retreat. 'Hey, can we play something else?'

'You choose,' he told her, smiling and shaking his head. Smailes poured himself a drink and looked around, warming up to the event. It really was typical of his wife to arrange such a gathering over his protests. He saw her over by the front door, talking with Iain, and headed towards them.

Iain Mack greeted his best friend with a bear hug and asked him how it felt to turn forty. 'Frankly, I feel cheated,' said Smailes. Clea laughed but excused herself, saying she had to keep helping in the kitchen.

Smailes stood back and inspected Iain. Mack's long hair was thinning also, and Smailes suddenly realized that he'd had it permed. Iain's vanity was the one thing about his friend that really irked him.

'Say,' said Mack conspiratorially, 'have you ever done it with a really tall, skinny woman?'

Smailes was taken aback and thought for a moment. 'No, I don't think so. Why?'

'It's sensational. Everything's at the right level – you don't have to adjust . . . I've just started a hot affair with my new research assistant – she must be five ten or eleven. It's great . . .'

'Why didn't you bring her?'

'Don't be daft, mate, she's married,' said Mack. Smailes felt an involuntary surge of envy, then an immediate stab of guilt at the thought of his adored daughter, asleep upstairs. He was about to respond when the door opened and Clea's parents entered, accompanied by Julie, Clea's ravishing but insecure younger sister. Iain disappeared with Derek's glass as Smailes accepted their handshakes and kisses. Peter Lynch headed for the bar as Julie went in search of her sister, and Smailes was left standing with Anthea Lynch, his mother-in-law. Smailes weighed a question about her new-found interest in Tibetan Buddhism, but she pre-empted him.

'How are you, Derek?' she asked evenly. Then, more pointedly, 'And how's Clea?'

Clea's mother was a wise and knowing woman whose counsel Derek had always valued. He exhaled slowly, then tried to explain as tactfully as he could Clea's ambivalence about the new baby.

'If she'd just agree to hire a nanny,' said Smailes.

Anthea Lynch shook her head. 'I didn't, so Clea won't,' she said. 'I know her too well.'

Iain Mack returned with their drinks, and Smailes introduced him. Anthea Lynch saw her daughters across the crowd and went to join them.

'Who's that?' asked Mack, nodding at Julie.

'That's Clea's sister, Julie,' said Smailes. 'You've never met her?'

'Not yet,' said Mack lasciviously. Derek gave his friend a punch in the ribs.

'Hey,' said Mack casually. 'You didn't hear anything about that Tory woman, did you? The one who got killed on the North Circular? I've got a contact at the Yard who tells me she may have done something naughty.'

Smailes's internal warning system switched to high alert, as it always did when his friend, a BBC news reporter, tried to pump him for information. Officially, Smailes couldn't even admit to him that he worked for MI5, which Mack found ridiculous.

Smailes looked puzzled. 'Who's that, then?' he asked. Mack pulled a sceptical face, and Smailes changed the subject, asking him about his work. Mack had recently won a producer's job on *Focus*, a new BBC documentary programme.

'It's going great,' said Mack. 'I just got my editor to approve a show on the rise of the Russian mafia. You know, how organized crime is in bed with the new civil authorities, since they're the only ones with both the capital and the know-how. Run it in the autumn, on the anniversary of the October Revolution – nice touch, eh? We go to Moscow for "recce" next month.'

The speakers began to blare out Bruce Springsteen, much too loud for comfort. 'Come over here,' said Smailes, suddenly feeling his age. 'I'll introduce you to Julie.'

Smailes actually enjoyed his party, drinking far more than his usual allowance. He was aware at some point, however, that his wife was avoiding him. As people began to leave, she eventually came over and took his hand.

'Nice party?'

'Terrific.'

'Tell me the truth – when did you guess?'

'The truth? On the drive home. I finally worked out why Iain called today.'

'I knew you'd seen his car as we drove up,' said Clea. Then she sighed. 'Derek, I'm sorry I've been such a bitch lately.'

'Well, I'm sorry for putting you up the spout.'

'Oh, I'm thrilled, really. It's just hard. You know, my plans . . .'

'I know, love.' He put his arm round her. 'Is Sarah spending the night?' he asked.

'I invited her to. Do you mind?'

'Not if she behaves herself. You remember last time, she lectured me for reading *Little Mermaid* to Lucy because it's too sexist?'

'Oh, I know. She goes too far. But she's having a difficult time. She just broke up with someone . . .'

'A woman?' Smailes asked.

Clea nodded.

'Is that what she's into?'

'Ideologically,' said Clea. 'But I think it's hard for her on, you know, a sexual level.'

'That's ridiculous,' said Smailes, despite himself.

'It is not,' Clea retorted. 'A lot of women today just don't find men, well, very trustworthy. Then there's the whole AIDS thing. A relationship with another woman is a logical alternative.'

'I don't think that's entirely fair,' said Smailes.

'Well,' asked his wife, 'how trustworthy is Iain?'

'Not very,' conceded Smailes.

'Look over there,' said Clea. She nodded across to the couch, where Iain and Julie Lynch were locked in intense conversation.

'Typical,' said Smailes.

'It bothers me,' said Clea. 'She's on the rebound from that chap Bert, you know . . .'

'I thought Tracy looked good tonight,' said Smailes, changing the subject.

'Could you tell she's on the pill?' laughed Clea. 'She's finally got some boobs.'

'Oh, *that's* it,' said Smailes, momentarily disoriented by the idea of his daughter's sexuality. Then he reflected that of his two daughters in the house that night, he had one on the pill and the other still in nappies, and felt even more disoriented. Clea was frowning.

'What's up?' he asked.

Iain and Julie, having found their coats, were making their way towards the front door.

'I've decided to go back up to town,' Julie said casually to her sister as they passed. 'Will you tell Mummy I don't need a lift?'

'You could tell her yourself,' said Clea archly.

'Oh, she's helping Sarah clear up in the kitchen,' said Julie. 'I don't want to make a fuss.'

Iain gave Smailes a leering wink. 'Give me a call. Let's have a drink,' he said, steering Julie towards the door.

'Sure thing,' said Smailes, shaking his head.

That night in bed, Clea unexpectedly rejected Derek's advances, leaving him crestfallen. 'What's the matter?' he asked.

'Oh, darling,' said Clea wearily. 'I'm just not in the mood. I suppose I'm depressed about getting fat again. It took me so long to get my figure back after Lucy was born. I feel about as sexy as a farm animal.'

She turned away from him, squeezing his hand, and Smailes reflected on how different this pregnancy was going to be from her first, when Clea had been so thrilled by the changes in her body that her libido had been enhanced. He cursed the presence of Sarah Sutcliffe down the hall, who always seemed to make Clea feel that Derek was one of the enemy. And he also realized, sadly, that despite their best efforts the rift between them was not yet healed.

Smailes approached the grim hulk of Curzon House along Bolton Street, which, unlike similar buildings in Washington, was not identified in any way. He stood beneath the camera where security could get a good look at him, then pushed the door at the buzzer's release. He completed the sign-in formalities and headed for the lifts. He had an early meeting with Standiforth about the Carne submission and wanted to review his notes first.

Derek Smailes, an assistant director of MI5, remained distinctly ambivalent about his employer, despite his recent elevation to management. On the one hand, he did not question the need for Britain, like any modern society, to protect itself from enemies from within and without. On the other hand, he knew MI5 remained a partisan, often pernicious organization which operated largely outside the law and whose excesses had been mostly unchecked by previous attempts at reform. He therefore questioned whether the Carne review, which he privately welcomed, was destined to fizzle out like its predecessors, despite all the fanfare and paranoia.

He had, however, become a keen student of MI5's internal culture. There were basically three kinds of staffers, to his mind: the old school, the household staff and the professionals. The old school was literally just that – men and women who had attended the same public schools and universities, who now belonged to the same clubs, lived in the same suburbs and played on the same golf courses. MI5 was in fact unusual in this one regard – the career opportunities it offered to women. The conventional Whitehall wisdom was that whereas men were preternaturally inclined to boast of their exploits, women, while addicted to gossip about trivia, were silent as the grave about matters of moment. Thus women had always done well in MI5's obsessive world, on occasion even rising to section or division head level. Rumour had it that one day a woman would run MI5, although Smailes couldn't quite imagine it happening during his career.

Generally, the old school had joined MI5 upon graduation and, despite the meritocratic Thatcher revolution, still ran the show. Their dominant culture had become MI5's culture – furnishing its peculiar slang, its peculiar politics, its peculiar social relations. These latter were often characterized by bitter distrust and rivalry, best illustrated by the relationship between Roger Standiforth and Miles Bingham. Both Standiforth and Bingham had attended Harrow and Oxford, were only a few years apart in age, and both exemplified the old school. But they had taken different career paths in the organization, and 'Standers' and 'Bingo', as they were universally known, hated each other's guts. Like others of the old school, both had been bitterly resentful of Williams's appointment as DG and were now the leading contenders for the job when he retired. Williams, typically, was known to the old school as 'Taffy' or the 'Chief Super', to emphasize his humble origins. Both Standers and Bingo were career officers and extended medieval webs of patronage throughout the organization, where they had recruited and bestowed favour.

A third prominent old schooler was Deputy DG Alex Corcoran – 'Corky' to compatriots. Corcoran was generally acknowledged the most gifted counter-intelligence officer of his generation, but his career had suffered from cruel misfortune. A victim of infantile polio, Corcoran had been confined to a wheelchair for most of his life, and although many changes had come to the British civil service during the Thatcher era, the career prospects of the physically handicapped were not among them. A recent mild stroke had further cast doubt upon his physical strength, and Corcoran was consequently ruled out as a contender for the Director-General's chair and the knighthood that went with it. He was a bilious, unpredictable character, but one who still wielded considerable influence in the organization.

Household staff fell into several categories. Women like Audrey Cole – from good families, often with military backgrounds – filled most of the clerical positions, and were the ranks from which the old school generally chose its wives. There were also former armed service types, NCOs or enlisted men, who were viewed as obedient and trustworthy and filled many of the non-management track positions. These were the people who, two generations before, would have been the secretaries, valets and butlers to the old school in their professional and domestic lives. Then there was the odd square peg, men like Les Townsend, the former safe-cracker who oversaw the vast workshops in MI5's basement. In fact, there were a number of reformed criminals on MI5's payroll, household staffers who owed their second chance to a specific officer who had recruited them. They were usually people of limited intellect and ferocious loyalty, whom it was wise not to cross.

Then there were the professionals, men like Derek Smailes, from law enforcement or military intelligence backgrounds who were late entrants into the service. Another such was Brian Kinney. Although Smailes had been recruited and twice promoted by Standiforth, the circumstances were in each case sufficiently ambivalent that he did not count himself a member of Roger's patronage circle, but instead felt allegiance to men like Kinney, fellow professionals from whom he had learned his trade. However, although their ranks had grown in recent years to include the DG himself, the professionals were under no illusions that they really called the shots at Curzon House.

Smailes was aware the latest gossip had it that Sir David was wearying of the continued friction at the top of the organization, and would opt for retirement at sixty when he became eligible in two years' time. The likelihood then was that the government would concede the appointment of an outsider had been a mistake, and the top job would devolve to one of the two insiders, Standiforth or Bingham. Provided, Smailes reflected as he unlocked his office door, that MI5 survived the Carne review and continued to exist in two years' time.

'So the idea is to see whether anyone has a firm idea who actually pulled off this raid, to give the investigation some direction,' said Standiforth.

'Exactly how do you mean, Roger?' asked Smailes. Smailes and his boss were seated in the transported clubland of Roger's office, where Standiforth had just completed a lengthy indoctrination of the Wakefield material.

'Well, the culprits could be either Libyan or Israeli, South African or Russian, which gives us quite a range of possible traitors, doesn't it? Bingham thinks up to sixty may have seen the information.'

'Okay. And what's the party's name again?'

'Prendergast. Wing Commander Mark Prendergast. He's based at RAF Locking, outside Bristol.'

Smailes scribbled on his pad, weighing his next question.

'So is this an extension of the Stap investigation, Roger?' Standiforth had not yet explained why Smailes had been indoctrinated into a file not obviously in his purview.

'Strictly speaking, no. But Stap and his secretary have to be the leading suspects, given what we know so far. We've already confirmed he was circulated the details of the mock attack.'

Smailes scratched his temple with the end of his pen. 'Surveillance turn up anything yet?'

'No. But Audrey Cole has to be the prime suspect, obviously. Where are you with your report?'

'Almost ready. I need to follow a couple more leads.' He paused. 'Frankly, Roger, I really doubt Audrey Cole acted solo. Military family, staunch Tories, IRA widow – it doesn't add up. My guess is she was Stap's cut-out, and maybe didn't even know what she was carrying. Her loyalty to Stap is the only thing I can think might override her sense of public duty.'

Standiforth's reply was larded with cynicism. 'We may not be talking conventional politics here. Maybe she was a closet Green, for God's sake, believing she was performing a public duty. If she gave the material to Nukewatch or Greenpeace, for instance, they could have sold it on the black market, just to be disruptive. Keep digging. See what Prendergast has to say.'

Standiforth implied their meeting was over, although they hadn't broached their original agenda.

'Roger – you want me to do some work on the Carne review submission for you?'

The reminder served to worsen Standiforth's mood. He lit a cigarette irritably and waved his hand in the air. 'You know what I learned this morning? His first submission is from that bastard Caldicott! I don't trust Carne's bloody bias.'

'The FO Russian desk chap?' asked Smailes mildly. It seemed only natural that Sir Herbert Carne would consult with Whitehall's top Russia expert, and Smailes couldn't see any particular significance in the order of witnesses. The whole subject of the Carne review seemed to render Roger irrational. Smailes watched as his boss struggled to rein in his emotions.

'Look, the whole thing is going to blow over,' he said eventually. 'It always does. No matter what a particular commission recommends, any prime minister can see that putting shackles on us would simply end our effectiveness. You can't have MPs snooping into our files, asking questions in the House – it's not on. And this PM is no different – he's going to realize he needs us on his side, no matter what Sir Herbert Snipcock tells him.'

'You want me to get involved?'

'Talk to Poynter about our argument against parliamentary oversight – he knows it by heart. And talk to Strickland about the rigmarole they have to go through in Washington – you know, the bureaucratic proliferation, the leaks, the scorn from other agencies. He'll talk your ear off. Give me a three-page synopsis.'

'When do you need this, Roger?' asked Smailes, feeling overloaded.

'First draft, next week. Any problems?'

Smailes exhaled. 'I'll let you know.'

That night in bed, Clea asked a series of pointed questions about how and when Derek planned to decorate the box-room as a nursery for the new baby, and Smailes had to concede he couldn't foresee taking any time off in the near future.

Clea returned to her study of a maternity catalogue with some irritation, and asked casually why he'd brought an office car home that evening.

'Got to go down to Bristol tomorrow and see a man about a nuclear bomb,' he replied sharply.

Graham Booth was annoyed. Instead of heading up the box for the Lubyanov honeytrap, he'd been dealt a humdrum assignment on a Tory politician with the personal habits of a robot. An occasional dinner at his club or a function in his constituency, otherwise home to Dolphin Square between six and seven, no movements and no visitors. Back to Reigate and the family each Friday. If Stap was rotten, he knew he was being watched and was lying low.

Tonight, however, there had been a variation. Booth and A Branch veteran Johnny Hooper had tailed Stap's taxi from Pimlico to an elegant crescent in Knightsbridge, where Stap had just entered an unmarked doorway mounted with a security camera.

'What's this place, then?' asked Hooper over his shoulder.

Booth squinted through the twilight before removing a paperback from his pocket and hunching down in the back seat.

'Don't ask me. Unmarked. Radio in the address – Number Eight Herbert Crescent. Looks like we're here until shift change.'

Booth reckoned he probably had half an hour's reading before it got dark. He was too much a professional to consider using a light after that.

6

Mark Prendergast was exasperated. He swung out of his chair and crossed to the window, through which Smailes could see sheets of rain drumming against the tarmac. A small but lethal-looking jet fighter taxied across his line of vision as Prendergast turned to address him directly.

'Look, I'm sorry, Derek. I've got nothing against MI5 as an outfit. Frankly, I think you do a bloody good job. It's just – I was against this stupid exercise from the start. And believe me, I find no satisfaction in being proved right.'

'What do you mean, Commander?' Smailes asked. He was on his very best behaviour, aware he was speaking with the single individual who knew more about British nuclear weapons security than any person alive.

'Mark, please,' he said, returning distractedly to his desk and tugging his tunic straight before sitting. 'It was unnecessary, that's all. There basically is no terrorist threat to our nuclear arsenal. Never has been. This exercise was devised to give F Branch something to do, plain and simple, since like everyone else these days, it has to try and justify its existence. I was against any mock attack that lowered our readiness at Burghfield in any way, for obvious reasons. I told Starling at NARO in no uncertain terms. I was overruled, and look what happens.'

Wing Commander Mark Prendergast, head of the Special Safety Organization, was probably five years younger than Smailes, and looked every inch the RAF officer. He was tall and trim, and his tailored light-blue uniform fitted him exactly. His office wall held a couple of heraldic plaques, with an old sepia print of a Spitfire behind his head. On the desk itself stood the gleaming white phallus of a model Polaris missile. Smailes felt a sudden jolt of envy at Prendergast's passionate rectitude, that sense of unwavering conviction to which he was largely a foreigner.

'You don't think this was a terrorist attack then, Mark?' he asked deferentially.

'Of course not. The only terrorist group with remotely this kind of knowledge and training are the Palestinians, who, thank God, have the least motivation of any outfit to go nuclear, given the geopolitics. No, the main threat to the British arsenal has always come from sovereign special forces – both hostile and friendly. Given what we know from the scene, I'm sure one of them is responsible.'

Smailes was intrigued. 'You mind if I take notes?' he asked, removing a pad from his briefcase.

'Well, it'll all be in my report, but no, go right ahead.'

'Which special forces do you suspect, specifically? You said hostile or friendly?'

Prendergast took a deep breath. 'Okay, this is a bit complicated. The precision of execution, the explosives used, the knowledge displayed – it all points to Spetsnaz.'

'The Soviets?'

'Well, Russian is more accurate. But yes, Spetsnaz is the former Soviet Army's crack commando outfit.'

Smailes waited. Prendergast adjusted the flawless knot in his slim black tie before resuming.

'The major physical evidence we've found so far consists of boot treads belonging to US Navy SEALs, traces of Semtex, and shreds of latex from the dampers they used.' He glanced down at a report.

'Aldermaston just completed its analysis of the latex and reports the composition is identical to that of a regulation Russian Army condom – they're so thick the squaddies call them "galoshes".'

'I'm sorry, you've lost me.'

'The raiders used a balloon-like device inflated with water to muffle the blast. Very clever – water is by far the best and simplest device. Looks like they used Soviet Army johnnies – God knows, the things are strong enough.'

'But the boot treads?'

'Doesn't mean a damn thing. Every Spetsnaz commando has several pairs, each with customized treads, so they can leave whatever trail they choose.'

'But it could be someone else, you say?'

'Well, yes – you've got to look at motivation. It could have been the SEALs themselves, wearing their own boots, using Russian Army condoms to point the finger in the other direction.'

'What would be their motivation?'

'Oh, you know, rub our noses in our own shoddy security. Teach us a lesson. You know, cowboy stuff. Portsmouth tells me there's been an American SSN in the Solent for the past week. It could have easily put ashore a SEAL team that night and picked them up again by dawn. I keep waiting for the phone to ring and some damn Yank to start crowing at me, "We told you so."'

'Anyone else?'

'Well, one or two countries have both the means and the motivation. Obviously, Operation Wakefield gave everyone the bloody opportunity. You can discount the Chinese and the French, I think. The South Africans – hardly. The Israelis – definitely. A *sayeret* squad would have both the technical training and the skill in deception.'

'Who're they?'

'*Sayeret* means "reconnaissance" in Hebrew. They're the IDF's top commandos. Their most famous operation was the Entebbe rescue.'

'What will your report say?'

'Well, I'll still opt for Spetsnaz, I think. For all the surgical precision, there was considerable risk here, and Spetsnaz has the strongest motivation, to my mind. Does Russian strategic command actually need American PALs? Not really – they have their own equivalents. But, given the opportunity, Spetsnaz desperately needs to prove itself capable of stealing them. Like everyone else, the Russian military is downsizing dramatically. Individual units need to prove their worth.' Then he paused. 'There is one other scenario, however, that I can't even commit to paper. But someone at MI5 should at least know of it.'

'Yes?' said Smailes expectantly.

'It could even be our own people – the SBS would be the most logical culprits.'

Smailes frowned. 'Special Boat Service stole American nuclear locks from a government weapons lab? I don't get it.'

'How much do you know about the history of the British nuclear deterrent?' asked Prendergast pointedly.

'Not much,' Smailes conceded.

'I can tell you this because I'm RAF myself, understand? This is all off the record, all right?' Smailes put down his pen and nodded.

'When the independent British deterrent was first developed, our strategic weapon was the free-fall nuclear bomb and its means of delivery the long-range bomber. So its sole custodian was the RAF, understand, which added to the tremendous prestige we'd accumulated since the war. To the detriment of the Navy, in their eyes. Do you see?'

'Yes,' said Smailes.

'Well, military technology changes rapidly, as you know, and the Russians and Americans both began to develop ballistic missiles. In the sixties the RAF was in line to get the American Skybolt, an air-launched thing, when suddenly the Pentagon scrapped it on cost grounds. Big hoo-ha. Macmillan rushed out to the Bahamas to meet with Kennedy and begged him for a replacement – this beauty.' Prendergast indicated the gleaming Polaris model with a delicate gesture of his hand.

'Of course, Kennedy coughed up. But the thing was, Polaris was sea-launched, a multiple-warhead missile, and since we had nothing like the plutonium-producing capacity of the big powers, the Air Force bombs had to be cannibalized to build the new Polaris warheads. So the RAF was no longer custodian of the deterrent and, after its Vulcans were scrapped, no longer retained any strategic role at all. Much to the indignation of RAF command, as you might imagine.

'But the other thing that rankled the RAF chiefs was that the Navy retained independent control of its missiles. Well, strictly speaking, they were under NATO authority, but the weapons were kept unlocked and the understanding was that in the event of the destruction of British central command, a Polaris commander would use his discretion about retaliation. This was thought essential for the credibility of the deterrent, to discourage a first strike. Of course, the RAF didn't quite see it that way. One chief of Bomber Command went so far as to say he thought the Navy was as big a threat to national security as CND or the Communist party. But his indignation was based mainly on the RAF's loss of prestige, in my view.'

Smailes was listening carefully, trying to follow Prendergast's logic. 'So the decision to install the American PALs . . .'

'Precisely. It reclaimed launch authority from the Navy, and subordinated it to the Americans in time of crisis, much to the delight of RAF command at High Wycombe and the gall of the Navy brass at Northwood. Then, lo and behold, the new PALs get stolen from Burghfield at the first opportunity!'

'And you think Special Boat Service might be responsible?'

'I think it's possible. SBS is officially a Royal Marine outfit, but they're essentially the Navy's special forces, just as SAS is the Army's. They're based down in Poole and could easily have made it up to Burghfield and back in a night. With stolen PALs they could learn how to disarm them and the Polaris commanders could remain quietly independent of the Americans. I could see that happening quite easily, with collusion at some pretty high levels, too.' Prendergast did not elaborate, and a silence followed.

'Mark,' said Smailes eventually, 'doesn't the end of the Cold War and the scaling back of nuclear weapons make all this obsolete? I mean, what's the likelihood of Britain's political leadership being destroyed these days, after all?'

Prendergast picked up his model missile and studied it, then smiled at Smailes for the first time during their interview. 'Derek, old chap, I can tell you're not a military man. We don't think that way. We don't think that way at all.'

If CIA station chief Loudon Strickland had the demeanour of a vindictive librarian, Boris Zhimin, his KGB counterpart, looked more like a professional gambler. Whereas Strickland was tall and pale, Zhimin was short and stout, with a florid complexion, thick wavy hair, and expensive tastes in clothing and accessories. Zhimin, the London *rezident*, was one of those First Directorate potentates who had inevitably survived the KGB's great purge, and for good reason. He had served in a half a dozen capitals, spoke as many languages, and knew how to run an espionage network. In short, he was a professional, and now served his anti-communist masters in Moscow with as much zeal as he had once served their predecessors. Zhimin and Strickland were meeting in the shabby living room of a Russian safe house in Slough, a dormitory town west of London near Heathrow airport. Zhimin's girth was spread expansively in a vinyl armchair, but Strickland remained standing, as if ill at ease in his former adversary's lair.

Zhimin had a low, rumbling laugh to accompany his stage villain's appearance, and was clearly enjoying his colleague's discomfiture.

'Relax and have a drink, Loudon. We should toast our success. Our people at the Academy of Sciences are very pleased with what we got from Burghfield. Very pleased indeed.' Zhimin folded his hands behind his head, displaying a large signet ring on his left hand.

'That would be premature, Boris,' said Strickland, adjusting his spectacles as he faced the window, the curtains of which were drawn, although it was still light outside. Then, more forcefully, 'Just keep your end of the bargain, that's all.'

Zhimin laughed again, then offered a pout of mock protest.

*

Although Derek Smailes and Iain Mack had known each other for most of their lives, Derek was aware their friendship had never been more important than of late. For Iain, Smailes knew he represented the single person he could unconditionally trust outside his media world of glad-handers and careerists. Also, Iain's mother had recently died, leaving his only close relative a married sister, whom he rarely saw. And for all Iain's accounts of a giddy social life, studded with names of celebrities and girlfriends, Smailes knew his friend was an essentially lonely man who slept alone most nights. For Iain, his career had become everything, and Derek Smailes the one dependable reference point outside it.

But Smailes often wondered whether Iain knew how significant the friendship had become for him in return. Iain knew Smailes better than anyone alive – better, in many ways, than Clea herself – and was his major link to the world outside the bell-jar of secrecy in which he was obliged to live. Smailes knew that many of his colleagues simply abandoned friends from their former lives, unable to cope with the continuous necessity for deceit. But despite frequent disagreements, Smailes knew that would never happen with Iain, although superficially this friendship between an investigative journalist and a secret policeman grew less and less probable with the passing years.

Although he had never confessed it, Smailes was aware his employers had at least once cocked an eyebrow at their friendship. Soon after his transfer to K Branch Smailes had been drinking at the very bar where he and Iain had met that evening, when a stranger approached him heartily, offering to buy him a drink. The character introduced himself as Harry and explained they'd met at Iain's Christmas party, and Smailes thought little of the encounter until Harry, who seemed drunk, told him conspiratorially that he'd been shocked by Iain's latest promotion at the BBC, since Iain was such a 'raving Trot'. Smailes laughingly discounted the characterization, until he suddenly realized that the worthy Harry must be a stooge, dispatched to probe the nature of the relationship. Smailes tripped him up over the location of Iain's flat, then drank up hurriedly and left, and did not disclose the encounter to either Clea or Iain himself. And sure enough, six months later, while visiting the Special Branch floor over at Scotland Yard, Smailes saw 'Harry' entering an office with a fistful of papers. It warned Smailes that MI5 kept a file on his friend, although he could never call it up on the registry computer. It also meant that MI5 was suspicious of Smailes's involvement with him, which made his determination to maintain the friendship all the stronger.

Smailes and Mack were seated over expensive lagers as Derek complained about his domestic plight. Eventually, Iain cut him off impatiently. 'I dunno, Derek. Seems to me you've got the perfect life. Lovely kid. Beautiful, intelligent wife. Rich too. You're finally super-cop . . .'

Smailes felt exasperated. He certainly wouldn't describe his situation as the 'perfect life'. But then he was reminded of the prism of envy through which they had always viewed each other. Smailes had always felt jealous of Iain's untrammelled life-style, and knew that in turn Iain romanticized Smailes's domesticity.

'Think you'll ever marry, Iain?' he asked.

'I dunno, Del,' said Iain, somewhat moodily. 'The commitment, you know. I'd run a mile . . .'

'No prospects for you and Julie?' he asked sarcastically.

Iain laughed. 'Not really. That was fun, you know, for a night, but she's a bit on the needy side for me. Besides, I've got my hands full with Nina.'

'The tall woman at work?'

Mack nodded guiltily.

'You know, when I saw you and Julie leave the party together I thought you might have an ulterior motive for taking her home. Listen, mate, I tell Clea very little about what I do, and she tells her sister absolutely nothing.' Smailes saw the look on his friend's face and immediately regretted the remark. No one needed an ulterior motive to sleep with Julie Lynch, after all.

Mack had taken immediate offence. 'Give me a break, Derek Smailes. You think I care enough about your work that I'd seduce your sister-in-law as a source? Give me a bloody break.' He paused, then looked directly at Smailes, his eyes narrowing.

'Your problem is, pal, you've always wanted to poke her yourself, and you're pissed off at the idea of me getting there first.'

Seeing his taunt was close to the bone, Mack sought to press home his advantage. 'So what the hell *do* you do, anyway, Mr Simon Templar? I can't tell you how stupid it is that you won't even admit you work for MI5.'

Smailes blew out his cheeks, peeved that Iain should turn a silly remark into a loyalty test. He lowered his voice. 'Look, all right, I work for MI5. I used to chase Soviet diplomats around London; now I travel the country asking low-level civil servants how they can possibly choose to leave government service before retirement. Hardly supercop, is it? And I could get put away for ten years just for telling you that, so keep it off the telly, okay?'

Smailes had grown annoyed in his turn, but Mack came right back at him. 'You know, that bloody Official Secrets Act is a one-way street. How come no one in the Cabinet office is ever threatened with it, when they leak stuff to us every day? And you know you've got your people sitting on our board, whereas we're not allowed to know a damn thing that goes on at your place.'

Smailes drained his glass moodily. 'Your round,' he said.

When Iain returned with their drinks, Smailes steered him into safer territory by asking about the latest political gossip. Mack immediately warmed to a favourite theme.

'It seems European monetary union may be back on the front burner, so the likelihood of an autumn election is all anyone's talking about,' said Iain heatedly.

'Are you serious?' said Smailes.

'Absolutely,' said Iain. 'If the PM is really going to sign back to that whole idea, he's going to have to go to the country, isn't he? Either that, or renege on his promise to seek a new mandate before committing Britain to anything so drastic.'

'Is it really so imminent? I thought monetary union had been postponed indefinitely,' said Smailes sceptically. He'd read the press speculation that MPs and business leaders had begun to exert heavy pressure on the Conservative government to take more decisive action against the worst recession since the thirties. But he didn't realize the spectre of monetary union had been revived. Try as he might, Smailes could not imagine ever going into his pocket and coming out with a fistful of ecus – it just wasn't British.

'It *had* been postponed,' said Iain conspiratorially, 'but things have changed. Look, mate, the world economy is in deep trouble. The American and Japanese economies are both stalled, so the Europeans realize they've got to look to their own house; but the German and French economies are both stuck, and unemployment here is still at Depression levels. So the consensus is building that only by removing the last trade barriers, by establishing a central bank and a single currency, can the big European powers jump-start their economies again. And they're betting the ecu would quickly replace the dollar as the medium of international exchange.'

'But blimey, Iain, wouldn't monetary union be pretty unpopular? Couldn't the Opposition campaign against it and win?'

Mack waved a hand in the air. 'Neither Labour nor the Lib Dems can cast themselves as anti-European, can they, mate? That's Stone Age politics. The only real opposition comes from the Conservatives' own Euro rebels, and they're effectively leaderless since Her Ladyship was booted upstairs to the Lords. The government can probably present monetary union as inevitable, you know – whistle the tune that Britain has to keep playing in the middle of the field in Europe. And I think most people would grudgingly accept it.'

'Are you certain of all this?' asked Smailes. The potential attitude of MI5's hardliners towards closer European union momentarily crossed his mind, but he dismissed the thought for later reflection.

'Nah,' said Iain. 'This is all just rumour level. But tell me this – why did the Chancellor just return from an unpublicized trip to Brussels? Why is the Lord Mayor of London, along with two top Treasury officials, currently touring European financial capitals?'

'I dunno. Why?'

'They're campaigning for London as the site for the central Eurobank and all the bureaucracy that goes with it, aren't they? Word is it's a head-to-head contest between London and Frankfurt.'

'Really? You think all this is going to happen, Iain?'

Iain sipped his beer and thought for a moment. 'My guess is the PM will wait for the next two sets of unemployment and trade figures. If they're still awful, I don't think he'll have much option. The pressure from industry, from the parliamentary party, will become overwhelming. The backbenchers are getting terrific grief in their constituencies every weekend, you know . . .'

Smailes asked whether *Focus* was working on a story, but Mack claimed he wasn't sure, he was preoccupied with plans for his own Russian mafia programme. He confirmed that he and a colleague were heading out to Moscow the following month for the preliminary 'recce'.

'You and Nina, right?' asked Smailes, laughing.

Iain grinned. 'Right. My editor doesn't suspect a thing. I'm more skilled at deception than you are, mate.' Smailes wasn't sure he'd received a compliment. His face clouded and he paused before continuing. He knew Iain had made two previous documentaries in the former Soviet Union, and that if MI5 kept a file on his friend, so did the KGB.

'Iain, be careful over there, okay? It's still unclear who's really in charge, and if you go around treading on toes, overturning stones . . .'

Mack held up a hand. 'Honestly, there you go again. You sound just like McAndrew.'

'Who?'

'Hugh McAndrew. He's the MI5 security bloke at the Moscow embassy. Been there for ever. Always gives us the same lecture when we arrive. "Keep your nose clean and your cock in your pocket . . ."'

Iain's parents had both been Scots, and he could brilliantly mimic a Glaswegian accent, which always made Smailes laugh.

'Well, I don't know him, but what he says is true, you know,' Smailes responded. 'People are under the impression that violence and repression are a thing of the past over there. It's just not true.' He saw the sceptical look on his friend's face. 'Listen, this isn't just party-line crap. I'm speaking as your friend, and I happen to know.'

Mack silenced him. 'Look, Derek, I work for the Untouchables. I'm not kidding. The BBC is the single most respected media outfit in the world. I sometimes find it laughable, but abroad it's like I've got almost clerical authority, I serve the secular God of the BBC. I say the three magic letters and *poof!* – doors just open.

'Besides, I've always followed McAndrew's advice. You know me, mate,' he added, giving Smailes a sly look.

Smailes was mollified. 'You're the professional, I suppose,' he conceded.

Roger Standiforth closed a folder, signifying the meeting with Sal Imodeo and Brian Kinney was over. Imodeo got to his feet and offered a sleek dark hand.

'I should have something by the end of the week, Roger. Monday latest,' he said.

'Please, Sal, we'd be eternally grateful,' said Standiforth, turning to look at Brian Kinney, who nodded gloomily. 'The more concrete evidence we have in the face of this damn review, the better.'

Imodeo gave Standiforth a sudden, dazzling smile. 'Oh yeah, what's the betting there, you guys? You got your résumés out yet?'

If Standiforth or Kinney thought the remark was funny, their expressions didn't show it. 'Herbert Carne is still in preliminary evidence stage. There probably won't be any decisions until later in the year,' said Standiforth frostily.

'Okay. Be in touch,' said Imodeo, turning on his heel and crossing jauntily to the door.

'Bloody wop,' said Standiforth as his footsteps retreated. 'He makes my skin creep. I wish we didn't have to ask the damn Yanks a bloody thing . . .'

Kinney leaned back in his chair and studied his boss neutrally. He doubted Roger was even aware of the schoolboy slurs that fell from his mouth so readily. He cleared his throat and chose his words carefully.

'Yes, well, the FBI computer might help us clarify Zhimin's order of battle, but it can't tell us much we don't already know about Comrade Lubyanov.' He opened his folder and passed a document to Standiforth.

'Really?' said Standiforth, brightening. 'The Hyde Park honeytrap? What have you got?' He studied Kinney's report quickly.

'Turns out SIS had a ream on him,' said Kinney eagerly. 'He's KGB all right, probably a major. He's served four consecutive tours . . .'

'First Directorate, senior grade?'

'Exactly. He's married, but he's a womanizer. His last posting was in Copenhagen, and it appears he had an affair with a Danish diplomat in the arts ministry.'

'No!'

'Apparently. He was recalled to Moscow and reassigned to London. Been here about three months.'

'Reassigned? Sounds fishy.'

'Could be. Or perhaps he simply wriggled out of it. Perhaps he used his connections . . .' Standiforth could tell from Kinney's feigned casualness that there was more to come.

'Connections? What connections?'

'Well, I got one of my new assistants to crunch his name through the other agencies. You know, Special Branch, the services . . .'

'Well?'

'She took the initiative to cross-check the wife's name too. It seems Yuri Lubyanov is married to the daughter of one Major General Osipov.'

Standiforth narrowed his eyes, as if trying to place the name.

'Military aide to the Mayor of Moscow, according to Aldershot,' said Kinney triumphantly.

'Lubyanov is the son-in-law of a big-time Russian general?' asked Standiforth, wide-eyed.

'Looks like it.'

'So who's the woman he's screwing?'

'A nobody.' Kinney consulted his report. 'Valerie Saunders. Aged twenty-six. Programme assistant at the Arts Council. Born Scarborough in Yorkshire; graduate of Essex University. Absolutely no access to classified information. It appears they met a few weeks back, in connection with an exchange programme for drama students.'

'Fantastic,' said Standiforth. He looked off into the distance, conjuring a vision of Lubyanov's ruin.

'Okay. Put the squeeze on the secretary, find out what she knows about Lubyanov's role. Then grab him and stick him on the grill. We've got pictures?'

Kinney nodded. 'Beauties.'

'Tell him he cooperates or Zhimin gets the prints. Complete order of battle, man by man. Names of British subjects in active collaboration. Sworn statements – something we can stick under Carne's nose. Then – only then – he gets a pension and reunion with – what's-her-name.'

'Valerie.'

'Right, Valerie.' Standiforth began to rehearse his tactics out loud. 'I'll need a sign-off from Taffy, but Corky will get on board, I'm sure. They'll understand this could really sit well with Carne . . .'

Kinney cleared his throat again, as if hesitant to disrupt the arc of Roger's fantasy. 'Are you sure this will work, Roger? You know, times have changed.'

'Not that much, they haven't,' Standiforth retorted. 'If Lubyanov's already been caught with his pants down once, then his career is finished, at very least. And if we set it up right, he could face criminal charges too. Comrade Lubyanov will see the light.'

'Well, we have another problem, Roger,' Kinney said. 'I've got no one to put on it.'

'What?' asked Standiforth, horrified. 'What about this new assistant?'

'Judith Hyams?' Kinney asked incredulously. 'Good Lord, no. She's bright as all hell, but she's only just joined us from KY, and has nothing like the experience.'

'Couldn't you take it on yourself?' Standiforth pleaded.

'Out of the question,' said Kinney. 'I've already got too many balls in the air as it is.' He paused. 'Actually, I was going to ask you the same thing.'

'Me?' asked Standiforth.

'Roger, if we're serious about Lubyanov, then we've got to use someone who knows what they're doing. I've got no one free with anything like the seniority or experience. Everyone's at full stretch.'

Standiforth was thinking. 'How about a temporary transfer?'

'If it's the right person.'

'How about Smailes?'

'I've got no problem with that,' said Kinney, brightening. 'Can he be freed?'

'Well, he's working on something for Taffy, but I could probably fix it . . .'

Kinney was warming to the idea. 'Do it, Roger, and I'll give him Judith Hyams as an assistant. They'd make a terrific team.'

Standiforth's mind was made up. 'Give me the Lubyanov honeytrap prints. I'll talk to Corky right away.'

At the opposite end of the fourth floor from Roger Standiforth's office, Sal Imodeo was reclining in Derek Smailes's considerably less opulent quarters. He was waving a languid hand in the air, offering his rendition of Standiforth's aggrieved baritone. For an American, it was a wonderful impersonation.

'"Please, Sal, we'd be eternally grateful . . ."'

Smailes hooted. 'I tell you, Sal, Bert Carne's put the willies up him. He's not himself. Sometimes, he's barely rational.'

'Well, it's no big problem. Just a question of getting in line for Big Bertha down at Quantico. And I've got to agree, it looks like Uncle Boris is doing some *serious* empire-building here . . .'

'Listen, maybe you could help me too, Sal. Officially, I mean. Roger has me summarizing the argument against parliamentary oversight for handing up to Carne's team. I'm supposed to interview Strickland . . .'

'Don't listen to him,' said Imodeo dismissively. 'He'll feed you some line about "meaningful partnerships". Truth is, since those oversight committees were set up after Watergate, they haven't made a damn bit of difference.'

'They haven't?' Even for a terminal cynic like Derek Smailes, this seemed a little strong.

'Not a damn bit. The congressmen that sit on those panels are all intelligence groupies, creaming their pants at whatever titbits the CIA feeds them. Whenever they need to, the professionals just ignore them. You know what the primary meaning of "oversight" is, after all, don't you?'

Smailes grinned. 'So what're you saying?'

'I'm saying it doesn't really matter whether you have legislative oversight or not. What has to stay secret always does, no matter how many laws get passed. It's the way it has always worked, in every government in the world.'

Imodeo was about to leave, but then lowered his voice conspiratorially. 'Say, on the subject of congressmen, I was right about those visitors you saw, I think.'

'Oh, right,' said Smailes. 'Who did you say? Senator Paul Wexford and his committee?'

'That's right. Unless one of them was a tall dude with light-brown hair and rimless glasses . . .'

Smailes thought back to the party he'd seen. 'Don't think so. Why?' he asked casually, looking across at his friend and noticing a wicked glint in his eye.

'Well, I got a friend in the CIA station who says Blane Morris is in town. Unofficially.'

'Who?'

'Blane Morris. Deputy Director of Operations. He's in charge of covert action and CIA offices abroad.'

Smailes laughed. 'Sal, I thought you drew the line at office romances.'

'Hey, I do – we're just friends. I was asking her about Wexford, and she told me about Morris. She knows I'm trustworthy.'

'Sure, Sal,' said Smailes, reflecting that Imodeo's revelation had just proved the contrary. The name Morris meant nothing to him, but he couldn't help reflecting on Wing Commander Mark Prendergast's theories, and wondering whether the surreptitious arrival in Britain of Langley's top spymaster had anything to do with recent events at the Royal Ordnance Factory, Burghfield.

7

Within the privileged landscape of London clubland, the Special Forces Club in Knightsbridge enjoyed a unique prominence. While not commanding the cachet of either White's or the Carlton, its entrance criteria nevertheless distinguished it from all others. Founded by veterans of Britain's wartime Special Operations Executive, its membership was restricted to the country's paramilitary, security and intelligence services, or, in the case of its handful of honorary members, to persons 'of such character and spirit that they might have served in the Resistance, had circumstances allowed'. As such, the Special Forces Club was spiritual home to the 'ultras', the extreme right-wing of British politics. The 'ultras', also known in MI5 parlance as 'hoorah boys', comprised a loosely knit group of soldiers, spies and bureaucrats, united by the virulence of their politics, their impassioned militarism and their devotion to the Crown.

The club was entered via an unmarked door in an elegant Knightsbridge terrace. The ground floor was occupied by meeting rooms, offices and a spacious lobby, from which a wide, curved staircase ascended. Here the club's famous heroes' gallery began – a cramped collection of framed black-and-white photographs, meticulously displayed together with typed accounts of each individual's exploits and decorations. The men and women honoured were by no means exclusively British – many were wartime Resistance figures of every conceivable nationality, who had collaborated with SOE in its sabotage efforts behind German lines. It was also clear from the tributes that many had paid for their heroism with their lives.

The curved gallery was interrupted at the first landing, from which led doors to a bar and dining room. The bar itself was presided over by a silent steward with an erect bearing, a shorn scalp and piercing, light-blue eyes. Two enormous oil portraits dominated the airy room – the first of Queen Elizabeth, the Queen Mother, patron of the club, the second of its current president, her grandson, the Prince of Wales. A further staircase led from the landing to private rooms on the second floor, along which the gallery resumed its chronicle of valour.

The doors along the upper landing were each identified by a legend and, where appropriate, a crest – the Donovan Room, the Belgian Room, the SAS Room. Behind this last a meeting was in progress. It was clear from the arrangement of furniture that what had been conceived as a bedroom had been redeployed as an office. Five individuals sat on folding chairs – the bed having been covered with a large board to serve as an extra desk. On the wall opposite the window hung an oil portrait of Prince Andrew, Duke of York, in naval dress uniform, and below it, engraved in brass, the lines from John of Gaunt's deathbed speech from *Richard II*:

> This royal throne of kings, this sceptr'd isle,
> This earth of majesty, this seat of Mars.

From this patriotic source the Sceptre Group, of which the steering committee was in session, drew its title and inspiration. As of this date in late June, very few individuals in Britain knew of its existence.

The Sceptre Group had come into formal being after a failed coup to wrest control of the Special Forces Club from its old guard of SOE veterans. Its main plank had been that Prince Charles was no longer a worthy president, since his increasingly provocative public statements revealed him to be either mentally unstable or dangerously left-wing. Some went so far as to suggest he was an outright 'pinko', a tool of the Labour party, and that since he was now legally separated from his wife, he was also unfit to succeed his mother as monarch when that sad day should arrive. The Sceptre Group vociferously favoured his younger brother as Special Forces president – a true prince who had flown Sea Kings under fire in the Falklands, who displayed both reliable views and, since his second marriage, a stable home life. (Privately, some also argued that Andrew would make a far better king. The previous Prince of Wales, they liked to point out, had proved a similar disaster and had abdicated, to everyone's relief, in favour of a courageous younger brother.) Although the Sceptre Group's slate of candidates had been roundly defeated in the club's spring elections, it had beaten only a tactical retreat to its second-floor office, where it continued to grumble beneath the portrait of its champion.

There were five individuals present, three of whom held military rank: General Sir Humphrey Porter, Lord Lieutenant of Greater London and retired commander of the British Army of the Rhine; Colonel Clive Halls, late of the Special Air Service regiment; and

Lieutenant-Colonel Timothy Crabbe of the Special Boat Service. The Sceptre Group chairman was Miles Bingham, CBE, head of MI5's F branch, who had just finished introducing the Tory party's spokesman on naval affairs, the junior defence minister Gerard Stap, MP. Bingham indicated with a grave gesture that Stap now had the floor.

'Well, what Miles tells you is all true, I'm afraid,' Stap began lugubriously. 'The Prime Minister has provisionally agreed to a special Eurosummit in early September, the main agenda of which is to be a new timetable for monetary union. And if it goes ahead, the PM will have to dissolve parliament and go to the country in October, obviously. If you ask me, unless something unforeseen happens, the momentum is going to be unstoppable. Then God only knows what will happen . . .'

'Well, *I* damn well know,' blustered General Porter. 'We just can't let it happen, that's what. It's outright treason!'

Porter, a white-haired, pink-jowled figure in Harris tweed, was the acme of the Blimp from the shires. Pensioned off as Lord Lieutenant after the BAOR had been stood down, he was technically in charge of crisis planning for the capital. In fact, he was the Queen's representative on the Defence Council, the shadowy group which oversaw British military policy.

'Because it's not just monetary union we're talking about, is it?' said Porter. 'It's the beginning of the end of British sovereignty, that's what! We'll end up governed by that rabble in Brussels, a bunch of self-appointed socialists!'

Bingham cupped his chin in his hand gloomily. 'I'm not sure I agree with you entirely, Humphrey. Monetary union by itself would be a disaster, if you ask me. Imagine, the Chancellor of the Exchequer with no more authority than some county treasurer – able to levy taxes, but with no jurisdiction over interest rates, exchange rates or economic policy. And what will he tell the unemployed if it doesn't work? Go demonstrate outside the Bundesbank? Ridley was right – Hitler's demented fantasies would be accomplished. Bloodlessly.'

Gerry Stap folded one pin-striped leg over the other. 'Frankly, I think you're *both* missing the main point. Can you imagine what monetary union and its political consequences would do to the future of NATO and our relations with the Americans? The Yanks would really get the message that they're unwelcome. And *that* would be Paris's greatest ambition fulfilled.'

'You're damn right, Gerry,' said Bingham.

Elaboration was unnecessary. Everyone in British military life knew that the French, ever since their withdrawal from NATO integrated command in the sixties, had been agitating for the formation of an exclusively Western European security order. The Germans were already on board, and only the British had dug in their heels over the continued significance of NATO and the Americans. Far better the Yankee pit bull than the French poodle, went the British military logic.

'Well, I agree with Humphrey,' said Stap. 'It's time to do something.'

Halls, the former SAS commando chief, spoke up. 'There are contingency plans, you know, gentlemen. Tim Crabbe and myself served on the committee that updated Britain's civil emergency measures in the eighties. Control zones around the ports and airports, an internment complex in the Shetlands. What was the name we gave it, Tim?'

'The Gaelic archipelago,' said Crabbe. Tim Crabbe was the youngest individual present, a taut, sharp-featured man. 'But I have to stress, Clive, those plans were for the event of a Warsaw Pact invasion, to facilitate civil defence and resupply. We would have to consider how our allies would see something so unconstitutional . . .'

'Who said anything about unconstitutional?' spluttered Porter. 'What do you know about the prerogative powers, man?'

Abashed, Crabbe conceded he knew nothing.

'The prerogative powers cede to the sovereign the right to intervene in times of extraordinary national crisis. She may direct troops. She may appoint a prime minister, if the parties cannot agree on one. If the country seems ungovernable, she may appoint a government of national unity.'

'You think the Queen is prepared . . .?' asked Crabbe.

'I *know* Her Majesty is prepared,' retorted the general, correcting Crabbe's lapse in protocol. 'From what I have divined in our own meetings, plus what I have been told in strict confidence by her closest equerry, she is concerned, gravely concerned, about the consequences of some headlong rush towards European union, despite what she has to say in public. Brussels might insist Britain adopt a written constitution, of all bloody things. Lord knows, the royal family has had its share of problems lately. I know for a fact they see European unity as the beginning of creeping republicanism. Except, of course, for that idiot Charles . . .' Here, Porter glanced up longingly at the portrait of Prince Andrew, his champion.

Stap chimed in. 'The polls are contradictory, but it's my intuition that any election over Europe will end up in a hung parliament. Then God knows what chaos will ensue . . .'

Porter took his cue. 'My strong belief is that the UK Commanders-in-Chief Committee would look directly to the Palace for guidance in any such crisis.'

'What about the Americans?' asked Stap, turning to Bingham.

'They're worried,' said the MI5 man. 'Very worried. I know it for a fact. They've got to hang on to NATO and keep both feet in Europe, if only for business reasons. I could sound out Strickland on how they would respond, if it was thought expedient.'

Porter slapped a hand down on his thigh. 'As Englishmen, we have no choice – it's time to act.' He turned to Crabbe and Halls. 'Gentlemen, we need those plans. In detail. Understood?'

They nodded.

'Miles, sound out the Americans – discreetly, I mean. Would they keep to barracks, even if intervention was requested by an elected government? I will speak to the Palace again, and try and sound out which way UKCICC would lean. But we'll need money, of course. Lots of it.'

Gerry Stap exhaled slowly. 'I don't think that should be a major problem. Miles, didn't you say you've already received offers?'

'Dozens,' said Bingham.

Porter was ploughing ahead, stirred by his vision of the apocalypse. 'And, of course, we'll need a political leader. Someone of sufficient stature to guide the country through the crisis, until any European treaty could be abrogated and new elections arranged . . .'

Porter looked from one man to another as the silence extended. Everyone knew whose leadership the general was invoking.

Eventually, Stap exhaled more slowly. 'Very well,' he said. 'I will speak to Baroness Thatcher at the earliest opportunity.'

'It's already been approved by the executive committee,' said Standiforth. 'A temporary three-month secondment to K5 to baby-sit Lubyanov, renewable for a further three months, if required . . .'

'Wait a minute, Roger,' Smailes protested. 'I can depute my day-to-day stuff to Godfrey Pawlett, but what about Wakefield?' He glanced anxiously across at Kinney, aware his former section head was probably not indoctrinated into the file.

'I've taken care of it. I'm assuming full responsibility for Wakefield myself. You can turn all your files over to Tennant.'

At the name of Roger's smooth-cheeked hatchet boy, Smailes's jaw tightened. Typically, he did not know what to make of this development, whether to feel flattered or insulted. He cleared his throat.

'Roger, are the prospects for Lubyanov so important that it's worth . . .?'

'Absolutely. If he cooperates – and what choice does he have? – we'll have cast-iron evidence to present to Carne of Zhimin's empire-building at the London residence.'

'He has a point, Derek,' Kinney interjected.

'Brian's department is at full stretch, so he asked for you, and after due consideration I assented. I think Wakefield's hit a brick wall anyway, don't you?' Kinney looked at Standiforth sharply, but said nothing.

Smailes shook his head. It was partly true, he had to concede. Surveillance of Stap had turned up nothing and F Branch had taken over the investigation into the Burghfield leak. Besides, he'd always enjoyed the rough-and-tumble of Kinney's department, and Roger had said it was a temporary transfer, not a demotion.

'What about back-up?' he asked, relenting. 'You want me to move back to my old office?'

'It's been taken, I'm afraid, old man,' said Kinney. 'Stay where you are. We can offer you Judith Hyams as an assistant. You remember, I introduced you the other day? She's proving very sharp. If you or Godfrey could make room for her . . .'

'Well, I suppose I could move another desk into my office,' he said, frowning. 'If it's temporary.'

'Three months should be quite adequate,' said Kinney.

'How strong are our cards with Lubyanov?'

'Very,' said Kinney. 'Wait until you see the surveillance shots. Plus, his wife's from a prominent military family.'

'He's not a dangle?'

'Unlikely, since he has a pattern of this,' said Standiforth. 'But of course, we need to check further. The important thing is to get going right away. I was scheduled to give my deposition to Carne next week, but I've postponed it by ten days. I'd love to drop something on his desk personally.'

'This is all approved?' Smailes asked, looking from one to the other.

'As I said,' said Standiforth impatiently.

'All right, ' he retorted with a shrug. 'Let's get on with it.'

Standiforth turned to his desk calendar. 'I'll arrange for Peter Tennant to debrief you on Wakefield this afternoon. Two o'clock all right?'

Judith Hyams sat on the edge of her desk, listening intently to her new boss. Smailes was seated in his desk-chair, twitching the swivel back and forth. He'd rearranged the furniture so the two desks faced adjacent walls and he wouldn't have to look across his desk to address her. He wanted a partner in this operation, not a glorified secretary. For her part, Judith was not yet settled in, having dumped a bulging concertina file on the floor and parked her personal laptop computer on her desk. As a section head, Smailes had his own terminal to MI5's registry, and knew that Judith needed special dispensation to bring in a personal machine. Given her skills, Smailes did not doubt Kinney had granted it readily.

To his relief, Judith did not appear cowed by her new surroundings or responsibilities, and seemed eager to get started on whatever Smailes might assign. He almost wished she would take a seat, since her long limbs towered above him from her perch. On the other hand, he appreciated her informality, since it would greatly ease their working relationship. Judith was dressed exactly as when he first met her – navy-blue business suit, conservative blouse, flat-heeled shoes. Her unruly red-brown hair was pulled neatly back from her face by a clasp, and she was regarding him mildly.

Smailes passed a file of photographs to her with a twinge of embarrassment over their intimate nature.

'She's Valerie Saunders, a programme assistant at the Arts Council. They've known each other a few weeks. He's deep cover KGB, on his fourth posting.'

Judith flicked through them and smiled. 'They seem to like each other,' she said.

'We know he's had affairs in the past. So do his bosses. So the question is, how come he keeps getting plum postings?'

'We don't say RIS yet?' asked Judith with a smile.

Smailes sighed. 'I suppose one day we might,' he said. 'Although you know they changed our name to Department Five of Intelligence a generation ago, and how many people call us DI5? I think they'll always be the KGB to me, whether they're calling themselves the Russian Intelligence Service or not.'

'Where do we start?' she asked.

Smailes handed across another file. 'I'm not satisfied with the background we have on his previous postings. They're all European, okay? So let's get on to domestic intelligence in each country and see if we can flesh it out. Then we need a clearer picture of his duties and activities here.'

Judith scanned the file. 'You want me to go through the embassies?'

It was a good question. 'Best way, definitely. Contact the military attaché or the head of station in person. Let them use their own protected links for the information, and we'll messenger it across London. The more we stay off the airwaves ourselves, the better.'

'Then what will be our first move?'

'The lovely Valerie, I think. You'll come along on that – she'll feel more secure.' Judith obviously relished the thought. She suddenly raised her eyebrows at the sound of Marjorie's tea bell in the corridor.

'Tea, sir?' she asked.

'Derek,' Smailes corrected her. 'Only if you understand there's no obligation for you to get it, ever, okay?'

She smiled again. 'All right. How do you take it, Derek?'

'Marjorie knows,' he said, returning her smile and pretending not to watch her lithe frame as it left the room.

Smailes allowed her to unpack and to order supplies and a telephone extension as he drank his tea. When she had finished, he gave in to his curiosity.

'So how do you come to be with us, Judith? With MI5, I mean?'

She laughed. 'You mean with two counts against me? Being both a woman and a Jew?'

Smailes understood that was exactly what he meant, although he hadn't realized it. He knew that Standiforth had begun to liberalize his recruitment practices, partly from necessity and partly to broaden his power base in the organization. But a young Jewish woman from an accounting background was still an anomaly in the professional ranks of MI5.

She cocked her head to one side. 'Oh, where do I start? Well, you see, I always wanted to join the police. Ever since I can remember.'

'Really?' said Smailes. 'I was in the force for ten years.'

'I know. Brian told me.'

'Go on.'

'Well, it's not that simple for a nice Jewish girl from North Finchley to join the police force. Not unless she wants to completely defy her parents. You see, my Dad is a taxi driver. Well, actually, he runs a

minicab business with my Uncle Mannie, his brother – where was I?'
'The police.'
'Right, well, my father wanted me to study for a real profession – accounting, law, dentistry – you know, something that Jews do.'
Smailes laughed.
'So I gave in. I mean, I studied accountancy at the University of Middlesex and then I joined Price Waterhouse when I graduated. Four years ago.'
Smailes nodded.
'But from the start I gravitated to forensics. It was just natural.'
Smailes laughed. 'Forensic accounting? Sounds like a contradiction in terms. You know, like investigative book-keeping.'
'Not at all, ' Judith replied. 'You'd be surprised what people get up to. Ninety per cent of what we did was corporate audits, and I suppose I have a naturally suspicious mind. Luckily, I was working for a partner who really backed me up when I uncovered my first fraud.'
'First fraud?' said Smailes. 'I'm impressed.'
'Well, don't be. It wasn't that difficult. A chemical company vice-president and his head of finance were skimming profits by padding their depreciation schedule. They didn't hide their tracks very well.' She paused for effect. 'They both got two years.'
'There were others?'
'Just one. But I was more proud of it. A clothing company in the East End run by an Orthodox family. I caught them bill-kiting.'
'Bill-kiting?'
'You get a vendor to issue false invoices, which you pay, then he reimburses you in cash, minus his commission. It lowers your net profits and therefore your tax exposure.'
'How did you catch them?'
'They were pretty clever. Built it up gradually, so you couldn't see big year-to-year fluctuations. But I compared their hauling costs to industry norms, and saw that theirs were wildly inflated. So we arranged a little sting with the Hackney fraud squad. The company's in receivership now.'
'Blimey,' said Smailes. 'I'd better watch my expense claims around you.'
'Anyway,' said Judith, intent on completing her tale. 'My Uncle Mannie always knew what my real ambitions were, and he arranged an interview for me with Special Branch. Behind my Dad's back, of course. My Uncle Mannie knows *everybody* worth knowing in north

London, believe me. Of course, I was thrilled to bits. I didn't even know I was being considered for the Security Service until Mr Standiforth introduced himself at the end, when he made the offer. Naturally, I leapt at it, although it meant a big pay cut.'

'And what did your father say?'

'He wasn't very pleased at first, but he calmed down a bit when I told him I was working for the government. You see, the civil service is a real profession to the Jews.'

'Unlike the police force.'

'Exactly.' Judith lowered her voice. 'David wasn't very happy though, I'm afraid.'

'David?'

'My husband. He's sort of the traditional type. We've known each other since school, our families are old friends.' She shrugged. 'It was almost an arranged marriage, you know.'

Smailes waited.

'Well, he'd rather I stayed home and had babies. He's a solicitor in Golders Green. I'm not sure I want to have babies, ever. My career's more important. And it's difficult that I can't tell him anything about what I do. He doesn't really understand.' She paused. 'You have a family, Derek?'

'I have a daughter from my first marriage who's almost as old as you are.'

'Go on!'

'It's true. Well, I married young, in my teens.'

'And you have a second family?'

'A two-year-old and another on the way. November.'

'That's nice,' said Judith, looking down. 'Does your wife manage by herself?'

'Sort of. We have a teenager who helps. Clea's on leave from the Foreign Office.'

'Oh,' said Judith, as if cowed by this news of his wife's status. 'I see.' There was a silence. Smailes weighed his next question.

'Excuse my prying, but did you have any problems in your interview? Women usually have decent prospects in this outfit, but I mean, over your Jewishness? It's just that Roger Standiforth has never struck me as the most pro-Semitic individual, frankly. I haven't offended you, have I?'

'No. No, of course not. It comes up all the time. You know, the double patriot issue. Can a Jew be exclusively loyal to Britain – what about allegiance to Israel? Is that what you mean?'

'I suppose so.'

'The question wasn't asked, and I think it helped a lot that the two chemical company executives I helped put away were both Jewish. Then the clothing company, that was Orthodox, top to bottom. So in a way I'd already proved my impartiality. You think Roger Standiforth is anti-Semitic?'

Smailes realized he was on dangerous turf.

'I think MI5 is anti-Semitic. And anti- just about everything else, for that matter. And Roger is MI5 old school. That's all I meant.'

'Right. Well, you don't have to be a genius to see there are no Jews anywhere near the top of this organization.'

'Exactly.' Smailes paused. 'Actually, Roger reserves his worst bile for Welshmen. He can't stand the buggers.'

'Really?' asked Judith, wide-eyed, until she realized Smailes was teasing. 'Oh, go on,' she said, waving a hand at him.

They were interrupted by a knock, and Smailes called out to admit the wraith-like figure of Peter Tennant, at which he shuddered. He simply couldn't stand the man, and knew the feeling was mutual. He glanced at his watch.

'Judith, you'll have to excuse us. I have a meeting with Peter here.'

'No problem,' she said airily. 'I'll get going on making some of these appointments, shall I? I'll use my old desk and phone until they install one here.'

She headed for the door in long girlish strides. For the first time, Smailes felt actively pleased to be dumping the Wakefield material on his despised colleague. He was confident he and his new assistant were going to make a great team.

It was close to the end of the work day and Judith had still not resurfaced when the non-secure line rang. Smailes answered the phone to his wife and was immediately stricken by fear of some emergency. By tacit agreement, Clea rarely called him during office hours.

'Everything all right?' he asked.

'Oh, fine, darling,' Clea replied breezily. 'I'm in Peckham. I was going to ask if you had plans after work.'

'Oh, right, it's Tuesday,' said Smailes with relief. 'I forgot. What've you been doing?'

'Oh, the usual. Filling out supplementary benefit forms. Trying to comfort women whose husbands beat the living daylights out of them.'

'How's Sarah?'

'Fine,' said Clea guardedly. 'Well, do you?'

'Have plans? No? What's up?'

'I thought we could have dinner in town. It's been ages, hasn't it?'

Smailes was delighted. 'It certainly has. Have you fixed it with Fidelma?'

'It's taken care of. Only, Derek . . .'

'Yes?' asked Smailes, wondering what was coming next.

'Mummy's talked me into going with her to a talk by her Tibetan lama friend. In Chelsea at half past five. I thought maybe we could meet up there.'

'You've got to be joking.'

'Oh, come on, Derek. Mummy's really proud of this fellow and wants to show him off. She'd be really touched if we both went.'

'Clea, it's not my bag.'

'It's not mine either. It's for Mummy's sake. Come on, it'll be an experience. And it's probably only for half an hour or so. I'll have the car. Then we can go to that Thai place we like near Harrods.'

'I could just meet you there,' Smailes offered.

'Don't be so narrow-minded. He's supposed to be really brilliant.'

Smailes sighed. 'Well, I suppose I could learn something about brainwashing. Where's he speaking?'

'Chelsea town hall, down the wrong end of King's Road. Five thirty.'

'What's his name?'

'Just a minute, I've got it written down somewhere. Lama Drukpa – I think that's how you say it.'

'Sounds like a Bolivian goatherd.'

'See you there, darling,' she said, hanging up.

Smailes felt distinctly uneasy as the dusty meeting hall began to fill up. The Venerable Lama Drukpa seemed able to command a good crowd, however, and by five forty there had to be almost two hundred people seated in rows of folding chairs. It was more the composition of the crowd that made Smailes feel awkward. There was a handful of people like himself and Clea – soberly dressed individuals on their way home from work. But by far the majority were from the post-hippie generation – shaggy young men and women wearing gaudy Himalayan jackets, flowered dresses, caftans and the like; Smailes could be fairly confident he was the only secret policeman present. Then there was a sprinkling of outright weirdos; in the row behind him was a bizarre-looking character in a Fair Isle sweater whose thin black hair had been slicked into two points which met in the centre of his forehead, and who wore a heavy Celtic cross around his neck. Smailes had taken an aisle chair and was relieved when the vacant seat across from him was taken by a man who was obviously a barrister. He wore an expensive dark suit and a blue shirt with detachable white collar, of the type successful lawyers favoured. He was bearded but carefully groomed. Eventually, a hush fell on the room as the lama entered the hall from the rear entrance.

Smailes had anticipated a Yoda-like figure, some diminutive holy man in saffron robes with no hair or teeth. Instead, he turned to see a tall, dignified individual walking slowly towards him down the centre aisle, dressed in a blue pin-stripe suit over a crimson Hawaiian shirt. He had a full head of jet-black hair and light-mahogany skin, and was leaning on the forearm of an attendant, as if partially lame. Lama Drukpa was of indecipherable age – anywhere between late twenties and early fifties. He kept a playful smile on his face as his party made its stately progress towards the stage at the end of the room.

The attendant, a young man in a blazer and trousers, made a fuss of helping the lama into his seat and attaching a lapel mike. Then he stood aside and tapped the bulb of a standing microphone at the edge of the stage and cleared his throat.

Smailes kept his eyes on the lama as his sidekick delivered a lengthy introduction. Smailes heard references to the lama's flight from Tibet in infancy, his exile and training in India under the tutelage of the Dalai Lama, then the doctorates from Oxford and the Sorbonne, the international travel and acclaim. Lama Drukpa seemed much more interested in the contents of his right nostril during this peroration, eventually parking whatever he'd extracted against the edge of a heavy glass ashtray on his side table. Then he took a long, slow drink from a glass containing a liquid that looked far too viscous to be water. What was it? Vodka? Tequila? At five o'clock in the afternoon? The gesture heightened Smailes's curiosity in this peculiar man.

Eventually, the attendant departed the stage and the lama began his address in high, lilting English. Smailes became fascinated despite himself, realizing that everything about Lama Drukpa was disorienting. The inscrutable face with its scalloped eyelids and high Mongolian cheekbones, the Hawaiian shirt and the business suit all had the effect of dramatically subverting each other. The lama's English was supple and idiosyncratic, delivered in a flawless BBC accent. He seemed at first to be intent on heaping ridicule on the crowd for its predilection for oriental clothing. He spoke of the wisdom of not rejecting Western traditions, and of Buddhism as the path of shedding ego, not of collecting exotic trappings. He warned against the danger of adopting a spiritual discipline simply as a means of embellishing a neurotic style. The audience seemed cowed, but the lama broke the mood.

'In San Francisco we would call this "Tripping on the tripless trip" ' and the crowd broke into grateful laughter. From this point, the lama delivered what to Smailes was a surprisingly convincing account of the relevance of the ancient wisdom of Buddhism to the modern world. Smailes's concentration drifted at times, and he found himself studying the rapt faces around him, but he followed enough of the lama's logic to recognize its simple truth. He felt slightly threatened by his lack of hostility, but had known intuitively that if his mother-in-law was involved, Tibetan Buddhism couldn't be complete twaddle nor its spokesman an outright charlatan. For her part, Anthea Lynch watched the lama with a proprietorial smile. Smailes reminded himself to ask her later what the hell he had in that glass.

At the end of the talk the lama invited questions, and a few individuals rose with respectful requests for clarification of his points. The lama answered in a lively, unpredictable way, often eliciting gales of laughter from the audience. It was then that Smailes heard a noise behind him and turned to see the Celtic warlock on his feet, waving a hand in the air. Lama Drukpa acknowledged him.

'Mr Drukpa?' the character began in a bizarre, high-pitched twang.

'Ye-es?' asked the lama mockingly.

'I'm confused by all these titles. Are you Mr Drukpa or are you Lama Drukpa? I mean, can you tell me, what is a mahatma?'

A titter rippled through the audience as the Tibetan took a belt from his drink and weighed his answer. The glass stayed at his lips for an unusually long time and Smailes realized at some point that the lama's shoulders were shaking. Eventually, he set his glass down carefully.

Lama Drukpa cleared his throat as if to speak but was seized by a violent shaking of the shoulders and put a hand over his eyes. The crowd realized the lama was laughing and began to join in – nervously at first, then with more vigour. Perhaps it was the contrast between the profundity of the lama's remarks and the inanity of the question, coupled with the outrageous demeanour of the questioner, but suddenly everyone was laughing – the lama, Smailes, his wife and mother-in-law, and everyone else in the room. The lama ceased to try and control himself and actually slid half-way out of his chair, helpless with mirth. This sent a new gust of laughter through the room, which got a further boost when the aggrieved questioner turned on his heel and stormed out, shrieking something incomprehensible. It was clear that the meeting was over, but no one was able to get out of his seat. People had literally become helpless, holding on to themselves and wiping their eyes. The lama had become a prostrate mass of quivering, pin-striped limbs straddling his chair. Across from Smailes, the barrister in the Savile Row suit had taken to the floor and was yapping like a Yorkshire terrier. Smailes himself was starting to grow hoarse. Clea grabbed his arm and said, 'We've got to go or I'm going to pee.' Anthea Lynch had begun to control herself, but at Clea's plea began howling again. With great difficulty the three of them made their way out of the room along with others who were sufficiently recovered to walk. Out in the street, Clea regained herself and told her mother, 'I see what you mean. He's quite something. What did you think, Derek?'

Smailes was still trying to control the giggles, and felt fundamentally grateful to any individual who could make him laugh so hard.

'Quite amazing, I agree.'

Anthea Lynch touched both their arms with pride. 'I'm so glad you could both come,' she said. 'I'm going home to relieve Fidelma. You two take your time and have fun.'

Smailes was dismayed to discover that once he and his wife had taken their seats in the restaurant, the atmosphere had chilled over into their now habitual, icy politeness. They inspected menus in silence and sat back to wait. Smailes decided to try and break the mood. 'So, any big developments in Peckham? Any news about that council grant yet?'

'No, not yet.'

'How's Sarah?'

'Oh, preoccupied. She's leading a seminar this weekend and is anxious about it.'

'What's it about?'

'You don't want to know.'

'Go on, tell me. I'm interested.'

'It's a masturbation workshop.'

Smailes gave a dry swallow. 'Sounds tiring.'

Clea missed the joke. 'They don't *do* it, silly. They *talk* about it.'

'That's the most ridiculous thing I've ever heard.' It was out of his mouth before he could catch himself.

'Yes, well, everything about Peckham Women's Centre is ridiculous to you, Mr Macho.'

'That's not fair.'

'It *is* fair. I don't know why you're so hostile towards everything I do.'

Smailes decided to try conciliation. 'Feminism makes me nervous.'

'I'm a feminist.'

'Yes, well, you make me nervous when you treat me like one of the enemy just because I'm a man.'

'I don't.'

'You always seem to whenever you spend time with Sarah.'

Clea fell silent. 'Sarah says you feel threatened. She says you find the prospect of staying home with the children and my being the wage-earner emasculating.'

Smailes's anger was rising. 'Well, maybe she's right. I just can't do it, Clea.'

'I'd compromise at one year.'

'What?'

'Just stay home with the children for one year. Then Lucy will be in playschool, and we can get a nanny.'

'Let's just get a nanny now, for Christ's sake.'

'No. You know my views. If you bothered to read any of my books, you'd know the first year of life is crucial to later development.'

Smailes held up his hand, unable to face this argument yet again. It was another sore point between them. To Smailes, parenting was an intuitive skill, like bicycling, and he had no interest in child development literature.

He reached across and took his wife's hand. 'I've considered it, darling. Honestly, I really have,' he lied. 'But if I took a year off work, I'd probably have to start all over again. Christ, in the current climate, I don't know they'd even hold my job for me.'

Clea could see that further discussion was pointless. A waiter had arrived and was standing awkwardly at her shoulder. She pushed her hair from her face, picked up her menu and ordered irritably. The conversation during the rest of their meal was stilted, and they drove home in a cocoon of bruised silence.

8

Judith Hyams eased the government Rover into the short-term car park next to the ferry terminus, then drove beneath the Cherbourg gantry towards the blue-and-white ticket kiosk. As the clerk leaned out, she held up her Home Office warrant card without rolling down her window or turning to meet his eye. He waved them through and Judith drove across the lane markings towards the public conveniences, outside which she parked and killed the engine. Smooth, thought Smailes. Very smooth.

Miss Judith Hyams had so far displayed a poise beyond her years in Jonquil – the codename picked for the Lubyanov operation. During the interrogation of Valerie Saunders, Lubyanov's girlfriend, she had played the instinctive good cop to Smailes's mean cop with aplomb, allowing Smailes to quickly cede the interview to her, as planned. Smailes then became an admiring spectator as Judith enlisted Valerie's full cooperation. Miss Saunders, a plain, good-natured Yorkshire-woman in her mid-twenties who also seemed a little naïve, was at first indignant at being grilled by the Security Service about her love life and refused to answer questions. But Smailes scared her by invoking the Official Secrets Act, even though it was obvious Valerie had no access to classified information. Then Judith had leaned across and placed a hand on her arm, explaining that her friend Yuri was probably a professional intelligence officer, and that the Security Service was simply trying to verify his activities. As hoped, Valerie Saunders jumped at the opportunity to exonerate her lover.

Yuri was an idealist trapped in a loveless marriage, she explained, who spoke longingly of building a new life in the West. He knew, however, that the authorities would never grant him an exit visa, because of the state secrets exclusion. This was a mere pretext, since Yuri was the cultural attaché and didn't know any secrets. The real reason was because his wife came from a prominent military family, and to permit his emigration would cause embarrassment. At first, Valerie refused to countenance that her lover could be an active KGB officer, describing him as an innocent and invoking their shared passion for the arts. But Judith Hyams won her confidence by showing her a document marked Confidential, condensing her research into Lubyanov's prior service. He was doubtless fairly low-level, Judith conceded, but his intelligence background was undeniable and the British wished to enlist his help in identifying others in the Russian diplomatic colony. In return for his cooperation, the British would help him resettle in the West with the offer of political asylum and a small pension. Then he and Valerie could be free to build a new life together, if they chose.

Smailes could see the tumult of fear and expectation that Judith's presentation engendered in Valerie Saunders. After pausing to gather her thoughts, she asked hesitantly what they required of her, and Judith explained they wanted a full account of her relationship with Lubyanov, and information about his activities and movements outside London. Meanwhile, she was to reveal nothing of their meeting, or the British would rescind their offer. Valerie took the plunge and decided to trust them, and during a lengthy description of her affair with Lubyanov revealed that Yuri had indeed hinted at a past intelligence role, and that he was scheduled to accompany a Moscow ballet troupe to Portsmouth at the end of the week, from where the dancers would take the midday ferry to Cherbourg. Smailes broke his silence and thanked her brusquely at the conclusion of the interview, making her swear once again she would not confide in her lover before that date.

MI5 had only a couple of days to locate and wire an appropriate interview site in Portsmouth, so Kinney and Smailes had insisted on Archie Keith, the top technician from S Branch, the technical division, as their advance man. Judith and Derek had driven down from London early that morning to meet Archie at Seacrest Manor, the modest bed-and-breakfast he'd chosen near the esplanade with a view of Southsea Castle and a 'No RN' sign in the window. Archie, an elderly Cockney with a superior manner, reviewed his recording system for them, then left haughtily to get his train, leaving Hyams and Smailes with ninety minutes before Lubyanov and his party of dancers were due to arrive from London.

Portsmouth's continental ferry terminus was in the same eastern reach of the harbour as the big Royal Navy base of HMS *Victory*. An ageing fleet of buses shuttled between Harbour Station and the departures building, where the Lubyanov party was expected to check in around noon for the one o'clock sailing to France. The British pair expected their target to emerge alone and take a taxi back to the station – the rank was directly outside the low white building. Judith and Derek guessed they had perhaps as little as thirty seconds after Lubyanov's re-emergence before he found a cab, which was why they chose to park their Rover next to the public toilets, just yards from the entrance. Smailes had resolved to let Judith drive. Then he would jump out, invoke Valerie's name and invite Yuri Lubyanov to get into the car. Lubyanov might balk, at which Smailes would mention their surveillance photographs. If the Russian still did not comply, they had resolved to drop him – Smailes and Kinney had ruled out coercion. Somehow, Smailes did not believe Comrade Lubyanov would prove resistant, given what Valerie had told them.

Judith and Smailes settled in to wait. Judith checked her watch. 'The London train should be arriving about now,' she said coolly.

'Ten or fifteen minutes, then,' said Smailes. Despite himself, he could not mask his excitement. He loved this kind of stunt – it made him nostalgic for the Cold War. Life would be very dull, he thought wistfully, if ever the Russians forsook their delusions of grandeur.

Judith checked her rear-view mirror.

'Derek, the law,' she said.

Smailes looked over his shoulder to see a policeman in shirt-sleeves sauntering over towards their car. It was illegally parked after all, well away from the car ferry lanes, and probably looked suspicious.

The copper, a lad barely out of his teens, tapped on Smailes's window. Derek rolled it down and handed the man his Home Office pass.

'MI5,' said Smailes quietly. 'Just ignore what happens here in a few minutes.'

The young policeman grabbed the peak of his distinctive helmet. 'Right you are, sir,' he said, and retraced his steps at the same nonchalant pace.

A few minutes later an ancient, cream-coloured bus with a red stripe drew up and tourists began to pile out. A stocky, grey-haired figure in a blue suit emerged and began to wave a succession of athletic-looking men and women into the building.

'That's him, Derek,' said Judith.

'Right on time,' said Smailes.

The party of Russians must have made alternative arrangements for their luggage, since the dancers each carried only a small overnight bag. After waiting until the last of them had descended, Lubyanov stamped out a cigarette and escorted a stately ballerina into the building. Smailes could feel his heart pounding.

The ferry sailed in less than an hour and there was plenty of activity outside the terminus. Twice the British pair almost made false starts as individuals of similar dress and build to Lubyanov appeared in the crowd outside the automatic doors. Then, suddenly, he was there, looking around anxiously as he fished in the pocket of his suit for his cigarettes.

'Go!' Smailes whispered urgently, and Judith swept the car around the semicircle to the taxi rank, where Lubyanov had joined a short queue. The brakes squealed as she pulled up. Smailes was on the pavement in an instant, standing next to the short, alarmed figure of Major Yuri Lubyanov, KGB.

'Yuri Andreyevich?' asked Smailes.

Lubyanov frowned. 'Yes.'

'Would you like to come with us? For a chat? We know all about Valerie.'

The tension appeared to drain from Lubyanov's face, and he waved at Smailes to get back in the car. Smailes opened the back door and the stocky Russian climbed in. Smailes got in beside him and slammed the door, and Judith, glancing in her rear-view mirror, drove off. The entire operation had taken perhaps fifteen seconds.

Smailes waited until Judith had pulled out into the dual carriageway back towards the city. He glanced out at the Marine guard in front of HMS *Victory*, who stood at ease holding his automatic rifle. All guards at British military installations were now fully armed since the IRA's latest bombing offensive.

Smailes turned to his charge. 'You know who we are?' he asked.

Lubyanov grinned sheepishly. 'Yes. British Intelligence. I have been expecting you. Valerie's behaviour was very strange when I last saw her. I guessed why.' He seemed almost relieved.

'I am Donald Sykes of the British Security Services. We have a proposal to put to you, Yuri,' said Smailes. 'We think you may find it attractive.'

Lubyanov exhaled slowly and folded his hands across his belly. As a professional, he knew the British would not attempt to recruit him in a moving vehicle, where recording was unreliable, and he settled back.

'Very well,' he said resignedly. 'But I must make an appearance at the embassy this afternoon. Otherwise there will be suspicions.' He spoke good, lightly accented English.

'We'll have you on board the two o'clock train,' Smailes assured him.

Lubyanov looked at his watch and shrugged again. He knew he was in no position to bargain.

Smailes didn't like Lubyanov. He seemed weak and had a foolish grin and a prissy manner. He was not without a certain seedy charm, however, with his fashionably long grey hair and expensive suit. He was probably about Smailes's age but looked older, with a strong-boned face heavily lined from too much alcohol and tobacco use. Smailes had anticipated Lubyanov might need fortification before his interview, and the Russian accepted a large glass of vodka thankfully. Then he sat down on the bed in the small room, since his hosts had taken the only available chairs. He took a long slug of his drink and lit a cigarette, accepting the large glass ashtray which Judith handed across to him. Archie Keith had deployed the telephone receiver at the Russian's elbow as the microphone for his recording system.

Smailes began peremptorily by reviewing Lubyanov's postings and career, and the KGB man made no attempt to correct the British information. He expressed surprise, however, that MI5 knew of his affair in Copenhagen, and was taken aback when Smailes demanded to know why he wasn't punished for it. He gave his foolish smirk and shrugged.

'I was given the benefit of the doubt, I suppose. I claimed I had seduced Katrina as a source, as part of my work. Of course, normally such activities are approved in advance. But you know my wife's father?'

'General Osipov?' asked Smailes.

'Correct. His career was flourishing at the time with the defeat of the reactionaries, and I think he may have used his influence. Anyway, instead of being fired, I was given a new posting. My wife had always wanted London. So now . . .' He shrugged again.

'And what is your brief here?' asked Smailes.

'Minimal,' Lubyanov replied. 'Most of what I do is actually the work of the cultural attaché, you may be surprised to learn. Like today. Now that we are both practically on the same side . . .'

'Not quite, Yuri.'

'Oh, it is a matter of time. You will see, we will be joining NATO, the EC . . .'

'So why is Boris Zhimin stacking his residence with techno-spies?' Smailes demanded.

Lubyanov pouted. 'That is precisely my point. If you would just let us join your organizations, we would purchase your technology instead of having to steal it.'

'How large is the KGB complement in London currently?'

'I don't know exactly. Twenty, thirty . . .'

'Don't make me laugh.'

'Well, perhaps more. Fifty, sixty. I am very marginal. I do not even know names.'

Smailes decided it was time to get tough. 'Listen, Yuri old pal, you'd better start getting less marginal. We want a complete rundown of Zhimin's order of battle. Names, ranks, areas of expertise. And soon.'

Lubyanov swallowed. 'I don't know whether . . .'

'And we want names of British subjects in active collaboration with any of your agent-runners. Understand?'

Lubyanov protested. 'Are you crazy? I am cultural affairs, understand? I listen to gossip in British intellectual circles. You know, your radical playwrights and authors, what are they up to? I have no involvement with the technical or industrial side. You think I am told these things?'

'No, but you're going to have to find out, mate. You eat lunch with your colleagues, don't you? You talk shop, don't you? You're just going to have to prick up your ears a bit. Janet?'

He turned to Judith, who was listening attentively at his side, and accepted his briefcase from her. He slowly removed the eight-by-ten glossies of Lubyanov and Valerie in various torrid poses and handed them across to him.

'You cooperate with us, and the Home Office will give you political asylum and ten thousand a year for five years. If you refuse, or fail to generate anything we consider worthwhile, these will land on Boris Zhimin's doorstep. I can't see your father-in-law saving your hide this time, can you? If we throw in the tapes of this meeting, you'll probably face espionage charges too, won't you?'

The colour drained from Lubyanov's face. 'Please, Mr Sykes. I know nothing of what you ask. If I begin to try and find out, my colleagues will get suspicious.'

'What about order of battle?'

'That too is difficult. I know maybe fifteen, twenty names myself. Others, I have to guess. Like you do. If there is a complete list, it is in Zhimin's safe, or Gropov's.'

'Who?'

'His deputy. The security officer.'

'Well, you're going to have to use your imagination, my friend. We are most pissed off at the way your government is exploiting the normalization of relations to try and rob us blind. You cooperate and we'll see you all right. If you fail, we'll throw you to the dogs.'

Lubyanov took another belt from his glass but said nothing. He was beginning to appreciate the depth of his predicament. Smailes looked at his watch.

'Drink up, Yuri,' he said. 'You've got a train to catch.'

Lubyanov listened ashenly as Smailes reviewed contact procedures. He handed Lubyanov a card with the details and told him to memorize them and destroy the card before he got to London. There were no smoke detectors in British Rail toilets, he explained. Lubyanov could burn it and flush away the ash. Lubyanov crushed out his cigarette.

'One last thing, Yuri,' said Smailes, standing. 'No more trysts with Valerie. No information, no nookie, get it? Produce the goods and we'll arrange for a reunion. Understand?'

Lubyanov got to his feet but had lost his voice. He nodded weakly.

It was a considerably less buoyant Major Yuri Lubyanov whom the British deposited at Portsmouth Central at quarter to two. As Judith Hyams watched the bowed figure disappear up the steps, she leaned back against her door and looked admiringly at her boss.

'You were terrific,' she said simply.

Smailes could not suppress a grin. He knew the burning of Lubyanov could not have gone more smoothly had it been a training exercise. Then his face clouded.

'You think he's legitimate?' he asked.

'Yes. Don't you?'

'I don't know. I've been wrong about Russians before.'

'Let's see what he produces. That's the best way to judge, isn't it?'

'You're right,' said Smailes, following the Southsea signs away from the station. He'd noticed to his amusement that he'd had no need to adjust the driver's seat – he and Judith were about the same height. 'Let's pick up our gear and get back to town.'

'So I'm Janet, am I?' she asked mockingly.

'Light cover, you know,' said Smailes. 'You pick a name with the same initials as your real name. Janet Hall,' he suggested.

'Janet Horowitz,' Judith countered, and Smailes laughed.

'Janet Horowitz it is,' he agreed.

*

The inevitable ensuing lull in Jonquil allowed Smailes to begin work on his Carne submission for Roger Standiforth. Roger had asked to see him at eleven on the Monday following the Portsmouth trip, and Smailes held a preliminary meeting that morning with Ed Poynter, MI5's resident legal expert. Five had countered parliamentary oversight manoeuvres so often in its past that Poynter was able to go straight to a fat file and hand it to Smailes. He also undertook to write a summary document condensing the prevailing wisdom as to why MI5 should not now, or ever, be directly answerable to the country's elected parliament. Smailes was taking notes from Poynter's enormous file when his secure line rang, signifying a call via the main switchboard.

Despite the faint distortion, Smailes immediately recognized the voice of Peter Lynch, his father-in-law, and his heart sank. Lynch wanted to see him urgently, he said, and was suggesting lunch. Peter Lynch liked to feign indifference that his daughter had married beneath her social class, but to Smailes it was an unconvincing act. His father-in-law was a financier and former Tory MP who never seemed to miss an opportunity to patronize him. He had 'loaned' them the down payment for their home in Coulsdon (no repayment schedule was ever mentioned) and Smailes had wondered whether Lynch might use the occasion of Clea's new pregnancy for further generosity. He also experienced a stab of familiar ambivalence. He was well aware that Clea's family money made things easier for him, and in fact had been a secret incentive for marrying her. But he felt embarrassed by Lynch's gifts and tacitly inculpated by them for failure to provide adequately for his daughter. But he could see no pretext for declining lunch and agreed to meet Lynch at one at the Oxford & Cambridge Club.

Smailes found Roger Standiforth in a supercilious mood. He congratulated Smailes unctuously on his initial success in Jonquil, having been present when Smailes and Judith were debriefed. He listened without apparent interest as Smailes brought him up to date on his research into Ed Poynter's files. Then he poked with his toe at a large cardboard box, which Smailes had not yet noticed.

'Take a look at this stuff, will you?' he asked.

Smailes leaned forward and fished out a handful of dusty pamphlets. It was anti-nuclear propaganda from CND, Nukewatch, Greenham Common Collective and the like. Smailes leafed through it absently – it all seemed so dated.

'Peter Tennant found this little stash in the study of our friend Brigadier Cole,' said Standiforth smugly.

'What?' Smailes couldn't believe his ears.

'Yes. I authorized an illicit entry after Peter brought me his file. Seems he was known in his later years as "the pink brigadier". Thought the country was going off the rails with overreliance on the nuclear deterrent. I think we've found the recipient of his daughter's stolen documents, don't you?'

This was entirely too ripe for Smailes. Although Roger Standiforth ordered burglaries ('illicit entries' in MI5 parlance) the way other people ordered take-out food, the physical removal of the documents contravened a most basic MI5 practice – never allow a target to know he'd been burgled. A written inventory or microfilm would have been more customary. Then again, Roger's pretext didn't make sense. Smailes had only met Alec Cole once, but he would swear he was what he seemed – an old soldier and Tory diehard – and certainly no closet leftist. Roger's claim seemed preposterous and left Smailes at a loss for words. Eventually he asked weakly, 'Pink brigadier? However did Tennant find that out?'

'It was in his file, old man,' said Standiforth tartly. 'Obvious place to look.'

It had crossed Smailes's mind to call up Alec Cole's file in MI5's registry, but he hadn't pursued it. He felt embarrassed.

'And all this stuff was in his study? Down in Hampshire?'

'Apparently so. I think between the brigadier and his daughter we've found two of Nukewatch's major sources, don't you?'

Smailes's mind was racing. 'The Burghfield leak?'

'Hard to say. But we can't rule it out.'

'Are we going to prosecute?'

'I'll send a memo to the Attorney-General, but I very much doubt it. There was nothing restricted in the box, I'm afraid. All in the public domain.'

'So there's no evidence he was receiving classified documents from his daughter.'

'None. Just the obvious inference.'

'Where does this leave Gerry Stap?'

'Good question. I think it raises the likelihood that he was telling you the truth, that Audrey Cole was acting without his knowledge. Surveillance hasn't turned up anything, and I think I'm going to suggest we wind it up. We're going to have to look elsewhere for the Burghfield leak, I'm afraid.'

Smailes was shaking his head, unable to assimilate these developments. Standiforth was clearly gloating that his own assistant had unearthed a file overlooked by the head of K9 – his exaggerated friendliness was his way of rubbing it in. Roger crushed out his cigarette and looked at his watch equably.

'Look, you'll excuse me, will you? I have an appointment. Keep up the work on that summary with Poynter – it's good to hear you're on top of it.' The remark was delivered without apparent irony.

Smailes got to his feet slowly and returned to his office, his confusion gradually turning to anger. As he sat down in his seat, Judith Hyams regarded him with alarm.

'Everything okay?' she asked.

'Yes, everything's okay,' he said irritably.

He didn't buy it. He didn't buy it for one second. He swivelled to his terminal and punched in his access data, then the characters for Alec Cole's file. Cole's file number came up, along with the response 'Y-Box'.

Y-Boxes were the most sensitive of MI5's files, locked in their own vault in K6, the domestic counter-espionage section. They contained the identities of MI5's secret agents, and personal files that were too sensitive for even the highly trusted registry queens to oversee. Y-Box data had been computerized also, but could not be retrieved without higher access than Smailes possessed. However, he could go to K6 in person and physically inspect the original file. He called Eunice, the K6 librarian, who told him the Cole file was signed out.

'Who to?' he asked.

She paused to consult her log. 'Roger Standiforth,' she replied.

Smailes hung up, fished out his address book, and put in a call to Brigadier Alec Cole. The telephone rang for a long time before it was answered. Probably out in his rose beds, Smailes told himself.

Smailes introduced himself quickly, then came straight to the point.

'Brigadier, have you been the victim of a burglary lately?'

'Yes,' came the crusty response. 'Last bloody weekend. I was up in town for the regimental dinner. Made the mistake of leaving the car at the station, so they knew I was gone.'

'What was taken? Anything much?'

'Not really. Just the video. Something they can flog for a quick sale.' Brigadier Cole ascribed blame to 'louts from the estate'. He would always be sure to take a taxi to the station in future, he said, and leave his car in the drive as a decoy. The brigadier added some sentiments about the deterioration of life in modern Britain.

'Nothing personal? No papers or documents?'

Cole sounded surprised. 'No. Nothing. Didn't even look as if they'd been upstairs into my study. Of course, I've nothing valuable there – that's all at the bank.'

'Quite. Yes, of course, Brigadier.'

'Why, has something turned up? How did you know about the break-in?'

Smailes had to think fast. 'Oh, we're investigating a pattern of thefts from former NATO commanders, that's all. Wondered if you'd been a victim also. No military papers missing, for instance?'

'Good Lord, no,' said Cole, alarmed. 'Nothing like that, I'm sure. Although I could check again.'

Smailes urged him to look and to call back if he discovered anything missing, although he knew he was wasting his time.

He turned to look across at Judith, who had returned to her study of papers on her desk. Sharing an office really was awkward when you were involved in multiple cases, he realized.

He sat and fumed. He didn't believe a bloody word of it. Brigadier Alec Cole was no more a closet pinko than Roger Standiforth. That box of anti-nuclear propaganda in Roger's office had come from some dusty F Branch vault, not Alec Cole's study. Peter Tennant had certainly broken into Rose Cottage, however, and nicked the brigadier's video to ensure his visit was duly reported – again, in direct contravention of MI5 practice. What it all meant was that Roger Standiforth was deliberately fabricating evidence in order to point a finger at Alec Cole and his daughter, whom Smailes was now convinced must be entirely innocent. The 'theft' also had the effect of exonerating Gerry Stap, MP, which Smailes had to assume was something else his boss wished to contrive. What Smailes could not begin to fathom, however, as he contemplated his lunch appointment with Peter Lynch, was why Roger had gone to such unusual lengths to accomplish it.

9

The Oxford & Cambridge Club in Pall Mall, a stone's throw from Buckingham Palace, was hardly Smailes's favourite lunch venue. Still, he conceded as he scanned the menu card, he'd begun to feel considerably less ill at ease there than he had on his first visits. As he looked around the dining room, he realized he'd become indistinguishable from the rest of the well-dressed, middle-aged clientele. The fact that he didn't have an Oxbridge degree didn't matter much either – neither did plenty of members he'd met. Smailes was aware he was eligible to join through his marriage to Clea, who was an Oxford graduate, but had always inwardly scoffed at the idea. Still, he told himself, the place was handy for the office, the luncheon rates were reasonable and the steward kept an excellent cellar. Then there were the squash courts in the basement, and Clea was always badgering him to take up some physical exercise . . . Peter Lynch's voice interrupted his thoughts; he was recommending a particular Beaujolais. Smailes murmured assent and shook his head in disbelief. Here he was, supposedly a man of the people, actually entertaining the idea of club membership. What was he coming to?

Smailes and his father-in-law gave their orders to the crisply dressed waiter and settled back. Smailes fingered his water glass and regarded his host. Clea's father was a boyish man of sixty, with a full head of brown hair, ears that were too large, and expensive but careless taste in clothes. He was wearing one of his signature Italian suits and a red tie with grease spots. To Smailes's surprise, Lynch seemed agitated, not his usual bumptious self.

'So what's up, Peter?' Smailes asked mildly. 'You said something about urgency.'

'You know Gerry Stap?' asked Lynch, coming straight to the point.

Smailes was taken aback. 'The MP? He's a junior defence minister, isn't he?'

'Right,' said Lynch. 'I knew him at Oxford.'

'Really?'

'He invited me to a private meeting at the Special Forces Club yesterday. Asked me for a donation – a bloody large donation – to something he called the Sceptre Group.'

Smailes said nothing.

'Seems it's based there at the club, in Knightsbridge. He mentioned some of the military people on the steering committee. I didn't catch the names.'

'What's its purpose?'

'Well, that's the point,' said Lynch forcefully. 'He said something vague about contingency plans in case of a breakdown in civil order if there's a general election over Europe this autumn.'

Smailes frowned. 'What breakdown?'

'Same damn thing I asked. He shilly-shallied a bit, then said something about approaching Lady Thatcher to lead a government of national unity in the event of a hung parliament. Then the penny dropped.'

'What penny?'

'Don't be stupid, Derek. They're talking about a bloody coup, that's what! They want to prevent any further steps towards European unity is what, and by force of arms if necessary. I can't believe Lady Thatcher would countenance any such idea . . .'

Smailes was alarmed by this news, but feigned indifference. He knew that the lunatic right had contemplated intervention in the democratic process on multiple occasions in Britain's past. The most recent, to his knowledge, was during the seventies when extremists had discussed installing Lord Mountbatten, the Queen's cousin, as head of a national unity government. Senior MI5 people had been involved in that plot, Smailes was aware, which had eventually come to nothing.

There was a pause as their waiter placed steaming plates of lamb before them and uncorked their wine. For a few minutes Smailes and Lynch ate in silence.

Derek wiped his mouth. 'I dunno, Peter,' he said carefully. 'I might have thought you'd be receptive to such an idea. I've heard arguments that if the economy doesn't improve, the PM might be talked into some accelerated timetable for closer European union. Shouldn't think you'd welcome that.'

Lynch put down his cutlery with a clatter and raised his voice. 'Are you serious, man? Do you know what you're saying?'

Realizing he was speaking too loud, Lynch regained himself and took a swallow of wine. He resumed in low, urgent tones. 'Listen, Derek, I've always been a staunch Thatcherite – you know that. And quite frankly, I share her concerns about the pace of European integration, about the independence of some of our institutions. But what Stap is proposing is outright treason! Not to mention, if a coup ever came off, which pray God it couldn't, it would be utterly counter-productive.'

'How so?'

'If there were any interference by the military in the political process, if it led to a change of government – no matter by whom it was led – Britain would become an international pariah, like Greece under the colonels! Can you imagine what that would do to business activity? Christ, Britain would end up a third-rate power, another Ireland! I'm astonished to hear you say such things!'

Smailes held up a hand. 'Just sounding out your views, Peter, that's all. No, no, I agree, this is potentially very serious. But it's hardly the first time the ultras have floated such an idea.'

'Well, that's my point too. I don't think you can class Gerry Stap as an ultra; he used to be Thatcherite, perhaps, but now he's almost a centrist, I would have said. If he's on board with such crackpots, how many others are? If they're approaching me for money, how many others have they talked to? How much have they raised?'

Smailes had gone pale. He had suddenly linked this development with the possibility that Gerry Stap was the source of the Burghfield leak. If someone in collusion with Stap had stolen American PALs and had access to a nuclear weapon, then perhaps this Sceptre Group, whatever it was, had some real ammunition with which to make good its threat to British democracy.

His father-in-law was still not convinced he was being taken seriously. 'Look, I assumed you'd be horrified by this news, as I was, but if you don't think it's significant, I'll bloody well go round you. I'm friendly with Standiforth, you know . . .'

'No, please, Peter, don't misunderstand me.'

'In fact, I saw him as I was waiting for you, and was in two minds whether to approach him on the spot. But you *are* my son-in-law, and I thought . . .'

'Really?' asked Smailes. 'Roger's here?' Then to himself, 'That's right, he said he had an appointment.' This news in itself was not surprising, since Roger and Peter had long been members of the same club. What was a little odd, Smailes thought, was that Roger should choose to conduct a private meeting here, when he was also a member of White's and the Athenaeum, both more prestigious clubs. Must be someone he didn't want to impress *too* much, he reflected.

'Yes, he and some guests have booked the Blomfield Room. Saw them going in from the bar. Look, I'm serious, Derek.'

'I know you are, Peter. I know you are. And I agree – conspiracies like this need to be monitored, even if they're doomed from the start. I'll speak to Roger this afternoon, as soon as I can. If he prevaricates, I'll go the Deputy DG. I'll make sure the information gets through. You've done the right thing, believe me.'

Lynch's feathers were still ruffled by Smailes's insinuations. 'Ultimately, this is not a party political thing, Derek; it's a question of accepting the inevitable. The only way the far right thinks we can continue as a world power is to cuddle up with the Americans. Well, that's not on any more. We need to rebuild our industrial infrastructure through partnership with Europe. If there is some dilution of our national sovereignty, well, that's just the admission price, I'm afraid. I agree we need to negotiate tough terms and retain important veto rights. But Europe is where the future lies, not across the bloody Atlantic. The diehards just refuse to see it.'

'Didn't know you were such an ardent European, Peter,' said Smailes, scanning the dessert card.

'You've got no choice these days, old boy, if you're in business,' said his father-in-law somewhat gloomily. 'Economic and monetary union are absolutely inevitable, eventually. There is no realistic alternative. The ultras just refuse to see it.'

'I see,' said Smailes. 'Sorry if I seemed unsympathetic at first. What did you tell Stap?'

'That's all right,' said Lynch grudgingly. 'I pretended to be interested but told him I needed a few days to think about it. The chocolate mousse was good last time I was here. By the way, how's Clea doing? She hasn't called for ages.'

Smailes realized with a pang of disappointment that his father-in-law was not about to offer them any money after all.

He was still weighing these developments as he handed over his ticket and accepted his raincoat from the cloakroom attendant. The cloakroom was next to the lift, between the bar and the private Blomfield Room. Glancing across, he saw there was a pay phone just outside its door. Curiosity got the better of him, and he fished out a coin and walked across to dial his office. As the line rang, he looked through the glass panel to see Roger Standiforth seated with his back to him, his profile wreathed in cigarette smoke. What surprised him more was the identity of Roger's guests. CIA station chief Loudon Strickland, in his trademark light suit, was stirring a cup of coffee, listening to a colleague seated at his left. Smailes did not recognize the second man, who was tall and brown-haired, with rimless glasses, but he answered perfectly the description of the CIA's chief of covert operations. What was the name Sal Imodeo had given him? Smailes hunted his memory – Morris, that was it. Blane Morris, deputy director for operations. Not that there was anything *ipso facto* unusual in such a meeting, except that Smailes knew Morris was visiting London clandestinely, and that his boss Standiforth had such legendary disdain for Americans that he would not normally give them the time of day, even at Curzon House.

Judith Hyams was excited. She'd just received a packet from the Dutch embassy containing a five-page dossier on Yuri Lubyanov, dating from the time he served in The Hague in the early eighties. It was in Dutch, of course, but translation ought to be a formality. And it confirmed that Comrade Lubyanov had a long and active history in the KGB, and was not perhaps such a low-level operative as he claimed. She eagerly anticipated her boss's return and the opportunity to impress him. The Lubyanov operation was proceeding magically – she'd never dreamed she would get involved so quickly in a real counter-intelligence operation.

However, when Smailes returned to the office he was clearly preoccupied, and barely glanced at the file when she passed it to him. He was on the telephone immediately with Glenys Powner, Roger Standiforth's secretary, asking for a meeting as soon as the head of K Branch returned from lunch. Judith knew better than to ask what had happened – she was quite aware Smailes found her presence irksome when he worked on cases in which she was not indoctrinated. They held a somewhat stiff discussion of how to approach the translation of the Dutch material – there might be no Dutch speaker on staff, in which case they would have to go through the Foreign Office or SIS, both unattractive options. Then the telephone rang and it was obviously Glenys telling him Roger would see him immediately, since he got out of his chair and took the Dutch file to his safe. As always, he was careful to shield the combination with his body – Judith was quite aware she would only ever know what she needed to know. Then, with a suggestion she inquire about MI5's Dutch speakers through Personnel, he left.

'All right, Derek. I suggest you repeat what you just told me. From the beginning,' said Standiforth.

Smailes realized his mouth was dry. He poured a glass of water from the pitcher in the middle of the DG's conference table, and cleared his throat. He felt nervous, but pleased to be on centre stage. It was his first time ever in the DG's suite.

Roger had been surprisingly attentive when Smailes rehearsed for him the information his father-in-law had given him over lunch. He asked a few pointed questions, but otherwise listened in silence. Once or twice he made remarks like 'I've been wondering about something like this' and seemed to grow steadily more concerned. When Smailes pointed out the possible connection between the Burghfield leak and the Sceptre Group, Roger actually sat up sharply. These responses didn't particularly surprise Smailes. While a staunch Tory like most of MI5 brass, Roger drew a distinction between himself and the 'hoorah boys', those whose jingoistic patriotism led them into all kinds of folly. Roger's Conservatism was of the deadly serious but pragmatic strain; if he sympathized with the agenda of the ultra right, he took care not to betray it.

At the conclusion of Smailes's presentation he said simply, 'We've got to nip this in the bud,' and placed a call to Deputy DG Alex Corcoran. Within five minutes a conference had been arranged later that afternoon in the DG's suite, and Smailes, to his surprise, had been drafted to repeat his account.

Actually, as he began speaking, Smailes's nervousness left him. He didn't question his right to be there, knowing he was at least as capable as the others in the room, excepting perhaps Corcoran, whose talents were legendary. The fact that Sir David Williams was an ex-policeman helped his confidence also, since he felt they were on a similar wavelength. Standiforth sat to his right, with Corcoran's wheelchair stationed opposite. Soon after he began speaking, the DG interrupted.

'What's this Special Forces Club?'

Corcoran gave a pout. 'Macho men,' he said. 'Our true defenders of Queen and country.'

Roger had gone to a file, from which he produced a print-out. He gave a potted history of the club, then an account of their recent annual dinner at the Dorchester Hotel.

‘Two hundred guests. Guest of honour, Prince Andrew. Speaker, General Norman Schwarzkopf. Significantly, Prince Charles, the club president, did not attend.’

Williams waved for Smailes to continue. Corcoran sat lizard-like with eyes half closed, chin on his hands, elbows resting on the arms of his wheelchair. Sir David Williams’s chair twitched back and forth between the ranks of grey computer screens. Roger Standiforth sat immobile.

Smailes spoke for perhaps ten minutes. No one responded when he invoked the possible link via Stap to the Burghfield leak. If Roger still espoused the ‘pink brigadier’ theory, he was keeping it to himself. When Smailes had completed his presentation, Williams asked immediately, ‘Who belongs to this Sceptre Group?’

‘Mr Lynch didn’t recall specific names, sir,’ said Smailes. MI5 culture decreed that the DG and his deputy were both ‘sir’. Everyone else was addressed by a first name or, preferably, a nickname.

‘Well, we need to find out,’ said Williams. ‘Who can we infiltrate?’

Roger said casually, ‘Well, I think you’ll find Bingo is already a member, sir.’

Corcoran shot him a quick look. ‘You don’t run anyone in there, Roger?’ he asked.

‘I wish,’ said Standiforth. ‘Otherwise I would have found out about this nonsense earlier.’

Sir David Williams had actually picked up his phone and begun dialling when Standiforth interrupted. ‘Don’t you think we should wait until we know whether Mr Bingham has any direct involvement with this Sceptre Group, sir?’

‘I’ll bloody well ask him myself,’ said Williams.

Corcoran spoke up forcefully. ‘I agree with Roger, sir. We should find out ourselves first who’s involved.’ Smailes noticed that Corcoran and Standiforth exchanged a knowing look.

Williams slammed down the receiver and blew out his cheeks. ‘Well, bloody hell, who can we run in there? Shouldn’t be too hard.’

‘How about Peter Lynch, sir?’ offered Standiforth. ‘He’s been pestering me for years to be used as a stringer.’

Now Smailes had heard everything. His own father-in-law to be drafted as an MI5 agent. God help the realm of Albion, he told himself.

Corcoran concurred. ‘He’s already been invited to make a donation. He could get further involved without arousing suspicion. He would just have to report back on their activities. Not too difficult . . .’

Unexpectedly, Williams turned to Smailes. 'What do you think of that idea, Derek?' he asked.

Smailes held up a hand. 'I plead conflict of interest, sir. I'm married to his daughter.' Everyone laughed.

'You think he'd agree?'

'I don't doubt it,' said Smailes.

Williams twitched his chair back and forth, regarding his minions. 'Set it up,' he said. 'Once we clarify the composition of the group, if he's not involved, we can turn it over to Bingham. It's an F Branch affair, obviously, and he's in the perfect position himself. See what Lynch can find out, and I'll alert the Cabinet secretary as soon as possible.'

'I'm afraid this is not the first time, sir . . .' said Corcoran.

'I know, I know,' said Williams. 'Probably all sound and fury. But Derek's right; if they've got some people with access to a nuke, and Stap helped them steal the locking device . . . Well, we've got to take it seriously.'

He turned to Smailes. 'Thank you, Derek. Admirably clear.'

Smailes straightened his tie in a glow of self-satisfaction. He knew David Williams was poorly regarded by the old school, but he was still Director-General of the British Security Service with a seat in the councils of state, bestowing particular praise on him, Derek Smailes. He folded his hands on the table in front of him and inspected the silver cuff-links Peter Lynch had given him. Then he winced inwardly. Since Lynch's schoolboy fantasies were about to be realized, his father-in-law was probably about to become insufferable.

'Well, you'd better try a little harder, Yuri, old boy,' said Smailes, grabbing Lubyanov's hand as it travelled towards his suit pocket.

'Do you mind waiting until you get outside, Yuri? It's such a dirty habit. Very bad for you, too.'

Judith Hyams found herself unnerved by Smailes's demeanour. He could clearly be extremely unpleasant without particularly trying.

Lubyanov was the picture of misery. Denied nicotine, he fidgeted, then got to his feet. The three of them were in the living room of an MI5 safe flat in Ladbroke Square, a short walk from the Russian embassy.

'Look, Mr Sykes, you must understand. To try and get the information you require, I have to alter my routines. To alter my routines arouses suspicion. Always. You know that.'

'I don't know what's so controversial about the KGB staff roster. I can't believe there's only a couple of copies.'

'What am I supposed to do? Steal one from a secretary?'

'No, we'll make it easy for you, Yuri. You just find one and memorize the names. Janet?'

Judith Hyams went to her briefcase and extracted a thick blue booklet.

'Thank you,' said Smailes, accepting it from her. It was the *London Diplomatic Roster*, prepared by the Foreign Office, containing staff lists of all accredited embassies. Smailes opened it at the page for Russia.

'You read this, and you mark each individual who you know is KGB and what their responsibilities are. Here's a pencil. You can start today.'

Lubyanov took the booklet and Smailes's propelling pencil, then hesitated. So far, he had not given the British anything. Now he was being required to cross the line, and his hands shook. Smailes knew what he was thinking.

'You can't turn back now, Yuri. You know that.'

'I don't know. This is all too fast.'

'All right. Take your time. Take the book home with you, if you like. We'll go over it at our next meeting.'

Lubyanov looked hugely relieved. 'Can I go?' he asked nervously.

'Of course, why not?' Smailes said expansively. 'We don't want to create any suspicions, Yuri – like you said.'

Lubyanov stuffed the booklet into an inside pocket and turned towards the door.

'One more thing, however. I have to remind you, Yuri, that order of battle is not enough. You could give me a hundred names, and I'll still turn you in to Zhimin. I want names of British subjects collaborating with you. Traitors – new, old, I don't care about the vintage. And I don't care how you get them. Those are the terms of the original deal, and they haven't changed.'

Lubyanov blanched. 'Mr Sykes, I have told you, this is most unreasonable . . .'

'Goodbye, Yuri. Until this time on Tuesday.'

'Mr Sykes . . .'

'Goodbye.'

Lubyanov gave Smailes a look of loathing, then slouched to the door. Smailes and Judith listened as his footfalls receded down the hall.

'Boy, you can be a real bastard, can't you?' said Judith. It didn't sound like a compliment.

'Nah. Complete pussycat, really.'

'You don't think he's telling us the truth?'

'He may be. But if I don't scare him, I doubt he'll stick his neck out.'

'And if his own side chops it off?'

'He should have thought of that before he climbed into bed with Valerie Saunders, shouldn't he? He's a professional, Judith. Never forget that.'

Judith thought of a rejoinder, but let it pass. She just hoped she never got on the wrong side of this man. He could be as hard as iron.

Smailes returned from the do-it-yourself shop on Saturday afternoon to find that Lucy and Fidelma had converted the dining room into a sprawling tent of chairs and blankets. Lucy was inside, making up beds for her animals. Fidelma came out sheepishly to the kitchen to apologize for the disruption. Smailes set his box of paint and rollers down on the table.

'No, that's all right, love. Play whatever games you like – I don't really have the time or the energy.'

Lucy came into the kitchen clutching Tweetie. 'Daddy go night night?' she asked.

'Believe me, I'd love to, love. But I've got to decorate the baby's room.'

'Mummy's tummy,' said Lucy.

'That's right, Lucy. The baby in Mummy's tummy.' Lucy and Fidelma returned to their game and Smailes shook his head sadly. His daughter was so precious, he ought to find a way to spend more time with her. Since Jonquil, he often wasn't home until after she was asleep.

Fidelma called out from the dining room. 'Oh, Mr Smailes, I forgot to say. Clea's Dad called you.'

Smailes winced. 'Thanks, Fidelma.' He'd been half expecting a call from Lynch. He suspected Clea was already over there, since she'd mentioned she'd stop in at Purley after shopping with her mother.

Peter Lynch answered the phone himself. Smailes could picture him, seated at the desk in his study, gazing out on to a future in which his exploits would be immortalized in a television mini-series.

'Derek,' he said casually, 'I wondered if you had a few minutes later this afternoon – maybe join me for a cocktail?'

Smailes sighed inwardly. 'Well, I was going to start decorating and I have to cook supper, but, well, if it's brief . . .'

'You probably know what it's about,' said Lynch darkly.

'Right,' said Smailes. 'Is Clea there?'

'Yes, I think I heard her and Anthea come in about ten minutes ago. You need to speak with her?'

'No. Just say I'll give her a ride home, though. About five o'clock?'

'Right.' Smailes looked at his watch – it was almost four. No point opening a can of paint today, he told himself.

Smailes recognized his mother-in-law's Peugeot outside the garage, but not the dark Volvo parked beneath the yew tree in the driveway. He thought it odd, also, that a formally dressed young man should be standing in the doorway, as if on duty. Had Peter Lynch invited someone from Whitehall to their meeting? On a Saturday? It seemed unlikely.

He skipped up the steps to the front door and the young man reached out to open it.

'I'm here to see Mr Lynch,' he said.

'Certainly,' said the stranger, pushing the door open.

In the hallway, another young man dressed in a blazer and flannels stepped forward.

'Is Peter Lynch here?' he said. 'I'm Derek Smailes.'

'Oh right, Mr Smailes. He's expecting you. He's in the study.'

Smailes frowned at the man, took off his jacket and hung it in the closet. The french doors to the sitting room were closed, but from inside Smailes could hear the murmur of voices.

He found Lynch where he'd predicted, seated at his desk nursing a Scotch. He looked peeved.

'What's with the security, Peter?' he asked.

'Anthea has her bloody Tibetan guru over for tea. She never asked *me* about it. Seems he never goes anywhere without at least two bodyguards. Honestly, I try to be tolerant about my wife's . . .'

'Lama Drukpa?' asked Smailes, brightening.

'You know him?'

'Anthea took us to a talk up in town. He's quite funny.'

'Yes, well, I don't think he's bloody funny. Believe me, I'd have his type deported. Sponsoring kidnapping, rejecting our laws, threatening writers . . .'

'Oh, he's a Buddhist, Peter, not a Muslim.'

Lynch scowled at him. 'Come on, man, they're all the bloody same. Scotch?'

Smailes suppressed a smile. 'Sherry, please, I think.'

Lynch strode across to his drinks cabinet as Smailes took a seat next to the low coffee-table. The oak-panelled study with its library shelves contrived to suggest a bookish man, but Smailes knew his father-in-law used it mostly as a retreat in which to drink and watch television in solitude.

Returning to his desk, Lynch came straight to the point. 'Alex Corcoran told me you know about my agreement to help keep tabs on this Special Forces outfit.'

'Yes. I said I thought it was a good idea,' Smailes lied.

'Really?' said Lynch, flattered.

'Well, I thought you could fit in pretty well over there.' Idiotically, Lynch took this as another compliment.

'Did you? Well, I've had some briefing from Corcoran, but I thought I'd check in with you, too. You know, how to comport myself. How not to arouse suspicion.'

What his father-in-law was really doing was preening, Smailes was aware. He'd probably been told not to discuss his role with anyone, but couldn't resist this display of new-found credentials before his son-in-law.

Smailes cleared his throat. 'You're going to wear a wire?'

'No. It was considered too risky. Just listen and report back.'

'To Corky?'

'Right.'

'Not Roger?'

'Roger was at the briefing, but no, Corcoran is my case officer.'

If the Deputy DG was running this infiltration himself, it was some measure of how seriously MI5 viewed this latest threat from the far right. Smailes was impressed, despite himself.

'Just act as naturally as possible. If pressed, give the kind of responses you think they'd want. I shouldn't think that would be too hard to dream up.'

'No, I know their arguments only too well.'

'Well, you don't need to push it too much. Some reticence would be expected. What have you told Stap?'

'That I'll give them ten thousand and act as liaison to the City. He was thrilled to bits.'

Smailes whistled. 'You're really going to do that?'

'Told him I've only got two grand at present. Corcoran assures me I'll get it back.'

Smailes wondered about that, but said nothing.

'And?'

'I'm to meet with the steering committee next week. At the club. Should be interesting.'

'I'll bet.'

There was a pause. 'Derek?'

'Yes?'

'Is there any danger here? I mean, if they found out?'

'I don't see how they would.'

'If they did.'

Smailes shrugged. 'No. They'd probably just give you an earful and boot you into the street. In my experience, these lunatic right folk are all bark and no bite.'

'Right,' said Lynch, sounding unconvinced. 'Good.'

Smailes and Lynch chatted about other subjects for another ten minutes, then Smailes stood to leave.

'Look, I'd better get going. Fidelma leaves at six. Is Clea having tea with the lama too?'

Lynch scowled. 'Don't ask me.' Then, more plaintively, 'I'll keep in touch.'

'All right, Peter. Stay in touch.' Smailes suddenly realized that his father-in-law, for all his preening, was in fact scared stiff.

Smailes moved into the hallway and saw Clea and her mother standing outside the sitting room, beaming. Number Two Bodyguard was standing at the banister, next to the downstairs toilet. There was a noise from within and Lama Drukpa suddenly appeared, wearing another of his Hawaiian shirts under a blue cashmere blazer. Anthea Lynch stepped forward.

'Lama-la, this is my son-in-law, Derek Smailes,' she said, and the lama approached and offered his hand.

Smailes accepted a firm, warm handshake and found himself transfixed by a pair of liquid brown eyes. As he recalled the encounter later, he felt as if he had stepped into a parallel reality, in which everything else beside the lama's face melted away.

'Have we met?' asked the Tibetan.

'No. I came to your talk in Chelsea though.'

The lama grinned. 'The mahatma?'

'Yes.'

The lama's shoulders shook for a moment, then he asked, 'What do you do?'

Immediately, Smailes knew that prevarication with this individual was impossible. Eschewing all his conditioning, he replied simply, 'I work in counter-intelligence.'

The lama's eyes twinkled. 'So do I.' Then he paused. 'Who is your enemy?'

Smailes thought for a moment. 'Potentially, everyone. Who's yours?'

The lama's eyes narrowed. 'Potentially, no one,' he said.

'Well, I don't think you can compare what we do,' said Smailes. 'You are trying to communicate something very important . . .'

'And you are trying to protect something very important.'

'Really? You think so?'

'The United Kingdom has an ideal form of government. You have Her Majesty and then you have her government and ministers. So the British people are all subjects rather than merely citizens. It is very important for people to feel they belong to something enduring, something uplifting in this way.'

Smailes felt embarrassed by his own cynicism. 'I've never quite seen it like that.'

'You must,' said the lama. 'You protect her kingdom by stealth, and that is also very important. It has been said: "What enables the wise sovereign to achieve things beyond the reach of ordinary men is foreknowledge."'

Smailes smiled in recognition. 'Sun-Tzu. *The Art of War*.'

'You see, you do understand,' said the lama, turning to his attendant and grasping a forearm. 'A pleasure to meet you,' he said. Somehow, from the lama's lips, it did not seem an empty courtesy. He released his grip and turned away, and it was only then that Smailes realized the lama had been holding his hand throughout.

He remained motionless as Lama Drukpa limped to the door and completed departure formalities with Clea and her mother. After the door had closed, Clea came across to him and slipped her arm through his.

'You look like the cat who swallowed the canary. Isn't he a lovely man? What did you talk about?'

'Counter-intelligence.'

'Really? You're kidding!' Clea well knew her husband's strictures regarding secrecy.

Anthea Lynch had joined them. 'Derek, I'm so thrilled I got to introduce you. If I had been certain he was coming, I would have invited you before.'

Clea looked at him archly. 'And what did you and Daddy talk about?'

'Gardening,' said Smailes with a smile.

10

There were many excellent restaurants in London's West End, but the Angus Steak House in Soho's Beak Street could not honestly be called one of them. The steaks were passable but its salads and vegetables were lousy, and the waiters were surly and spoke little English. Its clientele consisted mostly of tourists who knew no better, which was perhaps why it had been chosen as a lunch venue by Loudon Strickland, CIA station chief, and his British counterpart Miles Bingham, head of MI5's F Branch.

Strickland, dressed in his trademark light-grey suit, was sawing at his steak, then putting aside his knife and transferring his fork to his right hand, American-style. Bingham was mashing peas on to the back of his fork with a knife, then moving it across to his meat, cutting a wedge and lowering his mouth to receive its skewered contents, English-style. As he chewed, he spoke out of the side of his mouth. Strickland wiped his lips fastidiously before picking up his mineral water.

'So. Any chance of a response within the next few days?' Bingham asked.

'Actually, I received one just this morning. An eyes-only from the senior aide to the chairman of the joint chiefs.'

Bingham raised an eyebrow, impressed. 'And?'

'In the event of any civil disturbance in Britain, American forces would be ordered to remain on base. If it was understood this was the volition of the Palace.'

'Including aircraft?'

'Including aircraft.'

'What kind of confirmation of the Palace's wishes would that require?'

'A guarantee from your political leadership,' said Strickland impassively.

Bingham smiled and took a swallow of wine. 'That is no problem, Loudon,' he said.

'This is not an exclusively military decision,' Strickland emphasized. Bingham was even more pleased. 'I understand fully,' he said.

The next two meetings between Smailes, Hyams and Lubyanov proved unproductive. The Russian cultural attaché claimed to be working on breaching the *referentura*, the embassy's secure wing, where he felt he was more likely to come upon a staff roster. But his work gave him little pretext to visit, and he was anxious about arousing suspicion. Also, his wife had begun to remark on his altered behaviour, which he had attributed to an unanticipated and unwelcome visit from her father, who was on a trip to Brussels and London. This explanation seemed to have satisfied Madame Lubyanova, but her feckless husband claimed to be feeling extremely jumpy.

For his part, Smailes would not listen to excuses and insisted that Lubyanov produce something by the following week, or there would be repercussions. Smailes told him their investigation into his background suggested he was not nearly so marginal as he claimed. Actually, Smailes thought Lubyanov might be telling something close to the truth, but his own boss Standiforth was beginning to breathe down his neck. Smailes was aware that Roger had repositioned himself as one of the last of Sir Herbert Carne's deponents, but that time was running out for Roger to spring something on him.

At their first meeting the following week, however, there appeared to be a breakthrough. Lubyanov appeared on schedule and seemed highly agitated. He simply ignored Smailes's proscription against smoking and lit a cigarette as soon as he sat down.

'Well, I have something for you. I hope you are satisfied. I could probably get shot.'

'Ah, Yuri. This is good news,' said Smailes good-naturedly. 'What did you find?'

'On Saturday my father-in-law came to dinner. At our apartment.'

'General Osipov?'

'Yes.'

'Go on.'

'He had come straight from some meeting. My wife was preparing chicken. He wanted to buy wine. He left to go to the off-licence in Sussex Gardens.'

'And?'

'He left his briefcase on the sofa. My wife was working in the kitchen. I tried to screw up my courage. Eventually, I opened it. I had one minute, maybe two. I was very frightened.'

'What did you see?'

'I saw something about the movement of your nuclear submarines. It was obviously classified information. There was a British name – Daughtry, I think. I do not think that could be a codename, do you?'

'Daughtry? How do you spell it?'

Lubyanov attempted a spelling which Judith Hyams scribbled in her notebook.

'Are you sure?'

'No. I heard my wife's father returning and almost panicked. I got everything back into his case just as he rang the bell. I must have been sweating when he came in, because he made a joke about it.'

'Daughtry. Where does he work?'

'I do not know. It did not say. Of course, he may not be KGB. He might be GRU, a military spy.'

'All the same to us, Yuri. Well done.'

'Listen. I want to see Valerie. You promised.'

'Right,' said Smailes. 'We'll arrange it. Anything else?'

'I need a break. I feel like I'm heading for a heart attack.'

'I'm not surprised, Yuri, the amount you smoke,' said Smailes pleasantly. 'Okay, we'll skip a week, all right? How about a week Wednesday? Same place, same time.'

Lubyanov crushed out his cigarette. 'You are a bastard, Mr Sykes,' he said bitterly.

Smailes looked across at Judith, then back at Lubyanov. He shrugged. 'Hey, it's a tough business, Yuri. Nothing personal. Still working on that order of battle, are you?'

Lubyanov got wearily to his feet and gave Smailes a look of loathing. 'How do I contact Valerie?'

'Call tomorrow and we'll give you her new number.'

Lubyanov left dejectedly and Smailes slapped his knee. 'See,' he said, turning to Judith, 'I told you we just had to make him take some risks.'

Judith nodded dutifully and looked at her notebook. 'Shall I get on this right away?'

'Absolutely,' said Smailes.

The Knightsbridge premises of the Sceptre Group had expanded considerably over the ensuing weeks. The bedroom furniture had been removed from the SAS Room and replaced with a conference table. In the adjacent Belgian Room a modern office had been installed, complete with two secretaries, computers and a fax machine. In the conference room Prince Andrew still stood proud guard on the far wall, but facing him now was a large map of the British Isles beneath a sheet of perspex. Peter Lynch glanced up at its meaningless symbols scrawled in coloured marker. As he listened to Gerry Stap, he tried to act casually while remaining appropriately grave. The truth was, he felt extremely nervous and was afraid it might be obvious to the others in the room.

Stap was explaining to the steering committee Lynch's generous offer of financial and tactical support. Bingham sat in his chair at the head of the table, tapping his foot impatiently. Porter was sucking a meerschaum pipe, his hands folded across a canary waistcoat. Halls was leaning forward on his elbows, while Crabbe lounged in his chair, listening intently but avoiding eye contact.

'Delighted to have you on board, Peter,' said General Porter at the conclusion of Stap's introduction. 'Now, how can we help *you*?'

Peter Lynch cleared his throat and responded in what he hoped was a firm voice. 'I mostly need a sense of your overall planning so I can judge how best to approach others. Not that I need to convey any details, of course.' It was the question Alex Corcoran had primed him to ask.

'Yes, of course. Well, first and foremost, from my sources at the Palace I am assured of Her Majesty's support. In fact, the royal family as a whole, excluding Charles of course, can be relied upon to close ranks behind us. Naturally, there can be no *official* endorsement until matters are settled. But the crucial thing is that the Defence Council will instruct the Commanders-in-Chief that in the event of a constitutional crisis she will invoke her prerogative powers, if necessary. I will make this presentation myself.'

'What do the CICs say?' asked Bingham.

'Well, they're more guarded, of course. Have to be. But they've let me know any attempt to renegotiate our commitment to NATO will be fiercely resisted.'

Colonel Crabbe of the SBS straightened up. Although not in uniform, he exuded the coiled energy of a commando chief in peak condition. 'I'm confident our military leadership will look to the Crown in a time of crisis. It's the oath we all take.'

'Tim's right,' echoed Halls emphatically, although he himself had left the Army three years earlier under clouded circumstances and now ran a private security firm.

Bingham offered his own update. 'The Americans will welcome *any* government led by Lady Thatcher, period. And I'm told that US troops and aircraft will be grounded, if we can deliver the Palace.'

It was Stap's turn. 'Well, officially, Lady Thatcher's staff will offer no response, of course, which is in itself not surprising. Obviously, she'll bide her time – she'll wait for events to ripen, like Churchill did in 1940. Then, when the consensus, the national will to restore her to government is irresistible, she'll come in from the wilderness, like he did. And restore us to greatness in the same fashion.'

'Hear, hear!' said Lynch, immediately anxious that he had gone too far. Porter, however, was beaming across at him and Bingham clapped his hands together in satisfaction. Nothing about specific military plans yet. But not a bad initial foray for a new agent, Lynch told himself proudly.

Judith Hyams tapped a key and dark lines of type scrolled by on her miniature computer screen.

'See,' she said. 'No Daughtrys on any Ministry of Defence payroll. Nor with authorized contractors. I checked the Foreign Office too. There's a Janice Daughtry works in the canteen. I doubt she's the one we're after.'

Smailes was disappointed. 'Is that all we've got?' he asked.

'No,' said Judith.

'Go on.'

'Look,' she said, tapping another series of keys. 'I concentrated on the master personnel schedule, then did a search for possible homophones.'

'What?'

'Names that sound the same. You know, Haughtry, Sawtry, Daltry. In case Lubyanov had it wrong.'

'And?'

'There's a John Haughtry works as a civilian accountant at RAF Alconbury, outside Cambridge. No clear connection with the Trident programme.'

'Is that it?'

'Wait a minute. Then I decided to try a search by character order. You know, similar names that contain different letters.'

'Well?' asked Smailes, his expectation rising.

Judith tapped another series of keys triumphantly. 'Look – there's a Joseph Docherty working as a junior engineer at ROF Burghfield. That's where they service the missile warheads, isn't it?'

Smailes's heart jumped. 'You're damn right it is. Daughtry, Docherty – that's pretty close. Judith, I think we've got our man!' He moved from behind her shoulder to sit on the desk facing her. 'Or, more accurately, I think *you've* got our man. Incredible! How did you do it?'

Judith smiled modestly. 'Oh, it wasn't too difficult. After the proxy search pulled a blank, I really wanted to perform my own analysis. The MoD balked about giving me access to its data base, but I kicked up a fuss and Brian Kinney backed me up. You weren't around, and I thought . . .'

'No, no, you did the right thing. Then what?'

'I got them to download the files straight into this,' she said, tapping her slim machine.

'They can do that?'

'Of course.'

'It's got room?'

Judith laughed. 'Well, the fixed disk has only twenty megabytes' storage, but it has two full megabytes of RAM . . .'

'Hold it,' said Smailes, laughing in his turn, 'you've lost me. What you mean is it's a powerful little bugger.'

'Precisely.'

'Let's get Joseph Docherty's file,' said Smailes.

'I've already ordered it.'

Smailes put a hand on her shoulder. 'Judith, you're a doll,' he said. He realized he should have said, 'You're terrific,' or something more appropriate, and was momentarily alarmed she might take offence. But she put her hand up to his and said simply, 'Thank you.'

Smailes removed his hand, embarrassed. But he also felt gratified. Such a forward remark would doubtless have been greeted with a scathing put-down by Clea or one of her feminist friends.

By tacit agreement, Clea Smailes did not ask her husband direct questions about his work. So when he mentioned that he and his assistant were travelling up to Reading the next day to set up surveillance on a government engineer, she responded obliquely.

'Oh, how is Godfrey, anyway? Does he still get on your nerves as much?'

Smailes often complained about Godfrey Pawlett, his deputy in K9. Godfrey was a lifer, one of those superannuated denizens of Curzon House who'd been treading water for years in anticipation of his pension. It was only then that Smailes realized he'd never told Clea of his transfer, or that he was working with a new partner.

'It's not Godfrey, actually,' he said casually. 'Brian's department got overloaded and I've been seconded back for three months. My new assistant is a woman – Judith Hyams.'

'Is she young?' asked Clea suspiciously.

'Twenties, I think. She's married, Clea.'

Clea was undeterred. 'Is she pretty?'

'Not really,' Smailes lied.

'Is she thin?'

'Yes,' Smailes said irritably. 'Like a garden hoe.'

He reached over and snapped out his bedside light, and a moment later Clea did likewise. He knew better than to risk disappointment by reaching out to her. In numerous ways Clea had signalled that during this pregnancy, as far as she was concerned, sex was simply out.

The elderly couple who lived opposite the Dochertys' modest terraced house reacted with predictable fear and excitement when Smailes and Hyams arrived unannounced on their doorstep. However, after a check of credentials, the Markmans readily agreed to switch bedrooms so MI5 could install a watcher post in the front of their house, overlooking the Docherty residence. And they needed little prodding to tell all they knew about their young neighbours. The Dochertys were a quiet couple, they claimed, who had lived across the road for about two years. Joseph, they knew, worked at ROF Burghfield and Avril, his wife, worked in a High Street bank. They seemed upstanding citizens and were both regulars at St Aidan's Catholic church, where Joseph was active in the Scouts.

MI5, of course, already knew all this. The Dochertys were in fact both Scots and had moved south two years earlier when Joseph had been granted a transfer by British Aerospace. BAe operated both ROF Burghfield and the Royal Naval Armaments Depot at Coulport, near

Glasgow, which serviced the ordnance for Britain's nuclear submarine fleet. Docherty, an engineering PhD from Strathclyde University, had joined RNAD Coulport four years earlier. He had passed routine positive vetting at the time, and was not due to be revetted for another year. And since his leaving Coulport for Burghfield had been an internal transfer, not a departure, it had not come to MI5's attention at that time. But Smailes had little doubt the good Mr Docherty was their man. Which also made it likely he was the source of the Burghfield leak, suggesting neither Gerry Stap nor the 'pink brigadier' was the culprit after all.

MI5 technicians had been on stand-by and arrived while Smailes and Hyams were still drinking tea and interviewing Mr and Mrs Markman. Having determined the Dochertys were both at work, the watchers went about unloading and installing their gear. Smailes and Judith took pains to counsel the Markmans about maintaining their routines and, as far as possible, ignoring the strangers in their front bedroom. The Markmans understood the need for discretion, of course. Alf Markman had served in the Signals Corps during World War II, and assured Smailes he need have no qualms about their full cooperation. His wife nodded her vigorous agreement.

By late morning the watcher post was in place, and Smailes's old sparring partner Graham Booth was ensconced with a pot of tea and a tray of scones at his elbow. The watcher operation was not designed to determine criminal activity, but to identify routines and thus prepare the way for an illicit entry. If Docherty was a spy, the likelihood was there would be something on his premises that would incriminate him. Smailes bantered with Booth, who asked about Clea's welfare. Graham had known them both in New York before their marriage, before Clea's metamorphosis into a wife and mother and Smailes's into a K Branch bureaucrat.

'She's great,' said Smailes, knowing this was not strictly true. 'Expecting again in November.'

'Congratulations,' said Booth. 'Say, you two breed like rabbits, don't you?'

As often happened whenever he talked to Booth, Smailes soon felt like cuffing the little smart aleck.

'Obviously, I could hardly believe my ears,' said Lynch.

Neither could Smailes. They were seated in the bar of the Oxford &

Cambridge Club, and Lynch was expounding upon the grandiose fantasies of the Sceptre Group. Smailes found it all hard to believe – that British and American military leaders might actually sign on to such a crackpot scheme was beyond his conception. Still, he had to concede, he did not know the mind-set – not in the British high command, nor in the family wing of Buckingham Palace. Whereas it was easy to acknowledge the Sceptre Group members might be in deadly earnest, what was less clear was how serious the individuals with real power were.

Lynch had invited his son-in-law for a drink after work, as Smailes guessed, in order to brag about his exploits under cover for MI5. At first, Smailes had been disinclined to show any interest, knowing Peter Lynch was out of line by offering details. But his curiosity got the better of him, and Peter Lynch needed little encouragement to develop a full head of steam. Before long Lynch had given a complete account of his first encounter with the future saviours of British civilization.

'You didn't get a sense of what they're actually planning, did you?' asked Smailes.

'Not yet,' said Lynch. 'Just generalities. But they're not kidding around, Derek.'

'I never thought they were,' said Smailes, then paused. 'I say, Miles Bingham isn't involved, is he?'

Lynch exploded. 'Didn't I tell you? He's the bloody chair!'

Now Smailes had heard everything. He took a swallow of beer and weighed this news. He didn't like the sound of it. He didn't like it one bit. While he didn't doubt that Miles Bingham, Britain's counter-insurgency chief, was way to the right politically and a bona fide member of Special Forces, his involvement still struck Smailes as highly fishy. Not his participation *per se*, but the fact that he was fashioning an elegant noose for himself at the wrong end of a covert operation run by his arch-rival for the DG's chair, Roger Standiforth. Smailes corrected himself quickly – run by Alex Corcoran, with Roger Standiforth's connivance. This might be mere coincidence, of course. Or it might not. But he knew that Standiforth, whose thirst for power knew no bounds, would go to almost any length to secure MI5's top job. He seemed to have taken great pains to point the finger away from Gerry Stap with his 'pink brigadier' theory. But now Gerry Stap had led MI5 to Miles Bingham and the Sceptre Group. Could there be a connection? Suddenly Smailes became aware his father-in-law was regarding him quizzically.

'I say, you'll keep all this under your hat, won't you?' he asked.

'Of course, Peter,' said Smailes. 'Listen, I was wondering. If I applied for membership here, would you sponsor me?'

Peter Lynch leaned forward and clapped his son-in-law on the shoulder. 'Terrific idea, old boy! Of course, I'd be delighted,' he said, reflecting that perhaps Clea had not made such a stupid choice in this obtuse man after all.

Derek Smailes was seated in Brian Kinney's office, extolling the virtues of his new assistant.

'Honestly, Brian, she's incredible. What she can do with that machine of hers is amazing. Makes me feel so stupid. I hardly know the difference between a floppy disk and a hard one.'

Kinney grinned at the *double entendre*. 'Yes, well, she doesn't have your people skills yet, Derek. And she may never have. You've got to take the credit for shaking that name out of Lubyanov, you know. But I confess I did think you'd make a good team from the start. What do we know about the Dochertys?'

'Routines like granite,' said Smailes. 'Both leave for work about eight, back around half five. Honestly, they act like a couple thirty years older. No social life to speak of, apart from his Scouts and her church group.'

'No kids?'

'No, just the two of them.'

'What's the plan?'

'Well, it seems they have a cleaning lady Tuesdays and, lo and behold, they put a key out for her under the window box. Graham Booth got kitted out as the gas man and went and took an impression of it. Les Townsend should have me a duplicate by end of business. Judith and I go in on Friday.'

'Why wait? Why not tomorrow?'

'I'm sending her up to Scotland to research the Dochertys' background. She may turn up something we can use later at trial. She's taking the sleeper to Glasgow tonight.'

Kinney paused. 'She's got a particularly well-turned ankle, wouldn't you say?' he asked. This was an unusually forward remark coming from the proper Kinney.

Smailes hesitated. 'I dunno, Brian. Bit skinny for my taste.'

'She'll go far.'

'I don't doubt it.'

Smailes rose to leave, but hesitated. He'd been brooding over Peter Lynch's revelations about the Sceptre Group, unable to resolve in his mind whether it constituted a real threat or was just a bunch of disgruntled old soldiers beating their chests. That it might be the product of some demonic manipulation by Roger Standiforth also bothered him. One person who he knew might be able to clarify his thinking was Brian Kinney, who had worked in Army intelligence himself. While MI5 rules strictly forbade unauthorized indoctrination, Smailes himself had not been officially indoctrinated into the Sceptre operation and felt he could stretch a point. He also felt sufficiently confident of his ground with Kinney to risk going out on a limb.

He sat down again and asked Kinney whether he could ask his opinion in confidence. Kinney nodded. In a low voice, Smailes recounted what he had learned of the activities of the Sceptre Group of the Special Forces Club, Knightsbridge. It was late in the day and Kinney loosened his tie as he listened. Smailes did not specify his source of information, neither did Kinney inquire.

'Who's on their command group? Do you know?' Kinney asked eventually.

Smailes identified the civilians and Kinney raised an eyebrow and whistled. 'Interesting. And who're their military people?'

'The senior guy is a General Humphrey Porter.'

Kinney cast his eyes to the ceiling. 'That old shit. Is that it?'

'No, there's two commando types. Short names, I think. Wait a minute – Crabbe and Halls, that's it.'

At this news, Kinney physically flinched. Smailes pressed on. 'You know either of them? I mean, do you think they can be serious? Isn't it fishy that Bingo's involved, given that MI5 is getting reports on everything that's going on? Hey Brian, are you all right?'

Kinney had got up from his desk and walked across to stare out of his window of smeared bomb glass. When he finally turned round, he was wearing an expression Smailes had never seen before.

'What is it, Brian? You know these blokes?'

Kinney's voice was peculiar. 'I want to tell you something in confidence, Derek. Something I've only ever told my wife. Can you cope with that?'

'I think so,' said Smailes, alarmed. 'Of course.'

'I know Colonel Clive Halls only too well, and we have to take this group absolutely seriously if he's involved. *They're* deadly serious – make no mistake about it.'

'I see.'

'No, you don't. Not yet. You know the story about how I left Belfast? Back in '74?'

'You were burned in an ambush, I heard. Shot up. Lucky to get out alive.'

'That's the official version. The truth is slightly different. Colonel Clive Halls – he was a captain then – was my CO in Army intelligence. You may remember that in 1974 the political situation was extremely volatile.'

'I dunno, Brian. It's a long time ago. I was with the police at the time . . .'

'There was a minority Labour government elected in February '74. It hung on until October, when it went back to the country and won a working majority. Remember?'

'Oh, right. The first election came after the miners' strike and the three-day week and all that.'

'Correct. In the period between the two elections, the ultras on the far right were scheming for ways to bring down the Labour government. You must know the stories.'

'Of course. The smear campaign against Wilson.'

'That's right. And a group here at MI5 . . .'

'. . . was intimately involved. Everyone knows about it, Brian.'

'Yes. But do you remember this? Early in 1974 there was a general strike in Ulster, which brought down the power-sharing executive imposed by Westminster. A breakaway Independent Unionist party was formed in its aftermath, which put up candidates against the Official Unionists in the October election. The crucial difference was that the Independents were violently anti-Westminster and made it known they would refuse the Conservative whip. The numbers in parliament were so close, the Unionists potentially held the balance of power. Are you following?'

'Yes.'

'One week before the election, a big car bomb destroyed the headquarters of the Alliance party, the moderate Protestant group. It was timed to go off during rush hour and seven civilians were killed. Since the car had been stolen in a hard-line Loyalist neighbourhood, Protestant extremists looked like the culprits. Since most of the victims were also Protestant, the likely effect was to alienate the Independent Unionists from their political base.

'The problem was, a chap called White came forward to say he'd witnessed the car being stolen. He positively identified two Army intelligence officers, together with the licence plate of a car owned by us.'

'Blimey. So the British Army . . .'

'Precisely. Someone had ordered us to bomb a legal organization in order to try and discredit Protestant extremists and guarantee a Conservative majority in Westminster. Everyone at Lisburn HQ knew it was true. And when White went public, so did everyone else. And the bombing backfired completely, since the Independents won every seat they contested, and Labour got back in with a working majority.'

'White went public?'

'He was a brave man. Attempts to discredit him didn't work – he was a pillar of the community, a church warden. And he wouldn't give up. Pretty soon MPs were calling for an inquiry.'

'What happened?'

Kinney paused, then resumed in a quiet voice. 'Halls had him murdered. He ordered in a Regiment hit squad – he'd always had excellent contacts there. Went on to become one of their COs, you know.'

'The Regiment?'

'The Special Air Service at Hereford. In the Army it's known simply as the Regiment. This was back when the Labour government was still denying the SAS operated in Northern Ireland. Well, they didn't bloody know, did they? White had a weekend place in the country – County Antrim, I think. The SAS team ambushed him. Pumped eighty automatic rounds into him.'

'Jesus. Wasn't there an outcry?'

'Halls was very clever. He stuck a load of stolen television sets in a shed so it looked like White was in league with a Protestant crime syndicate. The Army pinned the murder on the IRA, and White's supporters in Westminster dropped him like a hot brick. One or two churchmen tried to keep the case alive, but it fizzled out.'

'So what happened to you?'

'We all knew what had happened. There was nothing official, of course, but Halls became very cocky. I suppose I had some kind of breakdown. I knew what had happened was a despicable crime, but I didn't know where the order had come from.'

'Could it have come from here? From MI5?' asked Smailes.

'It's possible. Or from someone in the anti-Wilson conspiracy who had sufficient leverage with the Army. Porter was Northern Ireland commander at that time.'

'Jesus Christ.'

'I wanted to report what I knew, but I was scared stiff. I didn't know how far up the line the conspiracy went. And I saw what had happened to White. I know it was cowardly, but Emma had just been born . . .'

'Brian, you don't have to excuse yourself.'

'So. I was out on my own one day, near Carrickfergus. I rammed a tree, then shot up the car with an Armalite I had in the boot. I threw the weapon into a culvert and smashed my head through the windscreen. I had to get out of there. I couldn't work for Halls and Porter any more.'

'So you got transferred . . .'

'Everyone seemed to buy it. Some people were sceptical, I know, and I've always wondered what Halls thought. But yes, I got honourably discharged and transferred into civilian intelligence. And I've lived with my secret ever since.'

'Brian, I still can't quite believe it. Seven civilians murdered? You hear the accusations, you know, but I never thought . . .'

'A lot of it's true, Derek. The British Army *has* committed atrocities as part of its campaign in Northern Ireland. How much has had political sanction, I don't know. But my point is Halls is a killer. I heard he was forced to leave the Regiment a few years back after the murder of that Lebanese businessman in Kensington. The word was mistaken identity, that the SAS thought he was a spotter for the group that did the Lockerbie bombing, but they got the wrong man.

'And listen – Porter is cosy with the Palace these days, I hear. Would British military command fall in with these idiots? I would like to doubt it. Would any unilateral action be repudiated by the Americans, and by Buckingham Palace? I'd like to believe it. But I don't know.'

'What you're saying is this threat is serious.'

'Damn serious. But it sounds like they've been infiltrated.'

'Corcoran's running it.'

Kinney exhaled slowly. 'Then it'll probably be handled properly. I'm sorry, Derek. This subject gets me rattled.'

'Brian, I'm not in the least surprised,' said Smailes quietly.

11

Judith Hyams was ecstatic. As she scurried down the platform towards her first-class carriage, she even gave a little skip in her flat-heeled shoes. Then, self-conscious, she pressed her overnight bag to her side with an elbow and forced herself to slow her pace.

Not that she had anything concrete to offer Derek Smailes yet – that was hardly the point. The point was he had entrusted her with this investigation unescorted, after only the most perfunctory of briefings, as if already convinced of her reliability. She knew he was not one to suffer a slow learner gladly – not that she considered herself slow, of course. But she was still very new, only recently a glorified data-entry clerk. Now here she was, travelling first class to Scotland and back, with full authority for what might become a crucial background check.

Her visit to Joseph Docherty's former home town of Helensburgh had only strengthened her suspicions – she could not believe any twenty-eight-year-old married man behaved like Docherty unless there was something wrong with him. His former supervisor at the Coulport arms depot had offered him nothing but praise, but seemed to have no idea what kind of a person his subordinate had been. Docherty seemed a complete loner, with no social contacts outside work, a man who did his work and kept completely to himself. A regular churchgoer was about all the chief weapons engineer knew about him. Docherty had requested the transfer to the south of England 'for a change'; that was the only reason he had given at the time. For Docherty and his wife, who had spent their entire lives in the Glasgow area, this did not ring true to Judith Hyams either.

Her meeting with Father Liam Daly of St Mary's Catholic church, Helensburgh, had been more instructive. Priests, who were used to listening to the most intimate of secrets, ought to be able to look a stranger in the eye, even if that stranger was an attractive young woman. But Father Daly, a portly Irishman with thinning hair and a pink scalp, fidgeted and looked away when asked to expound on the subject of Joe Docherty. Eventually he gave Docherty a glowing testimonial that contrasted sharply with his body language. Joseph and Avril were exemplary Catholics, Daly claimed, stalwarts of the church and their local community. Neither of them drank or smoked. The priest claimed to have no knowledge of Joe Docherty's motive for transferring to the south of England – he had assumed it was a promotion. When Judith asked about the Dochertys' involvement in church activities, Father Daly at first prevaricated. When pressed, he remembered that Joseph had helped with the youth group and Avril had taught occasionally at Sunday school. No, he said, he had had no further contact with them since their transfer. He hoped they were doing well. Neighbours near the Dochertys' former address had little to add about the lives of this preternaturally reserved couple.

As the train jerked into motion, Judith settled back into her seat and opened a magazine. Father Daly had been concealing something about Joseph Docherty, she was convinced – probably something to do with his uncharacteristic impulsive decision to transfer to Berkshire. She was sure she was right, and was fairly confident Derek Smailes would take her word for it.

Judith looked out of the window as the train eased out of the vast iron chasm of Glasgow Central station. She was developing a crush on her new boss, she realized. She sighed. How she wished she had trusted her instincts and resisted marrying David Hyams, a man whose horizons were bound by the pieties of middle-class Jewish life. Her ambition unnerved him, she knew, and increasingly their aspirations seemed incompatible. David, sensing her estrangement, had become morose and self-pitying, which only heightened her impatience with him. She flicked her magazine open irritably, determined to put such aggravating thoughts from her mind.

Derek Smailes sat at his desk, listening carefully to Judith's account of her inquiries in Scotland. He agreed with her – Docherty's sudden decision to transfer to Berkshire looked fishy, and the priest sounded like he was hiding something. Increasingly, however, Smailes found himself distracted in her company, and was aware it was because he was becoming increasingly attracted to her. He wished Brian Kinney had never invoked the subject, so he could have continued to ignore it. When Judith invited him to look at Docherty's employment record, he found himself standing behind her and instead inspecting the wisps of hair on the nape of her neck where they escaped from their silver clasp. The way she twisted in her chair and leaned against her desk dramatically emphasized the curve of her hip, he saw. Today she was wearing an elegant silk dress beneath a dark blazer and a cool, subtle cologne. Smailes decided to take the file back to his own desk for better concentration. He knew something approaching open flirtation had begun between them, although he was sufficiently confident of his own professionalism – and his steadfastness as a husband and father – not to feel threatened by it.

'So what's next, Derek?' Judith asked.

Smailes went into his pocket and held up a tagged key. 'We go in tomorrow, after the Dochertys have gone to work. We can take all day if we have to.'

'And what are we looking for?'

'That's what I need to talk to you about,' said Smailes, crossing and kneeling at his safe, which was concealed in a cabinet between their two desks. He opened it quickly, removed a folder and sat down again.

'Roger and Brian both agree you need to be indoctrinated into Wakefield before we begin taking Docherty's place apart. The likelihood is we'll find something that links him to it.'

'Wakefield?'

'It's the case I was on before we opened Jonquil. Looks like they might run into one another.'

Judith tried to conceal her excitement and folded her hands in her lap in anticipation.

'You know what a permissive action link is, Judith?' asked Smailes.

She frowned. 'Is that a computer term?'

'No, it's not – it's a nuclear weapons term. They install them at ROF Burghfield . . .'

It took only fifteen minutes to describe the botched F Branch attack which had led to the Burghfield break-in, the theft of the American PALs and the subsequent suspicion which had fallen on Gerry Stap and his secretary. Smailes left out other developments – the possibility of Brigadier Alec Cole's involvement, and the remote connection with the Sceptre Group. Standiforth and Kinney had agreed that technical details were all that were required on a need-to-know basis.

'So if Docherty is the spy . . .'

'We need to track him and find his controller. Then we can identify who stole the American technology, in all likelihood, and everyone can breathe a little easier, we hope. Not to mention that, with any luck, we get some arrests and a nice tight case to try.'

'And if he's not a spy?'

Smailes shrugged. 'Then we have to keep on looking, I suppose. What do you think?'

'I think he's a spy,' said Judith forcefully.

'So do I,' said her boss.

Judith and Derek entered the Docherty house just after nine the following morning. It was a cool Friday in July and a steady drizzle was falling, and they both wore raincoats and office clothes. Had anyone seen them, they might have been representatives of a bank or an insurance company. Smailes carried a briefcase which contained a portable copier, sub-miniature camera and other supplies. They walked directly up to the door and let themselves in with their key, which Smailes had just soaped in the Markmans' bathroom. It worked perfectly.

In the hallway Smailes and Hyams took off their coats and hung them on the rack. Smailes dropped to one knee and snapped open his case. He extracted his copier and handed Judith a pair of surgical gloves, which she put on. Then Smailes put on a pair of his own.

'I'll leave the camera right here, if you need it. You're confident how it works?'

'Yes.'

'You start downstairs. I'll take the upstairs.'

Judith, who had thought they would work together, was momentarily alarmed.

'All right?' asked Smailes.

'Yes,' said Judith, gathering herself. 'What am I looking for?'

'I don't know,' said Smailes. 'Just make sure you leave everything as you find it.'

Judith, who had been given this instruction several times already, resisted a retort. She watched as her boss moved noiselessly up the stairs, carrying his copier.

Derek Smailes mounted the stairs one at a time, walking on the outside of the runner like a professional burglar to avoid creaking steps. There was no one in the house, of course, but his caution was instinctive.

Once upstairs, he worked methodically. Nothing in the bedside tables except some cough medicine – no fruity literature, sex aids, anything kinky. Nothing in the dressing table or the tallboy either, except clothing meticulously ironed and folded. In a wardrobe he found a suitcase, but it too was empty.

The back bedroom looked like a workshop and office. Docherty seemed interested in electronics, since there was a partially disassembled video recorder on the table. No radio gear or anything incriminating, however. In a filing cabinet Smailes found correspondence and bank statements, and spent thirty minutes reading and copying. His examination again unearthed nothing unusual. There were letters from Joe Docherty's mother in Glasgow that contained references to their move, but they were unrevealing. The third bedroom was a spare room, containing a bed and a linen-cupboard. Smailes decided to check with Judith before he began sounding the walls and floors for hiding places.

He found her in the kitchen, struggling to ease a fridge back into its alcove.

'Anything?' he asked.

'No. Some computer and electronics magazines. Some needlework of Avril's, too. This couple are too good to be true.'

Judith checked that the feet of the fridge were exactly aligned with the indentations in the linoleum. 'How about you?' she asked.

'I've been reading his letters and bank statements. I can't see anything either.'

'What's next?'

'You're on the right track,' he said. 'Look for hiding places.'

'Damn it,' said Judith. 'I *know* he's rotten.'

'Let's keep looking,' said Smailes.

Judith looked up. 'It's stopped raining,' she said.

Smailes looked out down a long narrow garden. Judith followed his eye. 'What's that down there?' she asked, pointing out a small dilapidated building.

'Potting shed,' said Smailes. They looked at each other. 'Let's go,' he said.

They let themselves out of the back door and strolled down the concrete garden path between two strips of lawn. A woman two houses down had begun hanging out a wash, but appeared not to notice them.

Inside Docherty's small shed they found the first evidence of a hidden life. Old sacking had been thrown over an upturned bucket for a makeshift seat, next to which was a dirty ashtray filled with butts.

'She doesn't let him smoke in the house,' Smailes explained. 'He has to come out here.' A paraffin heater on the floor suggested the shed was Docherty's year-round retreat.

'Father Daly said neither of them smoked,' said Judith.

'Then I suppose Father Daly didn't know everything, did he?' said Smailes. 'Look around.'

Judith went straight to the drawer of a heavy work-bench stacked with plant pots and old magazines. It was locked.

'Find the key,' said Smailes. 'It'll be on a hook somewhere.'

Garden tools were suspended from nails around the walls, but Smailes and Judith could not find a key among them.

'Maybe he keeps it with him,' she said.

'No,' said Smailes, pointing out the drawer's heavy, old-fashioned lock. 'It's too big for a pocket. Keep looking.'

He crouched and began to feel around the inner surface of the table legs. He stood up with a grunt. 'Got it,' he said, holding up a heavy iron key. It turned in the lock with difficulty. From inside the drawer Smailes extracted a slim metal box, also locked.

'He'll have this one on him,' said Smailes. 'But the lock looks easy.'

Smailes fished out his small ring of picks. Feeling for the lock's internal spring, he prised it open with his first tool. He set the box down on the bench and opened the lid carefully. Judith gasped.

Inside were several thousand pounds in cash, mostly in used fifties. There were some floppy computer diskettes, and documents from the Burghfield Ordnance Factory stamped 'Classified'. There were also some magazines. Smailes picked one up in his gloved hand. It was called *Bambino*, and its cover depicted a flaxen-haired boy and the haunches of plainly older man. Grotesquely, a black box obscured the boy's eyes, but not the tumid penis the boy was taking into his mouth.

'The pervert,' said Judith with disgust.

'This is what the priest knew,' said Smailes.

'Then why didn't he tell me?' asked Judith indignantly.

'Learned it in confession, probably,' said Smailes. 'They're sworn not to repeat anything they're told. But I bet he agreed with Docherty's decision to leave town.'

'My God. The church youth club,' said Judith.

'I wonder what the parents of his Scout troop would say about this little trove?' asked Smailes.

'I knew they were too damn good to be true,' said Judith vehemently. 'You think his wife knows?'

'Get the camera,' said Smailes.'Quickly.'

*

A triumphant meeting was in progress in Roger Standiforth's suite, with Brian Kinney and Roger poring over a set of glossy eight-by-tens as Smailes and Judith exchanged a private look.

'He's even got his bloody computer disks labelled,' said Kinney.

'"Category D" and "Category F",' said Standiforth. 'That's got to refer to the PAL technology, hasn't it?'

'Absolutely,' said Kinney, shuffling his stack of prints. 'What're the documents?'

'A site plan of ROF Burghfield. Very naughty,' said Smailes.

'We need to catch him handing the stuff over. Any communications gear?' asked Roger.

Smailes turned to Judith, indicating with his eyes that he was deferring to her.

'No,' said Judith quickly, a little flustered. 'We spent an hour looking for another hiding place. Nothing.'

'My bet is he hand-delivers his material,' said Smailes. 'A radio would need a large hiding place in the house, and I don't think the little wife is involved. I reckon she's not allowed in the potting shed, where he stashes everything.'

'Well, it's a KGB operation, all right,' said Kinney bitterly. 'They buy the subscription lists from the outfit in Stockholm that publishes the kiddy porn, then scan them for anyone in government work.'

'So how long have they had their hooks into him, would you guess?' asked Roger.

'Depends how long he's been an active paedophile. Could even be since his university days, you know. They might have blackmailed him into classified work. I would say they almost certainly leaned on him to make the move to Burghfield.'

'You don't think he had to leave Helensburgh because of indiscretions at his church group?' asked Judith, emboldened.

Standiforth looked at her sharply.

'Possibly,' said Kinney. 'Either way, he ended up somewhere very useful to his masters, didn't he?'

'Watchers still in place?' asked Roger.

'Round the clock,' said Smailes.

'We need to find who's running him,' said Roger emphatically. 'Ten-to-one it's some embassy professional with immunity, but we may still get enough information to clean house over there.'

Standiforth gave Smailes and Hyams a thin smile. 'Well done, you two. A little more patience, I think, and our Mr Docherty may pay a big dividend.'

Smailes and Hyams rose to leave, Derek graciously holding the door for his young assistant. Lost in thought, Standiforth stared into space for a while after they had left.

'You going to take all this upstairs, Roger?' asked Kinney.

'Straight away,' said Standiforth. 'About time we had something like this to boost morale.'

'When do you see Bert Carne?'

'The beginning of next week.'

'Going to give him a slide show?'

'No, I don't think so,' said Standiforth slowly. 'I think I'll leave that to Taffy when he makes his own presentation.'

Kinney was surprised, but said nothing. Roger didn't usually miss an opportunity to strut his department's prowess, particularly in front of someone like Carne. But that was Roger. Whenever you thought you had him pigeon-holed, he did something to prove you wrong.

Iain Mack simply loved the Russians. Whenever he visited Moscow, he felt invigorated by a sense of privilege at just being in their company. In his view, the Russians had their priorities straight, period, and thus were able to cope with a level of adversity that would make most Western societies collapse from within. It was a society of which a sizeable chunk could recite by heart from Pushkin, a society which venerated courage and passion. In Britain nowadays, it seemed to Mack, most people revered sportsmen or comedians.

But in Moscow, he always felt a little ashamed of his cosseted lifestyle, which he took so completely for granted. The feeling was partly offset by his sense of heightened moral awareness, of being alive in the fullest sense. It made the experience of being in Moscow uncomfortably intense, so he always felt relieved, if a little guilty, to get home again.

Iain and his tall, elegant assistant Nina Gregory were seated in the living room of his long-time friend and collaborator, Stas Simonov. A former *Izvestia* correspondent, he had split with his wife since Iain had last seen him, and had recently moved into a surprisingly spacious three-room flat off Tchaikovsky Street. As with every other activity in Russia these days, an outsider like Iain needed a broker to help prepare a television programme, and Simonov was trying to line up interviews. The head of the Russian Central Bank had agreed to a preliminary meeting, and Simonov was working on the new police chief of the Anti-Corruption Task Force. The three of them were drinking sweet tea in Simonov's living room, and he was smoking one of the Marlboros Iain had brought him. Nina hooked her slim hands over a knee and tossed her dark hair over her shoulder. She'd removed her wedding band for this trip, Iain had noticed on the plane.

'And what if we could arrange a meeting with someone from the Georgian crime syndicate?' Simonov asked.

'The Georgians? They're big, aren't they?'

'The biggest. They control the black market in fruit and vegetables. Today this is more lucrative than oil.'

'Who do you have? Would he go on camera?'

'Maybe. For money. I don't know if I have him yet, though. These are slippery characters, you know.'

'Don't you ever get scared dealing with them, Stas?'

Simonov shrugged. 'It's business. As long as our dealings have mutual benefit, there is no real danger. This is the first principle of capitalism, no?'

Iain laughed. 'You blokes learn fast.'

Nina Gregory spoke up. 'What would be his motive? Does he have an axe to grind?'

'Possibly. Or he may be trying to spread disinformation. You know how that goes.'

'When will you know?' asked Iain.

'Tomorrow, probably. I will contact you at the hotel. You want something a little stronger to drink before dinner?'

Iain looked at Nina and shrugged. 'Why not?'

'Scotch? Vodka?'

'In Moscow I always drink vodka,' said Iain.

'Me too,' said Nina.

The British pair watched as their host shuffled out to his kitchen. Stas was a shabby man in his early forties, but he looked older, which was not uncommon in a country where male life-expectancy was barely sixty-five.

'You like him?' Iain asked quietly over the chink of glasses from the kitchen.

Nina smiled. 'He's great,' she said. Iain reached over and touched her hand. Simonov re-emerged with three heavy glasses held between his two hands. The three of them sipped icy liquid for a moment in silence. Eventually, Iain spoke.

'What is it with you Russians, Stas?' he asked. 'How is it you don't worry about the things I worry about? Why do I always feel so petty when I'm over here?'

Simonov shrugged. 'When a man is suffering from a terminal illness, my friend, he does not worry whether his cup is chipped. He thinks only of important things. We suffered from the terminal illness of communism for seventy-five years. We lost the habit of being concerned about things that do not matter.

'Also, we are poor. All honest people have no material goods, to speak of. I think that gives a greater authenticity in relationships, would you say?'

'You seem to be doing all right,' said Nina a little tartly, looking at him over the rim of her glass.

Simonov shrugged again. 'I am fortunate. Since I left *Izvestia*, most of my income comes from colleagues like Iain, in the Western media. I am paid in hard currency, so I belong to the new elite.'

Simonov took a slug of his drink and narrowed his eyes as he regarded his friend from beneath his craggy brow. 'But, Iain, you over-romanticize us, you know. We are also very corrupt. Your research will show you this.'

It was Iain's turn to be gracious. 'Graft is probably the only way to get this economy moving again, Stas.'

Simonov finished his drink, then looked at his friend and shook his head sadly.

On the short walk to his tube station the following evening, Smailes got the distinct impression he was being followed. Bolton Street was crowded with pedestrians as usual, but he thought he saw someone duck into a doorway behind him as he turned into Piccadilly. Instead of entering Green Park station, Smailes kept going, heading towards Piccadilly Circus and past the Ritz Hotel on his right. Then he stopped to examine the display in a shop window and saw the reflection of a figure behind him pause also, twenty yards back. He thought he recognized the face, but the body type was wrong. Then he saw the man advance towards him, smiling, and knew who it was. He turned and walked back through the crowd.

'Rudy, you old goat,' he said, holding out a hand. 'What the hell are you doing here?'

It was not surprising Smailes hadn't immediately recognized Rudy Kabalan, since he'd lost a good seven stone in weight since he'd last seen him. Rudy was an ex-CIA operative turned freelancer with whom Smailes had been involved in New York. They had become entangled in one memorable case together, after which Smailes had resisted Rudy's blandishments to stay in America and start up a doughnut business with him.

'Just visiting,' said Rudy, smiling broadly. 'Thought I'd check out your fieldcraft before announcing myself. Pretty good, Derek – you spotted me right away. Hey, you're looking good.'

'Rudy, you look *terrific*,' said Smailes. 'When did you lose all the weight?'

'End of last year,' said Rudy with a smirk. 'Finally found an incentive – I got married again.'

'Hey, congratulations. But look, let's not stand talking on the street. You got time for a drink?'

'Sure,' said Rudy.

'Where's the wife?'

Rudy laughed. 'Shopping at Harrods. This trip was her idea.'

Smailes saw that marriage had markedly improved Rudy's dress sense. He was nattily turned out in a light tweed jacket and turtleneck, whereas Smailes recalled a distinct penchant for brown polyester leisure suits.

'Unfortunately, there aren't any pubs around here,' said Smailes, looking up the street. 'But look, I'll take you to the Ritz.'

'Do I pass?' asked Kabalan, holding out his arms.

'Definitely,' said Smailes, laughing.

Over cocktails in the hotel lobby, Rudy Kabalan recounted his adventures in the years since Smailes had last seen him. His first doughnut shop in suburban New York had almost foundered, he confessed, because the training and quality control the Healthnuts franchise offered was so lousy. In response, Rudy had used some of his deception skills to enrol in a course at Dunkin' Donuts University in Massachusetts, the training ground for rival franchisees.

Smailes hooted. 'Dunkin' Donuts University? There is such a thing?'

'Don't laugh,' said Rudy gravely. 'Making a precision doughnut is no joke. Dunkin's got it down to a science – that's why they're so successful. I passed their final exam – 140 dozen doughnuts in eight hours. Hardest test I ever took.'

'Wow,' said Smailes, impressed. 'Then what?'

'Well, the economy finally began to pick up and my place took off like a rocket. I've opened two more outlets in Westchester since. That's how I met Carla. I hired her as manager for my third store.'

'Carla's your wife?'

Rudy grinned sheepishly. 'Carla Duffy's the best thing that's ever happened to me, Derek. I swear it. Great savvy too. She'd been a book-keeper at a Buick dealership – now we're partners. I'm staff and quality control, she's finance.'

Smailes sipped his drink. 'Remember you offered me a piece of your first shop, Rudy?' he asked.

'Offer still stands, actually,' said Kabalan in all seriousness. 'That's one reason we're here.'

'What?' said Smailes, alarmed.

'The suburban New York market has reached saturation – Carla and I don't think there's any more growth potential. There may be more room in the British market – Dunkin's been doing real well over here, you know.'

'So this isn't a honeymoon trip?'

'Well, it's a bit of both. We're gonna be here for a month or so. Stay in London a few days, then a car tour of Ireland. Carla wants to hunt for relatives in Sligo and Donegal. Then back to London and do some more business before we go home. Meet with the banks, the real estate people. And we're seriously in the market for British investors, Derek.'

Smailes held up a hand, flattered despite himself. 'Hold on a minute, Rudy. I'm actually enjoying my work these days, believe it or not. Don't you miss it? Intelligence, I mean?'

Kabalan looked at him sceptically. 'Tell you the truth, pal – making money's a lot more fun. I don't miss it at all. Anyway, it's all become just a scramble for turf. It's a dead-end business.'

'Things haven't changed that much,' said Smailes.

'Oh no?' said Rudy, intrigued. 'What's your field?'

Smailes explained his promotion to section head and his temporary transfer to help cope with revved-up Russian technobanditry in Britain. He hinted darkly about a nuclear engineer they'd just burned with his hand in the classified till. Looked like a classic KGB blackmail job, said Smailes.

'You work with the Yanks?' asked Rudy.

Smailes mentioned his friendship with Sal Imodeo, but Rudy didn't know him. He winced, however, at the name of CIA station chief Loudon Strickland.

'That jerk,' said Kabalan. 'God's gift to the CIA.'

'You know him?'

'Yeah, and his father – Loudon Strickland, Senior. One of Wild Bill

Donovan's right-hand men from the early days. Actually, he served here in London too until he was booted out.'

'Really? Why so?'

'You don't know the story? Back in the sixties, after Philby defected, the Agency made an open play to take over British counter-intelligence. Strickland Senior was head of station at the time and infiltrated a couple of moles into MI5 under cover as PEEFAB reps. They produced a report saying MI5 was basically incompetent and the Agency then made a direct pitch to Wilson to take over the whole show. The DG . . . who was it back then?'

'Hollis, probably.'

'Right, Hollis saw the report and hit the roof. He got Strickland PNG'd and fought off the attack. I'm almost surprised Langley gave the London position to Loudon Junior – kinda provocative, I would have said.'

'I don't really know him. But I can't say I like the look of him.'

'I don't blame you. Second-generation CIA people are the worst – kinda like Mormon missionaries,' said Rudy emphatically.

Smailes asked how much longer Rudy and his wife were in town, and when Rudy said three or four days, Derek invited them to dinner in Coulsdon the following evening. Rudy accepted enthusiastically, then glanced at his watch and said he had to get going. He and Carla were taking in a meal and a show, he confessed. Smailes smiled at his friend's reduced frame as it negotiated the revolving door. Rudy Kabalan, *Homo domesticus*, he said to himself, laughing.

12

The next day, Saturday, brought a quick breakthrough in Jonquil. In mid-afternoon the static team alerted their mobile unit that Docherty was leaving home by car, and the target was tailed to Reading station where he was seen boarding the London express. Crew chief Graham Booth managed to hop the train as it pulled out, and a panicked radio message to A Branch brought a back-up unit to Paddington to meet the train.

On arrival, Booth tailed Docherty's slim, hesitant figure into the station buffet, where he bought tea, chose a table and placed a large manila envelope on the seat beside him. Booth saw a three-man back-up unit spread itself out across the concourse and into the buffet itself. Then they all settled down to wait.

Within fifteen minutes there was action. A diminutive, jaunty-looking figure entered the snack bar and sat down opposite Docherty without bothering to line up for refreshments. Booth signalled with his eyes to Meg Pearson, the shabbily dressed woman hunched over a sticky bun near the door. She whispered into her lapel and moments later Johnny Hooper waltzed in, wearing his pin-stripes and bowler and clutching a briefcase. As he eased past Docherty's booth he raised his arm just long enough to get a couple of shots with the camera lens mounted in the briefcase clasp. Then he bought tea in a paper cup and left hurriedly.

Docherty seemed agitated whereas his natty friend looked relaxed, even garrulous. Booth sat across the room and could not catch what was said, but the contact, who had the air of a prosperous bookmaker, seemed in no hurry to collect whatever he'd been brought. Eventually, however, he stood and shook Docherty's hand, then accepted the envelope almost nonchalantly, which he slipped into the inside pocket of his suede jacket. Standing rules meant Booth would stick with Docherty, and he watched through the glass door as his colleague Bob Ferris, a gnarled young fellow with a beard and rucksack, peeled off from his study of the departures board to follow the little bookie out of the station. Presently Docherty drank up and rose to leave. He spent some time fussing in the newsagent's stand before buying a magazine, then crossed to the left-luggage area and unlocked a small locker. He extracted a tan envelope which he stuffed inside his folded magazine. Booth realized he must have palmed the key during the handshake – he was surprised he'd missed it.

Docherty's sequences were clearly well oiled since he had just enough time to saunter over to the platform where the Reading train was waiting. Booth waited until the last call was barked for the train, then trotted down the platform and hopped in the last carriage. Docherty would be home within forty minutes, Booth realized; barely two hours, start to finish.

The arrival of the foreign bodies of Rudy Kabalan and Carla Duffy later that same day did much to dispel the almost continuous tension that now pervaded the Smailes household. Clea, who had adopted the flat-heeled gait of the conspicuously pregnant, rose effortlessly to the occasion and seemed genuinely delighted to meet Derek's former sidekick from New York. The meal she prepared was outstanding – a salad, pasta with olives and capers, and an apricot flan. She and Derek were also both quite taken with Carla, a forceful, shrewd woman in her forties with a mane of dyed black hair and dramatic make-up. As she recounted their British plans, it was clear who wore the pants in their business relationship. Carla effortlessly reeled off statistics on profit margins and equity return, Rudy merely offering the occasional supportive remark as he sipped coffee doctored with a packet of sugar substitute from his pocket, having declined repeated offers of dessert.

'So anyway, we're not heading out until Wednesday,' Carla announced. 'Rudy and I have a meeting with NatWest on Monday, and the commercial real estate people on Tuesday.'

'Where?' asked Smailes.

'Croydon,' said Rudy.

Clea hooted and looked wide-eyed at her husband. Croydon was the largest Surrey suburb, a city in its own right, just miles from their home.

'Rudy, I told you . . .' said Smailes.

Kabalan held up a hand. 'Naw, I respect what you say, Derek. It makes business sense, that's all. The rents out here are lower, and sales analysis shows that commuters are our best customer base.'

Clea was puzzled. '*What* does Derek say?' she asked, resting a chin on her hands.

Kabalan looked at Smailes, who shrugged his assent. 'Derek knows we're in the market for British partners. But he tells me he's happy where he is.'

Clea's eyes widened with amusement. 'Oh, Rudy, you'll never get him into the doughnut business with you. He's hopeless. He believes he can be Director-General of MI5 one day.'

The remark was delivered affectionately, without sarcasm. The phone in the kitchen rang, and Smailes got out of his chair to answer it. Clea began to gather plates.

'Let me help, honey,' said Carla. 'You already got plenty to carry. When are you due?'

'Three more months,' said Clea, grimacing as she passed plates to her guest.

'Look, darlin', the second one's always easier,' Carla commiserated. 'I swear I barely made it to the hospital with my Bobby – he shot out like a greased football. Just don't wait as long as the doctors tell you.'

Clea laughed and looked across at Rudy, who was sitting in his chair like a tame bear. 'Have a seat in the living room, Rudy. We'll be right through.'

'Of course, they're teenagers now,' Carla continued. 'And, honey, it don't get any easier,' she confided.

'Great,' said Clea, kicking open the kitchen door.

The improvement in Derek and Clea's spirits continued throughout the evening and into their bedroom. Derek reached out to his wife and she actually responded, and they made love for the first time in many weeks. Not surprisingly, it was all over very quickly.

'Rudy and Carla are a hoot,' said Clea afterwards, as they lay together in the darkness.

'Great to see him again,' said Derek. 'And in such good shape.'

'Derek, I wish we didn't have to entertain knee-deep in toys,' she said, frowning. 'Do you think you could find time to convert the basement into a playroom before the baby comes?'

Smailes exhaled. 'I don't know, love. I'll be lucky if I finish the nursery at this rate.'

'What are you doing at work, anyway?' asked Clea, uncharacteristically. 'We hardly see you any more.'

'An operation against the Russians. Could be big. Listen, that was Iain who called earlier,' he said, quickly changing the subject.

'Really? He's back?'

'Yesterday,' said Smailes. 'But he's apparently not finished yet. He's trying to meet up with some Georgian gangsters who're being uncooperative. He's going back in a couple of weeks.'

'Is that what he called to say?'

'Not entirely,' said Smailes cautiously. 'He mentioned he'd fixed up a date this evening. On an impulse.'

'Who with?'

'Your sister.'

Clea propped herself on an elbow and looked down at him. 'With Julie?' she asked. 'Honestly, she's such a fool. Sometimes I wonder why you're friends with him, Derek. He's such a . . .' Clea hunted for a suitably pejorative word.

'Such a man?' Smailes suggested.

'Exactly,' said his wife.

'What does that make me?' he asked.

Clea stroked his cheek. 'Darling, you're hardly typical,' she said.

Armed with two excellent mug shots of their mystery bookie, it took Judith and Derek less than half an hour to identify him after Kensington Borough Council offices opened on Monday morning. The watchers had run the little fellow to ground in a flat above a dry cleaner's in Craven Hill, Bayswater, after he had employed some elementary but half-hearted fieldcraft to throw off a tail. He'd boarded a bus towards Maida Vale, but after waiting at a stop rather than jumping on one at random. Then he'd alighted after only a few blocks and sauntered back towards Paddington, stopping once at an Indian grocery to buy bread and tea. Ferris had little trouble allowing him a big lead and still keeping track of him. Forty minutes later Docherty's mysterious contact let himself into a flat above the dry cleaner's, itself barely a ten-minute walk from the station.

On examination of the council records, it appeared that one Mr Jurgen Klop of 26A Craven Hill, London W2, had found no difficulty making poll tax payments on time, and in cash – unlike many fellow Londoners. A visit by Judith and Derek to the dry cleaner's later that morning fleshed out Klop's profile further. The patron turned out to be an ill-tempered Cypriot called Costa who was at first distinctly unimpressed by their Home Office credentials. Costa refused to answer questions about his tenants, insisting he always declared his rental income. Only after Smailes convinced him they had no connection with the Inland Revenue, that they were from the anti-terrorist squad hunting an IRA fugitive, did Costa agree to share the secrets of his rent book with them. There were just two flats above the shop, he told them churlishly.

'Look, no Irish,' he growled. 'This one, 26B – Alison Zucker – she is American, at fashion college. Her boyfriend Ravi – he's Israeli.'

'Does she pay her rent on time?' asked Smailes, highly suspicious.

'Usually,' said Costa. 'No, look. She late twice,' he added, stabbing the page with a black-rimmed finger.

'How long has she lived here?'

'One year. A little more.'

'And who's your other tenant?'

'Mr Klop. A Dutch. Top floor.'

'Dutch?'

'From Amsterdam. Jurgen Klop. In books.'

'A publisher?'

'No. Sell to publishers.'

'A literary agent?'

'Yes, agent.'

'He pays on time?'

'Always. Look, first of month. Cash. Always. Very good tenant, Mr Klop.'

'How long?'

'Ah, almost three years now.'

'I don't like the sound of this American and Israeli couple. I want to see if anyone else is staying there. Are they out?'

'Yes, I think I see them go out already.'

'Give me a key and five minutes to look around.'

The three of them were seated in Costa's back office, which smelled strongly of naphtha and Greek tobacco. Costa hesitated and narrowed his eyes, but then went into a drawer and removed a fat ring of keys. He began working one loose.

'Look, no, don't bother. Just show me which is which.'

As Smailes had hoped, the keys were tagged. 'This one first floor, 26B, Miss Zucker. This one door to street,' said Costa.

'Thanks,' said Smailes, accepting the bunch. 'Back in five minutes.'

Smailes and Judith retreated into the street, where Smailes examined the door to the upstairs flats, making no attempt to open it. Instead, he led Judith back to their parked car, where he removed three tins of high-grade wax from his briefcase.

'You do it,' he instructed her. Carefully, Judith took impressions of the front door key, and the keys for the two apartments, 26A and B. Smailes received the keys back from her and wiped them with his handkerchief.

'If he gets half his rent in cash, you *know* he doesn't declare it, Derek,' said Judith, wiping her hands in turn. 'I hardly ever met a small businessman who would.'

'Yes, I thought of that,' said Smailes. Minutes later, they were back in Costa's office.

Smailes folded his arms gravely and gave Costa his most baleful stare. 'Okay, Mr Costa, we'll leave you alone now. Looks like there's been no guests. Just say nothing about this visit – to no one, understand – and we'll say nothing to the Inland Revenue about your undeclared tenant. Understood?'

'Understood,' said Costa, vastly relieved. He stuffed the keys back into his drawer. 'I run honest business.'

'No doubt.'

Smailes reached for a used cleaning ticket and scrawled his private number on the back. 'You see anyone you don't know coming and going, you call me, all right? Ask for Mr Sykes.'

'Okay.'

'Thank you, Mr Costa. And good day.' They didn't shake hands.

There were a few big literary agencies in London, then a host of smaller players, and it took Roger Standiforth barely an hour to massage his contacts and come up with a fuller picture of Mr Jurgen Klop, Dutch literary scout. It transpired Klop did indeed conduct a legitimate business, scouting manuscripts for the northern European market. He was a recognized sub-agent for publishers in Scandinavia, Germany and Holland, and seemed to specialize in mystery fiction and popular history. He had paid taxes to the British government on a reported income of twenty-four thousand pounds the previous year. Professional contacts in the publishing world found him an astute and dependable colleague who knew his markets well. No one in MI5's K Branch, however, had any doubts about Mr Klop's real nationality or profession.

An exultant meeting was hastily convened in Roger's suite. 'The watchers at the initial drop were sure they weren't spotted?' asked Brian Kinney anxiously.

'A hundred per cent,' said Smailes. 'Klop seemed very casual, unruffled.'

'No bloody wonder,' said Standiforth forcefully. 'He's been running this little shit in the heart of our weapons establishment for three years and no one suspects a thing.'

Judith frowned. 'Won't he be able to claim that Docherty is a professional client? You know, writing a book for him or something?'

'Not bloody likely. That won't wash – not with the stuff we'll be able to prove he's receiving.'

'What about his real identity?' asked Smailes.

'We need to get on it right away. Get these photographs across to SIS and over to Strickland. Then work down the list. The Dutch may know something. Has Winnie seen them?'

'She's still deliberating. But they haven't rung her buzzer yet,' said Kinney.

Everyone smiled. Whereas the CIA had a supercomputer in Langley that could analyse photographs against its vast data base, MI5 had Winnie Sewell, an elderly widow who'd worked for the service as long as anyone could remember, whose photographic memory had stored every Eastern Bloc officer's face to cross her desk. If there was a mug shot of Jurgen Klop anywhere in MI5 files, Winnie's memory would eventually retrieve it.

'He's young,' said Standiforth doubtfully. 'Winnie may not have the make.'

'Well, we'll get him eventually. If not, we can bloody well prosecute him under his alias,' said Kinney.

Standiforth gave his rare death's head grin. 'That's the good part, isn't it? No diplomatic immunity. A nice, juicy illegal. Think of the length of the sentence!'

'How long do we let him run, Roger?' asked Smailes.

'As long as we damn well have to,' said Standiforth icily. 'I want every damn bagman and traitor on his payroll. In the dock together. Do we have priority with A Branch?'

'It's taken care of,' said Kinney. 'Corky has walked them through it personally. Fall-off boxes, three shifts. Sod the other targets. He agreed we can't take it any other way. Klop may be over-confident, but he's obviously a pro.'

Roger gripped a pencil like a dagger and jabbed the air. 'Good. No, not good – excellent.' He picked up the photographs of Klop. 'Let Sir Herbert Carne stick these in his bloody pipe and smoke them.'

*

Gennadi Gropov was a career KGB man, a First Directorate lifer who had not yet overcome his indignation at the appointment of the absurd, perfumed figure of Boris Zhimin above him. According to seniority, London should have been his, but it was hard to know who called the shots in Moscow these days – he suspected Zhimin had been the protégé of someone close to the Russian Foreign Minister, in whose entourage he knew no one. Still, as number two in the KGB London residence, Gropov was responsible for embassy security and was determined to use his position to advantage. He now had clear evidence of compromised behaviour by one of Zhimin's appointees, and would not rest until the man was called to account. Zhimin had agreed to this meeting only reluctantly, at the end of business on Friday, as if apprehensive of his subordinate's agenda. Gropov waited patiently as Zhimin, his hair a brilliantined surf, fussed with some papers. Over Zhimin's shoulder, beyond the embassy grounds, Gropov could see the trees of Kensington Gardens, and away in the sunlit distance a children's playground.

'Yes, Gennadi Stefanovich?' Zhimin asked presently.

Gropov opened his file. 'You know Lubyanov?' he asked.

Zhimin frowned. 'No, I don't think so.' He went into a top drawer for his staff roster.

'You appointed him. Cultural affairs.'

'Ah yes, I remember now. Yuri Andreyevich.'

'Yes. I think he is a spy.'

Zhimin leaned back in his chair in surprise, then forward on his elbows, scowling. 'What has he done?'

'Routine debriefing at the end of last week suggested he has been trying to ingratiate himself with people from Industrial and Technical. You know, inviting himself to lunch. Asking questions.'

'So? He is new, isn't he? Trying to make friends is not a crime. Not even in the Russian Intelligence Service.'

'Perhaps. But this week I find he has made two attempts to sign himself in to the *referentura*. On the flimsiest of pretexts. Galina Maximovna reports . . .'

Zhimin interrupted. 'This is more serious. When was this?'

Gropov looked down. 'Monday and Wednesday. You appointed this man, comrade.'

'Not so!' said Zhimin angrily. 'He was recommended to me. Forced upon me, in fact. I know nothing . . .'

'I ordered his file from Yasyenevo. It arrived last night. Were you aware he had an unauthorized sexual relationship in Copenhagen? That he was recalled and faced a tribunal, but was cleared? That this action came only after the intercession of Osipov, who is his wife's father? Who recommended him to you?'

Zhimin was silent for a moment. 'What is your point?'

'I believe this may have happened again. Only this time the British have trapped him. He is working for them, trying to spy for them.'

Zhimin's eyes narrowed. 'Let me see his file.' He accepted it and read in silence for a few minutes. Then he looked up.

'Question him.'

'And if he denies it?'

'Give him one day. Then tell him we'll use active measures.'

'Here?'

'Yes,' said Zhimin impassively.

Sir Herbert Carne's borrowed premises in Bloomsbury gave some indication of how welcome his commission had been at MI5. Five's Gower Street outpost was cramped to begin with, but Carne's team had been consigned to a single poky office under the third-floor eaves, with barely enough desk space for the four of them. Today, however, Carne had poached the ground-floor conference room in which to receive his guests, and had made sure to pile the table high with multi-hued files to indicate the breadth of his knowledge of MI5's recent case history. For Sir David Williams and his deputy Alex Corcoran, although still technically on their own turf, the encounter felt like entering the lion's den.

Carne sat at the head of the table between his two senior aides and Williams sat to his right, flanked by Corcoran's wheelchair. Carne was a small but imposing man with heavy jowls, volcanic eyebrows and a booming voice. All were under no illusion about the importance of the meeting; it was the last chance for MI5 brass to state its case before Carne went to draft report stage.

Sir Herbert began a rumbling preamble designed to cow the bureaucrats before him.

'So the basic situation, I'm afraid, gentlemen, is that the government is committed to cutting the defence budget further, and this time MI5 must bear its share,' he said. As with most Western countries, the British domestic intelligence budget was concealed from public scrutiny in the 'black' portion of defence spending.

'We quite understand, Herbert,' said Williams evenly, one knight to another. 'We have brought our own proposals.'

'Yes, well, the pressure you've been applying to exempt counter-intelligence seems unrealistic. Your claims of increased Russian activity are unsubstantiated, and I don't see much evidence to justify spending at existing levels . . .' Carne indicated his pile of folders with a sweep of his hand.

'As for substantiation, there are some developments,' said Williams. 'We're about to get a complete rundown of order of battle at the Russian embassy, and it will confirm a level of espionage activity we haven't seen over there for years.'

'How?' asked Carne.

'We have an insider who's cooperating . . .'

'A double?'

'Not quite. A collaborator.'

'Coerced?'

'Yes.'

Carne folded his arms. 'I see. And when do you expect to get this rundown?'

'Any day now. But that's not all we have to tell you. Alex?'

Williams turned to his deputy and accepted a blue-edged file marked 'Jonquil'. He passed it to Carne, who glanced at it and flicked it open.

'What's Jonquil?' asked Carne.

'Possibly the single most important counter-espionage operation we've run in a generation,' said Williams calmly.

Carne was reading the file. 'The Burghfield leak? You've got him?'

'We think so. But read on. Look at the photographs. We've also got his controller. And he doesn't have immunity. We think he might be the Russian resident illegal.'

Carne's assistants exchanged a look of frank wonder. Everyone in Whitehall knew that MI5 hadn't caught a Russian illegal since Gordon Lonsdale in 1960.

'Really?' said Carne, examining the surveillance pictures. 'What's his name?'

'His alias is Jurgen Klop, and he's lived in London for the past three years. His cover is as a Dutch literary scout. We don't know his true identity yet.'

'You sure he's Russian?'

'No,' said Williams jauntily. 'But I'd bet all the coal in the Rhondda Valley on it.'

Carne was scanning the file. 'How did you get him?'

'By tailing our Burghfield man. We got *him* through our insider at Kensington Palace Gardens.'

Carne sat back in his chair, the massive eyebrows in involuntary motion. 'You going to let him run?'

'As long as we can. He's undoubtedly controlling others – we suspect the Burghfield engineer may be small fry. We could dismantle his entire network.'

'How about a disinformation exercise?'

'No,' said Corcoran, cutting in sharply. Everyone knew that feeding disinformation through a burned spy was a favourite SIS ploy; MI5 liked splashy arrests and trials.

'Excuse me, Sir Herbert,' continued Corcoran, correcting his tone. 'But we feel eventual arrests will have the maximum deterrent effect.'

'Is the Cabinet secretary getting briefed?' asked Carne.

'Daily,' crowed Williams.

It was Carne's turn to feel cowed. 'You said you had, er, your own proposals?' he asked.

Williams turned to Corcoran and accepted another file. Carne handed back the Jonquil material and took the new document.

'We think F and C Branches are the logical places to make cuts,' Williams said. 'Perhaps even an amalgamation, a new department.'

'Protective security and counter-subversion?' said Carne to himself. 'Well, there's some logic in that. What's your thinking?'

'Well, there's already considerable overlap . . .' said Williams, launching into his prepared pitch. Corcoran settled back into his wheelchair, his face impassive as a sphinx.

Peter Tennant was one of those MI5 staffers whom it was hard to classify. He definitely wasn't old school, since he was the product of a comprehensive and a redbrick, but neither could he be classed as household staff either. Perhaps he was closest to a square peg, since there were rumours that Roger Standiforth had plucked him from the entrance pool on learning of reputed 'infractions' during his university OTC career. What was clear to everyone, however, was that Peter Tennant was a young man of limited intellect and ferocious loyalty to his elected master. He only had one task at MI5, and that was to serve Roger Standiforth.

'He met an American,' Tennant was saying. 'Medium build, middle-aged. Then they had a drink at the Ritz.'

'How do you know he was American?' asked Standiforth, seated at his desk. Tennant, by contrast, was not in a chair, but was leaning against the side of Roger's desk, his arms folded.

'I followed the taxi when it left the Ritz, then spoke to the driver.'

'Where did he drop him?'

'A restaurant in Soho.'

'There's something else?' asked Standiforth.

'Yes. I think he's having sex with his assistant.'

'With Judith Hyams? The new K5 recruit?' Standiforth was all ears.

'I went into their office today. I knocked quietly and went straight in. She was seated on the edge of his desk, like this.' Tennant illustrated his point by parking a buttock on the corner of Roger's desk.

'Well?'

'They were laughing. She was wearing a short skirt – he must have been able to see right up it. They hadn't heard me come in. I startled them.'

'I've been wondering . . .' said Standiforth.

'I'd bet on it,' said Tennant.

Standiforth picked up his phone. 'Very good, Peter. Let me make a call, will you?'

Tennant straightened to leave. 'Stay on him?'

'No. No, I think we'll bring in someone else. But keep your ear to the wall.'

'Right, Roger.'

As the door closed, Standiforth consulted his Rolodex, then punched the buttons on his phone. After a pause, the faint peep of an answering machine could be heard through the receiver.

Standiforth spoke quietly. 'This is Richard Stiles. Please call me this evening. The number is . . .' Standiforth recited ten digits, an out-of-town number. The code was for Potters Bar, the Hertfordshire dormitory town where Roger had lived all his professional life.

13

Fall-off boxes were the most cumbersome form of surveillance MI5 could deploy, but also the most reliable, and with a fish as big as Klop to fry, no one on the fourth floor was taking chances. The method entailed a four-man team stationed at 'corners' around the target's residence. Then, when he left on foot for any reason, he would be tailed by the entire 'box' moving in tandem. What was different with the fall-off system, however, was that a separate crew would take over after only a few blocks, so that Klop would never notice the same faces around him for any length of time. The technique strained the watchers' resources to their limit, and other staffers, including even trusted spouses, were drafted into service. Both Smailes and Hyams took regular shifts on the Klop detail as MI5 painstakingly pieced together his routines.

They were annoyingly varied. During business hours Klop occupied himself visiting the disparate offices of literary London. Occasionally he would meet with writers or other agents in pubs or restaurants, although never, as far as MI5 could discern, in a railway station buffet. He conducted an active business by phone, the tap on which had been installed immediately, and received a continual stream of packages via the Leinster Gardens post office. These were also intercepted and rerouted through MI5's postal investigations unit, but were uniformly identified as manuscripts and correspondence with literary agencies and publishers in London and abroad, and scanning located no secret writing or microdot communication in them. Eventually everything was forwarded to its intended recipient. Once or twice Klop caused alarm by complaining on the phone about the whereabouts of a particular package, and MI5 had to route it to him hurriedly. But on the whole, the intensive surveillance of Jurgen Klop proceeded smoothly, and on the surface he was precisely what he seemed – a literary scout conducting an active and successful business.

But this was merely cover, MI5 quickly confirmed. Technical wizard Archie Keith was installed in a safe flat down the street and was able to determine via a non-contact tap when Klop used a powerful appliance, such as a short-wave radio. This was found to occur regularly each night between seven and nine, and Keith was quickly able to confirm the presence of a short-wave receiver, 'beat down' its frequency and listen in to Klop's traffic. As anticipated, this was enciphered material emanating from Moscow, undoubtedly using one-time codes, without access to which Klop's transmissions were impenetrable. Keith was able to identify Klop's range of call signs, but that was all. Klop appeared to use no transmitter himself, and Keith insisted this made perfect sense, since British/American counter-measures were now so accurate they could pin-point such an RF source almost immediately. Klop used runners for his own traffic, Keith insisted. However, his confirmation of a short-wave receiver listening nightly to enciphered Moscow traffic established beyond dispute what the Jonquil team had hoped – that Klop was a very big spy indeed. Given the volume of this traffic, he had to be the KGB resident illegal himself.

One priority which eluded MI5, however, was an illicit entry to search the flat and install listening devices. Klop frequently returned home between appointments and conducted much of his business by phone. Even if he strayed far afield during the day, it was simply too risky to conduct anything like the thorough search that was necessary. To break his traffic MI5 needed to locate his one-time pads, then copy and return them, and that required at least twenty-four hours. And predictably, since British publishing was concentrated almost entirely in London, Klop never seemed to leave the city.

Jurgen Klop was a sharp dresser who also seemed to cut a dash with the ladies. He was short and chubby but had a certain natty charm, and never seemed at a loss for female company. He appeared to have one steady girlfriend who worked for a literary agency in Regent Street and lived in Fulham. He never spent an entire night there, however, and managed to entertain a succession of other ladyfriends in his top-floor flat, although he usually seemed to get down to business by nine thirty or so in the morning. MI5 was kept at full stretch trying to check out all Klop's contacts and still stay out of sight. After two weeks they had failed to identify anyone else in Klop's acquaintance with anything like the classified access of Joe Docherty.

The Jonquil team was beginning to get impatient when there were two sudden developments. On a Saturday afternoon Klop made rendezvous again with Docherty in the Paddington snack bar. No envelope was exchanged, although the watchers were able to photograph the hand-over of the locker key in the parting handshake and shoot Docherty subsequently picking up his cash. It meant Klop had Docherty on a very short leash, meeting with him every two weeks to pump him with money, even when there was no drop. It was classic KGB practice with an agent they had hooked so deeply.

The following day, Sunday, Klop took a very peculiar route by bus, tube and taxi, eventually ending up in Whitechapel High Street near the Brick Lane open-air market in London's East End. Smailes was assigned to the mobile unit which tailed him, and he anxiously ordered back-up when Klop finally got out of his cab and sauntered towards the market. Smailes, sensing this could be a breakthrough, disembarked hurriedly, reassuring himself that tailing Klop through a mob scene like the Brick Lane market ought to be easy, even for a non-specialist like himself.

As with the shops and restaurants in Brick Lane itself, the market stalls were predominantly Asian in character, mostly Indian and Pakistani, but with some Middle Eastern thrown in. Smailes also saw a few indigenous Jewish *schmate* stalls, and watched from a discreet distance as Klop inspected a pair of flashy loafers at a West Indian booth. Klop stopped to buy a packet of Indian sweets, then pressed on through the crowd past a large converted mosque. Smailes quickened his pace, passing a stall selling prayer mats and playing devotional Islamic music. Then Klop suddenly turned right into a side street, just before a big modern brewery. This could be a counter-surveillance ploy, Smailes knew, so he hurried on past the turn towards the brewery. At the last moment he dropped his keys and shot a glance under his arm as he stooped to retrieve them. He saw Klop mounting the steps into a grocer's shop half-way down the block. Cautiously, Smailes doubled back to investigate.

Smailes entered a take-away kebab house directly opposite Habib Brothers Grocery, Fresh Fruit and Vegetables and Halal Butchers. He could see the back of Klop's head as he spoke with a shop assistant. For a resident of Bayswater, Whitechapel was not a logical place to buy groceries. Smailes bought a pitta sandwich and was about to take a bite when a voice at his elbow said quietly, 'That Chummy over there, then?'

Graham Booth was dressed in a headband, track suit and trainers. 'Yes,' said Smailes. 'You were fast.'

'You know what Halal meat is?' asked Booth.

'No.'

'Slaughtered in accord with the Koran. Chummy a Muslim, then?'

'Not that I'm aware.'

'Here he comes,' said Booth quietly. 'I'll take over, Derek.'

Klop was negotiating the steps carefully, a carrier-bag of vegetables in his hand. As he headed back up the street, Booth jogged out into the crowd. Smailes chewed distractedly on his barbecued lamb, looking across at the shop. Habib suggested a Lebanese outfit, he thought. Was this the base for Klop's runners, or just a dead drop? Should he stay and watch the action? No, he decided, the smart course was to look for property for rent in the area.

'Archie Keith was dead right,' said Brian Kinney with satisfaction. 'The Habib brothers are Klop's piano men, no question. And the name's not Habib. It's Basamalah.'

'No kidding?' said Standiforth, impressed. 'Who are they, then?'

'A couple of Yemeni brothers that the FBI identified running errands for the KGB in New York. Before they could expel them, they disappeared. That was three years ago – just before they resurfaced in Whitechapel and bought the Habib grocery business. Which was also just before Jurgen Klop moved into his flat in Bayswater.'

'How do we know all this?' asked Corcoran.

'The static post down the street got mug shots, and Imodeo had the make through his field office in New York.'

'So what's their operation?' asked Roger.

'Derek?' said Kinney. The four men were seated in Brian Kinney's spare but elegant fourth-floor office. Brian had recently managed to replace its regulation civil service furniture with a matching set in vinyl, chrome and glass. Smailes wondered how on earth he'd had the expense approved.

'One of the Habib brothers leaves every morning by van, around four, to buy fruit and vegetables at Nine Elms,' said Smailes. 'You know, the wholesale market on the South Bank.'

'Go on,' said Standiforth.

'Except, on certain mornings, the van never arrives. Once in the past week it was driven into Essex, and once into Kent. On each occasion it pulled over into a field and squirted a three-second radio message into the ether. Enciphered, of course.'

'How long has this been going on?' asked Corcoran.

'GCHQ has known about the mobile transmitter in the London area for the last couple of years. They get the coordinates immediately from Chicksands and Menwith Hill, of course, but by the time the local bobbies show up, there's no one ever there. When they slow the stuff down it's Morse, but unbreakable. Always switching frequency.

Now we know it's the Basamalah boys who are responsible, and Jurgen Klop is the sleeper they're servicing.'

'What else?' asked Corcoran.

'Their shop is a dead drop too,' said Smailes. 'Apart from its normal Islamic clientele, the grocery had a couple of conspicuously Caucasian customers this week. Their arrival corresponded with the docking of a Russian freighter at Tilbury.'

'Good God,' said Corcoran, aghast. 'They're still using the merchant navy?'

'*Plus ça change*,' said Standiforth wearily.

'So the Yeminis are probably servicing others besides Klop,' continued Corcoran.

'Probably,' Kinney agreed. 'Although we haven't made anyone else yet.'

'Can't we stop calling this fellow Klop?' asked Corcoran in exasperation. 'Don't we know who this bloody man is yet?'

'Not yet, I'm afraid,' said Smailes. 'SIS doesn't know him. Neither do the Cousins. The FBI is still searching. We're going down the line, but don't have anything yet. Actually, I was wondering, sir . . .'

'Yes?' asked Corcoran impatiently.

'Could we approach the Israelis? I've heard their archive is superb.'

Corcoran frowned and blew out his cheeks. British–Israeli relations were notoriously prickly, dominated by Arabists in the Foreign Office and tainted by the anti-Semitism of the British establishment. Whereas MI5 enjoyed cordial relations with most sister services, its relations with the legendary Mossad were distinctly cool.

'I don't know,' said the Deputy DG. 'I'll have to go upstairs on that. When can we arrest these, who are they, Basamalah people?'

'Whenever we like,' said Kinney, suddenly interrupted by a trilling phone. The gathering remained silent as Kinney exchanged staccato questions; the topic was clearly Jurgen Klop. He hung up excitedly and wheeled on Smailes.

'Derek, get over to Bayswater fast,' he said. 'Jurgen Klop just boarded a train to Birmingham!'

'Birmingham?' said Standiforth. 'Whatever for?'

'The watchers say he has an appointment with some academic from Aston University – something about a book on the rise of German neo-fascism. They didn't know it was definite until he actually got on the train. They're claiming he'll be out of London most of the day.'

Standiforth got the picture. 'This is our big chance. Derek, your kit's ready?'

'At all times,' said Smailes.

'Get his bloody pads,' said Corcoran.

Smailes hesitated and turned to Kinney. 'Maybe I should take Judith. You know, Brian, two heads . . .'

'Good idea,' said Standiforth, pre-empting Kinney.

Derek and Judith visited Archie Keith's listening post before approaching Jurgen Klop's flat. Archie, an elderly Cockney with a patrician manner who represented a dying breed at Five, clucked over Smailes's equipment.

'All right, all right. These will do, I suppose,' he said, examining the magnetic harmonica bugs Smailes was planning to install. Then he went into a tool-case and produced a small black device the size of a cigarette packet. 'You know what this is?' he asked.

'I'm not sure, Archie,' said Smailes.

'Standard bug detector,' said Keith. 'If Chummy is as big as everyone thinks, then he could have one somewhere in his flat. Watch.'

Keith flipped a switch on the box and told Smailes to activate one of his bugs. Smailes complied and Archie's contraption emitted a thin whine and a tiny red light came on.

'Picks up RF, see?' said Keith. 'If he's got anything like this on his premises, means he's wired for counter-surveillance and there's no way we can beat it without disarming his equipment. Which he might spot. So if you find one, forget about your bugs, right? We'll have to settle for what I can pick up through his telephone.'

'All right, Archie,' said Smailes obediently.

'I'm in touch with the unit at Euston, which is in touch with the Birmingham crew,' said Keith, indicating one of several hand-held radios on his kitchen-table command centre. 'So I'll know immediately he's on his way back to town. Chummy has his answer machine programmed to pick up after the fourth ring. I'll call twice and hang up immediately – you pick up the third time.'

'Right.'

'You along to take notes, love?' Archie asked Judith.

Smailes saw his assistant bridle. 'Judith is a senior case officer on Jonquil,' said Smailes. She gave Derek a look of gratitude.

Smailes and Hyams entered Klop's building from the top end of the street, so they didn't have to pass in front of Costa's shop. The hallway was dark, and dusty, but on the first landing a skylight gave better visibility. They stepped carefully past the door at the bottom of the second flight; Alison, or her boyfriend, or both of them, were listening to reggae. On the upper landing Smailes let them quietly into Klop's flat. There was no ancillary deadbolt, as Costa had promised.

The flat was small but neat. There was a floor-to-ceiling bookcase against the far wall stacked with fat manuscripts from which pink labels drooped like dry tongues. The rainbow spines of spanking new hardbacks occupied another, less utilitarian unit which also housed the television and stereo equipment. Smailes examined it carefully. It did not seem equipped to receive short-wave.

In one corner there was a small sofa, an oak coffee-table stacked with a neat pile of magazines, and a desk and a filing cabinet on which stood Klop's phone, fax and answering machines. Derek and Judith had agreed to communicate by sign as a routine precaution. Smailes touched her arm and indicated she should listen and watch carefully. He opened his briefcase and they both put on surgical gloves. Then Smailes removed a harmonica bug and carefully coupled it to its battery. They both heard a soft click. Smailes unhooked the bug and Judith walked across to Klop's work area. When Smailes seated the battery again, Judith waved to him eagerly. On Klop's desk was an old-fashioned pen and pencil set, mounted on a marble base. Inset in the base was a tiny, glowing LED light. Judith up-ended the set to reveal the housing of the bug detector in the hollow.

'Shit,' mouthed Smailes, uncoupling the bug again, at which the LED light went out. Judith raised her eyes in inquiry. He touched her arm and motioned her towards the bedroom door, indicating he would start with the living room/office.

He scratched his ear with a latex fingertip. He faced a huge task. Any one of Klop's scores of books could contain a hollowed-out hiding place. Any section of either bookcase could conceal a hinged cache. Not to mention the stereo and television cabinets. Somehow, Smailes knew to ignore Klop's work area. He did not doubt that all he would find there would be evidence of Mr Jurgen Klop's industry in the book trade.

Smailes started with the top row of hardbacks, removing and examining each in turn, then looking behind the shelf itself for evidence of a hiding place. He had begun on the manuscript shelf when Judith came back into the living room and gave a shrug. Smailes indicated she should examine Klop's desk and files.

He was half-way down the manuscript bookcase when the phone rang. His heart stopped. Then it was silent, and the pattern was repeated. On the third ring he walked across and grabbed it.

'Yes?'

'Chummy's on board the Euston express. Very short meeting, apparently. Conceivably, he could be there within an hour and a half. Wind it up, Derek,' said Archie.

Smailes hung up and swore quietly. 'On his way,' Smailes mouthed to his assistant. 'One hour.'

Judith looked startled and appealed mutely to Smailes for instructions. He pointed forcefully at the filing cabinet, then wheeled round, looking about. Instinct told him to keep checking the furniture.

He dropped to one knee, removed his gloves and felt around the rim of the coffee-table. His finger passed a minute impediment. He crouched and looked more closely. There was a sliver of clear adhesive tape, a few millimetres wide, between the underside of the table top and its base. He reached underneath and tapped the bottom with a knuckle. Hollow. He snapped his fingers softly but urgently, and Judith approached, removing her gloves also. She knelt beside him and examined the tiny tripwire of tape stuck to the underside of the table. He took her hand and examined her nails – they were much longer than his. Smailes pointed to the tape and Judith carefully picked it off and stuck it on the back of her hand. Then Smailes removed their Polaroid camera from his briefcase, took a shot of the pile of magazines, then moved them on to the sofa. Only then did he swing open the hinged table top. He gave a soft gasp. Inside was a trove of espionage gear, all the paraphernalia of a modern spy. Silently, Judith went to the briefcase and primed their camera. Klop also had a Minox in his cache, an earlier model than theirs. They saw the Burghfield documents and floppy computer disks that they had discovered in Joe Docherty's potting shed. There were chemicals and lenses for microdot manufacture, a modified microcassette recorder for compressing signals for burst transmission, and a tiny Morse key. There were no one-time pads. Working quickly and with complete coordination, the MI5 pair shot a Polaroid of all the materials in place, then removed each item and photographed it with the Minox camera against the neutral background of Klop's living room carpet. The entire exercise took almost thirty minutes. Then, working from their Polaroid prints, they restored everything to its place within the false-bottomed table and carefully repositioned the magazines. Smailes doubted Klop had used any fail-safe 'spotting' of these materials – they had been stacked neatly rather than seemingly haphazardly, which a conventional spotting technique would require. Finally, Judith knelt and replaced the tiny sliver of adhesive tape, then straightened to her considerable height and beamed at him. Smailes indicated his watch and jerked a thumb towards the door. They packed their briefcase and left hurriedly.

Out in the street, Judith slipped her arm through his. Whether for cover or from the simple thrill of success, Smailes did not object.

'No pads,' she said.

'They're stashed with his radio,' said Smailes. 'We'll find them next time.'

The main Pindar briefing room in Whitehall was an unassuming military command centre, and only its fluorescent light and the whisper of air-conditioning betrayed its location more than a hundred feet below the Ministry of Defence. The Pindar complex had recently been completed to replace COBRA – The Cabinet Office Briefing Room – which was only two floors beneath Downing Street and considered insufficiently bombproof. Ranks of computer screens and triplicated communications systems crowded a small conference table. On one wall was a darkened outline of the British Isles, within which other hardened command centres glistened as points of yellow light. MI5's deputy chief Alex Corcoran shifted his weight on the foam egg-carton on which he sat during all his waking hours and regarded Britain's senior military officer across the table. Brigadier-General Sir Nigel Denton, Chief of the Defence Staff and chairman of the United Kingdom Commanders-in-Chief Committee, was a short, squat figure with a boyish complexion and a small puckered fruit of a mouth which he tried to enhance with a stubby grey moustache. He was dressed in civilian pin-stripes and wore a laminated ID clipped to his breast pocket. He was about to respond to Corcoran's mute inquiry when the door opened and the head of the British civil service entered, looking flustered.

Cabinet secretary Sir Andrew Atkin was a tall, ungainly man who was all elbows, knees and chin. He stuck his tie back into his trousers and apologized profusely for his lateness, tossing a file folder down on the table with a light smack.

'Don't mention it, Andrew,' said Denton airily. 'We know you're a busy man.'

'Well, I wanted to be sure I had the story straight first,' said Atkin, leaning across the table to shake Denton's hand. Then he turned to his left. 'Corky, how're you?' he asked warmly, taking Corcoran's shrivelled claw into his fist.

'Well, Andrew. Quite well. So tell us what the PM thinks of all this nonsense.'

Atkin cocked his head, as if summoning inspiration. 'Well, he wants our advice, of course. It looks like the Paris summit on monetary union is a go, so it's no secret he may have to go to the country in the autumn. Naturally, he wants to avoid this Sceptre thing becoming a political football.'

'He's been regularly briefed?' asked Denton.

'Oh, I meet with him whenever I get updates. They go straight into his nightly box.'

'And what is his inclination?'

'To ignore them. He thinks arrests might backfire in the House.'

'Well, except for one nagging doubt, I would agree,' said Denton. 'In my opinion, Porter is off his rocker and ought to be confined to an institution – God knows where he's getting his information. I know for a fact the Americans have not been approached on any level.'

'Quite,' said Atkin. 'His impression of the Palace's thinking is way off beam too, from what I've been able to determine.'

'Couldn't believe it when he approached me in person,' said Denton, shaking his head. 'He's living in a fantasy world.'

'Well, arrests may be out of the question, anyway. At least so far,' Corcoran cautioned. 'As it happens, discussing a military coup is not a crime in this country, nor is trying to enlist others. Otherwise, we might have spent a great deal of our history arresting gin-soaked old soldiers. Our legal department says that successful prosecution under any existing statute would be very unlikely. Unless, of course, we can get written plans, something under Official Secrets.'

'This Boat Service colonel is their only active duty officer,' mused Denton. 'I'm pretty sure we can court-martial him, but we'll need something harder as evidence.'

'Surveillance tapes?' asked Corcoran.

'That's what I was thinking, yes,' said Denton. Corcoran scribbled a note.

'As for Porter, well, he'll lose his sinecure, of course, and be put out to pasture finally. Probably can't even touch this ex-SAS chap, though,' said Denton. 'What's his name again?'

'Halls,' said Corcoran.

'What about the others?' asked Atkin. 'I was a little surprised to learn of Miles Bingham's involvement.'

'We're planning to consolidate F and C Branches anyway,' Corcoran explained. 'I think Bingo might find it's a good time to retire.'

'And what about the politician?' asked the general.

'Stap?' Corcoran responded. 'We'll leave that up to the party leadership, I think. He may well find himself off the front bench after the next election, I would guess.'

'What was your reservation, General?' asked Atkin. 'You mentioned a nagging doubt.'

'It's the Burghfield business, that's all,' said Denton thoughtfully. 'We can't rule out that SBS stole the American locks themselves, can we? The refit is way behind schedule, but two of the boats have had their missiles modified. If SBS got the locks, they could possibly override launch control and create a very sticky situation. Those missiles still target Moscow, you realize. And SBS almost always has someone on board the subs. They deliver the patrol instructions, you know.'

Atkin and Corcoran exchanged a knowing look. They were both indoctrinated into Jonquil and knew that SBS was no longer the leading suspect in the Burghfield theft.

Atkin spoke up. 'I think you can rest assured, General,' he said. 'MI5 has identified a Russian spy in the retrofit lab where the theft took place. He's almost certainly the source of the leak, which means the Russians got them.'

Denton was clearly miffed to receive such significant news so offhandedly, but neither could he contain his relief. 'The Russians? Oh, that's much preferable. I've been in favour of handing the damn things over all along. Can't understand why the Pentagon has put up such a fuss.'

'Perhaps because the CIA happens to agree with you, General,' said Corcoran sardonically. Then, cautiously, 'You don't think this Sceptre Group could have got its hands on that missing Norfolk bomb, do you? The Oldham Three from a few years back?'

Denton waved a hand dismissively. 'Not a chance – that thing's at the bottom of a bog for all eternity, old boy. Believe me, no one got near the damn thing. Candidly, NARO think they may have got a bead on it with some new American monitoring device, but they can't get the dredging equipment near enough to find out. They'd have to drain half of East Anglia.'

'So what should I tell the PM, then?' asked Atkin. 'I don't think he's losing any sleep, but the subject does make him very irritable.'

'Tell him to ignore them for now. Our surveillance seems to be good. If a case develops, we could reconsider arrests. Certainly, if they try anything direct, we can intervene immediately. They are absolutely no threat. Wouldn't you say so, Alex?'

Corcoran shrugged. 'Yes. They're obviously up a gum tree.'

Atkin was satisfied. 'Well, I'm pleased, because I know this is what he wants to hear. He may well want to try and throw the book at them after the election, however.'

'If he's still in power,' cautioned Denton.

'Of course,' said Atkin with treacly politeness. He stood to leave. 'Need a push, old boy?' he asked Corcoran.

'Thank you,' said the MI5 man, manoeuvring his wheelchair towards the door.

At first, Alex Corcoran thought his old friend was merely being polite, knowing he needed help with the final escalator and wishing to spare him the indignity of waiting at the bottom while he summoned his driver. But as the lift moved silently upwards, Sir Andrew Atkin asked again about his health.

'Oh, I can't complain, you know, Andrew. I'm pretty well recovered. Probably got a good few years left before retirement.'

Atkin lowered his voice to a confidential tone. 'You know, it was a damn crime you didn't get the DG's job when it last came up, Corky. The PM now concedes they made a dreadful mistake bringing in an outsider. It won't happen again, I assure you. Looks like old Bingo's gone and scotched his chances, though.'

The lift door opened noiselessly and Atkin steered his friend's wheelchair towards the rolling mouth of the escalator. Corcoran looked back over his shoulder.

'Not a bad thing, Andrew,' said Corcoran. 'Standers will make a first-class Director when his time comes.'

'So you've really drawn a blank, Sal?' asked Smailes, disappointed.

The FBI man made an extravagant gesture of dismay. 'Hey, whaddya-want? Miracles? I made the Basamalah boys for you, didn't I? So Jurgen Klop hasn't served in the US – doesn't mean he's not who you think he is.'

Judith Hyams came back into the office carrying two cups of tea. 'Hello, Agent Imodeo,' she said coolly. 'Like a cuppa?'

Sal Imodeo grimaced. 'You've got to be joking – I've got work to do. You know, back in the States people think the thing about the English and tea-breaks is actually a joke.'

'Who says we're taking a break?' Smailes countered.

Imodeo gave Judith a raffish grin. 'Actually, Judith, I never touch the stuff. Maybe a cocktail sometime?'

'Too busy, Sal,' she said.

Imodeo shot Smailes a conspiratorial smile, then left.

Judith placed Derek's tea on his desk in front of him and sat down. 'Nothing?' she asked.

'The FBI doesn't know him,' said Smailes. 'Neither does Winnie. She's officially thrown in the towel. Let me hear the legend again.'

Judith opened the file on her desk. 'Jurgen Klop. Dutch gallery owner. Died of AIDS, Amsterdam, May 1987. Replacement birth certificate issued April 1987, Amsterdam. New passport issued July 1989, The Hague.'

'Clever, that,' said Smailes. 'Get the new birth certificate while the bloke is on the way out, but before there's any death certificate on file. And the Dutch say they don't know him?'

'No idea.'

'Neither do the Americans. Or the French. Or the Germans. Well, I suppose we're going to have to play our trump card. I've just got approval to approach Moshe Feldman.'

'Who?'

'He's the head of London station for the Mossad – they call him the *katsa*. You know what that means?'

'I don't speak Hebrew,' said Judith tartly.

'Frankly, I'm a bit nervous, Judith. We have zero contact with these people. You don't know anyone over there, do you?'

Judith exploded. 'No, I bloody well don't. Why would I?'

'Judith, I'm sorry. I just thought . . .'

'That because I'm Jewish I'm hand-in-glove with the Israeli embassy, is that what you thought?'

'No. It's just . . . I . . .'

'Honestly, do I have to spend my whole life trying to convince people I'm British? British, understand? I am not Israeli. I do not know any Israelis. I am a British Jew. It's different – get it?' Her chest was heaving.

Smailes was mortified. He liked Jews – didn't Judith know that? The thought that he might have been guilty of an anti-Semitic stereotype stung him deeply.

'Judith, look, I'm sorry. That was thoughtless. Of course, I don't think anything . . . Please, I apologize. Honestly.'

Judith Hyams flashed him an indignant look. 'It's all right, Derek. I'm sorry – just a sore point, that's all.'

'I'll talk to Feldman myself. It's no big thing.'

'Right, then,' said Judith, rising to leave.

The door closed and Smailes slumped in his chair, exasperated.

14

Yuri Lubyanov had panicked. Smailes had barely changed his clothes after reaching home the following Monday evening when the duty officer called to say Lubyanov had phoned in an emergency code. Smailes groaned. The truth was that ever since Lubyanov had unwittingly delivered the heavy goods on Joe Docherty and his controller, the British had all but lost interest in him. His contacts had been cut back to once a week, and while Smailes still cajoled him for a KGB staff roster, he too had become increasingly focused on the mushrooming Jonquil inquiry.

The emergency procedure entailed a meeting one hour from Lubyanov's call, with no fall-back. Smailes checked his watch and realized he needed to be in Notting Hill within fifty minutes, a virtual impossibility. Judith lived in North Finchley, a long way out, and Standiforth was in Potters Bar, as far north as Smailes was south. Smailes hung up and called Brian Kinney, who lived in St John's Wood, near Lord's cricket ground. Brian himself answered and Smailes quickly explained the predicament.

'Bloody hell, Derek. We've got tickets for a concert,' Brian replied irritably.

'I know, Brian, but what can I do? I could never get there in time. Neither could Roger. Judith, well, I don't think she really has the experience.'

Smailes heard Kinney exhale. 'What's your guess? What's happened?'

'Oh, take your pick. His wife has rumbled him. He's been grilled by embassy security. His girlfriend is pregnant and is threatening to expose him. All of the above.'

'Look, they can't get to Jonquil through him, can they?'

'I don't see how. I doubt Klop has any contact with the embassy. And Lubyanov doesn't know he gave us Docherty, does he?' Smailes felt uneasy using protected names on an open line.

There was a pause. 'So why not cut him loose?'

Smailes was horrified. Here was his Russian section chief, a man he looked up to in every respect, suggesting they dump an agent like an old boot so he wouldn't miss a performance of the Royal Philharmonic. Christ, it was a cynical profession.

'Look, Brian, personally I think Lubyanov is a worm, but a deal is a deal. If no one shows up to meet him, he might really panic. Then God knows what'll happen – he might try and flog his story to the tabloids or something. If you really can't make it, send someone from the duty office. Just tell them I'll meet with him tomorrow lunchtime, as usual. Or tell him to wait. I could be there in an hour or so, depending on traffic . . .'

Kinney muttered a rare obscenity. 'Oh, I'll take it, I suppose. Miriam can go to the bloody concert by herself.' Smailes heard a background protest, then a pause as Kinney cupped the receiver and spoke to his wife.

'The Ladbroke Square flat?'

'Yes. At seven thirty.'

'Call you later,' said Kinney, and hung up.

Now Smailes was getting the tale from the horse's mouth. Yuri Lubyanov was slumped forward in his chair, elbows on his knees, rocking slightly to and fro. A cigarette glowed in the back of his hand and any notion Smailes had entertained of Lubyanov's brazening out the situation had evaporated. He was clearly a broken man.

'I should never have listened to you,' he moaned. 'I should have gone straight to Gropov and told him I'd been a fool. I could have found work elsewhere. Why was I so stupid?'

He looked at Smailes in anguish. Judith squirmed a little in her chair, her briefcase held primly on her knee, discomfited by this tableau of wretchedness.

No wonder. Lubyanov had obviously not slept the night before and had also neglected to shave. He had fitted himself somehow into his business clothes, but was apparently unaware he was wearing odd socks. The cool weather had broken and London was now in the grip one of its increasingly frequent heatwaves. Lubyanov sat in shirt-sleeves, and beads of sweat shone on his forehead and upper lip.

'Where did you go last night, Yuri?' Smailes asked gently.

'Home, eventually,' said Lubyanov bitterly. 'I could not believe it when your colleague would not let me stay here. My life is in danger.'

'Come on, Yuri. Don't you think you're exaggerating? This could all be routine, after all.'

'Routine? Routine?' bleated Lubyanov. 'Did he not tell you? Gropov says if I do not provide a full confession in twenty-four hours, they will use active measures! You know what that means? Sodium pentothal! It makes you powerless. I will tell them everything, of course. Including what I found in my father-in-law's briefcase!'

He stared at Smailes with livid eyes. Smailes remained calm. 'Perhaps you'd better tell me what happened yourself, Yuri. Perhaps I'm not perceiving the situation correctly.'

'Why should I trust you?' Lubyanov shouted. 'Miss Horowitz – perhaps you will believe me! You must help me, or I am a dead man.'

Judith cleared her throat. 'We just want to know exactly what has happened, Yuri. Calm down. We'll keep our end of the bargain.'

Smailes wished he shared her confidence. Lubyanov crushed out his cigarette and fished miserably in his jacket for another. The Britons waited until he had gathered himself.

'At close of business yesterday, Gropov summons me. He is a reptile, this man. He has no humanity.'

'Go on.'

'He has my file from Yasyenevo. He talks to me insultingly. He says my behaviour has aroused suspicion. Talking with officers from other sectors. Asking to check the log in the *referentura*. You see, I told you I could not do these things!'

Smailes remained silent and Judith took the initiative. 'And what did *you* say, Yuri?' she asked.

'Well, I think I was suitably outraged. I denied his allegations. I told him he was imagining things.'

'And?'

'He was unmoved. He merely said he knew I had been compromised by you and had become your spy. And if I did not sign a full confession within twenty-four hours, I would be required to submit to an active interrogation. Ha! That is a good old-fashioned KGB word – "active".'

'And then?'

'I left and took a taxi to a pub. Then another. When I knew I was not followed I called as we agreed and went to our meeting. I was very angry neither of you were there. I thought I was betrayed.'

'Sorry,' said Smailes flatly. 'You weren't.'

'It is a miracle they do not have the handcuffs on me already. I am to see Gropov at five. I cannot go. You have to take me into your protection today.'

Judith looked at her boss and he shrugged, then turned to Lubyanov. 'Couldn't you just tough it out, Yuri? You know they have no proof.'

'Tough it out! Tough it out! You tough it out against a drug that makes you lose control of your bladder and bowels! That makes everything become a nightmare! You tough that out!'

'You're sure it will come to that?'

Lubyanov was defeated. 'Yes, Mr Sykes, I am sure. I was followed here, you see.'

'Followed?'

'Of course. You think I am any longer my own person?'

Smailes went to the window and peered over the wooden shutter. A beefy-looking chap with sandy hair lounged against a gatepost across the street. The bulge in his jacket might have been a radio, or something else. He was making no attempt to conceal his presence.

'Yes, I see,' said Smailes. 'Well, let's say I share your concern, Yuri. Janet's right, of course. We will keep our end of the bargain. If you wish, my government will offer you asylum and a resettlement allowance.'

'I wish. What choice do I have?'

'When?'

'Now, obviously. You think I want to be escorted back to the embassy by my friend over there?'

'Right, well . . . I'll make some phone calls. Perhaps Janet could get you some tea, Yuri – you look like you could use some.'

Lubyanov looked at Smailes in despair.

'They've got him!' said Smailes, bursting into his office waving a wax paper envelope.

Judith Hyams wheeled around in her seat. 'Who?' she asked in alarm.

'The Israelis have the make on Klop! Look!'

He tossed the packet on to Judith's desk and she extracted a set of photographs. The prints were old and indistinct, but there was no mistaking the plump little fellow in the safari suit.

'Where were these taken?'

'Tripoli.'

'When?'

'Right after that chemical plant of Qaddafi's burned down so mysteriously. Remember – the one that was a complete accident?'

'Yes,' said Judith mechanically. 'Rabta, 1990.'

'Wherever. Apparently he's Mikhail Ilyich Gontar, a former TASS correspondent and KGB PR man. The Mossad thinks he was brought in by Qaddafi to help exploit the propaganda opportunity.'

Judith was examining the prints closely. 'These were taken at a different time, right? The ones in the hotel?'

'Right. The Damascus Hilton. That was Gontar's posting in the middle eighties.'

'How much else do the Israelis know?'

'Not much. They think Gontar was living in Scandinavia, building the Klop legend before he was called in by the Libyans.'

'Friendly with the Arabs.'

'Obviously. I'll tell you, I'm impressed with their operation over there. Talk about lean and mean – there must be only half a dozen of them. How many do you think SIS has in Jerusalem?'

'Twice that number, I suppose.'

'At least.' Smailes was excitedly punching buttons on his phone. 'Roger? Hello – Derek. Can we call an *ad hoc* Jonquil meeting? The Israelis have the make on Klop.' There was a long pause. Eventually, Smailes spoke again. 'Yes – this afternoon. Yes, I was planning to.' He looked across at Judith before hanging up.

She seemed preoccupied. 'What's all that about?'

'He wants to know when we're taking our baby-sitting shift with Lubyanov. Apparently, the Russians have lodged a formal complaint over his disappearance with the Foreign Office and Roger had just had his ear chewed off by Caldicott.'

'Who?'

'Their Russia desk man. Naturally, the FO is very pissed off.'

'What did Roger tell them?'

'He's not particularly concerned – he's holding all the aces.'

'So what else did he ask? At the end there?'

'Whether you were on the baby-sitting detail with me. I think your star's in the ascendant there, Judith.'

She managed a smile.

'Come on, we've got a meeting in Roger's suite. Bring the snaps.'

Yuri Lubyanov was spending his second day in British custody at MI5's most opulent safe house in Chiswick, west London, and his nerves were apparently much steadier since the British had managed to deliver him in one piece from Ladbroke Square. Actually, the Russians had made no discernible attempt to tail him during the transfer. The burly escort across the street had spoken urgently into his lapel as the British car left, but they must not have believed Lubyanov was going to make a dash for it, since they appeared to have no mobile unit ready to follow him.

Smailes and Hyams were led into Graham Booth's presence and found him seated at the kitchen table. Modern cherry cabinets flanked the latest in kitchen equipment – the Chiswick house was often used as de-luxe accommodation for long-stay guests. Booth was clearly relieved to see them; a little of Yuri Lubyanov seemingly went a long way.

According to Booth, Lubyanov was still chastising himself over his folly and the misery of his predicament. Smailes didn't see what all the fuss was about – after all, Lubyanov was about to secure what he'd supposedly wanted all along. He was alternately touched and repelled by the spectacle of this weak, corrupt man, crushed by the weight of the enmity that still governed the secret world.

'He's all right, I suppose,' Booth conceded. 'Although the one-note samba gets a bit tiresome. He wants booze, but I overruled him.'

'Probably wise,' Smailes agreed. 'What's he doing now?'

'Watching television upstairs.'

'He hasn't asked for a radio?'

'No.'

'We may want to pull the plug on the telly if the story gets out. Apparently the Russian embassy has cried foul, and the FO has joined in the chorus.'

'Typical.'

Smailes turned to his assistant. 'Check in with him, Judith. See if you can cheer him up.'

Judith went upstairs as Booth and Smailes completed the paperwork for the shift change. 'Who's Long Tall Sally then?' Graham asked.

'You've met Judith, haven't you? My assistant? At the static post in Reading?'

'Not properly. I'd like to, though.'

'She's married, Graham.'

'I'm not.'

Smailes glared at Booth, then left to check on their charge.

Smailes could tolerate no more than twenty minutes of Lubyanov's bleating before he had to retreat back to the kitchen. Booth had already left. Presently, Judith joined him and they made tea. They made small talk for half an hour, then the phone rang. It was Standiforth.

'How's Chummy?'

'Feeling very sorry for himself. Wants to get drunk.'

'We've got problems. The Russians are insisting on a face-to-face meeting to convince themselves we're not holding him against his will.'

'I don't know about that, Roger. He's not in the best of shape.'

'Well, they're obviously taking the whole thing very seriously. Madame Lubyanov was on the first Aeroflot flight home this morning. They're playing all their high cards. And, of course, the Foreign Office has climbed into bed with them.'

'Great. You're going to capitulate? He's going to love this development.'

'Don't say anything yet. I'm still working on the details.'

'When?'

'Tonight, probably.'

'Terrific.'

Roger called back within the hour in a state of high dudgeon. 'This is getting bloody ridiculous. The Russians are insisting that their personnel officer attend the meeting. He happens to be one Boris Zhimin.'

'The KGB resident? Listen, Roger, don't agree to it. Lubyanov might fold.'

'That's exactly what I told them, but that bastard Caldicott has rounded up his minister and Sir Andrew Bloody Atkin and they're insisting the Russians be permitted to send in who they like. Taffy has appealed to the Home Secretary, but he's up in bloody Newcastle somewhere and they're still trying to find him. I think we're outgunned.'

'What shall I tell Lubyanov?'

'Tell him he has to meet with some embassy officials tonight in order to reassure them he's sought voluntary asylum. Don't for God's sake tell him who it's going to be. Prep him as best you can. Promise him whatever you want.'

'A night with his girlfriend?'

'No problem.'

'More money?'

Roger hesitated. 'Tell him it's a possibility.'

'A job with the government?'

'No way.'

'All right. What time?'

'We'll send a car at seven. It'll be at the Foreign Office, I'm afraid. Keep him sober.' Standiforth hung up angrily.

The meeting took place in one of those high-ceilinged, panelled rooms that bespoke Empire and the White Man's Burden. On an inner wall a procession of Foreign Secretaries in frock coats and whiskers gazed in oils on to sunsets that never touched their dominion. A boat-sized conference table reflected light from an enormous crystal chandelier, across which two groups of three men faced each other. On one side sat Francis Caldicott, Boris Zhimin and some KGB bagman masquerading as an interpreter. Opposite them were stationed Brian Kinney and Roger Standiforth, and between them their tremulous charge, Yuri Lubyanov.

The tableau was a study in the polarity of modern government. Caldicott was a huge tub of a man, clad in butter-soft mohair; Zhimin was suave and inscrutable, smoking contentedly. Opposite them sat the lean, compulsive figures of Standiforth and Kinney, and their battered prisoner – the hungry watchdogs of counter-intelligence pitted against the overfed mandarins of the foreign service. The two sides clearly despised each other. Caldicott opened the proceedings in a slack-jawed, Whitehall slur.

'Now,' he said, making a sound more like *nigh*, 'perhaps we can get to the bottom of this misunderstanding. Mr Lubyanov, your colleague here feels you must have made some *mistake*. Mr Zhimin?'

Zhimin was the model of unctuous politeness. For the benefit of the Britons, his pitch was conducted in English. The 'interpreter' sat impassively, holding a briefcase, which no doubt held a tape recorder among other hardware.

Yuri Andreyevich was labouring under some misapprehension, Zhimin insisted. His interview with Counsellor Gropov had been *routine*, a *formality*. Perhaps their colleague's manner was too stern – he, Zhimin, had reprimanded Gropov for his tactlessness. But if Yuri Andreyevich were guilty of some minor *indiscretion*, well, they would be understanding. He had the assurance of the *ambassador himself* that anything Yuri Andreyevich wished to tell them would be treated *in total confidence*. There was no need to go running into the arms of the British Security Service – they were not Yuri Andreyevich's *friends*. Madame Lubyanova had been deeply affected by her husband's actions and had returned to Moscow. Yuri Andreyevich's mother was also said to be upset. They both *implored* him to change his mind.

Lubyanov could not look at Zhimin and physically flinched at the invocation of these two names. Neither Standiforth nor Kinney spoke, but their erect bearing imparted their protectiveness.

Zhimin resumed his attack. He took a document from his henchman and waved it at Lubyanov. It guaranteed freedom from reprisal, signed *personally* by the ambassador, who had spoken *directly* with the Russian Foreign Minister. If Yuri Andreyevich wished *reassignment* in order to put this regrettable incident behind him, it could be arranged. However, if Yuri Andreyevich *persisted* in his foolish course, there would be repercussions, naturally. The threat was spoken lightly, but nevertheless left a chill in the room.

Lubyanov responded so meekly he could hardly be heard.

'I'm sorry, Yuri Andreyevich. You must speak up,' said Zhimin expansively.

'There is no turning back for me now,' Lubyanov repeated. It was hardly a ringing repudiation.

Brian Kinney looked with loathing at the larded figure of Caldicott, sensing how desperately he wanted Lubyanov to renege. He and Roger had briefly discussed indoctrinating Caldicott into Jonquil, but had decided against it – there would be plenty of opportunity to stick his fat face in it after the arrests. They trusted that Lubyanov, no matter how shaky, would weather this ordeal and uphold their agreement, since he had no realistic alternative.

'Are you *sure*, Mr Lubyanov?' asked Caldicott in dismay. 'Your cooperation is *entirely* voluntary?'

'Yes.'

Caldicott turned to Zhimin and shook his head; the wattle beneath his chin wobbled. 'Well, Counsellor, I don't think there's much more to say, is there?'

'You won't reconsider?' asked Zhimin almost humbly.

'No.'

'Well, the offer will still stand. For one week,' he said, standing and crushing out his cigarette. He left without turning round, trailed by his bodyguard. Lubyanov sagged with relief as the door closed.

'Well done,' said Kinney, clapping him on the knee.

'How about a drink?' asked Standiforth.

'Please,' said Lubyanov.

'We'll speak in the morning,' said Caldicott, waddling towards the door.

*

Peter Lynch was jumpy. The Velcro girdle around his waist made a bulge in the back of his jacket, which he was sure a trained commando might spot. He was particularly concerned about Halls, a man with dead eyes who looked like he wouldn't hesitate to bundle you into the Thames attached to a paving stone. His son-in-law had said the worst he faced if found out was a tongue-lashing; it was easy for Derek Smailes to say, shuffling papers over in Curzon House.

Peter Lynch had tried not to betray his dismay when Corcoran told him they needed surveillance tapes after all. Only a month before, it had been judged too risky – what had changed? However, he had assented gravely, assuming it was what was expected. He was in too deep to back out now.

Lynch rounded the first landing of the Special Forces Club and proceeded up the stairs past the gallery of dead heroes. He suddenly thought of his daughters and felt a lump in his throat. If he lost his life in the line of duty, would *they* think him a hero? Or a fool? He could not be sure.

The Sceptre Group had absorbed yet another top-floor office, Lynch noted. He tapped the door of the conference room and went in. To his relief, neither Halls nor Crabbe was present, just Bingham and the old general. It was a routine meeting to update a fund-raising list. The mike taped to Lynch's chest was voice-activated, Lynch had been told. All he had to do was start talking.

'Meet Lev,' said Stas Simonov. 'Lev Putiashvilli. Lev, this is Iain Mack, and Nina Gregory of the BBC. And this is Blair Harrison, their Moscow correspondent.'

Putiashvilli was a scrawny, unshaven character in an old suit who regarded the British trio with open distrust. He sipped his tea but offered no acknowledgement. The five of them were seated in the lobby of the Stalinist fortress of the Ukraine Hotel, where Mack always stayed in Moscow. Iain and Nina had been summoned back at short notice after Simonov confirmed he'd won the cooperation of a member of one of the Georgian gangs. Apparently, Putiashvilli was prepared to name names on camera, for a healthy but not unmanageable fee. Harrison, the seasoned and respected BBC reporter in Moscow, had come along to add weight to the British team.

Mack began in a slow, clear voice. 'We're very pleased you've agreed to talk to us, Lev,' he said. 'But we can't disguise you or use voice distortion. And we can't pay your fee until shooting is over and the programme is in the can.'

'When is this?'

'Some time next month.'

'You must say this will only be seen in England. Not CNN.'

Harrison and Mack exchanged looks. 'There's no danger of that, Lev,' said Harrison.

'Why are you agreeing to do this, Lev?' asked Nina, pushing her long dark hair behind an ear. 'What's in it for you, besides the money?'

'I'm sorry.'

Simonov translated hurriedly into Russian, and Putiashvilli babbled back at him.

'He says he has some very important information he wishes to give the BBC,' said Simonov.

'What information?' asked Mack.

'About corruption in the security forces. About the sale of military secrets.'

'How does he know all this?' asked Harrison, suspicious.

Putiashvilli spoke Russian again.

'Contacts,' said Simonov.

Mack was clearly intrigued. 'Can you speak English on camera, Lev? Or will you need a translator?'

'If not too hard, English,' said Putiashvilli.

'You'd better have a back-up,' warned Simonov.

'What about the Georgian crime syndicate, Lev?' asked Nina. 'This programme is supposed to be about the mafia groups, you know.'

'This too. This easy,' said Putiashvilli.

'I'd like to do some sound tests now, I think,' said Mack. 'Nina, you have the outline?'

'Up in the room.'

'Will you come with us, Lev?' asked Mack. 'For a preliminary interview?'

Putiashvilli looked alarmed. 'Not ready,' he said.

'Oh, don't worry. This is not on camera or anything. We just want to get an idea of the scope of your knowledge.'

Putiashvilli spoke to Simonov urgently in Russian. 'He wants me to come,' Simonov explained.

'I've no problem with that. Blair?'

Harrison shrugged and the five of them got to their feet.

15

It was barely nine o'clock but the crisis meeting had already convened in Roger's suite. Kinney read from notes as Standiforth stared at his hunting prints; Smailes pinched his temples and looked down at his feet; Judith sat primly, knees and ankles together. The heatwave continued and her complexion shone; the men were all in shirt-sleeves.

'Well, the static unit thought it bizarre when both principals got into the van in Whitechapel this morning. That was a first. Not much they could do, though, given the hour,' said Kinney.

'When?' asked Standiforth.

'Half past four.'

Roger grunted.

'So the van headed off into the Blackwall Tunnel and out towards Kent. Not a new route. The transmission site last week was near Dartford.'

'What kind of lead did we give them?'

'Up to a mile. You approved it, Roger.'

'I know, I know,' said Standiforth irritably, flapping a hand.

'Except today they didn't stop outside Dartford. They kept going all the way to Dover. Both Basamalah brothers boarded the seven o'clock hovercraft to Calais. The mobile unit found the van abandoned in the short-stay car park. Unlikely they've gone across to buy onions – they've flown the coop, Roger.'

Standiforth muttered an obscenity. 'Lubyanov – it's got to be.'

'How the hell, Roger?' Smailes protested. 'Zhimin had no way to connect the Klop network to Lubyanov, did he? You agreed that yourself before we let him come across.'

'A routine precaution?' Kinney offered. 'Closing down active networks in case Lubyanov had learned of them?'

Standiforth shook his head. 'Not standard. This is either an unfortunate coincidence, or the Basamalah brothers knew they were blown. Could they have spotted the watchers?'

'Very unlikely,' said Kinney.

'What about Klop? Has he done anything unusual? Who the hell tipped them off?'

Judith Hyams cleared her throat. 'I've already spoken with Mr Keith, Roger. He says there's been no apparent deviation in his routines. He hasn't been to Whitechapel in a week. He definitely hasn't called them from his flat.'

'From a coin box?' asked Smailes.

Kinney consulted his notes. 'Not according to our intercepts,' he said.

Standiforth had reached a conclusion. 'There's nothing we can do, is there? If Klop knows he's blown, he'll be leaving too. Today, probably. I don't think we can prepare an arrest on this short notice, can we?'

'Very difficult,' Kinney agreed. 'I can talk to Poynter, but I know he's hoping for a tighter case.'

'I'll get on to Corky right away,' Standiforth said. 'When is Klop due to meet Docherty again?'

'Tomorrow,' said Smailes.

'Well, if this is just a routine switch, or if those damned wogs left for some other reason, then Klop and Docherty will meet as usual, and we can arrest them both. Obviously, we can't let him run any longer.'

Smailes winced. 'That's a lot to accomplish in twenty-four hours, Roger.'

'I know, I know. Let's get moving,' he snapped, standing to signal the meeting was over.

MI5 soon decided against any quick arrest of Mikhail Gontar, alias Jurgen Klop. They needed to establish continuity of evidence between Klop and Docherty, otherwise they feared Klop might be able to wriggle off the hook, depending on what was found in their respective caches and the forensic evidence linking it. It was conceivable Klop could claim a professional relationship with Docherty, that he had never received classified information from him – if his cache was empty, the photographic evidence would prove insufficient for a conviction. Docherty's prospects were much weaker; given the unique provisions of the Official Secrets Act, the burden would fall upon him to prove his thefts had not harmed national security. Also, MI5 was fairly sure they could pressure him into a full confession. But with a professional like Mikhail Gontar, they needed a watertight case. So, despite the fear their prized illegal might escape, MI5 decided to prepare their arrests for the following day.

This decision was alternately challenged and buttressed throughout the day. The watchers quickly established that the Basamalah brothers had left in a big hurry. Their shop remained shuttered, to the mystification of employees who arrived for work, and a search of their abandoned vehicle revealed that the burst transmitter had not even been removed from its hiding place in a wheel well. All the evidence pointed to a panicked exit.

Klop, however, went about business as usual. He had made rowdy love to his girlfriend the night before, and spent the morning reading galleys. He left at lunchtime to buy newspapers and eat at a local restaurant. He then returned to his flat and appeared to take a nap – if he was perturbed about the sudden departure of his runners or his own imminent arrest, he showed no sign of it. Given Klop's level of expertise, of course, this might mean nothing. The Jonquil team had already resolved that if he hopped a taxi to Heathrow that afternoon, they would have to stand by and let him leave.

For Smailes it was a hellish day. He sat in his shirt-sleeves and baked, and as the hours crawled by he could focus on nothing but the periodic updates on Mikhail Gontar's movements. He was in impotent agony as Gontar took his lunchtime stroll, but felt scarcely reassured when he returned home without incident. The swirling preparations for the Paddington arrests largely bypassed him; Judith was working directly for Kinney and he hardly saw her. At four the Jonquil team was reconvened for a final review of logistics. Warrants had been prepared, and Special Branch and local police units selected and briefed. The physical lay-out at Paddington station was studied on a marker board, and individual roles rehearsed. Then there was nothing to do but wait.

Neither Smailes nor Judith felt like going home. As had become their practice, they decided to visit Archie Keith's listening post to check on Klop as he prepared to receive his nightly transmission from Moscow. If he was going to get a message to abandon ship, they wanted to be there to witness it.

Smailes also had a further motive for taking the short trip over to Bayswater. The heat was causing Clea great discomfort and she now insisted her husband sleep on a mattress in the partially decorated nursery, since nights had become a misery for her. He knew she was angry at his increasing absences, but she seemed equally resentful if he was there. The simple fact was she was suffering physically and he wasn't and since he could do nothing to alleviate her situation he contrived to avoid it. In the taxi Judith hinted darkly that she too was having problems at home, that she'd come to view her work as a refuge. Smailes did not inquire further.

Smailes and Judith found Brian Kinney already ensconced in Archie's kitchen command post. The three of them listened closely as one of Keith's underlings reviewed Klop's routines for them. Muffled sounds came over the relay from the hot phone on Klop's desk – this was Chummy doing his dishes; this was Chummy using the bathroom; now Chummy was watching the news on the telly. Long pause. This was probably Chummy breaking out the short-wave. Needles flickered in confirmation as Smailes visualized Klop seated on his sofa, tuning his dial. Within minutes, the four Britons heard the chirping of Morse. The S Branch man shrugged – who knew what it meant? He pointed out the call letters, a four-character burst *en clair*. It was a long message – almost twenty minutes – but eventually the machine was shut down and there was silence as Klop stowed his equipment and, presumably, began deciphering. The minutes ticked away, and Smailes and Kinney exchanged an anxious look. If Klop was going to bolt, it would be now. Finally, the recording equipment clicked on as Klop picked up his telephone and called his girlfriend in Fulham. He confirmed she was coming over, then told her in some detail what he planned to do to her in bed. Smailes sighed gratefully, knowing these were not the preoccupations of a man on the brink of flight. He smirked at Kinney, then across at Judith, not noticing she had flushed scarlet. He stood and threw his jacket over a shoulder.

'Time to get going,' he said. 'Busy day tomorrow.'

He arrived home after Clea was already asleep. She awoke as he was undressing, and he told her he had to work again all the following day. She sighed and turned over beneath her single sheet.

Paddington station was ideally suited for a stake-out. A small access road descended from Bishop's Bridge Road above the tracks on to the concourse itself, where taxis disgorged their passengers and station brass parked their cars. Smailes sipped his tea and looked out of the buffet window at his Rover and a carload of Special Branch officers parked nearby. He wished he'd been more involved in the planning – he thought the Special Branch car stuck out like a sore thumb. Worse still were the conspicuous figures of Roger Standiforth and Brian Kinney studying the departures board. It was another scorching day and Roger's idea of Saturday disguise was a lightweight blue suit. He was also chain-smoking. Brian at least wore a polo shirt and casual trousers, and looked something like a weekend traveller.

Judith sat opposite him studying a paperback. She was wearing a cream-coloured blouse and Levi's; he had chosen a safari shirt, khaki trousers and trainers. A couple of empty suitcases at their feet completed the picture of a young couple off on their holidays. A heavy-set Special Branch inspector sat just inside the door, munching on a doughnut. The tiny receiver in his ear looked gigantic. Smailes felt his stomach churn. Gontar had spent another night with his girlfriend, who had eventually left around eleven that morning. He had stayed in his flat ever since, listening to music. The MI5 team and their support units had been in place by three. Soon after, word came from Reading that Docherty had boarded his train as usual, and everyone had taken up position. It had already been decided not to tail Gontar – he would either show, or he wouldn't. Smailes guessed that if he knew he was blown, he would leave for this meeting as usual, then keep on going to catch a plane to safety, just to rub their noses in it. Docherty would be arrested, but the big prize would have flown. That was how Smailes would have done it if the tables had been turned.

Suddenly, Docherty appeared. Smailes had never seen him in the flesh, and he looked more frail and downtrodden than he expected. He wore a limp, open-necked shirt and held a green carrier-bag. He looked around nervously, as if ready to bolt. Judith had her back to the door and Smailes pressed his foot on hers. She glanced at him above her paperback, then resumed her pretence of reading. Docherty joined a line of customers at the counter.

Smailes took another sip of tea, which he had difficulty swallowing as Docherty took the vacant table directly opposite them. He cleared his throat awkwardly and saw the knuckles of Judith's hands whiten as she clenched her book. Smailes's heart was thumping. He was afraid Docherty would hear it. Docherty sat silently, staring ahead directly at the inspector with the ear-piece, or so it seemed to Smailes.

Gontar was there! Smailes didn't dare look at Judith, and instead examined his watch theatrically, then craned his neck to inspect the departures board. Gontar, his hair neatly parted and his girth cinched into a pair of burgundy trousers, sat down opposite Docherty, barely three feet away. There was no difficulty overhearing them.

Gontar greeted Docherty by name, but did not shake his hand. That came later, of course, when he passed him the locker key. Gontar was explaining they could not meet again this month – he was going abroad on business. The next meeting would be six weeks, maybe longer. He would get word to him. Of course, Smailes reasoned. Last night's long message had instructed Gontar to bail out, but not immediately. Docherty was too important a spy just to drop, so Gontar had been told to prepare him for a switch in controllers. Smailes's head throbbed; he wished he were invisible. Docherty said something, but he didn't catch it.

The plan called for Smailes to alert the Special Branch point man as soon as anything changed hands. The inspector would then whisper orders to the back-up unit in the car, which would enter and perform the arrests. Smailes and Judith would wait just long enough to confirm success, then signal Roger and Brian, who would in turn alert the police units in Reading and Whitechapel. Then Smailes and Judith would proceed to Gontar's apartment and complete their search. The flat would already have been secured by another Special Branch team waving a search warrant at Mr Costa.

Suddenly, Docherty hoisted his plastic bag on to the table. Gontar took it and Smailes got to his feet. He gripped his empty suitcase and told Judith with his eyes she should do likewise. This was not the plan, but he was reacting instinctively. He gave the inspector a conspicuous nod, who whispered quickly into his lapel. Smailes and Judith walked to the door, where they waited for what seemed an eternity; nothing happened. Gontar and Docherty were both on their feet, shaking hands. Smailes was in anguish. What the hell had gone wrong? All at once there was pandemonium. Two plain-clothes detectives burst in and rushed the two men. Another pair came in behind, shouting and drawing weapons. Smailes heard a scream, the crash of falling crockery, then the lead detective clearly announce their arrest for offences under the Official Secrets Act. The first detective grabbed the plastic bag from Gontar's hand. The second produced handcuffs and was fastening them to Docherty's wrists as he recited his rights. Neither man offered any resistance. Docherty looked stricken, crushed, but Gontar stood expressionless as the detective moved to shackle him. The back-up men stowed their pistols and hurried forward. The inspector was jabbering into his lapel. Smailes stepped out of the door, dropped to a crouch and threw Brian and Roger a thumbs-up. Then he and Judith were running towards their car.

*

Outside Craven Hill Dry Cleaners a baffled Mr Costa stood in the midst of a gaggle of what Smailes assumed were his patrons, next to a uniformed officer standing guard at the door to the upstairs flats. Smailes had parked the car with some care, knowing they might be there for hours, and he and Judith quickened their pace as they approached. Suddenly they were surrounded by a yelling mob. Camera shutters crashed around them, and Smailes realized with horror he was confronted by the press. He heard a shouted question and barked 'No comment' as he fished for his warrant card. He pushed through the throng and past the police sentry, pulling Judith's arm behind him.

'How on earth did *they* get there?' she asked angrily, slamming the door behind them.

'I'm not sure,' said Smailes, furious. 'But I've got a bloody good idea.'

Smailes's suspicions were confirmed upstairs, where they discovered Detective Chief Inspector Bill Moody holding court in Klop's apartment. A couple of minions were stuffing plastic evidence bags with the contents of his false-bottomed coffee-table. Moody stood over them, wielding a clipboard. Smailes lost his temper.

'What the hell's going on, Moody?' he demanded.

'Good afternoon, Derek. Collecting evidence, that's what's going on.'

'Who invited the press?'

'Don't ask me,' he said, turning away.

Smailes almost grabbed him by the collar. He could not believe Roger had not expressly overruled any participation by Moody, whose grandstanding was notorious at MI5. In particular, the Special Branch inspector had a long history of provoking K Branch by poaching on its preserve, preferably with a bevy of reporters on hand. Moody, with his idiotic pencil moustache and oiled hair, looked like a garage owner from Essex. Smailes regained his control.

'Bill, your instructions were to secure the premises until our arrival. Period.'

'Don't take orders from MI5, Derek – take them from the Police Commissioner. Got a search warrant here, and I intend to carry it out.'

'Give me those evidence bags and get out,' Smailes snarled.

'Sorry, mate. This is a criminal matter now. Out of your hands.'

With great difficulty Smailes asked Moody whether he would step into the bedroom.

Once inside, Smailes closed the door quietly, then manoeuvred Moody up against the louvred door of Gontar's wardrobe. He stood very close to his face.

'Listen to me, you stupid, greasy spiv. This is our biggest counter-espionage case in thirty years, and the agreement is we assemble and review the evidence, then turn it over to you. If you think I'm going to let you abscond with it, you're out of your tiny mind. Either you leave now and take your media circus with you, or I'll make it my personal mission to ensure you spend the rest of your career writing parking tickets. Leave me the evidence bags, the inventory forms and the warrant. Leave me the copper on the door. Then get out. The only criminal matter here is what I'll do to you if you resist.'

Moody was a big man, but he could see Smailes was in deadly earnest. He sucked his teeth for a moment, then retreated back into the living room. Casually, he told his men to pack up. Then he made a production of checking the evidence against the inventory and having Smailes sign for it. He looked around one last time, careful to save face with his subordinates, then sauntered out of the door. Judith's eyes were round with amusement.

'What on *earth* did you say to him?' she asked as the door closed.

'Oh, I appealed to his sense of reason,' said Smailes with a grin. 'Get your gloves on and let's check what they found.'

The contents of Gontar's cache were unchanged from their earlier visit. Smailes inspected the computer diskettes and the Burghfield site plan – he did not doubt Docherty's fingerprints were all over them. The espionage gear was also the same – easily enough to discredit any claim that Gontar was really a humble literary agent. Smailes and Judith lined the plastic bags up carefully, then resumed their search for Gontar's radio.

After almost an hour they were interrupted by a quiet tap on the door, and Smailes admitted the agitated figure of Brian Kinney. Kinney, usually the most phlegmatic of individuals, could not contain his excitement. Docherty and Gontar had been booked on a variety of charges at Paddington Green police station and would appear before the high-security magistrates' court at Arbour Square on Monday morning. There was not a snowball's chance in hell they would get bail. Gontar, predictably, was refusing representation and insisting on his fictitious identity and profession. Docherty had asked for a solicitor, but seemed a broken man; Kinney did not doubt he would sing like a canary at the first opportunity. The material seized in that day's hand-over wasn't great – a classified update on the PAL refit – but together with what they found in both homes it was enough to put them away for years. The only hitch in an otherwise flawless operation was that the story had leaked and the Home Secretary was annoyed at having his weekend disrupted by the press.

Smailes told him of Moody's presence at the flat and the likely source of the leak. He asked whether the media had cleared off and Kinney confirmed they had, apart from a couple of photographers. 'So what've you got?' he asked eagerly.

Smailes sat down and went over the inventory. 'You want to take this stuff away with you, Brian? We're still looking for the radio.'

'No,' said Kinney. 'I'm going home – I need a drink. Look, take a break, you two. It's been an awfully long week. We can secure this place and resume on Monday.'

Smailes looked across at Judith, guessing she shared his sense of incompleteness. 'Well, maybe I'll give it another hour, then knock off. Judith?'

'Fine,' she said. 'I'm not tired yet.'

'Suit yourselves,' said Kinney. 'And listen – well done. Both of you.'

As Kinney left, Smailes realized he was starving – he hadn't eaten all day. He ran his hand through his hair. 'Judith – you want to get something to eat?'

She laughed. 'I'm famished.'

'Chinese?'

'Terrific,' she said.

Smailes found Gontar's telephone directory and a restaurant nearby that would deliver. Judith made tea, and Smailes went downstairs at the sound of the doorbell. They ate directly from the cartons with plastic forks at Gontar's kitchen table. The light was beginning to fail. Smailes thought about calling home but let it pass.

'Ready?' he asked, wiping his mouth.

'Whenever you are,' she said.

They resumed in the bedroom. Smailes avoided Judith's eye as they stripped Gontar's bed. He noticed as she leant forward that she wore a blue cotton brassière beneath her blouse. She worked quickly and silently, the model of professionalism.

Smailes gutted the box spring with a kitchen knife, but they found nothing. Then he noticed dark smudges on the window sill. He opened the window and craned out.

'It's a flat-roofed building,' he said. 'It's getting dark. I'd better take a look.'

'Derek, be careful.'

'There's a drain-pipe right here,' he said. 'I think it's been used before.'

Smailes swung his bulk out of the window. Five minutes later he was back.

'Nothing,' he said. 'Damn it – I thought we'd found it.' He sat down on the wreckage of Gontar's bed. 'Come on, let's think this through. This isn't a big flat. If you were going to hide a short-wave radio somewhere, where would it be?'

'How big is it exactly?'

'Probably the size of a large shoe-box.'

Judith thought. 'Somewhere where there was an existing cavity.'

'The floor joists. We've tried them all.'

'Under a sink?'

'No – too obvious.'

'I mean where the pipes come in. Under the floor or in the wall.'

Smailes was on his feet immediately. The bathroom sink unit seemed undisturbed, but under the kitchen sink they found a movable panel of linoleum, and beneath that a section of flooring fitted with a brass ring-pull. Smailes tugged at it and it came up easily in his hand. Inside the cache were two rubber pouches, one large and one small. Smailes carried them both across to the couch. The radio was West German, a Braun, in excellent condition. Inside the smaller pouch were five miniature one-time pads, one of which was partially used. Smailes grinned hugely.

'Let's pack up,' he said. 'It's time to get going.'

It was almost ten by the time Smailes and Judith finally descended the staircase with their evidence. Derek carried the radio, Judith the rest. To their relief, there was no welcoming party in the street. Smailes told the uniformed officer that the flat was empty and secure. As they walked off down the street his radio squawked as he confirmed their departure with base.

Smailes had parked their car around the corner. He felt euphoric, the radio weightless in his arms. He set it on top of the car and unlocked the boot. Judith did not look at him.

He opened her door, then moved around to the driver's side and climbed in. She was waiting for him in the darkness as he reached for the ignition. He looked across at her.

Light from a street lamp cast shadows across her face and throat. She reached out and touched his arm and said something that he didn't hear. He hesitated a split second, then reached across and kissed her on the mouth. She drew away.

'Listen, Judith, I'm sorry,' he stammered, but she was suddenly back in his arms, and he realized she'd reached away only to unclasp her seat belt. She kissed him fiercely, her hands in his hair. Effortlessly, his hand found the soft fabric inside her blouse. He felt a small, round breast, the nipple firm to his touch.

'Judith,' he said through her kiss, 'this is professional suicide.'

'No, it's not,' she said, gulping for air. 'You'll be going back to K9 soon. We won't even work on the same floor.'

'You've already thought of this?' he asked, breaking away from her in the darkness.

'I've thought of nothing else for weeks. I wanted you to throw me down on that bed up there and make love to me. I couldn't look at you.'

'I noticed.'

'God, Derek,' she said, returning into his arms. 'Oh God.'

Their passion quickly escalated, her slim hand exploring him. He unbuttoned her blouse and pushed it away from her shoulders.

'Drive somewhere,' she urged. 'Find an alley, a car park. The seats recline.'

Smailes swallowed hard and started the car. Judith was clamped to his side, kissing his neck. In their absorption neither noticed a car parked down the block on the opposite side of the street, an infra-red telephoto camera mounted on its dashboard, its motor drive whining.

As he drove, Smailes's thoughts turned helplessly to his wife and child, both asleep at the moment in Surrey. It was one thing to have sexual fantasies about a co-worker, he told himself. It was quite another to consummate them. His face burned.

'In there,' Judith pointed. There was an alley next to a laundromat, leading to a small car park at the back entrance to some flats. Smailes parked and killed the engine. She began kissing him again, but knew immediately he'd changed his mind. She broke away.

'What's wrong?' she asked.

'I can't, Judith. I'm married.'

'So am I.'

'My wife's six months pregnant. If she finds out, my marriage may be over.'

'How will she find out?'

'She'll know. I'll either be so guilty I'll end up telling her, or she'll guess. She might want to forgive me and not be able to. You see, I tried it once before, Judith, and I ended up divorced.'

'Tried what?'

'Adultery.'

'That's such an old-fashioned word.'

'It's an old-fashioned practice.' He paused. 'You don't have any . . . any qualms?'

She frowned. 'David and I are going to separate, Derek. He's completely threatened by what I do, and I refuse to give up my career to pacify him. There's no other solution. It'll cause a big upheaval, but I'm going to leave him.'

'I'm sorry to hear that, Judith.'

'I suppose you're not quite at the same place,' she said quietly.

'No. Candidly, my domestic life has been hell too. We don't have sex and we can't communicate. Clea didn't want another baby yet, and, of course, I'm the villain. You're very . . . I'm very attracted to you, Judith. Obviously. But I know in my gut I have to stick with my situation. Things will turn around.'

'God, I wish I'd found someone like you,' Judith said bitterly. 'Life isn't fair.' She looked down and began fastening the buttons on her blouse. She moved across and pecked him on the cheek. 'Sorry. I got carried away. Let's go back to the office.'

Smailes backed out of the alley, his emotions in turmoil.

Nothing was spoken on the short drive to Curzon House. 'What are you going to do?' she asked as he parked.

'Oh, call Roger and Brian, I suppose. Book the stuff into my safe until Monday.'

'I mean about me. Are you going to recommend I be fired?'

Smailes was horrified. 'Good God, Judith – no. You're going to make it to the top. I'm as much to blame for what happened tonight. More. It was a mistake, that's all. Let's just put it behind us.'

Judith sighed. 'All right,' she said, her voice echoing his lack of conviction.

'You want to wait and get a ride home?' he offered.

'No. I'll walk down to Piccadilly and get a taxi.'

She leaned across and touched his arm. 'Good-night,' she said.

It was a warm night. Smailes watched her as she walked away, hugging herself with her long arms, her cardigan draped over her shoulders.

16

Iain Mack chewed a finger-nail irritably. His Georgian contact had failed to show up at all on Sunday, and only a desperate plea from Stas Simonov had persuaded Iain to delay his departure another day to try for one last meeting. Putiashvilli had been worried about visiting the hotel again, Simonov claimed. But he would consent to meet Mack outdoors, at one o'clock on Monday at the Leninsky Prospekt metro station, and would bring the proof the BBC was demanding. Realistically, Mack knew he had no alternative. His editor would never agree to put Putiashvilli on camera without evidence to back up his claims, and without Putiashvilli the programme wasn't nearly so strong. And after all, Mack was quite used to meeting Russians in neutral, outdoor locations – old habits died hard. So he and Nina had rearranged their flight for Tuesday afternoon, and Mack had taken a taxi from the hotel to the metro station at twelve thirty on Monday.

But now the little Georgian gangster was late again, and Mack was wondering whether he was getting the run-around. He had considered bringing Blair Harrison along, but knew Harrison was equivocal about continuing to work on a programme without an on-air credit. Then he and Nina had quarrelled over breakfast and she'd made it quite clear she'd seen enough Georgian mafiosi for one trip. So he had come alone. It was hard to pull rank on someone you were screwing, he reflected.

Suddenly Putiashvilli was there, tugging at his elbow. He had not emerged from the doors of the metro station, as Mack had expected, but from behind him. 'Let us walk,' he said gruffly. Lev was wearing his same baggy suit, although it was a hot August day, and carrying a shoulder bag. He pointed to the promenade along the muddy Moskva river.

They walked towards the Lenin Hills. People were swimming beneath the two-tier metro bridge, although Mack knew it was prohibited. An uninterested militia man watched them from the bank. 'What have you brought?' asked Mack.

Putiashvilli pointed up the slope to a small, clapboard A-frame. 'Up there,' he replied.

The two men climbed to the shelter and sat down on its bench. Putiashvilli went into his shoulder bag and produced a fat envelope, clumsily stapled and taped at both ends. He handed it to Mack.

'Here is proof. Details of top secret projects. Who sells them, who buys them. Dates. Photographs.'

Mack started to tug at the tape.

'No!' Putiashvilli warned, catching his hand. 'Wait until you go to your hotel. You do not see the policeman by the river?'

'He wasn't interested in us, Lev,' said Mack.

'You hope,' said Putiashvilli. 'When you leave?'

'Tomorrow. I'll be in touch, through Stas, about the exact taping schedule. Hopefully before the end of the month.'

'Yes. I go now.'

'You're walking back to Leninsky Prospekt?'

'No. To the Sportivnaya station. The other bridge,' said Putiashvilli, pointing down the river.

'All right, Lev. See you again. Soon.'

'Goodbye, friend.'

Mack watched for a few moments as the lone figure of Putiashvilli disappeared over the crest of the hill down towards the embankment. He considered breaking the seals on his package, but thought better of it. He decided to retrace his steps.

Mack emerged from the shelter and walked slowly back down the pocked roadway. An unmarked white van was making laborious progress towards him up the hill. Mack watched it with interest – this was not a public road. When the van was about fifteen yards away it stopped, and a man jumped out holding a video camera. A foreign crew? Mack wondered briefly. No – it wasn't professional gear. The side door of the van slid open and two men in plain clothes strode towards him. Then everything seemed to happen in slow motion. The first man, who had jet-black hair and whose face was contorted with tension, approached him and grabbed the package from his hand. The second walked behind him and forced his wrists together. Mack felt handcuffs. The third man was now only a few feet away, filming with his video camera. Mack did not resist; no word had been spoken. He looked away in the direction Putiashvilli had taken, his heart pounding. The second man pushed him towards the white van, which had drawn level with them. Only as he was bundled into the back seat did Mack fully understand what was happening. He had just been arrested by the Moscow security police, the domestic successor of the KGB.

Smailes leant forward across the bathroom sink, shaving. Lucy stood at his elbow on her plastic stool, smearing cream on her face.

'Daddy razor,' she said, pointing.

'You can't have Daddy's razor, darling. Sharp,' he replied.

Clea appeared at the door in her dressing gown, the Sunday paper in her hand.

'Derek – is this you?' she asked.

Smailes put down his razor and took the paper from her. The lead story was headlined 'Suspected Nuclear Spies Arrested' and was accompanied by a confusing photograph taken outside Costa's shop. Smailes was ducking his head, but it was recognizably him, tugging someone's sleeve off camera. The caption read, 'Detectives arrive to search the Bayswater premises of one of the spy suspects arrested yesterday.'

Smailes tucked the newspaper under his elbow and rinsed his face.

'That's me all right,' he said.

Clea lifted a coffee mug to her lips, impressed.

'So that's why you haven't been home in weeks. I see.'

'Lucy see,' said Lucy.

Smailes led his family into the bedroom and sat down to study the newspaper. The story must have broken just before the deadline for the late editions. It didn't say much, given British *sub judice* restrictions, but it revealed the identities of both suspects before they had even been arraigned. That bugger Moody, Smailes said to himself.

Lucy made a grab for the paper. 'Daddy?' she asked.

'There,' said Smailes, pointing out his picture.

'Daddy,' said Lucy triumphantly, marching off down the hall, leaves of newspaper trailing behind her.

'What's wrong with you?' asked Clea. 'You don't seem very excited.'

Smailes was buttoning his shirt. 'Well, it's all a bit of an anticlimax, really. The case will go upstairs now, then the Crown Prosecution Service takes over.' He managed a weak smile. 'Fun while it lasted, though.'

'Was it dangerous?'

'Not really.'

'So will you be home a bit more now?'

'I suppose so.'

'Rudy called yesterday.'

'They're back from Ireland?'

'They go home to America in a few days. He wants to invite us to dinner up in town.'

'When?'

'Monday or Tuesday?'

'Great. How are *you* feeling?' he asked.

'Hot,' said Clea, turning in pursuit of Lucy.

Iain Mack's panic had subsided slightly. Wedged between two policemen in the van's back seat, he watched as the driver drove past the government mansions on Sparrow Boulevard, down the hill and into the tunnel next to the giant titanium statue of Gagarin. The front passenger leaned over his seat, filming with his video camera. It was all a set-up, obviously. Putiashvilli was a stooge, sent to lure him into a trap. But it was also a big mistake, about to backfire on the Russians in a big way. Legitimate BBC journalists did not get arrested by security forces, in any country, for any reason. A call to Blair Harrison, a call to the British ambassador, and he would be released immediately with proper apologies. But then Iain reflected upon the supposed nature of the material he'd received, and his mouth went dry. There could be some pretty big fish with strong motives to suppress whatever the BBC was attempting to broadcast. This could get sticky, he realized.

He decided to remain silent. The van emerged on to the southern section of the Garden Ring, but then he had no idea where it went. Eventually, it pulled up at a gateway marked with a red-and-white No Entry sign, which opened to allow them to pass through into a cobbled yard. Mack was bundled out against a wall where he was photographed repeatedly with Putiashvilli's package stuffed into his handcuffed hands. Now he was genuinely frightened. When he was spun around for the last time, Mack demanded of the team leader, 'Where am I?'

'Lefortovo,' the man repeated coldly.

Mack's bowels froze. Every foreign correspondent in Moscow knew the name of Lefortovo prison, the notorious Tsarist fortress where the Russian state had imprisoned its opponents since the days of Catherine the Great.

Without ceremony he was frog-marched through a door, up two flights of stairs and down a corridor smelling of floor polish and disinfectant. The party wheeled left then stopped outside Door 200. Mack was ushered into a spartan office from which a window gave on to the inner courtyard. There were two desks, several telephones, and a clock on the wall, but that was all. The clock read one forty.

A squat, expensively dressed figure turned to face him. He was about sixty, with iron-grey hair combed straight back from a low forehead. A younger assistant with hollow cheeks and a receding hairline came towards him and barked something at Mack's escorts. He felt his wrists being unshackled and involuntarily drew them to his chest and began rubbing. The assistant held out Putiashvilli's package to the senior man as he stepped forward. The two policemen took up sentry positions by the door.

'Good afternoon, Mr Mack,' said the older man in passable English. 'You have been arrested on suspicion of espionage against the state of Russia. I am Gasparov. Colonel Nikolai Gasparov, internal security. I have ordered your arrest. And of your accomplice, Putiashvilli.' The photographer stepped forward and resumed shooting with a still camera. Mack said nothing.

Gasparov had taken the package from his assistant and tore open the staples. He tipped the contents on to a desk. 'What have we here?' he asked theatrically. 'Well, let me see. Blueprints for the propulsion system of the Energiya rocket. Diagrams of the Topaz-2 space reactor. A site plan of the Plesetsk missile centre. Very interesting.' Classically, Gasparov made no attempt to inspect the material or to disguise his prior knowledge of its contents. 'Stand here, please.'

He positioned Mack next to the desk and its pile of classified documents. The photographer backed away, his camera shutter clicking. Mack held his fingers at his crotch in an inverted V-sign, a gesture instantly recognizable by any Briton that the scene was fake. He had regained some composure, having forced himself to remember the British embassy's security briefings.

'Colonel Gasparov,' he said in a firm voice. 'I demand my right under Russian law to call my ambassador.'

'Certainly, certainly,' said Gasparov expansively, waving at the photographer to leave. 'In time. In time. First, I must ask you some questions. Please sit down.'

*

There was a festive air about the fourth floor of Curzon House on Monday morning, but Smailes did not share the mood. He was still preoccupied by his weekend encounter with Judith and could not distinguish which feeling was stronger – remorse at the lapse in professionalism represented by his making a pass at a co-worker, or guilt at the implicit betrayal of his wife. That he had pulled back at the last moment did not really exculpate him, he knew, and he doubted the incident could be dismissed quite as airily as he had suggested. He was acutely aware he was going to have to continue sharing his office with an assistant with whom he was painfully infatuated. He could request her transfer, but knew it would look odd. Jonquil was almost wrapped up, and Judith would soon be transferred to other duties. He arrived early and to his immense relief she was not yet there.

Smailes was not surprised to find a note from Glenys Powner, Roger's secretary, instructing him to report to Alex Corcoran's office on arrival. But he was a little more taken aback by what he discovered in his safe. It had long been his practice to 'spot' its contents between hairline pencil marks, so he would know whether anything had been disturbed. It was a tip from Kinney when he first joined K Branch – since the only officers with the combination to a given safe were the division head and the DG himself, 'spotting' allowed you to know when Big Brother was looking over your shoulder. To Smailes's knowledge, his secure files had been disturbed only twice, most recently after he had made an unorthodox recommendation on a K9 case. Both times, Smailes was sure, the culprit was Standiforth, trying to second-guess him. Smailes, of course, had never mentioned either incident.

On Saturday night he had carefully checked all Klop's material into his safe after verifying it against the inventory form. For space reasons he had discarded the plastic evidence bags, positioning the computer diskettes on top of the inventory sheet and tracing faint pencil marks around them before locking up. The radio, too large for his safe, had been booked in with the duty office. Now, on Monday, Smailes saw that the computer diskettes were still in position, but nowhere near their original marks. Which meant they had been removed, examined and replaced – by Roger Standiforth again, without doubt. Probably copied, too, Smailes reflected as he left for the seventh floor.

The Monday morning papers were spread out across Corcoran's conference table, each one leading with the story of the Docherty and Klop arrests. Clearly, Roger had been playing his Fleet Street orchestra, and favoured journalists had been rewarded with rich lodes of inside information. The *Daily Telegraph*, for instance, had a linked front-page story on the disappearance of the Basamalah brothers and the Special Branch raid on their shop in Whitechapel, and even an exclusive that the 'real' Jurgen Klop had died in Amsterdam almost eight years earlier. The tabloids attacked the story with customary gusto, dubbing Docherty and Klop 'Top Nuke Spies' and extolling the intrepid British spy-catchers. One or two of the heavies ran accompanying pieces on the recent history of British counter-espionage and concurred that, if convicted, Docherty and Klop would represent the biggest scalps on MI5's belt since Geoffrey Prime and Gordon Lonsdale, respectively. Most stories credited unnamed 'senior Whitehall officials' as their source. Smailes could not help remembering his friend Iain's complaint about the one-way nature of the Official Secrets Act – had anyone but a top government official leaked such information, they would probably be facing prosecution.

The mood in the conference room was contented rather than euphoric. The DG dropped in to offer his congratulations and to ask for an update. He was told that the flat above the Whitechapel grocery shop had yielded a second transmitter, along with some one-time cipher pads and secret writing chemicals. Docherty's potting shed had disgorged its grubby trove of banknotes, nuclear secrets and kiddie porn. Smailes confirmed the discovery of Klop's radio. 'Looks like we have them stone-cold dead all right,' said Sir David pleasantly, and left his minions to their conjuring of Docherty and Klop's doom.

Kinney confirmed that Klop had been charged under his assumed name and was still refusing legal representation. They would hold back their knowledge of his true identity until interrogation began in earnest. Docherty, unfortunately, had retained Jeremy Parsons, a left-wing solicitor who had successfully defended a recent Secrets Act case. Kinney had visited Docherty in his Paddington Green cell the previous day, however, and was convinced they might still get a confession and a guilty plea out of him. Kinney and Corcoran, along with Ed Poynter, were preparing the brief for the Director of Public Prosecutions – rumour was the Attorney-General would try the case herself. Nothing had been handed over to Special Branch yet – MI5 had a strong interest in proving to Crown prosecutors that they were at least as adept at preparing such a case as the police. If recent precedent held, both Docherty and Klop were looking at twenty years in jail, minimum.

Corcoran's phone rang and he held it out to Smailes, who edged his way behind the wheelchair and took the receiver. It was Judith, telling him in her most businesslike manner that S Branch was planning a follow-up sweep of Klop's Bayswater flat and wanted someone from the Jonquil team along. Smailes hastily agreed she should go, and resumed his seat. He looked across at the impassive face of Standiforth, who lit another cigarette and regarded him pleasantly.

'By the way, I think special congratulations should go to Derek and his able assistant,' he said. 'They've done a splendid job. Was that her, Derek? Is she joining us?' he asked mildly.

'Yes,' he said. 'I mean, no. I'm sending her along with Archie's team for the sweep of Klop's flat.' He felt his face glow involuntarily and looked away. The telephone rang again, this time for Kinney.

Brian Kinney exchanged staccato questions, then cupped the receiver. 'It's that arsehole Caldicott,' he said. 'Apparently, the Russian embassy has called, demanding that Lubyanov's wife be allowed to speak to him from Moscow. Caldicott is insisting we comply for "humanitarian reasons".'

'Who?' asked Standiforth, momentarily nonplussed. 'Oh right, Lubyanov.' He wheeled on Smailes. 'Hasn't he gone up to Bovingdon yet?'

'No, we promised him a night with his girlfriend, remember? That was last night. He's due to go up this afternoon, isn't he, Brian?'

'Yes,' said Kinney impatiently, still cupping the receiver. 'So what do I tell Caldicott?'

Standiforth looked across at the hunched figure of Corcoran, who shrugged. 'All right,' said Standiforth irritably. 'One bloody call, that's it. And make sure it's taped.'

Kinney gave the confirmation over the phone and hung up.

'Was his bedroom bugged last night?'

'Of course,' said Kinney testily.

Iain Mack lay on a cot in his small, foul-smelling cell, his stomach churning. He looked around for the source of the stench, and saw an iron toilet cone with an ill-fitting wooden lid which rose directly from a sewer pipe at the end of the cell. Towards the top of the wall was a small, smeared window partially open to the grille outside. He fought to discipline his thoughts. Harrison had been confident, encouraging, but Iain had never felt so alone in his life.

Gasparov had subjected him to four hours of mocking, repetitious interrogation before finally allowing him his call. Iain had stuck doggedly to his story, insisting he was working on a television documentary on organized crime, that Putiashvilli was a contact he had met through Simonov only the previous week. Gasparov played the slow-witted policeman with exasperating skill, insisting Mack go over details again and again until he inevitably made mistakes. There were also glimpses of an ominously thorough file on Iain's prior activities in the Soviet Union. Gasparov, for instance, asked whether Putiashvilli had been a source for his documentary on the military withdrawal from Afghanistan, and Mack had said wearily no, he'd explained he'd met the Georgian for the first time the previous week. For Mack's part, it was impossible to penetrate Gasparov's pretence that Putiashvilli was his 'accomplice' and not working directly for the security police. What was more painful, as Mack now lay sweating on his cot, was the likelihood that his trusted friend Simonov had also been instrumental in the set-up. He remembered Stas's spacious new apartment, his warning that all Russians were corrupt, and winced.

It had been after five when Gasparov finally indicated the telephone, and Iain decided against phoning McAndrew, the security man at the British embassy. The likelihood was McAndrew would have left for the day, and Mack would be stuck trying to explain his predicament to some duty officer. Instead, he had called the BBC's Moscow bureau, and to his relief Blair Harrison had answered the phone himself. Harrison was immediately reassuring, saying Interfax had put out a wire that afternoon about the arrest of a Western journalist, and when Mack had failed to return from his appointment, he and Nina had been afraid it was him – they had already warned London. Harrison confided he had feared the security forces might try something like this if they learned of Putiashvilli's collaboration. Then he dropped his bombshell. Talking with head office, Harrison had learned that the big story in Britain was the weekend arrest of two nuclear spies, one of whom was a likely Russian national. There was the distinct possibility that Mack had been grabbed in retaliation as a bargaining-chip. He told Mack to sit tight. He would get word to the British ambassador and the BBC brass. With the time difference, he would also be able to file a story that would make the lead on the evening news that night. The story would make international headlines, and the Russian government would stand condemned in the eyes of the world. Neither the BBC nor the Foreign Office would tolerate his continued incarceration. He would be released the next day, if not that night.

Mack wished he shared his confidence. His thoughts were interrupted by a banging on the food hatch. He peered out to see a stained white coat stretched over an ample bosom. An incomprehensible voice barked a command in Russian, and he reached out to accept an aluminium bowl of buckwheat and cabbage gruel. An assistant reached in with a dented tin mug and a pot of tea, then the hatch banged shut. Iain set the food on the floor. It smelled awful.

He closed his eyes and thought bitterly of his phone call and of the voice of his lover, Nina Gregory. Just a minute, Harrison had said – Nina wants a word. Predictably, Nina had been hysterical, her thoughts only for herself. Should she go back to the hotel? Were the police going to arrest her too? Had Iain said anything about her involvement? Angrily, he told her to follow Harrison's advice and demanded that Blair be put back on the line. So much for true love, he thought to himself sourly, pouring tea.

To his dismay, Iain's voice had cracked when Harrison came back on the line. 'Blair, I'm not a bloody spy,' he almost sobbed.

'Iain, everyone knows that,' said Harrison.

'But I want out of here. If they want to swap me for a real spy, I don't care. Understand?'

'I understand, Iain. Don't worry – we'll get you out.'

Then, as an afterthought, Iain said, 'Get word to Derek Smailes. He's my best friend – he works for the Security Service in London. Tell him I need his help.'

'All right,' said Harrison. Gasparov looked at him knowingly, but Mack ignored him.

'Anything more you want to say to Nina?'

'No,' said Mack.

'Sit tight,' said Harrison. 'You're not alone.'

Easy for you to say, thought Mack. He bent to sip his tea and the tin cup scalded his lip.

Derek Smailes returned from lunch to discover Judith Hyams seated at her desk. He closed the door and launched into a prepared speech about his regret for his behaviour on Saturday night, how he was determined not to let it prejudice an excellent working relationship. But he still could not look at her. From the corner of his eye he saw she was wearing an oatmeal linen suit and a fawn blouse. She was also waving a slip of paper at him.

'Derek, you've got to phone a woman at the BBC right away. I just took her call . . .'

'Don't be daft, Judith. I can't field inquiries about the Docherty arrest,' he said, finally looking at her directly. She seemed agitated.

'It's not that. She works on *Focus* with your friend Iain. She says they heard he's just been arrested in Moscow. They're accusing him of espionage.'

Smailes grabbed the paper and strode urgently to his desk.

Tim Crabbe looked out across Poole Harbour towards the Isle of Purbeck, scanning the second-largest harbour in the world after Sydney, Australia. He could see the hills above Swanage against the horizon, and the anchorage of six camouflaged landing-craft amid a flock of pleasure-boats in the middle of the bay.

'Shouldn't you have all that cordoned off?' asked Miles Bingham, following Crabbe's gaze.

'People ignore us, Miles,' said Crabbe. 'It's secure. We only exercise at night.'

'In theory, people could sail right up here, couldn't they?' asked Gerry Stap.

'In theory, yes,' agreed Crabbe. 'But they never do.'

Stap's bald pate shone in the strong afternoon light. He wore a light nylon jacket and canvas shoes; Bingham sported a blazer and grey flannels.

Crabbe, Bingham and Stap were standing on the small jetty of the Special Boat Service's Amphibious Warfare Training Centre on Hamworthy Beach, outside Poole. 'Beach' was something of a misnomer, since its sand had all been removed for sandbags during the war and never replaced. A few sunbathers lounged on the rocks beyond the chain-link fence; kids with buckets peered into pools as their mothers sat in deck-chairs, knitting. It was a very British scene. Crabbe turned around to face the low, prefabricated buildings painted camouflage grey.

'So is it definite?' he asked.

'Yes,' said Bingham. 'The PM has agreed to a summit in Paris next month and has cancelled all leave indefinitely. Porter thinks we might have a one-week window after the election.'

'We have a date?'

'Early October, probably,' said Gerry Stap. 'That's what the Chief Whip is saying.'

'Let's go to my office.'

Tim Crabbe had a small office without windows off the repair shop. He went into his floor safe and retrieved a Ministry of Defence envelope. His two guests took seats on metal folding chairs. Crabbe spoke in low tones.

'I don't know if you're aware, but the Trident retrofit is way behind schedule. HMS *Vanguard* has been in short refit in Rosyth, and now she's going to have to put to sea without her new PALs.'

'When?' asked Bingham, leaning forward.

'August 30. I just received the patrol instructions from Northwood.'

'What's your thinking?'

'We're not scheduled to join this patrol – they've had to cut it short as it is. But I don't think it would be difficult to alter the orders . . .'

'And?'

'Two of us could overpower the commander and the weapons officer. We could convince the crew it was a training exercise. Those missiles are still targeted to destroy half the Russian population.'

'You could fire them?' asked Stap, impressed.

'If we had to.'

'Porter will like it,' said Bingham quickly. 'Hopefully, we won't need to use the sanction.'

'But it's useful to hold in reserve. If needed,' agreed Stap.

'Precisely,' said Crabbe, catching a glimpse of glittering water through the reinforced window of his door.

17

A series of frantic calls to BBC Television Centre and, after numerous attempts, to MI5 liaison Hugh McAndrew in Moscow gave Smailes a clearer picture of what had happened to his friend. It was obvious that Iain was the victim of an elaborate KGB sting, and Smailes made the immediate connection with the Docherty–Klop arrests, their presumed plan to barter a real spy for a fake one. Though he cursed inwardly, the tactic in itself did not surprise him. The KGB had always cast off its Joe Dochertys – experience had taught him that most of its officers had open contempt for their Western collaborators; shit-eaters, they called them. But the KGB usually tried to rescue its own, no matter how desperate their straits, and the outrageous frame-up of Iain Mack proved how highly Gontar/Klop was valued. Clearly, the Russian security police and, by extension, the Russian government were prepared to jeopardize precious international credibility by such an arrest, reminiscent of the worst excesses of the Cold War. Smailes refused to believe anyone would credit the monstrous charge that a respected BBC journalist would actually engage in military espionage.

But neither did he doubt that the British Foreign Office, protective of its relations with Moscow, would favour a swift, no-questions-asked trade. MI5, together with its Home Office overlords, would doubtless insist on standing firm and prosecuting its two captured spies. It looked like a classic stand-off between age-old rivals within the British establishment; Number Ten would probably have to arbitrate. Smailes thought of his friend Iain, stewing at the moment in some KGB dungeon, and shuddered. He asked himself whether their friendship might have contributed to his plight, but quickly dismissed the thought. Judith was watching him. He felt almost relieved to have some concrete emergency to which to respond, and briefed her on developments; she made the connection with the British arrests immediately.

Smailes gathered his hastily scribbled notes and started for the door.

'Derek,' she said, 'I was going to ask Archie Keith for data on

Klop's radio traffic. You know, to perform my own analysis. If you thought it worthwhile.'

Smailes was already in the corridor.

'Fine,' he said over his shoulder. 'Why not?'

Smailes barged into Roger's outer office without knocking, to discover CIA liaison Loudon Strickland seated next to Glenys Powner's desk. Smailes ignored him.

'Is he in?'

'No, Derek. I think he's across with Brian. Do you want an appointment? Mr Strickland here is . . .' Glenys caught herself, since Smailes had already ducked back into the corridor.

Smailes found his superiors standing over a document on Brian's glass desk. Both men were in shirt-sleeves, and Brian's tie was loosened. Kinney looked up at Smailes distractedly, but was immediately alarmed by his expression.

'Derek. What's happened?'

Smailes walked to the window in agitation, then turned to address the two men. Standiforth sat down wearily and lit a cigarette. In five minutes Smailes had given them a garbled version of what he'd learned from the BBC and McAndrew in Moscow.

Standiforth got out of his chair, livid, and struggled into his jacket. 'God damn it! No bloody deals. I'm going to tell Taffy to stand fast.'

Brian walked across to his wall unit and punched on a television monitor. He surfed through the channels, hunting for news, but there was none. He muted the sound angrily. Standiforth had crushed out his cigarette and grabbed the phone.

'Glenys – get me the Director-General of the BBC. Put the call through to Sir David's office. And tell his secretary I'm on my way up. Well, tell Loudon we'll have to reschedule . . . I have no idea, do I?'

He banged down the receiver and wheeled on Kinney, pointing at Smailes. 'Send him down to Chiswick right away. Find out what the bloody hell is going on.' Cursing under his breath, Roger swept out of the room.

Smailes was confused. 'What's *he* on about?' he asked, taking Roger's seat. Kinney ran a hand through his hair and pushed the document on the desk across to Smailes.

'Take a look at that. It just came up from transcription.'

Smailes skimmed a transcript of Comrade Lubyanov's pillow talk with Valerie Saunders the previous evening.

'Seems our Russian Casanova couldn't perform last night, despite Valerie's best efforts,' said Kinney bitterly. 'The bloody fool is having second thoughts. He's even entertaining accepting Zhimin's offer and returning to the fold.'

'You're kidding?' said Smailes.

'I'm not. If we'd realized his bloody state of mind, we would never have consented to his wife's call from Moscow.'

'When's that supposed to happen?'

Kinney consulted his watch. 'Any minute now.'

'Has he coughed up any order of battle?'

'Piffle – twenty names. We were saving the real grilling for Bovingdon. The car's booked for four.'

'So what do you want me to do?'

'Get down to Chiswick right away. Find out what's going on. Tell Lubyanov he can't change his mind now – Zhimin will castrate him.'

Smailes took a deep breath and exhaled slowly. 'What's happening, Brian? A few hours ago, we were in clover . . .'

Kinney picked up his phone and waved him from the room.

Smailes stopped at his empty office before leaving the building. He'd remembered Iain's relationship with his research assistant and wondered whether she might still be in Moscow. He called back his contact on *Focus* and was given Nina Gregory's name and the BBC's Moscow telephone number. He tapped his foot impatiently as the circuits were busy on his first three attempts. Then the call got through and Smailes was connected with Blair Harrison. Harrison quickly explained that Nina had returned to her hotel and gave him the number. He apologized for not having time to talk – he was racing against a deadline for the evening news. Five minutes later Smailes was speaking to a very frightened Nina Gregory at the Ukraine Hotel.

To his relief, she knew exactly who he was and readily gave him the background to Iain's arrest. She had not trusted Putiashvilli from the start, she claimed, and had refused to go to their clandestine meeting that day. For that matter, she had never really trusted Simonov either, Iain's contact who had brokered the meeting – he had seemed too much of a fat cat to be a legitimate journalist. It was now clear Iain had walked into a trap. She was terrified that at any minute the security police would arrest her too. Smailes had interrupted her packing – she would spend the night with Harrison's family, then return to London the following day, if the Russians allowed her. Smailes felt like urging her to stay and show solidarity with her colleague and lover, but let it pass – the woman was clearly scared out of her wits. Smailes made her go back over their earlier meeting with Putiashvilli and what he had promised. He could quite understand how Iain would be unable to resist such an offer, despite what seemed, with hindsight, obvious risks. Then he inquired carefully about Simonov's role. It was clear that Iain was being set up much earlier in the summer – long before MI5's interest in Docherty and Klop. This in itself was not unusual: Smailes knew the former KGB often ran insurance files against Western visitors for use in just such a contingency. What was surprising was how little things had changed. Knowing his call was probably monitored, Smailes ended with a clear statement that Nina should not fear any reprisals from the Russian security police, since she was innocent of any intelligence role, as was Iain Mack.

Graham Booth was Yuri Lubyanov's reluctant jailer, just as he had once been Smailes's jailer in New York, in vastly different circumstances. Smailes followed Booth down the hall into the elegant kitchen and sat down.

'How's Chummy?'

'Terrible. He just got off the phone with the little wife ten minutes ago, and I think he's still recovering. He was in really bad shape during the call.'

'Any idea what they talked about?'

'Nah – all in Russian. But they were both blubbering a lot. My guess is she was begging him to change his mind.'

'So what happened this morning?'

'Valerie Saunders left before nine. She was upset too, I was told. I didn't come on until ten.'

'I saw the transcript. Chummy couldn't get it up.'

'Too bad for Valerie. He stayed in his room all morning until his call came through. Then he came down and asked for a drink. I overruled him.'

'He's in the living room?'

'Yes.'

Smailes got to his feet and went to the drinks cabinet. It was locked. Booth threw the keys at him. Smailes poured a large vodka and locked up again. Then he went in search of Lubyanov.

He was seated on the sofa, smoking, his face puffy from emotion. They'd given him a change of clothing, but the shirt fitted poorly; he looked pathetic. Smailes held out the glass. Lubyanov took it and gulped hungrily.

'Thank you, Mr Sykes,' he said presently. 'I need this. Your colleague, he does not seem to understand.'

'What's up, Yuri?' asked Smailes mildly.

Lubyanov looked into his glass bitterly and took another swallow before replying. 'I am a disgrace,' he said quietly. Smailes did not speak.

'I suppose I have always been a disgrace, but until now I have been able to spare my family. Oh, it is not so much my wife – ours has been a loveless marriage for many years. Although I feel bad she will now lose her apartment and have to move back with her parents. At her age. But my mother . . .' Lubyanov was momentarily at a loss for words.

'My wife says she thinks the humiliation may kill her. She is apparently hysterical with grief. It is all my fault,' he said despairingly. Then he turned on Smailes.

'I wish I had never got into the car with you that day in Portsmouth! I wish I had just gone straight to Gropov and confessed. Oh, I would have been reassigned – fired probably. Yes, and divorced too. But none of this disgrace would have happened. I could have found another position. Like that.' He snapped his fingers, then took another drink of vodka. Smailes cleared his throat.

'I can understand your feelings, Yuri,' he said carefully. 'But we will arrange an adequate life-style for you, and you'll have Valerie . . .'

'Valerie! Valerie is hateful to me now. Last night I could not even screw her! I want nothing more to do with Valerie!'

'Yuri, there's no turning back for you now,' Smailes warned.

'Yes. Yes, there is, Mr Sykes. Zhimin said their offer would stand for one week. I have two more days.'

'Yuri, the car comes in one hour to take you to our reception centre . . .'

'I will not go!' Lubyanov shouted. 'I want more time to think. If I had not given you those twenty names . . . But it is nothing, is it? You probably knew them already . . .' Lubyanov was clearly weighing an awful alternative.

'Yuri, you can't turn back now. Surely you know what will happen to you.'

'Yes, but I would rescue my honour. Ha! That would be a first!'

Lubyanov was getting drunk and there was a manic edge to his voice. He drained his glass and set it down clumsily. 'I will not go, do you understand? You must give me another day to think. If you try and force me, I will not cooperate with you in any way. Understand?' he asked sarcastically. 'More vodka!'

'Not yet, Yuri. We need you sober.'

Smailes found Kinney and Standiforth in a foul temper and his tidings only made matters worse.

'Spineless bloody fool,' said Standiforth bitterly, forgetting these were the very qualities which had recommended Lubyanov to them in the first place. 'Well, I'm not going to waste my time worrying about him. If he wants to sign his own death warrant . . .'

'What's happening upstairs?' asked Smailes.

Roger reclined in his big padded chair and looked up at the ceiling. 'Well, we've packed Taffy off to an emergency Cabinet meeting to state our position.'

'Which is?'

'Mack's arrest is an act of state terrorism and any willingness to negotiate implies his guilt and is therefore out. Unconditional release is all we'll accept.'

'Sounds fair enough,' said Smailes.

'Yes, well, will Taffy have the backbone to withstand the bloody onslaught? That's more the question.'

'What onslaught?'

'Think about it, Derek,' said Standiforth patronizingly. 'Every damn ministry with a stake in cosy relations with Moscow will be in favour of striking a deal. That includes the Foreign Office, Defence, Trade and Industry – God knows who else. It'll basically be Taffy and the Home Secretary against the rest. Of course, if the PM's serious about this Paris summit and an autumn election, he can't afford to seem weak-kneed. Unless, of course, the polls were to suggest . . .'

'It's the cards the Russians are holding that worry me,' said Kinney. 'I've seen several of these tit-for-tat arrests over the years, and each time the KGB has put together an impressive prima-facie case. Entirely concocted of course, but carefully done. I don't think they would have grabbed anyone as prominent as a *Focus* producer without something fairly convincing.'

Smailes told them of his discussion with Nina Gregory, and how it appeared the Russians had been setting Iain up since early summer, long before MI5 showed any interest in Docherty or Klop.

'Well, that's precisely my point,' said Roger. 'I can hear the arguments now. "If we take Klop to trial, the Russians will do the same to this BBC chap. If we produce evidence of guilt, so will they. Et cetera. MI5 has fired a shot across the KGB's bows, so there's no need to send Klop off to prison. Expel him, and let the Russians do the same to Mack. End of crisis. After all, that wretch Docherty will go to prison for ever, which is what MI5 really wants."'

'Well, don't we?' asked Smailes.

'No, we bloody well don't!' shouted Standiforth, banging down a hand. 'If we let the Russians get away with this, we're sending entirely the wrong message! We're being bloody overrun, man! I want Gontar in the dock at the Old Bailey, facing twenty years, like he deserves! That's the only kind of message they'll understand.'

'Well, Number Ten probably doesn't have enough information to make any hard decisions yet,' said Kinney. 'But one thing is certain – nobody in Whitehall is going to want this thing to drag on. Not with an election over Europe in the offing. The longer it continues, the more pressure will build for a settlement.'

The phone rang and Roger picked it up angrily. 'Yes, he's here,' he said, passing the receiver to Kinney.

'You called off the Bovingdon car?' Standiforth asked Smailes.

'Like you said, Roger. Booked for tomorrow.'

Standiforth cupped his chin in his hand gloomily.

'You've got to be bloody joking!' yelled Kinney into the phone. 'Listen here, Francis, this is going too far! Too bloody far!' He paused. 'Look, hold on, will you?' He cupped the receiver and turned to his colleagues.

'It's bloody Caldicott again. Now he's saying Lubyanov's *mother* is demanding the right to speak to him from Moscow! They're standing by to connect her.'

'Don't do it, Roger. I don't think Lubyanov can handle it,' warned Smailes.

Kinney looked painfully at Standiforth. 'I don't know, Roger. Having allowed the wife, I don't really see how we can deny the mother.'

Standiforth was thinking. 'All right. But tell Caldicott that if we allow Lubyanov's mother to speak with him, Iain Mack can call whomever he chooses from . . . where are they holding him, Derek?'

'Lefortovo prison.'

'From Lefortovo. Got it, Brian? It's an absolute condition.'

Kinney spoke rapidly into the phone, then hung up. Roger struggled into his jacket. 'Let's listen in to this one,' said Standiforth. 'S Branch can patch in a relay from Chiswick, can't they?'

'Of course,' said Kinney.

Derek Smailes got wearily to his feet. It had been a long day.

Clea Smailes sat amid the toys on the living room floor, playing distractedly with Lucy. It was difficult; she was still reeling from the news she'd just seen on the BBC that Iain had been arrested in Moscow on espionage charges. Lucy prattled on, but Clea ignored her, her mind swimming with television images. File shots of Iain. The Prime Minister standing in front of Number Ten, insisting on his immediate release. The head of the BBC announcing he was flying to Moscow that evening. The BBC political correspondent stationed in front of Big Ben, describing the worst East–West crisis since the end of the Cold War. Blair Harrison in Moscow interviewing some steely-eyed Interior Ministry official. A diplomatic expert querying the recent arrests of the nuclear spies in London, invoking precedent. Clea felt her eyes moisten, her chest growing tight. The front door banged open, and Lucy ran squealing into the hall. Derek came into the living room, their daughter in his arms, and Clea broke down.

'What is it, love?' asked Smailes, alarmed.

'Derek, they've arrested Iain in Moscow! I've just been watching the news. Oh, Derek, will he be all right?'

'Of course,' said Smailes, crouching to comfort his wife. Lucy, frightened, began crying also.

'You know all about it?' she asked.

Smailes quickly explained how he'd learned the news, his conversations with Blair Harrison and Nina Gregory. Clea got to her feet and gathered herself, accepting the wailing figure of Lucy from her husband. 'Lucy, everything's all right,' she said.

'Mummy cry,' said Lucy.

'What did the PM say?' asked Derek.

'That he won't negotiate. The Russians have to release him unconditionally.'

'Good.'

'Will they?'

'Too soon to say. Of course, they want to barter for the bloke we arrested on Saturday. He hasn't confessed yet, but he was their senior spy in Britain.'

'Good grief,' said Clea, wiping her eye with a sleeve. 'Well, the BBC had someone on speculating about that.'

'Any official Russian announcement?'

'The Moscow reporter interviewed someone who said they had evidence of Iain's crimes . . .'

'Crap,' said Smailes.

'Crap,' said Lucy.

'Derek, you don't . . . I mean, when Iain comes back from Moscow, you don't . . . ask him things?'

'No, I don't,' Smailes snapped. Clea had struck a nerve.

'All right, all right. Just asking,' said Clea.

'Sorry,' said Smailes. 'Look, I'm counter-intelligence, Clea. I'm not interested in Iain's tittle-tattle from Moscow. Not that he would ever tell me anything, anyway.'

'Of course,' said Clea, still wounded.

'I'm sorry,' said Derek again. 'This business with Iain has really got to me.'

'Crap,' said Lucy again.

'Crap to you, little miss,' said Smailes, grabbing her wrists. 'Come and help Daddy change.'

'Rudy called,' Clea shouted after them. 'We're on for tomorrow night, six o'clock.'

Smailes turned on the stairs. 'We may have to cancel that, darling,' he said wearily.

Alex Corcoran put down his telephone and shook his head in disbelief. Of all the exotic aspects of Roger's scheme, Peter Lynch's recruitment had to be the most outlandish. Here was Lynch, on a non-secure line no less, yammering about the latest Sceptre Group meeting at which an SBS move against a nuclear sub at Faslane was mooted. Lynch said he would turn over his tapes the following morning, but he was sure Corcoran would want the information immediately, before close of business. Corcoran had put his hand over his eyes and asked Lynch to repeat his account. Heavens above, he thought. If I hadn't offered to run this clown myself, Lord knows what might have happened.

Corcoran issued practised words of reassurance. No, there was no need to run the tapes in tonight – tomorrow would be fine. Yes, he would await their transcription eagerly. Yes, well done, Peter. Well done indeed.

Corcoran cleared his desk and called for his car. He reflected that Ian Fleming had a lot to answer for, making grown men believe the intelligence business was a chiaroscuro world of glamour and intrigue, when in fact it was tawdry, grey and corrupt. But then he corrected himself – no one in their right mind would call Peter Lynch a grown man, after all.

Iain Mack looked across at Colonel Nikolai Gasparov and knew he was hopelessly outmatched. In the course of a sleepless night, Iain had resolved to be as compliant as possible while maintaining his innocence, relying on British efforts to secure his release. If it was true that he'd been set up for a swap with some Russian spy arrested in London, he knew there would be intense manoeuvring behind the scenes. Gasparov had told him yesterday that he was entitled to legal representation, but he didn't want to make any decisions until he'd spoken with someone from the embassy or the BBC.

Gasparov ignored him, reading in a file and occasionally scribbling notes. The clock on the wall said eleven, although it seemed much later to Iain; his sense of time was already woefully distorted. The day had begun around six, he guessed, when a guard opened the food hatch and barked at him to get dressed. Then he was marched to a bathroom in the basement where he was allowed to shower, under supervision. The guard offered him a pair of prison overalls which looked freshly laundered, but he refused them, reasoning he was more likely to retain his dignity wearing his own clothes, no matter how grubby.

Then he was marched to another windowless room with a padded bench and cabinets and told to wait for the doctor. She turned out to be a po-faced woman in a turban and bloodstained smock, and her examination consisted largely of taking his blood pressure with a greasy tourniquet and peering up his behind with a dented torch. She spoke no English, so Iain had no idea of her conclusions, but he found the entire procedure humiliating. Give me the torch, Olga, he felt like saying – let's see what yours looks like.

Then he was frog-marched back to his cell, where he tried to doze on his cot as the air grew hotter and more fetid. Suddenly he was awakened from a fitful dream and escorted into the presence of Colonel Nikolai Gasparov.

The balding, hatchet-faced assistant was also present. Gasparov motioned for Mack to take a seat, then ignored him.

Presently, he looked up from Iain's file and smiled at him. 'Good morning, Gospodin Mack,' he said expansively. 'And congratulations. I have good news for you.'

Involuntarily, Iain's heart surged, but he said nothing.

'The British ambassador and the chief of the BBC have been granted permission to see you. They will be here this afternoon.'

'Will I be released?' he asked.

'Not so quickly, my friend,' he said. 'You are facing serious charges. Our investigation is continuing.'

'This is a sham,' said Iain. 'You picked me up to swap for that spy of yours in London. I am innocent. Everyone knows it.' Immediately, he regretted his confrontational tone.

'Also, to make a phone call. To anyone you like. International call, if you choose.'

Mack frowned at him, suspecting a trap. Gasparov continued in the same reasonable tone. 'Perhaps you would like to call this man Smailes in London. Your controller.'

In the back of his mind Iain must have been expecting this, since it did not throw him completely. But he mentally rebuked himself for sending the impulsive message through Harrison the previous day.

'Derek Smailes is my oldest friend. We were at school together. It's just coincidence that he works for MI5. Anyway, he's counter-intelligence, isn't he? You probably know that. He spends his time finding out why people leave government service. He's not interested in me or what I know about Russia.'

'You know a lot about our country, do you, Gospodin Mack?' asked Gasparov pleasantly.

'A bit,' said Mack. He saw no point in pretending Russia had not been a particular interest.

'Well, I am counter-intelligence too, as you probably know also,' said Gasparov. 'But I have many friends in the foreign intelligence service. As no doubt does your friend Smailes. He is what we call a cut-out. He debriefs you after you return from your visits, and passes your intelligence along to colleagues with more direct interest. Yes?'

'No.'

'You deny that you have made thirteen visits here in the last eight years?'

'Of course not. I have made three documentaries here. Well, I'm working on my third.'

'Yes, and very interesting subjects too,' said Gasparov, looking down at the file. 'The withdrawal from Afghanistan. The conversion of Soviet heavy industry. And now, supposed criminal elements who steal military secrets. All of great interest to your intelligence services, I would think. And to their masters at the CIA.'

'I wouldn't know,' said Mack.

'You are a very clever spy, Mr Iain Mack,' said Gasparov admiringly. Iain found the accusation chilling.

'I am not a spy,' he replied weakly.

'Well, we think you are,' said Gasparov. 'Let me show you something.'

He lifted a flimsy document from the file and passed it across the desk. Its contents made Iain's stomach turn to water. The document appeared to be a British embassy cipher form with 'Top Secret' stamped across the top and 'Destroy Upon Transmission' across the bottom. It was completed in block capitals and read CALEDONIAN MATERIAL DIPLOMATIC BAG WEDNESDAY. MCANDREW. It was probably a forgery, but Iain could tell it was a good one.

'You know who is McAndrew?'

'Of course,' said Mack as firmly as he could. 'He's the security man at the embassy. He briefs us whenever we come to Moscow.'

'Yes. He is MI5 man at your embassy. You see, we have someone who helps us in the cipher room. Sometimes this person finds things before they are destroyed. Like this document. Did you notice it was dated yesterday?'

'No.'

'Caledonian. That means Scottish, doesn't it?'

'Yes.'

'Your background is Scottish, no?'

'My parents were born in Scotland. I wasn't.'

'Yes. And you don't think this "material" refers to the package you received yesterday from your accomplice, Putiashvilli?'

Iain felt helpless. 'He's not my accomplice. He's your accomplice.'

'Well, this is not what Putiashvilli says. He has already confessed. He says you pressured him into getting specific information on the new space reactor and the Energiya rocket. These are fields in which the West still lags behind us, no? Well, I'm sure you already know this.'

Iain Mack was at a loss for a reply. 'Now, let's talk again about your accomplice, Putiashvilli,' said Gasparov. 'Tell me again how you met.'

18

'Smarmy little prat,' said Moody, jabbing a cheroot into his mouth. 'I'd like to stick my fist down his throat.'

'I know just what you mean,' said Kinney, raising his voice above the thunder of a passing bus. 'They're a disgusting breed, people who betray their country for money.'

Moody looked surprised. 'No, I'm not talking about Docherty. I'm talking about his lawyer – Parsons. He's the type that really makes me puke.'

Kinney laughed. 'Docherty's entitled to representation, you know, Bill. It's the law. You can't expect him to pick someone sympathetic to us.'

Moody dipped his face into a fan of flame from an old petrol lighter. 'I suppose not. Parsons isn't going to get him off, is he?'

'Not a chance,' said Kinney emphatically. 'Their story just won't wash.'

Brian Kinney and Detective Chief Inspector Bill Moody were standing beside the security bollards outside Paddington Green police station in Edgware Road, waiting for their respective drivers. They had just completed a lengthy interview with Docherty and his lawyer, in the course of which Docherty had made a voluntary statement. Kinney was frustrated; with a less confident solicitor at his elbow, Docherty might have been badgered into a full confession in exchange for some consideration at sentencing. Instead, he'd given them a cock-and-bull story in the misguided hope his lawyer might get him off the hook altogether.

Docherty was claiming that Jurgen Klop had approached him with the idea of his writing a book on the British nuclear weapons industry in the aftermath of the Cold War. The money he had received had been part of a publication advance, he claimed. When confronted with his obvious betrayal of the Official Secrets Act which he'd signed on employment, Docherty tried to claim he was acting in the public interest. Despite explicit disqualification in the Act, this 'whistle-blower' strategy had worked all too often in the past with recalcitrant juries. Docherty's story had all the flavour of a concoction prepared by Mr Jeremy Parsons.

Kinney was still more exasperated by Docherty's refusal to admit his leak of the MI5 mock attack at ROF Burghfield. No Burghfield employees knew of the exercise in advance, Docherty claimed – the first anyone had suspected was when they had reported for work the following morning. He admitted supplying his 'agent' Klop with computer disks on the American PAL hardware – it was material Klop had requested specifically, and disks were simply easier to remove than full-sized documents.

'Well, we'll get him on kid-diddling, looks like,' said Moody with a sniff. 'The little wife has made a statement that she had no idea about his espionage, but knew all about his thing for little boys. Claims it was why they had to leave Scotland. Reading CID has been interviewing the Scout troop and it looks like there's a couple of lads he may have been naughty with. We're trying to convince the families to press charges.'

'The money?' asked Kinney. 'His wife wasn't curious about all the money?'

'Doesn't look like he ever spent any of it,' said Moody with disgust. 'Pathetic, isn't it?'

Moody's car drew up at the kerb. He squeezed the glowing tip off his cheroot and stuck the stub back in his packet. Kinney caught his eye.

'Look, Bill, we were a bit upset by that scene at the flat on Saturday. We had explicitly requested . . .'

'Listen, come off it, Brian,' said Moody heatedly. 'I've got to keep my people happy, haven't I? Just like Roger Standiforth does. Jesus Christ, he practically wrote the stories in the Monday morning papers himself. No harm done, was there?'

'Well, that's not quite the way I heard it.'

'From that tosser Smailes?' Moody growled. 'Listen, Brian, you've got to keep an eye on that bloke – he's unstable.'

With that, Moody ducked into his car. Kinney shook his head. He couldn't believe that MI5 continued to balk at being granted executive powers; he'd give anything to be rid of these Special Branch goons.

MI5 had circled its wagons, and Sir David Williams had descended from his cave of computer screens to join his executive committee around his large conference table. If he was to prevail in the turf battle that had blown up over the Mack arrest, Williams knew he needed all the support he could get.

Miles Bingham was hot and agitated. Whether or not MI5 had to bargain away its prized illegal, he knew his rival Standiforth would accrue kudos for both the investigation and the arrests. Although Bingham could now maintain the Burghfield leak had been a K Branch responsibility all along – they should obviously have interrogated the traitor Docherty when he transferred from Scotland – the thought gave him little consolation.

Roger Standiforth, by contrast, seemed in complete control. He lit a cigarette slowly as he listened to Corcoran's peroration. Corky, the man with the steel-trap mind, was the committee's automatic choice as their chief strategist in the crisis.

'Well, we've got big obstacles on several fronts, it seems to me,' said Corcoran, speaking rapidly. 'Mack seems to have strayed into some very dangerous turf. I say "strayed" because I can't believe he would have done this deliberately.'

Bingham gave a sceptical grunt.

'In the free-for-all that is contemporary Russia,' Corcoran continued, 'everyone is trying to sell everything to anyone.'

'The triumph of the free market,' Standiforth offered pleasantly.

'Quite. Since the old KGB was in charge of military security, they have direct access to the most sensitive secrets. The most valuable too, obviously. We've known for some time that a lucrative trade has developed in the sale of blueprints to the West. Anything is for sale, literally – for the right price.

'So when Mack wandered into this territory, the KGB had to stop him. It doesn't really matter whether his Georgian contact was working directly for them or not – they could have learned of his research any number of ways. Of course, they could have simply confiscated his tapes and booted him out, but our arrest of Gontar probably gave them the incentive to respond in kind. They want Gontar back, obviously, although they haven't acknowledged that yet. But our main problem isn't with the KGB. It's with the Kremlin. What's the text of the Russian President's announcement, Roger?'

Standiforth looked down at a document. '"The journalist Iain Mack has been apprehended red-handed in possession of Russian state secrets. He could only have come by this material illegally. The matter is now a judicial one, in which I have no power to intercede."'

'That's ripe,' said Bingham.

'Well, the point is the KGB must have something on him, mustn't they?' said Corcoran. 'Something big, otherwise he would never permit them to jeopardize his precious relations with the West. He must have no room to manoeuvre.'

'What do you mean?' asked Bingham.

'Think about it, Bingo. The Russian President must have his hands dirty in the secrets trade too. It's obvious.'

David Williams cleared his throat. 'I just spoke with Sir Colin at SIS. They run someone inside his Cabinet, and it's precisely what they're hearing.'

'It's McAndrew's opinion too,' said Corcoran.

'Damn,' said Standiforth.

'What else?' asked Williams.

'Sir Andrew Atkin called me this morning,' said Corcoran.

'The Cabinet secretary? Really?' asked Williams, impressed.

'We're old friends. Andrew told me the PM is planning to send Bert Carne to Moscow to mediate. He also said both he and Carne are leaning towards a settlement, if they can find some way of dismissing the charges against Mack while getting Klop to acknowledge his guilt . . .'

Standiforth spluttered a protest.

'They're his two most knowledgeable advisers, Roger, and both are officially neutral. If they recommend a deal, you know the PM is going to have to accept it.'

'Now, wait a minute,' said Standiforth.

'Oh, I don't know,' said Bingham gloomily. 'We've made our splash. I'm sure Herbert Carne reads the newspapers.'

'What has Gontar said?' asked Williams.

'Nothing yet,' said Corcoran. 'He won't admit his identity, and he won't comment on what we found in his flat, or on his relationship with Docherty, or with the Basamalah brothers. All we can get out of him is that he'll make a statement at his trial. It's as if he *knows* it won't get that far.'

'Jesus wept,' said Williams. 'I'm not letting him go unless he admits who he is – a full, signed statement. That's final. Can we still prosecute Docherty if we let Gontar off? What has he told us?'

'I don't know,' said Standiforth. 'Kinney's over there this morning. But it's a good question. Kinney and Poynter hope to have the file to the DPP by the end of the week. And I for one will be bloody upset if we don't chuck the book at both of them.'

'Damn it. *Damn* it,' said Williams. 'The bloody BBC – can't they keep their noses clean?'

'Apparently not,' said Standiforth, exhaling smoke evenly through his nostrils.

Alex Corcoran reclined in his wheelchair, silently appraising Roger Standiforth's performance.

'All right, Rudy. See you at five thirty. The Running Footman, Charles Street,' said Smailes, hanging up.

Smailes had bantered with Rudy a little about his trip to Ireland, apologizing for his cancellation of their dinner and citing 'work pressures'. Rudy, who had been reading the papers, inquired no further, but was obviously disappointed. He and Carla had the rental car one more day, he said – they could drive out to Surrey that evening if that worked better. Smailes was touched by Rudy's loyalty, but couldn't face the prospect of small talk with their wives when his best friend was being grilled by some KGB bone-cracker. Instead he promised Rudy a last drink together, having confirmed they were returning to the States the following day.

His thoughts returned to Lubyanov, particularly the final phone call from Moscow and the impotence Smailes had felt as Lubyanov degenerated into a blubbering wreck on the line with his mother. Roger had corralled a Slav from the translation pool who hunched over the tiny speaker, providing a simultaneous English version – the mother pleading for Lubyanov to spare her more heartbreak, Lubyanov whining that he had gone too far, but that he would try and think of a way out. It made galling listening. Eventually, the mother made a remark about the arrest of the British spy in Moscow and the British claim that a Russian spy had been arrested in London. Was this true? Was it Yuri? Had Lubyanov in fact been arrested, held against his will? The translation lagged the actual speech by about a sentence, and Standiforth angrily cut the line dead when he heard the question. He cursed colourfully – the last thing MI5 wanted was for their cold-footed Casanova to know anything about the wider world of British–Russian relations. It had seemed an appropriate end to a truly awful day.

Judith came into the office. To Smailes's relief, her appearance provoked little reaction in him; their weekend encounter had now been completely overtaken by events. He looked at his watch and saw it was almost noon; he wanted to find out whether Kinney was back, what Docherty had said, but Judith seemed preoccupied.

'What's up?' he asked.

She crossed hurriedly to her desk and tossed down a file. 'Just had a meeting with Archie,' she said.

'You two seem to be making up for a slow start,' he said. Judith ignored him and booted up her tiny computer; it began to whine and peep.

'I worked late last night,' she said. 'Really late. Remember I wanted to do an analysis of Gontar's radio traffic?'

'Right,' said Smailes. 'Anything interesting?'

'Yes,' she said. 'Look at this.'

She pointed at the screen and tapped a series of keys. 'Archie got me GCHQ's raw data on Moscow intercepts for the past three years.'

'Raw data?'

'Everything they couldn't break. A lot of stuff – I had to dump most of my files to load it.'

'What were you looking for?' asked Smailes. The black numbers streaming in front of his face meant nothing.

'I sorted it by call sign. To see if I could find out how much of it was going to Gontar.'

'Right. Okay.'

'Look,' she said, pointing to a row of totals at the bottom of her screen. 'For the past three years, as long as we know Gontar's been in the country, he's been getting between five and eight hundred groups a month, according to the call signs we've been able to attribute to him.'

'All right.'

'Now look.' Judith hit another key and more columns scrolled by. She pointed to another total and tapped the screen with her nail. 'In late June that figure dropped to between three and five hundred groups.'

'So?'

'This was just before we put him under surveillance, right?'

'Yes, but . . .'

'Derek. Do you believe that Mikhail Gontar is the KGB resident illegal?'

'Of course.'

'And how many spies would you expect him to run?'

'Well, several. But . . .'

'And how many did we identify?'

'Just Docherty. But I've already thought of that. It could be . . .'

'Do you believe that your friend was arrested in Moscow in retaliation, in order to trade for Gontar?'

'Absolutely.'

'It's not a coincidence? He's not the victim of some independent counter-intelligence operation by the Russians?'

'Come off it!'

'When was he arrested?'

Smailes scanned his memory. 'Around one thirty, Moscow time. That was Nina Gregory's best guess.'

'Yesterday.'

'Monday, yes,' said Smailes.

'Which is ten thirty, GMT,' said Judith.

'That's right.'

'So some time between our arrest of Gontar – around five on Saturday – and, say, ten yesterday morning, the Russian embassy had to tell their colleagues in Moscow to stage a tit-for-tat arrest of a Briton, right?'

'Absolutely.'

Judith flicked open her file and handed Smailes a document. 'This is the GCHQ schedule of cipher transmissions from the Russian embassy, between Friday at five and yesterday at noon. Archie requested it for me.'

'None?' said Smailes, incredulous.

'Actually, one,' Judith corrected him, pointing. 'Their first transmission was yesterday at eleven. Half an hour after Iain Mack had been arrested.'

'Hold on a minute, Judith,' said Smailes. 'Those instructions could have gone some other way. Secure phone link, for instance.'

'Do you believe that, Derek?'

'It's possible.'

'But not probable, is it? And consider this. The KGB sees its single most important spy in England arrested on a Saturday evening. The story is all over the Sunday papers. But the KGB residence doesn't send *any* transmission to Moscow until Monday at eleven? That's not credible.'

'You're right. That is bloody weird. What are you getting at, Judith?'

'The Russians knew we were on to Gontar. They made him drop his other spies just before we tagged him, to protect them. His radio traffic fell off accordingly at the same time. Docherty is a discard. His other spies are safe.'

'Wait a minute.' This was too far out for Smailes, too much like knee-jerk counter-intelligence paranoia. 'Why would the Russians discard Docherty? He was a pretty big source. Or allow us to arrest Gontar? Why not just bring him home?'

'I don't know. But how did the KGB in Moscow know to arrest Iain Mack? By telepathy?'

The phone rang, but Smailes didn't answer it. Then he picked up the receiver absently, a second before the call rolled back to the switchboard. 'Smailes,' he said.

The telephonist's voice greeted him, followed by a howl of static, then a distant voice jabbering in Russian followed by an instantly recognizable voice.

'Derek? Derek, is that you?'

'Iain! Bloody hell! Where are you?'

'I'm in the KGB Hilton. Where do you think I am?'

'I thought for a minute you might be out!'

'Some hope. They let me make a call, and after stewing about it I decided to call you. Who else was I going to call? My editor? My sister? It's probably stupid, since they think I'm a spy and that I work for you.'

'That's crap,' said Smailes angrily. But he quickly gathered his wits, realizing the call, unexpected and undoubtedly monitored, was a big opportunity.

'You're an innocent man, Iain. The whole world knows it. The story is lead news everywhere. People are saying your arrest shows the true face of Russian democracy.'

'What's the British government doing?'

Smailes chose his words with care. 'It's a stand-off. They won't negotiate, because they're insisting on your innocence and on your unconditional release.'

Smailes could hear Iain's disappointment. 'Well, I understand their position, Derek, but these boys have got me pretty well stitched up. They planted a packet of military secrets on me, then produced an embassy form with McAndrew's name on it, referring to me as "Caledonian".'

Smailes swore under his breath. It sounded typically thorough – a classic KGB sting.

'Look, Derek, I want out of here. I don't care about the fine print –

understand? That's all I called to say. I thought you might be able to pass on the message.'

Smailes understood his friend perfectly. Iain was saying that if his reputation was smeared by being traded for an actual spy, he didn't care.

'How are you being treated?'

'All right. Well, it's no picnic. It's hot. My cell stinks.'

'What's happening?'

'One interrogation session per day, so far. The ambassador and the Beeb are supposed to be here later this afternoon. I was hoping I'd be able to leave with them. Probably not, is that what you're telling me, right?'

'I don't know, Iain. Listen, you want me to call anyone? Your friend Nina?'

'Don't mention her name to me.'

'Janet?'

'Oh, I suppose so. Tell her I'm all right, if she's interested.' Smailes knew Iain had not spoken to his sister in years.

Smailes couldn't think what else to say. 'How was your programme going?' he asked.

'Derek, I never want to see this bloody country again.'

'I don't blame you. Listen, mate, hang in. Everyone's on your side. This story is not going to go away. The Russian government is going to have to step in and get you released. They can't afford to alienate the West.'

'Right,' said Iain. Then, more poignantly, 'See you soon.' His voice cracked on the last syllable and Smailes's eyes smarted.

'Drinks are on me,' Derek managed. The line went dead.

Smailes reached for his jacket and bolted for the door. 'Don't do anything yet,' he said to Judith. 'I need to go over this whole thing with you again.'

Smailes was told that Roger was in Brian's office, but when he barged in he found Kinney holed up with Ed Poynter, MI5's legal man. Poynter was old school, but an eccentric; he had refined taste and manners but a face like a boxer, which he had apparently once been. He looked up and Smailes could tell immediately something was wrong.

'Brian, Ed . . .' he began. 'What's going on?'

Kinney looked haggard. 'There are some bloody mistakes in the Gontar warrant. Not enough to throw out the case, but a clever lawyer could make things sticky.'

'Mistakes?' asked Smailes helplessly.

Poynter swivelled on him. 'Someone put the wrong flat number on the damned search warrant. 26B instead of 26A. You searched the wrong bloody flat, Derek.'

'Jesus,' said Smailes. 'I didn't even look.'

'It wasn't *your* fault,' said Poynter. 'But there's worse. The warrant ought to have been reviewed by a circuit judge so we could remove privileged material – you know, documents pertaining to Gontar's "clients". Special Branch had this thing signed at Arbour Square – by a bloody stipendiary magistrate! Roger's staff and Moody's people are trading accusations over who's responsible.'

'Where *is* Roger?'

'In emergency session with the DG and Corky. There's no way we can keep this from the defence lawyers. They'll spot the discrepancies immediately.'

'I thought Gontar had refused a lawyer?'

'He'll probably change his mind when Docherty's people try and disqualify the evidence taken from his flat,' said Poynter.

'Is that crucial for a conviction?' asked Smailes.

'In Docherty's case, no. There were prints on the stuff you found in Gontar's cache, but they weren't his. Luckily, we have enough from what we found in Docherty's potting shed – thank God there was nothing wrong with *that* warrant. No, it's the case against Gontar I'm concerned about.'

Smailes reflected on the likely impact of these developments on the government's resolve not to trade Mack for Gontar, but said nothing.

'Iain Mack just called me from Moscow,' said Smailes. 'He wants out, on any terms. The Russians have a nasty case against him, including fake cipher blanks from the embassy.'

'Jesus, I knew it,' said Kinney. At that moment, Roger Standiforth came back into the room, flustered.

'*There* you are,' he said to Smailes. 'I've been looking all over for you. Get down to Chiswick right away. Lubyanov has just refused to get into the car to Bovingdon. He's claiming he's changed his mind – he wants to be handed back to Zhimin.'

'God damn it,' said Smailes.

'I've dismissed the car, but for Christ's sake get him to see reason.

Explain that Zhimin will sew his testicles into his face before he's finished with him. Tell him we're going clean house at the embassy from that order of battle he gave us, and that he'll probably get twenty years in a labour camp, at least.'

'What about Docherty?' asked Smailes.

'No, don't say a damn thing about Docherty!' He turned to Poynter. 'Those bloody mistakes weren't made in *my* office. That material was *scrupulously* prepared by Peter and Glenys, and they both *swear* . . . Well, never mind.'

'What does the seventh floor say?' asked Kinney.

'Corky's going to talk to Andrew Atkin. This might tip the scales at Number Ten.'

'Shit,' said Poynter.

'Well, we'll still have Docherty,' offered Smailes. He was by now sufficiently attuned to Iain Mack's plight to no longer really care about the prosecution of Mikhail Gontar.

'We're going to have a fight on our hands,' warned Kinney. 'Parsons is going to use the whistle-blower defence, and Docherty is denying the Burghfield leak.'

'Derek says Iain Mack just called him from Moscow,' said Poynter.

Standiforth wheeled on Smailes. 'He's out?' he exclaimed.

'No, no, from Lefortovo,' interrupted Kinney. 'Remember the condition we imposed to allow Lubyanov to speak with his mother?'

'Don't remind me.'

Smailes began to recount his conversation, but Standiforth cut him short. 'I'll get the details later. Right now, I need you in Chiswick. Do whatever you can, but get Lubyanov to stay on board.'

'We care that much?' asked Smailes.

'It's the bloody *principle* of the thing, Derek,' said Standiforth. 'But, look, if he won't budge, get that fat bugger Caldicott off his behind to do the hand-over. We can't have Zhimin showing up in Chiswick himself, can we?' Smailes thought of relaying some of the doubts Judith Hyams's research had cast on the whole operation, but knew Standiforth was in no mood to listen. The post-mortem would come later, when the Jonquil case was well and truly dead.

Smailes pointed the government Rover west and headed for Chiswick. Iain's voice haunted him – he hoped his friend trusted that he, Smailes, had never done anything to compromise him. But Derek had been proved right in one respect: the KGB certainly ran an active file on him, and Iain had seriously underestimated the dangers of contemporary Moscow.

Reluctantly, his mind returned to Judith Hyams's allegations. He thought it likely they were true – it *was* odd that Gontar only ran a single spy, Docherty, but in the excitement of the chase no one at MI5 wanted to cast doubts. And the KGB London residence would *unquestionably* have been required to file an immediate report on the Paddington arrests, certainly using one-time radio cipher, the traditional, most secure method. That suggested Docherty and Gontar were both discards, except that Gontar wasn't a *real* discard – he was about to be released and would live to spy another day. It was likely that even if their case against him had not begun to unravel, the British would have been forced to trade Iain for the Russian illegal. But if the Burghfield spies were discards, what on earth was the Russian motive? It could only be to protect some other, more important spy. Who? Smailes's mind was impelled towards the inexorable conclusion – it had to be someone in the British establishment, the *real* source of the Burghfield leak, no doubt. In which case, Docherty's denials were in fact true.

Smailes's mind made the next, obvious connection. If Gontar was rotten, so was Yuri Lubyanov, the man who had dished him up in the first place. And surprise, surprise, here was Yuri the poltroon about to risk his life for 'honour'. It meant the Lubyanov honeytrap was a dangle, a classic KGB ploy. What was it Judith had said? Let's see what he produces – that's the way to evaluate whether he's genuine. In their hunger for success, the British had overlooked elementary precautions which might have cast doubt on the operation earlier.

Smailes suddenly felt like a marionette, his strings manipulated by unseen hands. Whose? They could only be Zhimin's, the suave KGB potentate. But how had he tricked everyone? Had it needed only some elementary computer analysis to expose his deceptions?

Smailes drove through Hammersmith, his knuckles white against the wheel. He rewound the entire operation in his mind in its new light, more and more convinced Judith's analysis was correct. Lubyanov had seduced the hapless Valerie, then paraded in a public park until the watchers spotted him. He had eventually coughed up the name of 'Daughtry' and allowed the British to use their deductive brilliance to pin-point Joseph Docherty at Burghfield; then the magical surveillance operation of Gontar and the Basamalah brothers, who had been recalled before they too could be caught in the net; the triumphant arrests at Paddington and the reciprocal seizing of Iain Mack, ensuring that Mikhail Gontar would never spend more than a few days in a British jail. There had certainly been some high-level British collusion – the Russians had known precisely when to arrest Iain Mack, without being alerted by their London embassy.

By the time Smailes drew up outside the Chiswick house, his jaw was set in anger. There was nothing he could do – Roger was doubtless scurrying around Whitehall trying to put out fires, and Kinney did not have sufficient authority to rule on his conjectures. Smailes could return to Curzon House, demand an emergency meeting and let Yuri Lubyanov stew in his own juice. But he and Judith would need a carefully documented case before they had anything like adequate grounds to go before a tribunal. So Smailes had no choice but to play his part in what he was now convinced was a charade.

The door was answered by A Branch veteran Johnny Hooper, who looked downcast. 'Sorry, Derek. I couldn't get anywhere with him. He flat refused,' he said.

'I doubt I'll do any better,' said Smailes. 'Where is he?'

'In the living room. He's been playing cards.'

It sounded like odd behaviour for someone who had supposedly made the most fateful decision of his life, but Smailes didn't comment.

'Put the kettle on before you turn on the recording gear, will you, Johnny?' asked Smailes, opening the door to the tobacco clouds of Lubyanov's presence.

For an hour Smailes tried his best to play his part as Lubyanov's thwarted suitor for the sake of the post-mortem, but his heart wasn't in it. He now knew Lubyanov was acting, and his act seemed transparent. But Lubyanov had a retort for each of Smailes's gambits and kept up his pretence assiduously.

'You'll go to Siberia, you know, Yuri,' Smailes goaded. 'We're going to boot out those diplomats you named and Uncle Boris is going to be very pissed off with you.'

Lubyanov countered with his foolish grin. 'I do not think so, Mr Sykes. My mother tells me things are quite tense between London and Moscow right now. Each has arrested a spy, she says. I do not think your government is going to make things worse by expelling diplomats, do you?'

Smailes pressed on into unauthorized territory. 'How do you know this spy we arrested wasn't as a result of your information?'

Lubyanov glared at him. 'Impossible. And if it were, it could never be traced to me. I will deny everything!'

'Still hoping your father-in-law will get you off the hook, Yuri?'

'Actually, yes. Together with what I can provide in debriefing about your tactics, I think I can avoid a jail sentence. Oh, I will be fired, certainly, but that will be a relief.'

'Lucky you,' said Smailes.

'And I will have my honour. My mother will not go broken-hearted to her grave.'

'Right, Yuri, your honour,' he said, unable to disguise his sarcasm.

Smailes and Lubyanov trotted around this circle a few more times until Smailes felt he could officially quit.

'Right, Yuri, you can have your wish. I'll arrange for you to be handed over to your embassy.'

'Today?'

'Today,' he confirmed, and went out into the kitchen to make his calls.

After speaking with Kinney and then Caldicott's people, Smailes decided to go one last round with Lubyanov. He had told Brian that he thought the whole thing stank, and Brian agreed with him, not picking up on his meaning.

Lubyanov was sprawled on the couch, smoking and reading a magazine – really tortured by his predicament, Smailes thought. He looked up at Smailes but kept on reading.

'Well? Soon?' he asked.

Smailes crouched at his side. 'Listen, Yuri,' he said quietly, although he knew the recording system was off. 'I know you're a sham. You've conned us from the start, and we fell for it, so I guess you win. But don't think you fooled everyone. If I'd worked it out sooner, you'd be up in Bovingdon right now, facing some of our own active measures. Some sleep deprivation, a little hooding, I think we'd get the true story out of you quite quickly. You see, Yuri, I believe you really *are* a coward.'

Lubyanov was instantly back in character. He sat bolt upright. 'What are you talking about?' he cried. 'Honestly, thank God I will be finally quitting this crazy business! Everyone is paranoid! You think I made all this up?'

'Yuri, I know you did. You and Zhimin together,' Smailes said, and left the room.

It was after two and Smailes had not eaten. The hand-over was arranged for five, and Smailes had to stay and complete the formalities. He told Hooper sourly he was stepping out for a bite to eat.

He found a snack bar and ordered a sandwich, feeling angry and impotent. To his relief, he realized he would no longer be able to keep his appointment with Rudy. He asked the waitress for a pay phone and she pointed out a booth by the door. Smailes searched his wallet and called the number for Rudy's hotel.

A strong French accent told Smailes that Mr Kabalan was not answering his phone. Was there a message? Smailes said yes, that he was sorry, he would have to cancel their appointment. Was that all? The receptionist wanted to know. Smailes made an impulsive decision.

'No,' he said. 'No, there's more. Ready? "Smelly Russian about to fly the coop, five o'clock. Surveillance would be greatly appreciated."' Then, aware he was putting his career in jeopardy, he appended the Chiswick address. Appealingly, the French clerk asked him to spell the word 'coop' but not 'surveillance'.

19

The stately hulk of Francis Caldicott cruised into the Chiswick kitchen flanked by a diminutive aide, like a liner escorted by a tugboat. He was late but clearly immensely pleased by this turn of events, and stooped to confront Smailes, who did not stand.

'*Nigh*,' he drawled, 'where is our Prince Hamlet?'

'Upstairs,' said Smailes, 'rehearsing his lines.'

Caldicott ignored the taunt. 'Well, I must say, this is all for the best. *Some* of us try to move the clock forward, you know, while *others* keep trying to turn it back. And look what happens. Can't you fellows see your antics are a thing of the past?'

Smailes felt his hackles rise. He hadn't met Caldicott before, though he knew him by reputation. He didn't doubt that in his deposition to the Carne commission Caldicott had done his level best to state the case for MI5's extinction.

'Well, the exercise wasn't without results,' was all Smailes said. 'Johnny? Fetch him down, will you?'

Hooper was stationed at the door and retreated to summon Lubyanov from his bedroom. Caldicott's aide delved into a briefcase and produced a legal folder which his master inspected briefly, then handed to Smailes. Smailes scanned the contract quickly. It contained an MI5 boiler-plate for collaborating foreign diplomats, with a few custom clauses for Lubyanov, probably composed that afternoon by Ed Poynter. In it Lubyanov agreed to indemnify the British government against all claims, to state that his treatment had been 'acceptable and humane', and to leave the country within forty-eight hours. It also declared void undertakings any government representative may have given him, verbally or in writing. It affirmed Lubyanov's decision to be returned to representatives of Russia was made of his own free will, and that he accepted all consequences. Typically, the forms were in quintuplicate. Francis Caldicott had already signed them all on behalf of Her Majesty's Government.

'What's the procedure?' Smailes inquired, although Kinney had already told him.

'We'll drive our friend over to the Shepherd's Bush roundabout, where he will be transferred to First Secretary Zhimin.'

'You weren't followed?'

Caldicott frowned, then said wearily, 'No. Our Friends arranged counter-surveillance. We are assured not.'

'Friends' was the Foreign office moniker for SIS, which meant MI5's arch-rival now knew the address of their Chiswick safe house. Roger wouldn't like that.

Lubyanov duly appeared and made a production of anxiously perusing his contract before signing all five copies. Smailes found his temper rising again – he could sense Lubyanov laughing at them. Finally, the three of them shuffled down the hall and out into a black government limousine. Smailes stood at the bay window, looking up and down the street at the rows of parked cars. As Caldicott drove away, Smailes waited several minutes to see whether any vehicle was going to pull out in pursuit. There was none. The SIS crew had probably peeled off, and either Rudy hadn't received Smailes's message, or, just as likely, he had chosen to ignore it. Smailes returned dejectedly to the kitchen and called K Branch. Kinney took his call, but told him everyone else had already left for the day. Johnny Hooper then got on to his crew chief and was told to come back in. Smailes handed him the Lubyanov documents and asked Hooper to book them in for him. Then he went dispiritedly out to his car – it was almost six.

Clea Smailes had made a determined effort to appear less resentful around her husband, although she knew she wasn't always successful. She greeted Derek's arrival cheerfully enough and offered to get him a drink, noticing immediately that he seemed depressed. Smailes sat down wearily on the floor with Lucy, who began recounting an incomprehensible tale about Fidelma and a big dog.

'You all right?' Clea asked.

'Iain called me from Moscow today.'

'Iain?' she shrieked. 'Is he out?'

'No.'

'How did he sound?'

'Scared, demoralized. The Russians have concocted a nasty case against him.'

'What is MI5 doing?'

'The wheels have started to come off our own case against the

Russian bigwig – we'll probably have to agree to a trade. Iain will be out in a day or two.'

'So is that why you're depressed?'

'I suppose so. No . . . well, it's a long story.'

Clea disappeared into the kitchen, then returned to lean against the door frame.

'Maybe Daddy can put you to bed tonight, Lucy,' she said, immediately regretting her archness of tone.

'Yeah,' Lucy cried. 'Daddy tell story!'

Smailes looked up at his wife.

'Do you mind?' she asked belatedly.

'No,' said Smailes, getting up with a grunt. 'It's my turn, I suppose. Is there a beer in the fridge? I've got to change.'

Smailes came downstairs and resumed his attempt to play with his daughter. The phone rang and Clea answered it in the kitchen.

'It's for you,' she said coldly. 'Judith.'

Smailes got to his feet, embarrassed. He took the call as his wife tossed lettuce busily at his elbow.

'Yes?' he said.

'Derek? Look, I'm really sorry to call you at home. I wanted to call you at Chiswick, but Brian wouldn't give me the number. Can you believe that?'

'Yes, well, everybody's been under a lot of stress. What's up?'

'I've got some more information on Lubyanov.'

'What?'

'I looked for you . . . I was told you had gone down to Chiswick.'

'Right.'

'Lubyanov. Has he, you know, done a bunk?'

'Yes.'

'I decided . . . Well, if the whole thing was fake, then he had to be fake too.'

'I couldn't agree more.'

'So I put another trace on him. Wider than I'd done before.'

'How?'

'It was a long shot, but there's a publication in America, in Ohio, called *The Current Digest of Soviet Press*. We used to use it in KY.'

'Go on.'

'Well, it's defunct now, but they keep an archivist, and I got him to do a search on Yuri Lubyanov. It didn't cost much. I wired them my own funds.'

'And?'

'He got back to me just before close of business. Apparently there's a Yuri Lubyanov who got great reviews from the *Literary Gazette* for his performances in a Chekhov play at the Mkhat Theatre in 1975.'

'That bastard is a professional actor?'

'Exactly.'

'God damn it! Well, that confirms it. This whole bloody thing stinks, Judith. We've been led up the garden path.'

'That's what I think.'

'Look. We'll put our case on paper first thing in the morning, then call a meeting of the Jonquil team. It may affect how we proceed with Gontar.'

'All right. You don't mind my calling in like this? Normally, of course, I . . .'

'No, don't be daft. You did the right thing.'

'All right. Thanks. But, Derek – what on earth is their game?'

'Good question. Give it some thought. Give me a number in case I want to get back to you.'

'Just a minute,' said Judith. A moment later she came back on the line and gave him a number.

'You don't know your own phone number?'

'I'm staying with a friend in Muswell Hill.'

'Oh, right,' said Smailes. 'Well. Talk to you later.'

'What was all that about?' asked Clea coolly.

'Like I said,' said Smailes, 'long story.'

He went back into the living room to find Lucy, but the phone rang again. This time he came back into the kitchen and answered it himself.

'Derek?' said a familiar voice. 'That you?'

'Rudy!' Smailes yelled. 'Where the hell are you?'

'Sluff,' said Rudy.

'You mean Slough,' said Smailes, laughing. 'What're you doing there?'

'Well, it's where the Russian boys went after they picked up their guy at the big roundabout.'

'You tailed them? You got my message?'

'Yeah, although not till around five. Thought I might be too late. I'd already sent Carla off on her own, so I thought what the hell, for old times' sake.'

Smailes hooted, then said, 'But I watched from the window – I didn't see anyone follow our limousine.'

'You don't think I'm dumb enough to park in the street, do you? Lucky I didn't too, because there was a back-up team down the next block. Made it a bit tricky . . .'

'Rudy, you're a pal. What happened? They went to Slough?'

'Yeah, right. They did a hand-over at that big roundabout, then the Russian car headed west. Both British cars headed back into the city.'

'How were the Russians behaving?'

'Hard to tell – I gave them a long lead. Although, when the car pulled up at a light, I could see all three – that's the driver, the little fat guy in the back, and the guy who's been picked up, who's sitting in front – light up smokes. Then the guy in the front threw back his head, like he'd been stuck with a lit cigarette or something.'

'Or was roaring with laughter?'

'I dunno. Could be.'

'Then what?'

'Well, I thought it weird they weren't heading back to their embassy, but then I think no, they're going to the airport.'

'They didn't?'

'No. They drove right by the exit and pulled off at Sluff. Then they drove into this tacky housing development and all piled out into a shitty little house. I'm calling from a laundromat round the corner.'

Safe house, said Smailes to himself. He could tell there was more coming. 'Then what?'

'Well,' said Rudy, 'it's the damnedest thing, but I'm parked round the block, up a little hill, wondering what to do, when a second car pulls up and another guy goes in.'

'So?'

'Well, I couldn't be a hundred per cent, 'cause it's years since I've seen him, but I'd swear it was that asshole Strickland.'

'Loudon Strickland? The CIA station chief? Entering a Russian safe house?'

'Yeah. I figured this is getting weird, I should give you a call.'

Smailes's mind was racing. 'Rudy – you got a camera?'

'Sure, but it's back at the hotel.'

'Where are you? Exactly?'

Rudy gave him the address, motorway exit and rough instructions how to find him.

'Sit tight. I'll be there in half an hour or so, depending on traffic.'

'You wanna tell me what this is all about?'

'When I get there. Just keep your eye on the place, okay?'

'Okay. But Derek, I dunno . . .'

'Rudy, I'm going to owe you one. A big one. See you soon.'

He hung up, wheeling round. He saw Lucy sitting in Clea's lap and four eyes regarding him evenly.

'Now what?' asked Clea.

'Where's the camera?' he asked.

'On the bookcase. Derek, you're not going out, are you? You promised Lucy . . .'

'I've got to, Clea. That was Rudy, in Slough. I can't really explain, but he may be on to something really important.' He rushed into the living room.

Lucy had realized what was happening. 'Daddy tell story?' she asked anxiously.

Clea came into the living room after him, carrying Lucy. 'Where are you going?' she demanded.

'Slough,' he said, checking the camera for film.

'Honestly, Derek, I'm just sick of this. We're all sick of this. You have a family too, you know.'

'I know, Clea. Look, I'll explain, I promise. Lucy, I'm sorry. I've got to go back to work. I'll tell you a story tomorrow night.'

'Daddy tell story!' Lucy howled. Clea glared at him as he hurried out of the door, but he ignored her. She held the wailing child in her arms and watched from the front window as her husband reversed hurriedly out of the drive, then roared off.

'Oh, Lucy,' she said angrily. 'Do shut up.'

Traffic on the M25 was heavy in places, but Smailes made it to the Slough exit in just under forty-five minutes. During the drive he sketched the outlines of the story he would give the Jonquil team the following day. Collusion between the CIA and the KGB was now confirmed; between them they had obviously cooked up the sting involving Lubyanov, Gontar and Docherty. Why? Smailes knew the CIA had favoured giving the Russians American PAL hardware all along, which made Strickland the probable source of the Burghfield leak. Which in turn had required the Russians and Americans to dish up a real spy at Burghfield – Docherty – to foreclose further British investigations. The scheme was intricate and expensive, but had a certain warped logic. Smailes negotiated a series of roundabouts, his mind set on finding the Russian safe house before it got dark. He desperately wanted recognizable prints of Strickland and Zhimin emerging, hopefully together.

The housing estate was on the western edge of town, one of those sixties developments in which the attempt at variety only emphasized the essential uniformity of the three-bedroom, semi-detached boxes. The houses were faced with stucco, tile or panelling, with garages attached or recessed. Streets were named after local flora, and Smailes found Rudy's rented Escort in Vine Crescent, around the corner from Foxglove Drive, where Rudy had said the targets were holed up. Smailes parked quietly and slid into Rudy's passenger seat.

'They still there?' he asked, not looking at his friend.

'Yeah,' said Rudy. 'Getting to be quite a party.'

'What do you mean?'

'Another guy just showed up. Ten minutes ago. Came on foot from the other end of the street.'

'What'd he look like?'

'Tall, fiftyish, white hair. Pin-stripes. Smoking a cigarette. Brit, I'd say.'

Adrenalin flooded Smailes's system, constricting his chest. The description was unmistakable.

'Standiforth!' he spat. 'I should have bloody well known it. God, I'm so stupid!'

'Who's Standiforth?'

'My boss.'

'Your boss? Hey, no kiddin'! Derek, where the hell are you goin'?'

Ignoring him, Smailes struggled out of the tiny car, his face purple with rage. Rudy climbed out and ran around to restrain him.

'Don't be stupid, Derek. Derek . . . Derek!'

Smailes shook off Rudy's grip and strode angrily down the street. Standiforth, of course; Roger Standiforth, the master manipulator. The operation had betrayed Roger's hallmark all along, if only he'd looked; instead, he'd been a complete nincompoop. There was no counter-espionage triumph here – just a cosy deal between three secret warlords carving up turf. Smailes no longer cared about photographs or presentations to the Jonquil team. He just wanted to see Roger's face when he burst in and confronted him with his real associates – Boris Zhimin, Yuri Lubyanov and Loudon Strickland.

Smailes passed a dwarf poplar and was reaching down for the latch of a low metal gate when a movement caught his eye. Looking up, he saw a pale figure at the top of the street drop into a crouch, a dark blur in front of his face. Then he heard a single report, and pain exploded in his midriff. Looking down, Smailes saw blood bathe the front of his shirt and trousers as fire flowed up into his chest and neck. He pitched forward in terror, then passed out.

*

Clea Smailes had just completed the awkward task of getting her disappointed daughter to sleep and was changing into her nightdress when the phone rang. She sat on the bed and took the call, pushing a sticky strand of hair from her face. It was Rudy, speaking rapidly.

'Clea? Yeah, look, it's Rudy. Yeah, listen, Derek's been shot. But they say he's going to be okay. Well, he lost a lot of blood, but the head nurse just came out, and said, well, he's in the operating theatre right now . . .'

Panic flooded her. 'Derek's shot? Where? Where are you? What happened?'

'In the gut somewhere, I think. We're at the hospital. Wexham Park hospital. It's just outside the town, Sluff. The ambulance got here pretty fast, luckily. Listen, Clea, I've got to go with the cops. They're waiting for me.'

'Rudy, wait! Which town? Slough?'

'Right, whatever you call it. Look, I'm sorry, Clea. I couldn't stop him. I knew it was real dangerous. I gotta go. Don't worry, he's gonna pull through. I'll call you later.'

The line went dead and Clea fought her emotions as she fumbled in Derek's bedside table for his address book. Her hands shook as she punched the buttons. Brian Kinney's wife answered, and it seemed an age before Brian himself came on the line. At the sound of his voice she broke down completely. It was a long minute before she could gather herself to relay Rudy's horrific news. Brian checked a couple of details, said he'd meet her at the hospital and rang off.

Clea stood paralysed in the middle of the bedroom. She had to get to Slough. She had to get a sitter for Lucy. She had to change. She pulled the nightgown over her head and stood naked and bewildered in front of her wardrobe. She reached in for a dress but it fell from her grasp. She sat down on the bed and began to whimper. Then she forced herself to make her calls, first to her next-door neighbour, then to her mother, using as few words as possible. She pulled on her underwear and dress, struggling against the heat and her size. She could hear her neighbour Alice tapping on the back door. Gathering herself, she walked slowly downstairs, careful not to wake Lucy.

On the way to Slough, Clea suddenly realized the meaning of the expression 'beside oneself'. She felt disembodied, observing this preternaturally controlled woman who was driving at breakneck speed in the fast lane of the motorway. She felt no violent emotion, just an icy dread that her husband would die. Worse, that he would die believing her heart was hardened against him. She felt a searing regret.

It wasn't Derek she had resented, it was her situation. Had he understood that? But Derek was all she had had to blame. Clea made desperate bargains with a deity in whom she had never believed, that if her husband survived she would somehow make amends. What had she overheard in the kitchen? The Russians? The CIA? What had Rudy said? He tried to stop him? What on earth had Derek done to get himself shot in the stomach – in Slough of all places?

Luckily, the hospital was signposted from the first exit, and Clea followed the ring road around to the north of town. She pulled into the access road to a low, modern hospital with a central tower block, instinctively following the sign for Accidents and Emergencies past the main entrance, incongruously set back between shop fronts for a florist and a radio station. She parked and hurried across to the automatic doors, outside which an ambulance was parked. Her heart was in her throat. She did not think she could maintain her control much longer.

In the reception area she immediately saw Brian Kinney, standing next to a fenced children's play area. She thought of Lucy and her unborn child, and collapsed into tears. Brian's wiry arms caught her.

'He's going to survive. He's out of surgery,' said Brian.

'Oh, thank God. Thank God,' said Clea, weeping uncontrollably against his shoulder.

'They'll see us in the family waiting room,' said Kinney. 'The surgeon asked to be told as soon as you arrived.'

Brian gestured to a nurse and led Clea slowly to the waiting room where, mercifully, he produced a large handkerchief. Clea sat down and sobbed tears of gratitude and release. Feeling better, she took a deep breath and looked at Brian.

'What happened?'

'I'm not sure. I was waiting for you. I'll go over to the police station and try and find out. Apparently, Derek met a friend . . .'

'Rudy,' said Clea.

At that point the heavy metal door opened and a young man came into the room. He was wearing Levi jeans, a short-sleeved shirt and tie, and looked like he needed a shave.

'Mrs Smailes?' he asked.

'Yes,' Clea managed.

The young man squatted on his haunches and took Clea's hand. 'I'm Mr Alan Smallwood, the senior registrar. I performed the operation on your husband. He was very lucky. He should make a full recovery.'

Clea was momentarily confused, forgetting that in the National Health Service surgeons were 'Mister' and that 'registrar' was a medical, not an administrative rank. Seeing her puzzlement, Smallwood pressed on.

'I'm head of the trauma team, the senior surgeon. We were ready to operate on him in Resuscitation, but the ambulance crew had done an excellent job of stabilizing him, so I was able to get him down to the OT. The bullet transsected the renal artery and macerated his right kidney, I'm afraid, so we had to take it out. But luckily there were no other internal injuries . . .'

Clea was horrified. 'You took out his kidney? And he'll be all right?'

'Oh yes,' said Smallwood brightly. 'He'll do just fine with one. Lots of people do.'

'So he isn't . . . he wasn't in any real danger?'

'Oh, I wouldn't say that. His friend saved his life really, getting the ambulance there so quickly. Loss of blood is the major threat with abdominal wounds, and the damaged artery was bleeding profusely. But the ambulance crew was there within minutes of the call, and they were able to make up his fluid deficit and get him into the Mast trousers.'

'Mast trousers?' asked Brian.

'It's an inflatable garment that's pumped up to constrict the blood vessels of the legs and maintain blood supply to the vital organs. They've become real life-savers with abdominal wounds.'

'Can I see him?' Clea asked meekly.

'I thought you'd ask that,' said Smallwood. 'He's in ITU, on a ventilator, but I'll let you look in, to prove to you I'm telling the truth.'

'ITU?' asked Clea.

'Intensive Therapy Unit,' said Smallwood. 'It's a routine precaution, for twenty-four hours or so. Then we'll transfer him to Recovery. He'll be fine in a week or so. You'll see.'

Reassured by this young man's obvious skill and confidence, Clea gave silent thanks for the existence of the National Health Service.

'Actually, will it be a private room?' asked Smallwood, turning to Kinney. 'I heard he's a civil servant.'

'That's right,' said Kinney. 'Private room. We'll accept all costs.'

'Right, then,' said Smallwood. 'Follow me.'

Brian halted in the reception area and told Clea he needed to get going – would she be all right? Clea smiled for the first time since Rudy's fateful call. 'I'll be fine, Brian,' she said. 'Will you call me at home later? Just tell me what you can. I understand, you know, if you can't tell me much.'

Clea's heart was suffused with gratitude and appreciation. What a lovely man Brian was, she told herself. And so good-looking! And this young doctor – what a hunk! She followed him down an antiseptic corridor lined with children's drawings, her eyes fixed on his skinny, jean-clad hips. Outside a door guarded by what looked like a welding kit, Smallwood paused.

'All right, don't be alarmed – the life support equipment is purely routine. We'll start taking it off when he's awake. He'll he transferred to Recovery tomorrow. The nurses are still getting him settled, so just stand inside the door and look.'

Clea and the surgeon entered the ward and Smallwood drew back a privacy curtain. Clea's eyes watered – Derek looked so helpless. He was sprawled on his back, most of his face obscured by a mask and a corrugated plastic tube. His head was immobilized by a plastic neck brace, and intravenous lines fed into both arms. Pads and wires encased his bare chest above a thick white dressing from which tubing led into a receptacle on the floor. Monitors peeped and whirred; green digital numbers glowed and screens pulsed. He seemed to be in safe hands.

'Oh, darling,' she said to herself, her heart bursting with love. 'The things you get yourself into.'

Ignoring Smallwood's instructions, she stepped forward and touched the little finger of his right hand. It stirred slightly. Smallwood caught her shoulder and frowned, and they retreated back into the corridor.

'Sorry, doctor,' she said. 'I just had to . . .'

'That's all right. Now, if you'll excuse me . . .'

Clea shook his hand. 'Thank you. Thank you so much. I don't know what to say.'

'You just did. Actually, it's a pleasure.' He glanced down at the fullness of her figure. 'When are you due?'

'November.'

'Congratulations. Look, if you want to wait, he'll be awake in an hour or so. Actually, I wouldn't advise it. He'll be very disoriented and in a lot of pain, and we'll need to run more tests. The front desk can explain the visiting hours. Can you find it again?'

'I think so.'

'Well, then. Goodbye, Mrs Smailes. Your husband is a lucky man.' Before Clea could decide whether this was a forward remark, Mr Alan Smallwood's skinny hips had disappeared around the corner.

20

Rudy Kabalan felt like an idiot. He cursed the impulse which had made him accept Derek's bizarre request in the first place, knowing it would make Carla furious. She'd made him forswear his cloak-and-dagger past before agreeing to marry him and, at the time, Rudy had consented willingly. Now he would have some explaining to do. What would be worse, of course, was if the British detained him for further questioning and they missed their plane home. That would send Carla through the roof. It had been a long trip and she was anxious to get home.

Rudy sat on a hard chair in the waiting area of Slough police station. His statement to Detective Inspector Bill Cartwright had been circumspect, to say the least. Rudy knew the gulf that separated the law enforcement and intelligence worlds only too well, so had offered only the barest outline of events. In his statement Rudy had professed ignorance of the identity or nationality of the individual he'd followed on his friend's behalf. He did not know why Derek wanted him followed, or why Derek had tried to enter the house. He had not seen anyone fire the gun – this much was true. Neither had he seen anyone leave the scene, since he had run into a nearby house to call an ambulance – this much was not true.

A policeman had stuck his head in the door and said that a Mr Kinney from the Security Service also wanted to interview Mr Kabalan. Could he please wait? Rudy, of course, had been happy to oblige.

Rudy now watched as a thin, intense-looking man in a golf shirt and brogues entered by the main doors and looked around.

'Are you Rudy?' he asked.

'Yeah,' he said, standing. He wasn't sure whether a handshake was in order, and he shifted his weight awkwardly. 'How is he?'

'Out of surgery. He's going to pull through.'

Rudy was vastly relieved. Kinney stepped forward and offered his hand. 'I'm Brian Kinney – Derek's section head. Let me see if I can find us a room.' He strode up to the heavy oak counter and spoke to the desk sergeant.

At first, Rudy was suspicious. 'I thought Derek's boss was a guy called Standiforth,' he said as they took their seats across a grey metal table. Inspector Cartwright had taken up his position at Kinney's elbow.

'That's right,' said Kinney, and explained Derek's temporary transfer back to his section. Then he took a microcassette recorder from a trouser pocket and set it on the table. 'Now, can you tell me exactly what happened?'

Rudy pointed at the CID detective and frowned. Kinney understood immediately.

'Look, Bill, give us a private session, will you? I'm sure Mr Kabalan is prepared to cooperate fully.' Cartwright scowled, but left the room. Kinney clicked on his machine. 'Now, Rudy, what the bloody hell is going on?'

Rudy trod carefully, since he realized something big was going on in that little house in Slough – it sounded like a covert summit of honchos from three supposedly hostile intelligence services. And Rudy wasn't sure what Kinney knew or what he was supposed to know. But Rudy was in a jam and realized he'd better show good faith or he would never be on that plane to New York the next day.

This time around, Rudy's version of events was more expansive. He explained his discovery of Derek's message at his hotel, giving the word-for-word text, since he reasoned MI5 could easily learn it from the desk clerk. Kinney was clearly shocked, and asked about Rudy's relationship with Smailes. Rudy explained he was an ex-CIA contractor, and that he and Derek had worked together in New York but were now just social acquaintances. He and his wife were visiting London on their honeymoon trip and had looked up Derek and his family. They were due to leave for the States the next day, he said pointedly.

He went on to describe his tailing of the British limousine from Chiswick, the hand-over at the roundabout, and his subsequent tracking of the Russian car to the Slough housing estate. He had then called Derek, who had shown up within the hour.

'What else did you see?' asked Kinney.

Rudy described the two guests who had arrived while he was waiting, but did not pretend to identify either. Derek had brought a camera with him, he explained.

Kinney's expression remained impassive.

Rudy then explained Derek's violent reaction at the description of the second party, and his attempt to storm the house.

'Did he say who he thought it was?' asked Kinney.

'He blurted a name, I think,' said Kabalan. 'I didn't catch it.'

'Go on.'

'I knew it was dumb for him to go barging in there. I tried to restrain him, but he shook me off. He's a big guy. I . . . I'm afraid I just stood and watched. I was already sorry I was there.'

'No doubt.'

'So when he got to the gate, I saw him look round, up the street. Then I heard the shot. He fell.'

'You didn't see who shot him?'

'No, whoever it was, he was up the street, out of sight.'

'What did you do?'

'For a few seconds, nothing. I was in shock.'

'What happened?'

'The people in the house started bailing out. The three parties in the original car climbed in and drove off. It was out front. So was the second guy's car.'

'The pale man in glasses?'

'Right. He drove off real fast too. The third guy was out on the sidewalk by now. A car screeched up and he climbed in. They were all gone within seconds.'

'Did you get any licence plate numbers?'

'No,' Rudy lied.

'What did they do about the body lying there?'

'They just stepped round him, like he was so much dead meat. I could see blood on the sidewalk – a lot of it. People were coming out of their houses. I ran into the nearest one. The lady called the ambulance, the cops. I went to see if Derek was still alive. There was a crowd around his body. I could see he was breathing, but it looked real serious. Gut shots usually are. Luckily, the ambulance was there right away. Then the cops. I told them what I'd seen, and they brought me to the hospital and let me call Derek's wife. The nurse came out and said they thought he was going to be okay. Then the cops brought me here. I gave them a statement. Confidentially, Brian, it's not nearly as full as what I just told you. I figured, well, you guys would be handling this yourselves, maybe you wanted to do it your way.'

'I understand.'

'Listen, Brian, I got one major question. Now that Derek's gonna be okay, and I've told you what happened, can I get my plane home tomorrow? Otherwise, my wife is gonna kill me.'

Kinney had already thought of this. Smailes was no doubt going to recover, and would have no choice but to give them the full story himself if he was going to save his neck. From Kabalan's description, it sounded as if Zhimin, Strickland and Standiforth had been meeting to debrief Lubyanov, far-fetched as that sounded. He wasn't sure Kabalan had told him the whole truth, but he was confident he would get a more complete story out of Smailes. As far as he could tell, Rudy had broken no British laws. He was a material witness and could probably be recalled, if necessary. Somehow, Brian doubted it would come to that.

'Well, all right. If you understand you may be recalled, and if I can clear it with the police.'

'You can swing that, can't you, Brian?'

'Probably,' said Kinney. 'Now, let's start again at the beginning. Tell me how you know Derek Smailes.'

Clea Smailes was lying wide awake, her thoughts streaming, when the phone rang just after midnight. She picked it up on the first ring.

'Clea? Hi, it's Rudy. It's not too late?'

'No. No, that's all right. I don't expect I'll sleep much tonight.'

'He's okay?'

'Yes, he's all right. They let me see him. They had to remove a kidney, but that's apparently not serious.'

'Jesus. Look, Clea, I'm really sorry. I couldn't stop him . . .'

'Rudy, it's not your fault. I know Derek when he's in that mood. Wild horses couldn't stop him. Can you tell me what happened? Derek's boss was supposed to call me, but he hasn't.'

'Kinney?'

'You met him?'

'At the police station. Seems a decent guy. He's letting me and Carla leave tomorrow, at least,' he added.

'How's Carla?'

'Pissed as all hell. She's not speaking to me.' There was a pause. 'Listen, I don't know what I can really say, but Derek had me tail this guy from west London.'

'A Russian.'

'I guess so. I called your house when they got out in Slough – that's how you say it?'

'Yes,' said Clea, sitting up and pushing her hair from her face.

'Then a couple of other guys show. I describe them to Derek when he arrives, and he freaks out. He obviously wanted to bust up their party. He was shot when he got to the gate.'

'By whom?'

'I couldn't see. A look-out, I would guess.'

'Will they catch him? The person who shot him?'

'Depends on whether anyone got an ID or a plate number. Probably not – the guy would likely have diplomatic immunity, anyway.'

'What's going on, Rudy? What made Derek so angry?'

'Beats me. I think you'll have to ask him yourself, honey. Look, I may try and stop in tomorrow on the way to the airport. But if I don't, you tell him from me it's time for him to find a less dangerous profession, understand? From someone who knows.'

'You tell him, Rudy. He won't listen to me.'

'Yeah, well.' There was an awkward silence.

'Rudy, don't feel bad. The surgeon said you saved his life.'

'Me? How?'

'By calling the ambulance so quickly. The bullet punctured the artery to his kidney and he would have bled to death if they hadn't been able to operate so fast.'

'Well, hey, that makes me feel better. Actually, a lot better. Maybe if I tell Carla, she'll cool off a bit.'

'Do that, Rudy. And say hello from me. Tell her I'm sorry we didn't get together again.'

'Yeah, next time. Good luck with the baby, Clea. Good luck with everything. So long.'

'Bye, Rudy. And thanks for everything.'

'Yeah.'

Clea hung up, feeling oddly euphoric. Derek had been reprieved, her family had been reprieved, and she felt perhaps even her marriage had been reprieved. She wished Derek were there beside her now, potent and alive. She thought of Brian, the dark hair on his wiry forearms, and of the young surgeon with the Mick Jagger hips. Lucy stirred in her sleep and called out. There was little chance of sleep for her tonight, she knew. God, it was so hot! She touched herself gently beneath the sheet, easing her bulk down the bed.

Smailes awoke to the ministrations of a tall, lithe nurse with ebony skin and a flashing smile.

'Good morning,' she said. 'And how're you feeling today?'

Smailes's first reaction was one of relief, tinged with pride. He'd stopped a bullet and survived. He dimly remembered waking the previous evening, impaled by life-support equipment, feeling a distant panic, then an intense pain. A nurse and a doctor had been quickly on hand to uncouple some of the devices. A remote, disembodied voice told him a bullet had been removed from his abdomen but he was doing fine. The doctor examined him and spoke about matters Smailes could not recall. The solutions in his intravenous bags were changed, for the pain, he was told, and for sleep. Then the white fog descended again.

Smailes tried to hoist himself on his elbow and cried out in pain.

'No, sir,' said his nurse firmly. 'You lie still.' She began to remove the dressing around his waist. Smailes's next fear, remembering the blood on the front of his trousers, was for his manhood. Peering over his chest he saw that he was naked.

'Am I intact?' he asked.

'You certainly look it to me.' She gave him the flashing smile again. 'No cause for concern there.'

She adjusted something between his legs and Smailes gasped. 'What the hell is that?' he asked.

'You've been catheterized, sir,' she said. 'We've got to monitor that kidney for a while.'

Only then did Smailes think of his wife and daughter; he was stricken with remorse. His lunacy had almost left Clea a widow, Lucy fatherless, not to mention their unborn child.

'My wife? Has she been called?'

'I'm told she was here last night, before you were awake.'

'Can I talk to her?'

'Not yet. You'll be taken to Recovery, if Mr Smallwood says so, some time today. There're phones there. Now, I need your cooperation here. You've got to lift your buttocks for me. Slow, very slow. Good.'

Smailes suffered her attentions in silence, clenching his teeth against the pain, his mind a jumble of images from the previous night. He visualized the house and the street, and suddenly knew, with crystalline certainty, the identity of his attacker. A young doctor appeared at that moment and exchanged some gibberish with the nurse before consulting the monitors flanking Smailes's bed.

'I'm Alan Smallwood, head of the trauma team,' he said. 'I performed your operation last night. How do you feel?'

'Sore,' said Smailes.

'You will for a while. But you're a lucky man. The bullet damaged your right kidney, so we had to remove it. But that was fortunate – you happen to have two of those, and it's housed in its own cavity, behind the peritoneum, so the bleeding is contained. If you'd been hit in the liver or spleen, we might not have saved you.'

'I've lost a kidney?' Smailes gasped.

'Don't worry – you don't really need two. You can resume a completely normal life. I'm going to have you moved to Recovery this morning, as soon as we have a room ready. You should be home in a week or so.'

Smailes had a hundred questions, but one was paramount. 'Doctor, can you get this thing out of my penis? It's really uncomfortable.'

'No, not for another day. It's a Foley catheter, and it's monitoring the performance of your surviving kidney. Once I'm confident it's doing its job properly, I'll remove it.'

Smailes winced.

'Mr Kabalan is here to see you. I think he probably saved your life, calling the ambulance so quickly. Normally we'd put off visitors another day or two, until you're installed in your own room. But he says he has a plane to catch. I'll also make an exception for your wife, since she wasn't able to talk to you last night. I've told the police, and the people you work for, that you can't see anyone until tomorrow afternoon. Now, do you want to see Mr Kabalan?'

'Definitely.'

'I'll show him in.'

The nurse gave him an injection in his buttock, then covered him up. Presently, Rudy shuffled backwards through the door, hefting an enormous basket of fruit. 'I'll take that,' said the nurse, lifting it from his arms and leaving them alone.

Rudy regarded his friend sheepishly. 'Hi,' he said.

'Hi,' said Smailes.

'Look, I'm really sorry, Derek.'

'Don't be daft. You saved my life.'

'I shoulda wrestled you down. I knew there had to be a look-out.'

'You wouldn't have been able to.' Smailes paused. 'You get a look at him?'

'No. He was up the street.'

'No matter. I saw him.'

'Look, Derek, Carla's out in the car. We gotta get to Heathrow. I just wanted to see you were okay, give you something.'

'What?'

'I told your guy last night I didn't get any plate numbers.'

'Who?'

'Kinney. I talked to him at the cop station. He's the one who fixed it for us to leave. The cops, well . . .'

'He's a good guy.'

'Well, I did get the plate number of the car that picked up the last guy.' Rudy went into his wallet and pulled out a business card. He held it up in front of Smailes's face, then reversed it.

'That confirms it,' said Smailes. 'That's Roger's car. That was no look-out who shot me, Rudy. That was Roger's hatchet boy, a little prick called Peter Tennant. I saw him a split second before he fired.'

Kabalan crouched at his friend's side. 'Listen, buddy, I told this your wife last night, but I'll tell it to you, okay? It's time to get out. Getting shot is bad enough. Getting shot by your own team is worse. Much worse.'

'You worked it out, didn't you?'

'Yeah. I figured if the shot came from the same direction as the party on foot, it had to be his driver. If the Russians had a look-out, most likely he'd be inside. If you were right, that was your boss, then it's real bad news.'

'I'm going to get him, Rudy. I'm going to bring him down.'

'Derek, cut your losses. You got out alive, minus a kidney. Call it quits.'

'I thought you knew me better than that.'

'I do. But see reason. This is not a level playing field, guy. You don't know how high this thing goes. And count me out. I didn't see nothing, okay? I can't go to bat for you on this, Derek – I'd end up divorced. Carla is pissed I insisted on coming out here this morning. Real pissed. But I felt I owed it you. Now I'm outta here. Understand?'

'I understand, Rudy. Thanks. Leave me that card.'

'No way.' Rudy stuffed it back into his wallet. 'So long.'

'So long, Rudy. You coming again soon?'

'Within six months, probably. It's a go, I think, the shop in Croydon.'

'No kidding? Hey, Rudy – thanks.' He managed a weak wave, his IV line flapping.

Against her better judgement, Clea decided to bring Lucy to the hospital the next day. She was anxious about her Daddy's whereabouts, and Clea decided the best way to allay her fears was to show her Derek was all right. After confirming her husband was out of ITU, she told Lucy she could come along too, upon which Lucy clapped her hands and demanded a complete change of outfit. If Derek still looked frightful, Clea reasoned, she would make up an excuse and cope with Lucy's tantrum on the spot.

It turned out to be an inspired decision. Clea and Lucy found Derek in a fourth-floor recovery room, sitting up and wearing a hospital smock, his arm tethered to a lone IV. Derek and Clea were each too moved to speak at first. Clea drew up a chair and took her husband's hand, and Lucy tried to clamber on to the bed, saying 'Daddy, boo-boo?' Clea restrained her gently and explained that yes, Daddy had a boo-boo, but that he was going to be all right. She turned to Derek and kissed him lingeringly on the lips as the tears ran freely down her face. It was Derek who broke the silence, speaking through their kiss.

'You'd better stop, love. I've got something the size of a drinking straw up my willie, and I'm not sure of the consequences if you keep going.'

Clea giggled and sat down, and Derek reached for the Kleenex next to his bed. He wiped his eyes and blew his nose theatrically in the way that always made Lucy laugh. Lucy cried out with glee, then spied Rudy's basket of fruit.

'Geeps!' she cooed, stretching up and coming away with a handful of grapes. Clea wiped her eyes and laughed.

'Rudy,' explained Smailes, pointing. 'He came on his way to the airport.'

'He said he might,' said Clea. 'He called me last night.' She paused. 'The doctor says you were very lucky.'

Smailes squeezed her hand. 'I'm the luckiest man on the planet,' he said, at which Clea began to cry again.

'I'm sorry, darling,' he said eventually. 'It was a really stupid thing for me to do.'

'You survived. That's all I care about. As I was driving here last night, I was afraid you would die believing I hated you. I couldn't face that. I've been so awful to you, Derek.'

'Die?' asked Lucy, through a mouthful of grapes.

'Well, I didn't, and I don't, and you haven't. All right?' said Smailes.

Lucy had swallowed her fruit. 'Daddy die?' she asked, trying to climb on to the bed again.

'No, but I just might if you clamber on me, little miss.'

Clea grabbed her and planted her on her lap, where Lucy seemed content to roost. She stuck her thumb in her mouth. 'Geeps,' she said again into her hand.

Neither Derek nor Clea had any interest in matters of weight. His brush with mortality had burst the dam between them, and they sat together, holding hands and prattling, laughing at Lucy's antics, or saying nothing. Smailes's heart was bursting, and he felt a perverse gratitude for the trauma that had brought about this reconciliation. Deep shit lay ahead of him, he knew, but in this warm family cocoon he was able to put his predicament from his mind.

Presently, a nurse put her head in the door and said firmly that Mr Smailes had to rest now. Clea stood to leave.

'These nurses are ferocious,' Smailes explained. 'They wouldn't allow me any visitors today until Smallwood intervened.'

'Good,' said Clea. 'I'll be back this afternoon, around five.'

'Clea, you can't drive from Coulsdon to Slough and back, twice a day.'

'Who says I can't?' she asked. 'It's all arranged. Mummy's coming across to give Lucy supper.'

Lucy creased her brow. 'Granny come,' she explained gravely, in case Derek had missed the point.

'All right,' Smailes said, touching Clea's fingertips. 'See you later, then.'

'Do you need anything?' she asked.

'Yes. Ask a nurse to come and take this thing out of my willie.'

Clea grinned. 'A pretty one?'

'Any one will do.'

Smailes noticed a telephone had been installed when he woke from an afternoon nap. He eyed it suspiciously, since he hadn't ordered one. He was compelled to confront his situation: if Roger was in collusion with the CIA and KGB, and knew Smailes knew, then he would probably prefer to see Derek dead. At very least, he would want to bug Smailes's hospital room. Smailes had not formulated a course of action yet. But now, as his euphoria ebbed, he was forced to make plans. The phone rang and he picked it up, his wound smarting. Smailes felt unsettled to hear Judith's voice.

'Derek! How are you? Honestly, I've been worried to death! All we were told was that you'd been shot last night but were out of danger. Brian told me which hospital you were in, and I've been calling all day trying to get through. What happened?'

Smailes let the silence extend on the line, not sure how to respond.

'Well, it's a long story,' he said eventually. 'It's difficult to know what to say. Do you know what I mean?'

It was Judith's turn to pause. This was a test of how sharp she truly was, Smailes told himself. How much had she worked out?

'I'm not sure,' she said. 'How do you feel? Are you all right?'

'I'm sore as hell and am missing a kidney, but apparently that's not a big deal. The surgeon says I'll be home in a week.'

'Honestly, what a relief! Derek, who on earth shot you?'

'I can't really say.'

This time Judith seemed to get the message. 'Oh, I see. Do you want to talk about it? Can I come out and visit you? Tonight?'

'No,' said Smailes, a little too sharply. 'It's not a good idea.'

'Well, okay, then,' she said. 'Is there anything I can do for you?'

'You could pass on a message for me.'

'What is it?'

'Tell Brian he's the only one I'll speak to. Tell him that if Roger Standiforth tries to stick his nose in here, I'll have hospital security evict him.'

Judith couldn't contain her curiosity. 'What happened with Lubyanov?'

'I'll tell you later.'

'All right. I'll call again.'

'I wouldn't bother, Judith.'

He had the sense she had understood his warnings, but could tell he'd hurt her feelings. 'Yes, well, all right. Get well soon,' she said, in an injured voice.

'Thanks.'

Smailes hung up, and the phone rang again almost immediately. It was Brian. After checking Derek's condition, he came straight to the point. 'Look, I've spoken with Smallwood, and after some badgering he says I can visit you this afternoon, if you feel up to it. He had to override the ward sister, but I told him it was urgent. Slough CID are chomping at the bit, and you and I really need to get some things straightened out first.'

'Fine. No problem. Come out as soon as you're ready.'

'Right. About an hour.'

'Brian?'

'Yes?'

'Who ordered this phone?'

'I've no idea. Maybe it goes with the room. I didn't.'

'Right. See you soon.'

Smailes hung up and reached for the call button for the nurse. He didn't care how loud he had to shout and scream – he had to get this tube out of his urethra or he would go crazy.

21

Miles Bingham was not surprised by the summons to Sir David's office. He'd learned of the latest crisis – the shooting of that K Branch chap out in Slough last night – on his arrival, and no doubt some new fire-fighting team was being assembled. If he got the opportunity he would give Williams his candid opinion – that such fiascos were the logical outcome of Standiforth's cowboy tactics. Although he had little time for Williams – a lower-class bore, totally unsuited to the job – he was damned if he was going to let Roger reap all the rewards of Jonquil uncontested. Bingham had every intention of moving into Williams's office when it became vacant, if he was not called to higher service first.

At first Bingham thought he had a good opportunity, since Williams and Corcoran were alone, with no other division heads present. Corky, however, appeared to have another agenda, and produced a document from a file folder for Bingham's inspection.

'This is the working paper Sir David and I presented to Herbert Carne last month,' Corcoran began. 'As I think we discussed, one of our major recommendations was the amalgamation of F and C Branches, in the general interests of economy.'

Bingham had mounted a vigorous defence at the time, although he knew the withering of Soviet sponsorship of domestic subversion had long ago put his fiefdom in jeopardy. There was a time when the Communist party of Great Britain had provided work for a hundred staffers, but then it had to go and vote itself out of existence; not even the expansion of the IRA's mainland campaign had been able to plug that gap. So in the end, grudgingly, Bingham had acquiesced. He knew he had fifteen years' seniority on Dunning, the head of C Branch, and would be capturing new turf to compensate for that which he relinquished. Undoubtedly, droves of his staff would be made redundant, but one had to move with the times, after all.

'Well, we've received confidential word through the Cabinet office,' Corcoran continued, 'that Carne recommends acceptance of our proposal. Which will entail some major restructuring around here. Soon.'

Bingham sat across the conference table, his hands folded across his paunch, listening politely. Then Corcoran dropped his bombshell.

'We've called you here today, Miles, to tell you that Charles Dunning will be offered the position as head of the new domestic security division.'

Bingham spluttered his outrage. 'Dunning? That man's not even forty – I have more than a dozen years' seniority over him. I won't serve as deputy, do you hear? It's a damned insult . . .'

Williams held up a hand to silence him, then clicked on a microcassette recorder in front of him which Bingham had not yet noticed. Sir David adjusted the volume wheel, then sat back in his chair. The proceedings of a recent Sceptre Command Group meeting filled the room, the audio quality remarkably sharp. General Porter could be heard giving his enthusiastic assent to Lieutenant-Colonel Crabbe's plan to hijack a Trident sub. Other voices chimed in as tactics were debated and ironed out – the voices of Clive Halls, of Gerry Stap and, unmistakably, that of Miles Bingham, CBE.

Williams let the tape play for a few minutes, then snapped the machine off. Bingham's face had turned a furious red.

Corcoran resumed. 'You may be interested to know that military authorities arrested Colonel Crabbe last night as he attempted to deliver adulterated patrol instructions to the commander of HMS *Vanguard* in Faslane. He will be charged with high treason. Regrettably, there is nothing we can particularly charge *you* with, Miles, beyond an outrageous lapse in judgement. But don't worry, there is no question of your being offered the position of Dunning's deputy. In fact, we think it's time you chose to retire.'

Bingham exploded. 'Don't you bloody well talk down to me, Corcoran! You ought to *applaud* what Sceptre's been doing! Christ, don't you understand? We serve the Crown, not the bloody elected government! Her Majesty does not *want* her realm to become a province of Brussels. She does not *want* her Constitution tampered with or her kingdom dismembered! We know this for cold fact! That's the treason, to stand by and let it happen! I'm shocked, shocked at you. I don't expect the likes of *him* to understand,' he said, jabbing a finger at Williams. 'But you! You're one of us!'

Corcoran sat motionless in his wheelchair as Bingham's fury spent itself. Then Williams spoke for the first time. 'Alex, have security assist Mr Bingham in emptying his safe and clearing his desk. Then have him escorted from the building. Now.'

Kinney and Smailes eyed each other warily. 'I hear you've been very lucky,' said Kinney eventually, pulling up a chair.

'That's what they tell me,' said Smailes. 'Excuse me if I don't feel it, although I've just had a catheter removed, which has cheered me up no end.'

'I'll bet. You're sore?'

'Very.'

'Listen, Derek, I'd have left you alone, but we have some sticky issues to resolve. Some of your actions yesterday appear to have been, well, a little unorthodox.'

'I know. But do me a favour first, okay? Take that phone and put it on the floor, then bury it under one of these pillows, will you? It makes me nervous.'

'Aren't you overreacting, Derek?'

'I don't think so. You didn't order it, and I certainly didn't. My bet is Roger did.'

Kinney looked sceptical, but complied with Smailes's request. Then he produced his miniature tape recorder and set it on Smailes's tray table. 'Well, I intend to use this, if that's all right,' he said.

'That's fine, Brian. I happen to trust you.'

'All right, why don't we start at the beginning?'

Smailes had resolved that his best hope was to lay the whole confusing story before Kinney and trust he would believe it. He knew he couldn't possibly confront Standiforth with his imputed treachery unless he had at least one major ally – he and Judith would simply be laughed out of court. He was also aware that his conduct had violated any number of protocols, and that he was probably facing the chop unless someone of Brian's seniority agreed the circumstances warranted his actions. Rudy was right – Smailes didn't know how high any conspiracy at MI5 went, but he was confident Brian couldn't be part of it. In addition, he felt a pressing need to lay his and Judith's theories before a third party and have them adjudicated. He had been unable to work out their full implication himself, an inability probably compounded by the volume of painkillers in his bloodstream.

Smailes began his story with Judith's discoveries the previous afternoon – the fluctuation in Gontar's radio traffic at the beginning of the summer, and the curious absence of any cipher messages between the KGB London residence and Moscow during the weekend of the arrests. To both Smailes and Hyams, this cast doubt on the authenticity of the whole operation, suggesting Gontar and Docherty might be discards.

Kinney made a scoffing gesture. 'Come off it, Derek. Gontar and Docherty are the biggest spies we've caught in years. Why would Moscow discard them?'

'I don't know yet. That's where I need your help.'

'Go on.'

'I came looking for you but found you all in a big flap over the Gontar warrant, and then the Lubyanov crisis blew up again and I was sent down to Chiswick. None of you was in any mood to listen to my doubts. The timing wasn't right.'

'I'll agree with that.'

'But on the drive down to Chiswick, I began to think it through. If Gontar was a discard, then Lubyanov, who dished him up in the first place, had to be rotten too. And lo and behold, here he was doing his big repentance act, volunteering for oblivion. I suddenly saw his behaviour in a new light.

'When I got down to Chiswick I did my best to get him to change his tune, but by now I was convinced he was acting. I tried to warn you I thought the whole thing stank when I called in, but you missed my meaning.'

'I certainly did,' said Kinney.

'So, anyway, since it was clear I was going to be stuck in Chiswick for hours, I had to cancel an appointment with a friend of mine.'

'Rudy Kabalan.'

'That's right. He wasn't at his hotel, so I left a message for him. Then, on impulse, I asked him to tail Lubyanov when he returned to the fold – just to see whether anything unusual happened. Rudy's a good friend, an ex-freelancer from New York. A bloody good one too.'

'That was a little irregular, Derek.'

'I'm aware of that. Just let me finish, will you? So I stood back while Caldicott and his henchman did the paperwork and carted Lubyanov off. I watched them leave, and there didn't appear to be any tail. I called you, then went home.'

'About six.'

'Correct. Around seven I got two calls. The first was from Judith, who'd put a wider trace on Lubyanov and discovered the bastard used to be a professional actor in Moscow. That swung it for me. Then Rudy called, from Slough, where he'd managed to follow the Russians after the hand-over. And he told me he'd seen a second party enter the house whom he identified as Loudon Strickland. He knows him personally.'

Kinney swore. 'He didn't tell me that.'

'I'm not surprised. So, I told him to hang on and grabbed a camera and drove like hell over to Slough. It was still light when I got there, and I thought I could get some recognizable shots.'

'Also irregular. We have a whole department for those tasks, Derek.'

'When I got there, Rudy told me a third party had just shown up on foot. Brian, he gave me a perfect bloody description of Roger Standiforth.'

'Yes, he gave me a similar description last night,' said Brian evenly. 'Did he know Roger personally?'

'No.'

'Then what happened?'

'Well, I'm afraid I just saw red. It meant the whole thing was a stunt cooked up by the three of them, and there they were, meeting to toast its success. We'd all been played for fools, and my best friend was stewing in a Moscow prison thanks to them. That's obviously part of the script, Brian, the way for the Russians to get Gontar back. We're left with that little prat Docherty as a consolation prize.'

'So you decided to storm the house and were shot by the Russian look-out when you got to the gate,' Kinney prompted.

'Brian, that was no Russian who shot me,' said Smailes heatedly. 'That was Peter Bloody Tennant. I turned and saw him the split second before he fired. He was baby-sitting Roger's car around the corner and shot me before I could break up the party.'

Kinney snapped off his machine. 'Do you know what the hell you're saying, man?' he hissed.

'I know exactly what I'm saying, Brian. I'm telling you the truth.'

Smailes saw the turmoil in Brian's expression. He was, after all, both Britain's second-ranking counter-intelligence officer and Smailes's mentor. He left his machine off.

'All right. I suppose you deserve to know the official version, at least what will appear on the news tonight.'

'There's an official version already?' asked Smailes.

'It seems the house in Foxglove Drive is leased to Aeroflot,' said Kinney.

'Surprise, surprise.'

'The airline claims they use it for the recuperation of their Heathrow crews.'

'No doubt.'

'At first they denied there was anyone in the house when you were shot, and the Russian embassy wouldn't comment. That was until this lunchtime. The Russian ambassador has just issued a statement.'

Kinney reached for his inside pocket and extracted a curling fax sheet. 'The statement confirms that at the time of the incident the house was being used by First Secretary Boris Zhimin to debrief a diplomatic colleague, Cultural Attaché Yuri Lubyanov, who had spent an extended period in the custody of the British authorities. This is what it says exactly. "Attaché Lubyanov had requested to be returned to Russian authorities and was scheduled to take an evening flight to Moscow from Heathrow airport. During this meeting in Slough, two Russian security officers arrived separately to interview Attaché Lubyanov. Shortly after this, an unidentified man attempted to enter the house and was challenged by the head of embassy security, Senior Counsellor Gennadi Gropov, who was stationed nearby. After the individual failed to respond, Counsellor Gropov drew his weapon and shouted another warning. When the individual still did not halt, Counsellor Gropov fired. The Russian diplomats then left the house in great haste, understandably fearing for their safety. It has since come to our attention that this individual was Special Police Detective Derek Smailes. We deeply regret this incident, which we attribute to the unfortunate state of tension that currently exists between the British and Russian governments. Had Detective Smailes, who had no authority to enter the house, heeded the order to halt, he would not have been shot. However, the Russian government is pleased to learn that Detective Smailes is expected to make a full recovery from his injuries.

'"An internal inquiry has established to my satisfaction that Senior Counsellor Gropov, who has full diplomatic immunity, was completely justified in his actions. However, Counsellor Gropov has already been recalled to Moscow and will be reassigned to other duties. Once again, the government of Russia deeply regrets this incident, which it now considers closed."'

'Total crap,' said Smailes. 'Roger wrote that. Those were no security officers – they were Strickland and Standiforth. And it was Tennant who shot me. I saw him with my own eyes.'

'Derek, you have no proof. None at all. None of the neighbours saw anything.'

'I do have proof. Rudy was here this morning, on his way to the airport, and gave me the licence number of the last car to leave. It was Roger's car, Brian. Tennant was driving it.'

'Why didn't he tell me that?' Kinney cried.

'Because he wanted to get back to America with his marriage intact.'

'Damn it. I knew I shouldn't have let him go.'

'So I'm a Special Branch detective now, am I?' asked Smailes sarcastically.

'For public consumption, yes. You know what the seventh floor thinks about publicity.'

'And what is Special Branch saying?'

'That their inquiry is continuing. That's all they're going to say, too.' Kinney reached forward and snapped his machine back on.

'So what is your theory for why the head of K Branch was meeting secretly with senior officials of the CIA and KGB?' he resumed in a formal tone.

'I'm not entirely sure, but it has to be some kind of three-way swap. My guess is it's connected to the PAL theft from Burghfield – the Russians get the American hardware, and in return they dish up an expired network and Roger Standiforth gets to look like Mr Counterspy, which will strengthen his chances for the DG's chair. What's in it for the Americans? I don't know, except they've wanted the Russians to have those nuclear weapon locks all along, I was told.'

'Sounds very far-fetched, Derek.'

'Oh yeah? Who made those mistakes in the Gontar search warrant, which will probably convince Number Ten to trade him for Iain Mack?'

'That's unclear, Derek. It could have been . . .'

'Peter Tennant made those mistakes. Deliberately. Come on, Brian. You must see it.'

Kinney clicked the machine off again, then leaned back in his chair. He passed a hand through his hair wearily.

'What are you going to do?' asked Smailes.

'Write up my report and present your case exactly as you state it.'

'And what do you think?'

Kinney paused. 'I'll concede there's an outside chance it could all be true, as you claim. But it would be more bizarre than anything I've encountered in twenty years in the business. There's a much more plausible explanation, Derek.'

'Which is?'

'Lubyanov was real and experienced a genuine change of heart. It's hardly surprising he was once an actor – he was their cultural affairs man, after all. The fluctuations in Gontar's traffic in early summer were just that – fluctuations. The instruction to pick up Mack was relayed to Moscow some other way – secure phone link, for instance. Lubyanov was taken to Slough before being bundled on to a plane home and the two parties Kabalan saw were exactly who the Russians say they were – KGB heavies coming to rough him up a little. They happened to bear a passing resemblance to Strickland and Standiforth – no more. When you overreacted to false information and tried to storm the house you were shot by Gropov, the Russian look-out. Bill Moody's office made the errors in the Gontar warrant.'

'You really believe all that?' asked Smailes, crestfallen.

'It's a lot more plausible than your version, Derek,' said Kinney. 'I don't doubt it's what the seventh floor will believe.'

'That's not what I asked.'

Kinney leaned forward and spoke in a low, urgent voice.

'Look, Derek, I don't trust Roger Standiforth any further than you do. Of course I know he's capable of something like this. Maybe that *was* him and Tennant in Slough last night. But don't you think they'll both have cast-iron alibis? Do you think he could have overlooked that? And consider this. The Docherty–Gontar arrests are MI5's biggest counter-intelligence success in a generation, even if Gontar is swapped for Mack. And the timing is impeccable, given Carne's review. No one on the seventh floor is going to be interested in your version, that the whole thing is a sham, are they? So it doesn't really matter what the hell I think, does it? You can't win this one, Derek.'

Smailes knew what Brian was saying. He was telling him that he was out on a limb, and that Brian Kinney was not about to climb out and join him on it.

'So what's next?' asked Smailes bitterly.

'The DG has appointed a committee of inquiry. He wants a report as soon as possible.'

'Who's on it?'

'Me, Corcoran and Standiforth.'

'Not Bingham?' asked Smailes, reasoning the DG might want someone ostensibly neutral.

'Miles Bingham's been fired, Derek,' said Kinney. 'He was escorted from the building at eleven this morning.'

Smailes leaned back against his pillows and gave a low whistle. 'The Sceptre Group association?' he asked.

'No official reason was given, although I heard that SBS colonel, Crabbe, had just been taken into custody up in Faslane. So, probably yes.'

Smailes shook his head in disbelief, his mind racing. 'So what are you going to do?' he asked eventually.

'I told you. I'll report your whole story. Word for word.'

'Not that, Brian. What will you recommend? You're my section head, after all.'

'I'll say that you had some justifiable suspicions, in the context of which your actions can be understood, if not excused.' Kinney managed a thin smile.

'Thanks,' said Smailes, knowing it was the best he could hope for. 'So what do I tell the police?'

'As little as possible. I've already explained there are national security concerns here. There's a clodhopper called Cartwright in charge. Tell him you rushed the house because you thought the KGB were torturing Lubyanov, or something. I wouldn't go giving out any number plates, if I were you. Everyone's going to swallow the official version, Derek. Surely you can see that.'

Kinney reached down and shook Smailes's hand. 'I'm not going to let him get away with it, Brian,' said Smailes quietly.

'Don't do anything stupid,' said Kinney. 'Just maybe I can save your hide.' He turned to leave.

'Brian,' Smailes said as Kinney reached the door. 'Protect Judith. She's going to be a star.'

'You're famous,' said Clea, breaking away from their kiss. 'I heard the news on the way over. Those poor Russians sound very concerned about you. Did you hear you've been transferred to Special Branch?'

'Damn,' said Smailes, pointing at the headphones hooked over the bed rail. 'I was going to listen. I fell asleep again. Brian told me the Russian ambassador's statement this afternoon. What else did the news say?'

'A commentator said this will only increase the pressure to resolve the diplomatic impasse. Nobody wants people to start getting hurt.'

Smailes said nothing.

'Derek,' asked Clea carefully, 'are you in trouble?'

'Yes. Giving the safe house address to Rudy is probably my biggest problem. The seventh floor isn't going to like that one bit. Together with all the publicity – they hate that worse than anything.'

'Can you tell me anything? What happened?'

'I don't have it all worked out myself yet. But I'm convinced that big case we just wrapped up was stage-managed by Roger and the Russians to make him look good. Clea, that was Roger's assistant who shot me last night, not any Russian look-out.'

Clea drew in her breath sharply, but was distracted by an odd, muffled ringing. 'What's that?' she asked.

'The telephone. It's under the pillow over there.'

Clea found it and answered it. Smailes put his hands to his head as he heard Clea attempting to pacify his mother.

'No, Elsie, it's me, Clea. No, he's fine. He's right here. Yes, fine, really. Of course you can speak to him.'

She lifted the phone to Smailes's tray table and he looked up at her in anguish. 'You didn't call her?' he mouthed, cupping the receiver.

'I've been in such a dither,' Clea whispered. 'I meant to, but I forgot.'

Smailes put the instrument to his ear. 'Hello, Ma. I'm sorry, I meant to. Look, I've been asleep most of the day. No, I'm all right. Well, they took out a kidney . . . Ma, Ma, calm down. Of course you can visit. No, no, don't come tonight.'

He cast his eyes to the ceiling and settled in for what he knew was going to be a long call. Clea looked at him in amusement and began peeling a banana. She gestured to his nether region and raised her eyebrows. Derek gave her a forlorn thumbs-up.

The next eight days of Smailes's recuperation were uneventful. He settled into a routine of receiving visits from Clea and Lucy each morning, and from Clea alone each evening. In between visits he read a little and flirted with the nurses. Smallwood stopped in daily and pronounced Derek's progress exemplary. His mother and sister journeyed down from Cambridge, and Smailes tolerated their flustered entreaties that he take up a safer line of work. His mother scolded him for threatening his family's future, and Smailes was duly contrite. He took a call from Yvonne, his ex-wife, who told him Tracy was on the continent with her boyfriend, but that she'd try and get word to her about her father's 'accident'. Smailes told her not to bother.

No one from MI5 called or visited, and the story soon dropped out of the news. Smailes began to regret his harshness with Judith, and wondered how she was surviving the internal inquiry. Smailes realized that Standiforth could now identify her as his accomplice, making her a marked woman. He was also hungry for office gossip in the wake of Bingham's departure, which Judith could have supplied. He thought about calling Brian, but had resolved to use his telephone as little as possible.

On a couple of occasions Smailes almost broached the topic of his dalliance with Judith with his wife, but each time backed away. He was reluctant to jeopardize their restored good will and besides, he rationalized, Clea seemed sufficiently concerned about their immediate future to have to cope with anything else.

He knew he would probably get fired. He didn't doubt Roger would dismiss his accusations as the ravings of an embittered hothead. The divulgence of the safe house address to a foreign national would be judged unpardonable, in addition to the sin of getting himself publicly shot. In the final analysis it was either Roger or him, and he doubted even the intercession of Brian Kinney could save him.

But Smailes was resolved not to go down without a fight. He had plenty of time to reflect, and his anger continued to reinforce his determination. Each time he reconstructed events in his mind, Roger's plot grew more demonic. He was damned if Roger was going to rob him of a kidney and his livelihood too. There were formal grievance procedures for civil servants – he would invoke these and threaten to go public. He could appeal independently to the DG or Corcoran; Kinney was probably correct that no one wanted to believe Jonquil was a sham, but if Bingham was out of the picture, someone might want to curb Roger's power before it was too late. Most of all, Smailes was determined that the little shit Tennant was not going to get away with nearly killing him. If he was going down, then he would take Peter Tennant with him at very least. In his brighter moods Smailes thought he might have an even chance of getting Roger too.

Clea tentatively inquired about Derek's plans on his release, but he was evasive. She made him promise he would not do anything foolish, and he agreed.

He did receive other visitors that week. The day after his interview with Kinney, Detective Inspector Bill Cartwright of Slough CID showed up. Cartwright was clearly deeply annoyed that an attempted murder investigation should be wrested from his grasp by national security concerns. He made Smailes go over Tuesday night's events once again, which Smailes did with due conciseness. At the conclusion of his account, Cartwright leaned forward to address Smailes confidentially.

'Tell you what I'd do, Derek, if it was up to me.'

'What's that, Bill?'

'I'd have the SAS storm their bloody embassy, like we did with the Iranians. Ten-to-one that wanker who shot you's still in there.'

Smailes said he would pass on the suggestion.

On the fifth day Smailes received an unexpected visit from a doctor calling himself Muldoon, who said he'd been sent by Personnel to perform an independent examination in order to validate Smailes's disability leave. Smailes submitted reluctantly to Muldoon's brusque handling, which included a particularly gratuitous rectal examination, and was relieved when he finally left. He was left with the suspicion that Standiforth, not anyone at Personnel, had been the author of Muldoon's mission.

The day before his discharge, Smailes was both sickened and relieved to hear a BBC news report that both Iain Mack and Mikhail Gontar had been released into the custody of their respective embassies. Sir Herbert Carne had brokered the deal in Moscow, by which the charges against Mack were dropped unconditionally, provided he undertook never to return to the Russian Republic. The same day, the Director of Public Prosecutions appeared before the Arbour Square magistrate to say the Crown Prosecution Service was dropping its case against Jurgen Klop, alias Mikhail Gontar, for lack of unimpeachable evidence. The DPP was careful to reaffirm the government's conviction of his guilt, and told the court that once the charges were dismissed and immunity confirmed, Gontar had agreed to sign a voluntary statement detailing his activities in Britain, which would prove invaluable to the Security Service's continuing investigations. Gontar was banned from ever returning to Britain. The deal was roughly symmetrical and both sides appeared to have won something and, more importantly, to have saved face. Smailes listened to the news cynically, fully appreciating its choreography. But he was greatly relieved that Iain was free; Gontar, of course, had been a straw man from the start, whom the British were never meant to prosecute. It wasn't in the script.

On a Thursday morning at the end of August, Clea Smailes drove her husband back to their small suburban home, which he found festooned with balloons and streamers, courtesy of Lucy and Fidelma. Anthea Lynch was on hand to help Derek to his armchair and bring him tea. He truly did feel lucky to be alive, back in the bosom of his family, and the world of Whitehall seemed almost irrelevant, a distant, malevolent planet.

22

An entire day in an armchair proved enough for Smailes. The next morning he excused himself as Clea made preparations for a trip to Purley, saying he preferred to stay home and potter. Clea looked at him askance, but knew better than to argue. As soon as his wife and daughter had left, Smailes called a taxi, then went upstairs and changed into his best suit. An hour later he was leaning on his walking stick beneath the security camera at Curzon House, waiting impatiently for admittance.

Judith Hyams's desk and personal effects had been removed from his office, to his relief. Internal mail had accumulated in his in-tray, but he ignored it. He sat down and tried to gather his wits. His wound ached violently and his mouth was dry. He thought of tea, but dismissed the idea. No time like the present, he told himself.

Glenys Powner looked alarmed to see him, but tried to force a smile. 'Derek!' she cried. 'My, you're looking so well! Take a seat and I'll buzz him that you're here. We weren't expecting . . . Derek?'

Smailes ignored her and limped towards Roger's inner door. He knocked once, then advanced. The familiar aroma of leather polish and cigarette smoke greeted him. Roger sat at his desk beneath his hunting prints, Tennant at his shoulder, examining documents on his blotter.

'Derek!' Roger exclaimed mildly. 'What a pleasant surprise! I wasn't expecting you for weeks yet. You should have called . . .'

'That bastard owes me a kidney,' said Smailes, jabbing his stick at Tennant. 'Get him out of here before I castrate him with this thing.'

Standiforth turned to his hatchet boy. 'Perhaps you should give us a few moments alone, Peter. We can wrap this up later.'

Tennant advanced towards the door, giving Smailes a vindictive smirk as he passed. Keep your temper, Smailes told himself. There's no need to shout to convince him.

'Do sit down, Derek,' said Standiforth solicitously. 'Golly, you must be violating *all manner* of doctor's orders by coming in so soon. I was told it might be *weeks* before you were up and about.'

Smailes sat down carefully, resting his hands on the cane between his knees. He did not look Standiforth in the eye until the pain from his exertion had ebbed. He kept his voice hard and cold. 'I'm going to bring you down, Roger. You're not going to get away with this – I don't care how much prestige you've won. I'm not going to go away. And I'm not going to keep my mouth shut.'

'I see,' said Roger more carefully. 'Naturally, I had wondered whether you were going to continue insisting upon your bizarre theories. Frankly, most of us round here put them down to post-operative delirium.'

'Damn it, Roger!' said Smailes, raising his voice despite himself. 'Don't you get it? I know everything, front to back! You think I'm going to let you shoot me down, like a dog in the street, and do nothing about it?'

'I'm *sure* you saw the ambassador's statement. The Russians accepted full responsibility . . .'

Smailes took a deep breath. 'All right, if you insist, I'll start at the beginning. The night Audrey Cole was killed on the North Circular, with the Trident document in her handbag, where was she going? She was going to *your* house, Roger. The route from Wembley to Potters Bar would take her right through Finchley, wouldn't it? And why was she on her way to visit you? Because Gerry Stap is your man on the Conservative front bench, isn't he? You needed to know exactly when those warheads would be in the retrofit lab – right? You weren't indoctrinated into Wakefield, so you couldn't have been the leak there. But Strickland was, wasn't he? He was the one who told the Russians when Burghfield's defences would be down, when the PAL hardware would be sitting on a workbench, waiting to be stolen. It was *his* role I couldn't work out for the longest time. But then I remembered something my friend Rudy told me about Strickland's father and his empire-building in London. What have you promised the CIA at Curzon House when you become DG, Roger? A whole floor?'

Roger Standiforth had lit a cigarette and was regarding Smailes evenly. The heatwave had finally broken and Roger was wearing his most formal mandarin outfit, the broad blue pin-stripes with the burgundy shirt and white collar. He said nothing.

Smailes resumed. 'Now, to your annoyance, I was assigned the Stap investigation by the seventh floor. You didn't like that, in case I discovered he was your agent and smelled a rat. So you got me transferred back to K5 when the Lubyanov ball began rolling, and then invented the absurd "pink brigadier" theory to explain Audrey Cole's actions. Then, surprise, surprise, Gerry Stap leads the watchers to the Special Forces Club, where your biggest rival is in bed with a gin-sodden old general and a couple of mad commandos. How convenient! Then Stap's approach to Peter Lynch, of all people, an agent-in-waiting since he was in short trousers. That had to be your riskiest gambit, Roger – I couldn't believe the seventh floor signed off on that. Of course, Peter Lynch blabbed the whole thing to me, as you must have feared he would. And I suspected your involvement from the start, Roger. Tell me, do you think Miles Bingham knows you trussed and roasted him like a turkey, or does he believe he and his pals had a real chance of overturning the government?'

Roger remained impassive, enjoying his cigarette. Smailes was beginning to enjoy himself too.

'Mind you, it was a deft touch to feed the Sceptre Group all that gossip from the Palace – that really got their patriotic juices flowing. Of course, everyone knows you run people over there too. What did you have to promise your pet equerry to have him whisper all that rubbish into Porter's ear? A life peerage? Hey, cheap at the price! And let's not forget your new pal Strickland. He did his bit by insisting the US joint chiefs were on board, that the Americans would sit on their hands if those idiots started anything. The Americans and the Palace, that's all the encouragement they really needed, wasn't it?'

Standiforth's appreciation of Smailes's harangue seemed to be growing. He leaned on an intercom button at this juncture and ordered tea, then indicated that Smailes should continue.

'But let's get back to the central deal, shall we? The great counter-intelligence coup that has done so much to restore MI5's lost prestige! All right, so Sir Herbert Carne is brought in to finally adjudicate who gets what in the aftermath of the Cold War. Big panic at Curzon Street! In fact, big panic right here in this office. I saw your reaction – you've probably had your sights set on the DG's chair since you were flogging your fags at Harrow, right, Roger? Twenty-five years working your way to the top, then suddenly there might be no MI5 left to run!'

Standiforth had begun playing with a letter-opener and gave Smailes a thin smile at this remark. Smailes pressed on.

'I don't know where this idea originated, but I would guess it was with the Americans, with Strickland and his boss Blane Morris, the head of covert operations. You see, I happened to see you that day, meeting with Strickland and Morris, over at the Oxford & Cambridge.

Roger Standiforth, who would hardly give a Yank the time of day, cheek-by-jowl with the barbarians! They knew you had to be desperate to impress Carne, so that's why they drafted Uncle Boris and his merry men, wasn't it? In exchange for the Burghfield leak and the opportunity to steal American PALs, the Russians dealt us the Docherty network, which was judged sufficiently meaty but expendable. Of course, we were never meant to hold on to Gontar, or to catch his Yemeni back-up team – nothing *really* valuable. The odds were that the post-mortem at Burghfield would have uncovered Docherty, anyway. And, of course, let's not forget Comrade Lubyanov and his role of a lifetime. Actually, I'd say your acting was at least as good as his, Roger, and he used to be a professional. "I'm going to tell Taffy to stand fast! No deals for Iain Mack!" What a joke!'

At this point Glenys Powner entered with a bone-china tea service which she set before her boss. Roger poured himself a cup, then lifted his eyes to Smailes. Smailes was parched, but declined. Standiforth offered a smile of sympathy.

'Obviously, the presence of the press at Gontar's apartment the night of the arrests was no accident. The story had to be milked for maximum publicity, to show the country, and particularly Bert Carne, what a crack outfit MI5 still was. That's why Bill Moody was set up in charge, knowing he would bring his media circus with him. And his reputation was bad enough round here to conceal the real source of the errors in the Gontar search warrant. Of course, stupid Bill Moody had put his foot in it again! Actually, Roger, was that really necessary? The British government would have *had* to trade Gontar for Mack in the end, or allow him be sent to jail. After all, you'd dealt Zhimin a British diplomatic cipher blank so his comrades in Moscow could construct a cast-iron case, making it look like Iain was a spy run by McAndrew through the embassy. But I don't really think you've thought this through properly, Roger. Don't you know how badly Iain will want to go public, after all he's been through, when I tell him who was *really* responsible for his ordeal?'

Smailes's side was aching, and he was aware he was pushing the bounds of his self-control. Why didn't Roger react and say something? How could he just sit there sipping tea?

'Actually, I appreciated the cleverness of discarding Docherty so the finger of suspicion for the original Burghfield leak would point at him and away from you big shots. But you made another mistake there, Roger. Perhaps the Russians didn't get everything they needed on the night of the break-in, since Docherty was told to steal more PAL software, which ended up back in my safe. Someone removed it and copied it, which could only have been you, Roger. I don't doubt it has reached its intended customer by now.

'And there were other mistakes, inevitably. Gontar's radio traffic wasn't maintained at pre-Jonquil levels, which would have been a sensible precaution. Neither was the Russian embassy told to send dummy traffic through to Moscow on the weekend their biggest spy in thirty years had been arrested, and when they were supposed to be instructing their colleagues to retaliate by grabbing Iain Mack. Then a trace turned up the fact that Yuri Lubyanov had been a professional actor.' Smailes deliberately left Judith Hyams's name out of these discoveries, although he was well aware Roger knew of her role.

'But, for all these slips, your stunt would have succeeded brilliantly if you'd been able to resist toasting your cleverness with Zhimin and Strickland, and if I hadn't had the luck to draft one of the best freelancers in the business, who identified your smug faces when you entered the Russian safe house. My big mistake, of course, was to lose my cool and rush the house instead of waiting to photograph your guilty faces as you left. Then I think I'd have had you stone cold, Roger. But I've certainly paid for the lapse – Peter Tennant saw to that. But you'd better believe I'm going to bring you down, Roger. I'm going to see you charged with treason, and that little shit Tennant with attempted murder, if I can swing it. Nothing you can do will deter me.'

Smailes's chest was heaving, but, infuriatingly, Roger remained unruffled. Presently, Standiforth reached into a desk drawer and produced a file folder, then began discussing Smailes's medical condition.

'It seems Muldoon fears you may never make a one hundred per cent recovery from your injuries, I regret,' said Roger sympathetically. 'Something about the likelihood of recurrent peritonitis. Accordingly, I asked Personnel to update me on the procedures for a disability discharge. Apparently, with a certified disability, you retain full pension rights – in a lump sum distribution, if you prefer. In your case, with the carry-over from your police service, that's something like thirty thousand pounds . . .'

'No way,' Smailes responded fiercely. 'You're not buying me off, Roger. You've deceived everyone – Williams, Carne, the Prime Minister, not to mention the bloody British public. My friend spent two weeks in a Moscow jail thanks to you. I was nearly killed. You think I'd let you buy me off?'

'Now, this friend of yours to whom you divulged the address of the Chiswick safe house. He's an American, you say?'

Smailes did not respond.

'Well, that's a rather serious matter, Derek. In fact, as I'm sure you're aware, it's an offence under the Official Secrets Act. Punishable by up to ten years in prison, should we choose to prosecute. Then we have these . . .'

Standiforth went into the back of his file and handed Smailes a set of glossy, eight-by-ten photographs. They were grainy infra-red prints, but quite distinct. They showed Derek Smailes and Judith Hyams in a series of passionate clinches – violently kissing, her hand in his hair; foreheads together, his hand unmistakably inside her blouse; Judith's head thrown back, her blouse unbuttoned, her shoulders and throat dramatically shadowed. They made Smailes's face burn.

'This is also very irregular, I'm afraid, Derek. You're both married – to other people, I don't need to point out. This kind of sexual liaison contradicts Clause 6 of the Personnel manual, the terms of which you accepted in writing upon employment. The maximum sanction is termination and forfeiture of annuity rights.'

'Who has the negatives?' Smailes managed to ask.

'Well, the DG has the negatives, of course, along with Kinney's report of your ridiculous allegations. As for your claim that Peter Tennant and I were in Slough that night, I think you'll find the security log indicates Peter and I left Curzon House together just before eight, at the very moment you were getting yourself shot by Comrade Gropov so foolishly. I'm afraid you've made rather a laughing-stock of yourself, Derek.'

Smailes sat motionless, his thoughts careening. Suddenly, all bogus concern left Roger's voice. He leaned forward across his desk and spat his words.

'Take your miserable pension, Smailes, and get out. And count yourself lucky. Or get fired and get nothing – it's your choice. You can sign the papers in Ed Poynter's office on your way out.'

Smailes took the photographs and struggled to his feet. 'I'm going to the seventh floor,' said Smailes. 'I don't care what ammunition you have. I'll go to the DG, to Corcoran. If I get nowhere with them, I'll go to the Security Commission, to the Civil Service Appeals Board. I'll fight you every inch of the way, Roger.'

'Be my guest,' said Standiforth, closing the folder and returning to the scrutiny of the papers on his desk.

*

Smailes emerged from the lift on the seventh floor, his face hot with shame. He'd succeeded in folding Roger's prints vertically into an inside pocket, where they bulged accusingly. He limped down the corridor and turned into the door for the DG's secretariat. Gwyneth Rees oversaw her own modest staff, above whom she sat at an elevated desk. She, too, reacted with alarm when she saw Smailes, and came down from her rostrum to head him off.

'Hello, Derek,' she managed pleasantly. 'I'm afraid Sir David isn't in. I don't think he has office hours until tomorrow. Would you like to make an appointment?'

Smailes hesitated. 'No, Gwyneth. Well, perhaps. I'll come back.'

He turned into the corridor and around the corner towards Corcoran's suite. Smailes found Corcoran's secretary working at her computer – he didn't know her name. He explained his business and took a seat awkwardly as she spoke on an internal phone. 'You can go right in, Mr Smailes,' she said.

Alex Corcoran was seated in his wheelchair behind his desk, scanning a report with a propelling pencil. Smailes hobbled to a chair and sat down. Eventually Corcoran looked up.

'Yes?' he asked.

'Did you see Kinney's report?' asked Smailes. 'My account of what happened in Slough?'

'Of course.'

'You know it's all true, don't you?'

Corcoran tossed down his pencil in exasperation, then leaned forward. 'Go away, Mr Smailes. Go away, and take your money with you. Otherwise Roger Standiforth will destroy you.'

Smailes was appalled. 'How can you condone what he's done?' he cried.

'Listen,' Corcoran hissed, 'Roger Standiforth has single-handedly guaranteed the future of MI5, that's what he's done. Sir David is over at Number Ten right now, being clapped on the back by the PM and raising his glass to Herbert Carne's draft report. MI5 is to retain full authority for domestic counter-intelligence, with an increased budget. For this feat alone, Roger Standiforth deserves to be the next Director-General.'

A horrible awareness was dawning on Smailes. 'You've been in on this from the start, haven't you? My God, who else was part of it?'

Corcoran seemed affronted. 'Well, since no one's ever going to believe a word you say, no I wasn't. But I worked it out quite early on and acquiesced. Bloody clever plan, I thought.'

'Clever? Wouldn't cynical or corrupt be more accurate?'

Corcoran sighed. 'Mr Smailes, you're obviously a bright fellow, so try and understand. Roger devised an inexpensive way to win us some high-profile success in a very tight political situation. And, of course, the world will be a much safer place with the KGB in better control of Russia's nuclear weapons. Anyone can see that.'

'Inexpensive? What about the Americans? What about their price? What about MI5's autonomy?'

Corcoran shrugged. 'That's been inevitable for years, I'm afraid. It will happen to SIS too, sooner or later. God knows, it's already happened to our armed services.'

'I'm going to demand an interview with the DG. I'm going to insist he hears the whole story,' said Smailes, an edge of panic in his voice.

'You *are* a tiresome fellow, aren't you? Listen, Taffy is not interested in your crackpot theories, even if a tiny part of his tiny brain suspects they might be true. Roger Standiforth has made him a bloody hero, hasn't he? He's been a dead loss at this job, and now he'll go out in a blaze of glory, one of the most successful directors in history! You think he'll want to listen to your tale of woe? You don't stand a chance.'

Smailes was speechless, frightened of what was building up inside him.

'Look here, laddie. You divulged a safe house address to a bloody ex-CIA man – penalty, ten years. You were screwing a married co-worker – penalty, dismissal, forfeit of pension rights. Make one false move and you'll drown in a vat of your own shit. Roger will destroy you and destroy your marriage. And understand something. MI5 is not for the likes of you. Or of him,' he said, waving a hand towards the DG's suite. 'Never has been, never will. Count yourself lucky Tennant is a lousy shot. Get out.'

Shaken, Smailes stumbled from Corcoran's office and down the corridor to the lift. Back on the fourth floor, he let himself into the lavatory and locked himself in a cubicle. He broke down and sobbed; tears of rage, tears of shame, tears of defeat. Corcoran was right – Roger had crushed him, he was helpless. He felt an idiot for ever believing he could beat him. Brian had been right too – Roger was just too thorough, too ruthless, to have left himself vulnerable. He took out the incriminating photographs and looked at them again, his face burning. What had he been thinking? What would Clea say if she knew? He recovered himself and walked from the cubicle to a sink.

Mercifully, the room was empty. Slowly, a course of action began to suggest itself. Perhaps he could salvage something from this mess, he told himself, splashing water in his face.

Smailes entered Kinney's office and Brian looked up from his desk, his face grim. 'Derek – I heard you were in the building. Are you all right?'

'Have you see these?' asked Smailes, tossing down the photographs. Kinney glanced at them.

'Yes. I demanded an explanation when Roger insisted Judith be transferred back to KY.'

'He's got me by the short ones, Brian.'

'I know. That's what concerned me in the hospital, when you seemed so determined to go up against him.'

'You believed me, didn't you? That the whole Jonquil operation was phoney?' Smailes demanded.

Kinney hesitated, then nodded.

'Did you also realize that Audrey Cole was the courier between Roger and Gerry Stap, that Stap was his man in the Tory party? That through Stap he was able to set up Miles Bingham and the Sceptre Group and then cut off his legs?' Smailes sat down awkwardly and Kinney looked at him with concern, then sighed.

'Yes, eventually I worked it out. There had to be an explanation why Roger wanted you off the Stap investigation so badly. He claimed it was my idea, you know, to transfer you back to K5. It wasn't – it was his. The more I thought about it . . .'

'Corcoran was on board. I just came from there.'

'I'm not surprised. Do you think the DG . . .?'

'Apparently not. But Corcoran's right – Roger's made him a bloody hero. He would never listen to me.' Smailes paused. 'Did you work out what the pay-off is to the Yanks, for Strickland's contribution?'

'I've been afraid to.'

'British counter-intelligence to be run from Langley in the future, as far as I can tell.'

Kinney winced, then said, 'Gontar flies home tomorrow.'

Smailes managed a smile. 'What did he tell us?'

'Nothing, like you'd expect. He conceded his identity, that was all. Claimed he was sent over exclusively to run Docherty, whom they'd had for five years. Total crap. The board tore up Lubyanov's order of battle. No expulsions – Zhimin's residence stays intact.'

'Terrific,' said Smailes. Then, after a pause, he asked, 'Brian, what did you tell Judith when she was transferred?'

Kinney was obviously embarrassed. 'Well, that Roger had evidence of a . . . of an indiscretion between you and her. That her transfer was a disciplinary action. I didn't show her the photographs. Derek, I . . .'

'I know, Brian. I've been a bloody fool. In lots of ways.'

'What are you going to do?'

'Take the money and run. They're letting me cash in my pension.'

'You're lucky.'

'Probably. What will *you* do?'

The question was painful for Kinney. 'There's been a siege mentality around here since Bingham got fired. Word has leaked that F and C are going to be reorganized. Everyone's afraid for their job, Derek.'

'Well, don't worry about K Branch. Williams is round at Number Ten now, raising his glass to an expanded counter-intelligence budget – Roger's major goal accomplished.'

Kinney gave Smailes an anguished look. 'What *can* I do, Derek?' he asked. 'I ought to resign on principle, I know. But we've got one girl at Oxford and two still at school. Have you any idea what we pay in fees? And what could I do? Private security really isn't my line. I heard Bingham's been made managing director of Halls's company, by the way.'

'What a surprise!'

'I'll soldier on, I suppose. K Branch still has a job to do. I'm sorry . . .'

'Don't apologize, Brian. I'm the one who ought to apologize.'

'Derek, it took a lot of guts to do what you did.'

'Guts? Stupidity would be a better word. Will you do me a favour? Lend me your office so I can make some calls and talk to Judith?'

'Of course. You want me to call her for you?'

'Thanks.'

'And Derek – stay in touch, all right?'

'Don't worry.'

Kinney made a call and asked Ms Hyams to report to his office. Then he rose to leave and offered Smailes his hand.

'Don't stew about it, Derek. Remember what's still intact, what's really important.'

'Right, Brian. Thanks.'

Judith Hyams knocked and entered with a downcast expression which changed to shock, then confusion, when she saw Derek Smailes.

Like Smailes, she was girded for battle in her most conservative blue suit. He got to his feet slowly.

'Judith,' he said.

'Hello,' she said guardedly. Smailes had anticipated more emotion, maybe even a move to embrace him, but she stood near the door, as if afraid. 'How are you?'

'On the mend, I suppose.'

'Derek, what did you tell Brian? Out at the hospital? Did you hear I've been transferred?'

'I didn't tell him anything, Judith. Roger had these.' He indicated the photographs on Brian's desk top. Judith moved past him to examine them. Smailes caught the scent of her cologne as she passed, then heard her sharp intake of breath. 'Oh, that beast . . .' she said, turning to him indignantly, her colour rising.

'I've been fired, Judith.'

'Oh, Derek!' she cried, raising a hand to her mouth. 'I've been so worried. And so furious with you. I don't know how I've survived the last week. Nobody would tell me anything.'

'Furious?' he asked.

'Yes, furious!' she said. 'How did you expect me to feel? What exactly was your opinion of me? That I was all right for a quick grope in the dark, but that I wasn't fit to speak to you? Or to visit you in the hospital? That I didn't care?'

Smailes was stricken. 'I'm really sorry, Judith. I regretted what I said immediately. But Roger had bugged the phone, I'm sure, and my family was coming out to the hospital every day. It wouldn't have been right . . .'

'Roger?' she asked, baffled.

'He was behind the whole thing, Judith. Jonquil was a stunt cooked up by Roger, the Russians and the Americans to make him look good, so MI5 would survive the Carne review. The Russians got the American PALs. And the Americans get MI5 when Roger takes over.'

Judith was searching his face, uncomprehending. 'You're not serious?'

'*You* made me question the whole thing, Judith. Lubyanov was a dangle. Gontar was a discard. Look at it – we end up with nothing except Docherty.'

'How did you find out . . .?'

'I had an American friend tail Lubyanov when he was handed back to the Russians. He followed them to Slough, where he saw Strickland

and Standiforth go in after Zhimin. I got clever and tried to storm the place, and Peter Tennant gunned me down.'

Judith looked horrified. 'Peter Tennant? God, Derek, you can't let them get away with it!'

Smailes shrugged and gestured to the photographs. 'With these things sitting on the DG's desk? Having divulged a safe house address to an American? I'm dead in the water, Judith.'

'Do you think Roger put us together deliberately?' asked Judith cautiously, looking down at the prints.

'I wouldn't put it past him.'

'Oh,' she cried, 'and I've been thinking such terrible things about you! That you told Brian and Roger I was a tart to get me out of your hair. That you thought I was stupid and unreliable, unfit for K Branch.'

Smailes touched her sleeve. 'Judith,' he said softly, 'I think you're amazing.'

Judith choked back a sob and threw her arms around his neck. 'Derek, Derek, I love you,' she said into his ear.

Smailes reached up and took her wrists gently, breaking the embrace. With his stoop, he found he was actually looking up at her. 'That's very, very flattering, Judith. In other circumstances, I might have fallen in love with you too. But I'm married. Very married.'

'David and I have separated,' she said quietly.

'Well, that's not going to happen to me. What happened between us was foolish and unprofessional, and I'm completely to blame. Now, you get back to KY and get your head down. I don't want to wreck two careers.'

'You can't mean that.'

'I certainly do. Look, Brian knows how good you are. He's going to be head of K Branch one day, and he'll bring you back up.'

'Does he know everything?'

'Yes, and he's going to tough it out. So should you.'

'What are you going to do?'

'I'm not sure,' said Smailes enigmatically. 'They're giving me some money to go away and keep quiet. Maybe open a restaurant.'

'Derek, can we . . .?'

'No, Judith, we can't. You'll never see me again.'

Judith hesitated, then came to a decision. She straightened up and offered him her slim, cool hand, the way she had the very first time they'd met. Smailes took it gratefully.

'Goodbye, Derek,' she said. Then calmly, and with great dignity, she left the room.

23

Clea Smailes was seated on the big living room sofa, sipping mineral water and reading a magazine. Her husband came slowly into the room and sat down in his armchair. He was carrying his jacket and had loosened his tie. She looked at him accusingly.

'I knew you were going to the office. You could have said.'

'I got fired, Clea.'

She drew in her breath sharply. 'Oh, I'm sorry, Derek. What reason did they give? Giving Rudy the Chiswick address?'

'Not only that. They had these too.'

Smailes handed the buckled photographs to his wife. She looked at them slowly, one by one, her hair falling in front of her face. Eventually she said in a small voice, 'You said she wasn't pretty.'

'I lied.'

'Did you . . . did you make love with her?'

'No. I came to my senses before then. But I don't claim that exonerates me.'

'Derek, I'm pregnant – how could you?' She looked up at him through angry tears. Smailes felt his face flush with shame.

'Because I'd become an egomaniac, I'm afraid. You were right, what you said to Rudy, the night they were here. I really *did* think I could make it to the top of MI5. That whole phoney operation of Roger's was a huge ego-trip for me. Judith flirted with me and I was flattered. It was a power thing. It wasn't her fault . . .'

Clea was looking down at her hands again. 'No, but it was partly mine, I suppose. I've been such a bitch to you, Derek, since I got pregnant. I can't really blame you. Not entirely.'

Smailes marvelled at his wife's generosity of spirit. He had half feared she would march upstairs and begin packing. 'Clea, I'm not looking to make excuses . . .'

'No, I mean it, Derek. When I found out I was pregnant again, I was faced with a choice between going back to work and feeling guilty, or staying home and feeling resentful. So I chose resentment, and you bore the brunt of it. It wasn't your fault, it was an accident, but I had to blame someone.'

'Well, you don't have to make that choice now. I called Rudy this morning, before I left Curzon House. They're letting me cash in my pension – thirty thousand quid. I'm going to start up the Croydon doughnut restaurant with him. Except, for the first six months, I've told him it'll be strictly part-time, since I'll be home a lot with the new baby. You can go back to work, Clea.'

'Derek, that's very sweet of you, but you don't have to do that for me . . .'

'I'm not, Clea. I'm doing it for all of us. I've already made up my mind – as long as I can have Fidelma at least four hours a day.'

Clea began crying. 'Derek, are you serious?'

He moved to the sofa and put his arm around her. 'Do you forgive me?' he asked.

Clea looked at him through her tears. 'No,' she said. 'She's too skinny.' She got to her feet.

'Where are you going?' he asked.

'To burn these pictures. I don't want Lucy finding them.'

'Where is she?'

'Asleep.'

Smailes remained motionless upon the sofa, his emotions churning. Had he made the right decision? Or had he acted impulsively, out of guilt?

Clea came back and sat down next to him and laid her head on his chest. He put his arm round her again. 'Oh, this has been so hard, Derek. So many things have happened. Is everything going to be all right?'

'Yes, everything's going to be all right. I was never going to fit in over there, ultimately. It took something like this to make me realize it.'

'Doughnuts, Derek?'

'Hey, it's a living,' he said. She looked at him and laughed, then kissed him tenderly.

'We haven't had sex in ages,' she said. 'No wonder you got frustrated.' She began to stroke his thigh.

'Clea,' said Derek. 'The doctor said nothing strenuous.'

She got up and pulled him to his feet, then embraced him. 'You'll have to let me do all the work, then,' she said, leading him towards the stairs.

*

Derek Smailes leaned back against the pillows, savouring an oceanic contentment. The window was open and a breeze played over his haunches and the dressing on his stomach, beneath which his wound ached distantly. As he made the desperate bargains with himself on his taxi-ride home, he hadn't thought his confession scene would end like this. It was much more than he deserved. Clea came back into the room, nude, and paused to study herself in the wardrobe mirror. Smailes looked with awe at the marvellous white spheres of her body. She moved to join him and he took her hand. 'Have I told you recently how beautiful you are?' he asked.

'No,' she said.

'You take my breath away,' he said. She squeezed his hand but looked away.

'Derek, she wasn't working for him, was she? For Roger? In order to blackmail you, in case you found out?'

'It crossed my mind. But no, it couldn't be – her discoveries led me to suspect the whole thing in the first place. She's fatally compromised too. He'll wait a while, then get rid of her. I can't plead entrapment, Clea.' They fell silent again.

'Are you really going to do it, Derek? Open the restaurant with Rudy? Can I really go back to the Foreign Office?'

'Absolutely,' said Smailes. 'Rudy's over the moon. He doesn't want to open until the spring, so he wants me to go over to the States, when I'm well enough, to learn how they run the business over there. But I should have plenty of time to finish the baby's room and get the basement done before he arrives. In some ways, I'm glad this all happened. I feel reprieved.'

'That's the way I felt when I knew you had survived your operation. Like we could start again.' She seemed lost in thought. 'It was the lama, wasn't it?' she asked eventually.

'What?'

'Lama Drukpa. That day in Purley. I couldn't believe you had talked to him about your work. He said something that convinced you to leave. Am I right?'

'No, it was the reverse, actually. He had this totally starry-eyed notion of MI5's protecting the sovereign through stealth. I wonder what he'd say if he knew the reality, that it's utterly corrupt, a jungle of dinosaurs fighting over turf.'

Clea shrugged.

'So you forgive me?' he asked again.

'Not yet. No,' she said, still not looking at him.

He put his hand on the taut drum of her belly. 'How's *he* doing?'

'Fine,' said Clea. 'He's asleep.'

'Surprising, really.'

'He's like his father. When he wants to, he can sleep through anything.'

'Anything?' he asked, his hand roaming.

'Derek. Honestly.'

'I can't help it. I feel like celebrating.'

'Wait,' she said, pushing her hair behind her ear. 'I've got a better idea.'

Iain Mack came out to Coulsdon the following weekend to an emotional reunion in the Smailes' kitchen. Then, over Clea's protests, Derek and Iain immediately repaired to the pub. Smailes was walking unaided by now and brought beers out to the garden in the back. The two friends found a vacant table.

'Here's to the KGB,' said Smailes, raising his glass. Iain smiled and drank deeply.

'Boy, I learned a tough lesson there. I've always had this completely naïve, romantic view of the Russian soul, while all the time my best friend in Moscow was setting me up with the goon squad. He gave me veiled warnings about the depth of Russian corruption, but I missed them. I was a sitting duck.'

'He wasn't the only one setting you up, mate.'

'What do you mean?'

'I wish I could elaborate. But one of the conditions of the termination agreement I signed was that I wouldn't discuss events with any third party or undertake "any journalistic collaborations with Iain Mack". It named you specifically.'

'Fuck that,' said Mack, growing excited. 'You wouldn't believe the book offers I've had since I got back. I'm going to have to get an agent.'

'Believe me, it's frustrating for me too, Iain, but I just can't. They've already let me off with one Secrets Act infraction. If I spilled anything to you, they'd come down on me like a ton of bricks.'

'Come on, Derek. Give me the gist.'

Smailes sighed. 'All right. Your holiday in the Russian slammer and the bullet in my gut were part of the same script. It involved the

Russians, the Americans and the British. It was very cynical and very clever. I found out about it, so they fired me.' Smailes was aching to tell Iain his full story, but already regretted he'd said so much. Predictably, his words were like a red rag to a bull.

'Come on, man. You can't stop there.'

'Look, tell me what happened to you. From the beginning.'

Smailes listened with awe to his friend's account of his roller-coaster ride in Lefortovo prison. In some ways, it was much worse than what Smailes had been through. 'All right. Your turn,' said Iain finally, not relenting.

Smailes changed the subject, asking Iain about Whitehall gossip. Iain told him the inside story was that plans for an autumn election had been scrapped. Although no one believed opinion polls any more, recent international events had apparently damaged the Prime Minister's approval rating, and he was no longer confident of an outright majority if he went to the country. In addition, the most recent trade and unemployment figures had been unexpectedly good, so the British had been emboldened to drop monetary union from the agenda of the upcoming Eurosummit, at which the Germans had refused to attend, scotching the whole process. Effectively, economic and political union had been shoved back on to the back burner and the Conservative government had resolved to try and tough it out. Smailes listened with considerable interest – how Iain would love the story of the Sceptre Group, he realized.

'So come on, Derek. Tell me what happened to you.'

Smailes shook his head. 'I'm sorry, Iain. I just can't. I'm a family man. I can't spend the next ten years in jail for the sake of revenge and a bestseller.'

Mack was studying his empty glass thoughtfully. Eventually he said, 'How about fiction? How about if I wrote a *novel* about a journalist who gets arrested in Moscow, and a British agent who gets shot when he finds out why? Any resemblance to living characters would be *entirely* coincidental, of course.' He gave his friend a shrewd smile.

'Iain, let me think about that one, will you? That's a very provocative idea.'

It was the first week in October when Derek Smailes walked into a Soho wine bar wearing his buckskin jacket and cowboy boots. Judith Hyams was waiting by the window, sipping soda water.

'Red or white?' he asked. Judith said she preferred white.

Smailes bought a bottle of Alsatian Riesling, took two glasses and sat down. He watched Judith carefully as he poured their wine, noticing she was wearing tweed and had had her thick hair cut short. As he expected, she looked poised and beautiful.

She took a sip of wine. 'This was a big surprise,' she said.

'No doubt. I wanted to ask you – was it your own idea to seduce me, or did Moshe Feldman instruct you?'

Judith's mouth fell open and she began to respond, but then she stopped herself and took another sip of wine.

'Who?' she asked.

'Moshe Feldman, the *katsa* at the Israeli embassy. The Mossad chief. Your controller.'

'Derek, I don't know what you're talking about.'

'There was one piece of the whole puzzle I couldn't work out. The scientists at Burghfield said those raiders got away with a complete engineering package – hardware and software. But Docherty was specifically instructed by Gontar to steal more PAL software, which ended up back in my safe the night of the arrests. Why? If anything was missing, it could have been discreetly passed to Standiforth or Zhimin, since they were all in it together. No, it was meant to be found, in order to point the finger more firmly at Docherty as the source of the original leak. But someone took that software from my safe, Judith. They removed it, copied it and returned it. I use an elementary spotting technique, so I knew immediately those disks had been disturbed. I assumed it was Roger Standiforth, although that didn't make much sense the more I thought about it.'

Judith said nothing, but did not look at him.

'Well, last week, I finally got round to checking in with Brian. A sense of duty, I suppose. We chatted about this and that. I asked how you were doing. He said fine, keeping your head down, like we both hoped. I don't know why it came into my mind, but I asked him, on the spur of the moment, to check the log for the weekend of the arrests. Just a hunch, I suppose. He took a little cajoling, but he eventually agreed. He got back to me yesterday. It seems that at one o'clock on the morning after the arrests, you signed back in to Curzon House. Out again at one twenty. Why? You told me you were going home in a taxi, remember?

'You went back up to our office, Judith. I must have become careless operating the safe, you'd watched me enough times to work out the combination. You removed those disks and copied them into your laptop. At some later point you passed the data on to the Israelis. That's why you reacted so violently when I asked you whether you knew anyone at their embassy. Accused me of racial stereotyping, as I recall. Well, you already knew Moshe Feldman quite well, didn't you? He'd placed you in MI5 in the first place.

'You knew Gontar had been stationed in Tripoli and Damascus, which meant maybe the PAL technology had been dealt to some of the Soviet Union's former Arab clients. No doubt you felt justified, as a Jew, in handing the material to Feldman. Now the Israelis can build their own PALs, can't they, step up their nuclear readiness, keep pace in the Middle East arms race.'

'It's not true, Derek,' Judith said weakly.

'It *is* true, Judith. All the while I was lying in that hospital, trying to piece together Roger's game, I assumed I was the victim of a diabolical double cross. But I was wrong, wasn't I? It was actually a triple cross. Either admit it to me now and resign tomorrow, or I'll have Brian run tests on those disk sleeves. If your prints show up there, along with the evidence of the security log, you'll end up in the dock, Judith. Remember, we used gloves in Gontar's flat. Both of us.'

Judith was silent for a long time. She drank some more wine, then looked away, her eyes bright with tears. Eventually she looked across at him and began speaking slowly.

'It's a complex thing, Derek, being Jewish. You're right, partly. Moshe Feldman approached me soon after I got the job with K Branch. I realized, looking back, that my Uncle Mannie must be one of his *sayanim*, since he was the one who had pushed me into classified work in the first place.'

'His what?' asked Smailes.

'*Sayanim,*' said Judith. 'It means assistant in Hebrew. It's how the Mossad manages to be so lean and mean, as you put it – there are literally thousands of unpaid *sayanim* in London alone. They're everywhere, in all the professions. They provide services secretly. I suppose my Uncle Mannie gives them vehicles, things like that.'

'Together with your father?'

'No. I don't think Dad knows anything about Mannie's activities. And I'm only guessing about Mannie.'

'*Sayanim,*' said Smailes. 'I thought you told me you didn't speak any Hebrew.'

Judith shrugged.

'Go on,' he said.

'Feldman asked me to keep my ears open for anything of use to Israel. I was furious. I screamed at him, sent him away, told him never to contact me again.'

'Really?' asked Smailes sceptically.

'Yes, I did,' Judith said angrily. 'Getting a job in counter-intelligence was my dream come true. Do you think I was going to jeopardize it for a sleazy little spy like Feldman? No way!'

Smailes said nothing.

'But the crucial thing was, I didn't report his approach. It's drummed into you in orientation – if you don't report an approach, it's the same as if you accepted it. But I couldn't. I'm convinced no secular Jew ever would.'

'Why?'

'Look, Derek, you don't have to approve of the Israeli government, or of the Mossad, to support Israel's basic right to exist. As a Jew, you can't deny that right.'

'What would have happened if you'd reported Feldman's approach?'

'He might have been expelled. My Uncle Mannie could have got into trouble. Derek, I just couldn't, all right? I never intended to have anything further to do with him.'

'But you did, didn't you?'

Judith emptied her glass and Smailes poured her a little more wine.

'You're right about Gontar,' she resumed. 'I got worried when it became obvious he'd worked for the radical Arab states. Feldman got the make for us, didn't he, so I suppose I felt an obligation. I don't know, it might have been his motive for supplying us the photographs in the first place. They can be very cunning.

'So, nothing might have happened. Maybe I would just have given him a verbal report when it was all over. But you told me you were going to put those disks into your safe! My computer was up there. Yes, I knew the combination. It took just a few minutes . . .' She began to cry softly, then looked up at him angrily.

'How dare you suggest I was instructed to seduce you! In my recollection, it was *you* who made the pass at *me*. What happened between us was completely genuine on my part. I thought so on yours. It's a vile thing to say!'

'I'm sorry,' said Smailes. 'I retract it.'

'Derek, don't make me resign,' she implored. 'I swear, nothing will ever happen again. Ever. I don't know if David and I will make it. If I lose my job, I'll have nothing. Please, Derek, if I meant anything to you, let it go. Please.'

It was Smailes's turn to search for words. 'I can't, Judith,' he said eventually. 'I just can't. It's not that I give a damn about MI5 or its bogus concern for national security. Believe me, I don't. But when Roger becomes DG, Brian will be made head of K Branch, and if you're still there I know he'll promote you. You'll be a time bomb waiting to go off whenever something crosses your desk that you think is vital to Israel's existence. You have admitted as much yourself, haven't you? I can't do that to Brian, Judith.

'Listen, tell them you're resigning to save your marriage. Go back to accounting. Work it out with David. Believe me, there is life after MI5.'

The tears were running freely down her face now. He reached for her hand.

'Look, Alex Corcoran said something before he showed me the door – MI5 is not for the likes of us, Judith. Never has been, never will. You're a threat to Roger, and he'll be looking for a way to get rid of you. Accept reality and go.'

Judith withdrew her hand and picked up her bag. Then, without another word, she stood and left the bar.

Clea and Derek Smailes's second daughter was born in early November, just after midday, following a short but dramatic labour lasting three hours. Smailes had thought they were looking at an all-day event, like the first time, but suddenly doctors and midwives were running everywhere with lamps and instruments and stainless steel pans, and the baby was born before they could remove the bottom half of the delivery table. The actual birth was totally shocking and miraculous, all over again. The midwife asked whether Smailes wanted to cut the cord, but he felt too shaky and said they'd better find someone more qualified. Then the furious, waxy face of their daughter was placed on Clea's breast and they looked at her for the first time, blinking back tears.

'She's beautiful,' said Smailes.

'No, she's not. She looks like a Pekingese,' said Clea, laughing.

The baby sucked at her mother distractedly for a few seconds, then resumed howling. A young doctor lifted her away to be examined, and Smailes took his wife's hand.

'Well done,' he said.

'Piece of cake,' said Clea as the medical team worked feverishly down at her far end. Smailes glanced up and saw needle and thread, then looked back at Clea quickly.

'We were going to call him Stephen,' he said. 'We don't even have a girl's name.'

'Stephanie?' asked Clea.

Smailes screwed up his face, and Clea laughed.

'Sally?' he tried.

'Sally Smailes. I like that,' said Clea.

The doctor brought their daughter back, swaddled tightly now, and held her out to Clea.

'Let her father take her. He needs to get used to it,' said Clea.

Derek Smailes accepted the tiny parcel and took her on a walk around the room. Her eyes were screwed tight against the light. Smailes found himself transfixed by the miraculous scroll of her ear. Then, suddenly, a pair of deep blue eyes were regarding him quizzically.

'Well, hello,' said Smailes. 'Welcome. Let me introduce myself. I'm your father and I'm in the doughnut business. That's your mother over there, the one on the table with her knees in the air. She's a diplomat.'

The midwife looked up from between Clea's legs and smiled. 'They make a good team,' she said.

'Don't they just,' said Clea contentedly.